Zui! What a joy it's been to get to know you this year. Much love, Farrah xxx

Zui, Zui,
Anuna min yar (ee).
An original writer, a special person, the best picnic creator this side of Kansas City.
Giddy up Vagabond!
Love Yaz xxx

PROSE FICTION

Zui,
Reading your pieces has been such a treat. Your writing is gold, the world is waiting for it.
Anushe

Dear Zui,
While moving out of Dalls I saw the Christmas card you made Dec '21. I just think you're so stupid. I will always have a lot of love for you and I'm so grateful that our paths crossed.
You're going to do great things. I said this from day 1.
Love,
Rabia

Zui, you're a legend. Phir milenge har manzil pe xx

PROSE FICTION

UEA MA
Creative Writing Anthologies
2022

CONTENTS

V

AMIT CHAUDHURI
Foreword

My first experience of a Creative Writing department was the term I spent at Columbia University in 2002 (teaching not writing but literature and modernism at the department during a one-off stint). The students were intellectually open and unafraid, but weren't (at least that's the impression I got from what I heard) encouraged to raise literary questions in the writing class. Creative Writing, in America, felt, implicitly, different from literature. Thinking about literature and working on writing were meant to be two different things – in some ways, they may have also been seen to be opposed to each other. I may be wrong. And maybe this isn't the case any longer. But there was a sense I got at the time – others did too – that Creative Writing programmes in the USA involved a process of homogenisation as students 'worked on their writing', and that part of the homogenising was to do not so much with adhering to a handbook of rules but a model of style. As we know, the model at the time was Raymond Carver, or Gordon Lish's version of Carver.

I don't wish to compare, but comparisons are inevitable when you only know two forms of something. I came into contact with the second form that a Creative Writing course might take when I started teaching (if that's the right word) the MA in Prose Fiction at UEA in 2008, two years after I'd made a first tentative foray in the department, offering, as I had at Columbia, an MA on modernism. It took a while for me to understand that, though UEA's adoption of the original Iowa-type 'feedback' model wasn't very different from comparable courses in America, something unlike America was happening here as far as the writing emerging from the MA was concerned. For one thing, there was no equivalent of Carver directing the production of proto-Carvers. I encountered a diversity of styles: realist, poetic, satirical. I even read stories that were written about, of all places, Norwich. This was not some kind of incipient English regionalism being practised by local students. To gesture towards a regional tradition, one needs the idea of the local to have some sort of glamour. Norwich didn't have that. And yet, the Norwich stories (I invoke them as one example of the unexpected discoveries I made reading or examining students' work) made me, through their intelligence and humanity, look at both Norwich and 'creative writing' in a new way. So did the other kinds of stories: about the historical, or the everyday, or the contemporary, or the future. In fact, there seemed to be greater variety and nimbleness in the Creative Writing MA than there was in the domain of published novels. This was a revelation, because the suspicion and expectation (as in American anxieties about the creative writing industry) is that the opposite will be true. Anyway: I did not, in the twelve years I was associated with that course, come across instances, or note the presence, of one recognisable, dominant creative writing style. What I did find were varieties of excellence, as I do in this anthology, and it took me a few years to understand this. I don't know how this variety both survives and flourishes: both students and teachers must be responsible for it, as must an unspoken, maybe unconscious, pact between student and teacher.

The world 'out there', of publication and 'finished copies', is far less heterogenous and possibly less interesting. That's why these yearly anthologies seem important to me now, in retrospect, because the project seems to grow in significance and probably has the potential to point a way, devoid of mainstream mediation, to what a truly burgeoning and many-sided contemporary literary practice might look like. I hope there will be more anthologies: maybe a quarterly could be introduced, as well as anthologies of the excellent critical prose students write.

You will be struck by the various momentous events, human habits, and insights recorded in these pages – from speaking to diced carrots to the fact that the depredations of human history are most powerfully present in a dentist's waiting room (and other such revelations).

I have always admired the UEA MA writers, and I wish this latest talented group well, and I wish them courage.

Amit Chaudhuri
July 2022

TESSA MCWATT
Introduction

*The world of a writer is doing and, when circumstances
allow, this doing is in fact writing.*
   —Tsitsi Dangarembga (PEN Pinter Prize Address 2021)

Here are the circumstances.

We'd come through something catastrophic. We're still coming through, with more crises on the way, but at that moment in September when we first met in a seminar room in the Elizabeth Fry Building – named after the social reformer who advocated for shelter, for refuge – we huddled together in the shadow of the pandemic. We were cautious, but we were excited to be in person after so long behind the flat light of screens. No masks. No, those would come out again over the course of the year as Covid waned and raged, as directives changed many times in response to global health uncertainties. But for the moment, there they were: forty new students and eighteen returning part-timers – the numbers having swelled beyond normal levels due to a range of consequences of the pandemic. There we were, eager for the writing we would share with one another.

These new and returning students were from the UK, Ireland, Hong Kong, Nigeria, the USA, Kenya, Thailand, Pakistan, Germany, India, and Israel. The diversity of their stylistic, thematic and canonical reference points was evident from the first workshops, where the world came into focus, where the next wave of literary concerns and voices became apparent. This richness was in part thanks to the inaugural year of our International Chair of Creative Writing programme, which now supports writers from Africa through our Global Voices Scholarships, in addition to our on-going Miles Moreland scholarship. It was also thanks to our new Sonny Mehta India Scholarship and the Sonny Mehta Scholarship for Writers, along with generous funding from our well-established scholarships.

Tsitsi Dangarembga took up her role as International Chair of Creative Writing in September 2021, and throughout the year she and our Director of Creative Writing, Jean McNeil, were involved in outreach events across several African countries. For our MA students this meant workshops, masterclasses and seminars from this Booker Prize nominated author, along with special seminars on African women writers given by acclaimed South African/Namibian journalist and fiction writer Dr Margie Orford.

In the spring we were honoured to have a masterclass from Caine Prize-winning author Irenosen Okojie. We were also fortunate to have two weeks of masterclasses and tutorials from Irish novelist and poet Elaine Feeney, our Rathbones Folio Prize Fellow. The value of having Elaine engage with our MA cohort is without measure, and we are truly grateful for her generosity.

Over the course of two semesters this cohort of students went through various stages of exploring their own writing and the writing of others – published authors as well as the in-progress drafts of their classmates. They celebrated, they got Covid, they flagged, they rallied, and their writing grew in proportions that showed us just how precious in person learning is. It was a delight to watch how some of the writers in this anthology found their voice, how some lost their voice only to find a new and better one, how many took risks, experimented and, no matter what, brought to the page the varying contours of their imaginations. The process of this intense year allowed them to step back and look at their craft in new ways. And as Dangarembga says in her interview with novelist Madeleine Thien, 'Stepping back is sometimes more painful than going in. A writer once said to me, "I thought I was writing it out, but actually I'm writing it in!"'

Writing it in. Yes.

They impressed us, challenged us, and taught us about the ever-changing parameters of literature. Nowhere was this more obvious than in the lunchtime sessions coordinated by Naomi Wood. Students whose creative practice engages with issues of anti-colonialism offered lectures to our School which outlined strategies for thinking differently about literature. Kaeya Zui Kumar-Reddy, Boo Sujiwaro, Kinjal Sheth, April Yee, Tahira Yaqoob and Hanna Thomas delivered seminars on topics that ranged from 'The Sublime, the Subtext and the Subaltern,' 'East Asian Narratives, Autofiction and the Art of Webnovels,' 'Postcolonial Aesthetics,' 'Who Gets To Tell Our History?' 'Docupoetry,' and 'The Centre(s) and the Margins.' We are grateful for those dynamic interventions into our conversations around what literature can be.

'We all have our dreams,' says Dangarembga. In this anthology you will discover dreams come to life on the page, through literary experiment, through humour, fantasy, horror and characterful interactions in, this, our current world under strain. This year's bounties have been immense, despite circumstances that were perpetually in flux. It was a year of in-person action – writing, communing, growing. It is the energy of doing that gives us hope, and it is with this energy that I commend these marvellous writers to you.

Tessa McWatt
June 2022

This diverse anthology comprises the latest work from the 2022 cohort of prose writers studying UEA's renowned Creative Writing MA.

CIARA AARON

Ciara Aaron is a London born writer. In 2019 she graduated from University College London and was awarded the HW Fisher Scholarship for Curtis Brown Creative's novel-writing course. She writes short stories about sex and the weather.

ciaramariaaaron@gmail.com

Counterparts, 21
A Joyce Rewriting

Curtains open and Tuesday morning hits the window. She's slept in. She was up late last night watching porn on her laptop. Her body feels thick and damp like washing in the machine left too long. She's glued to the mattress with sweat and something close to soured cream. The phone on the floor keeps buzzing, not a ring but a buzzbuzzbuzz as if the carpet has a pulse of its own. Grabbing the phone, she draws the password on the screen, the one that looks like a smiley face but upside down, and the phone gives way to a warning:

DEBORAH WORK

Of course, Deborah, who presumably wants to talk engagement, who enjoys breaking her syntax into little pieces, digestible word chunks running the course of the phone screen like brain Tetris on and on, over and again, no space for interjections, not even an emoji to suspend the stream of afterthoughts ahead of the actual thought.

> *Had some really*
> *really bad hitback on our post last night*
> *fucking intern*
> *didn't read the translation*
> *cut n paste job*
> *now we're in the shit*
> *big time over*
> *pronouns*
> *purple news all over it*
> *already about to blow*
> *can't ppl think these days!!!*
> *can you sort*
> *pls????!*
> *need statement post ASAP*
> *sim to black square but*
> *tweaked, obvs*

Laura?
Laura??????
Lauara?????????

Shit. *Sorry, phone died*, she types. I'm on it.

She's all over it.

She's all over her bed. She's all under the covers and her hands, having momentarily thrown the phone back to the floor are moving down now past the navel, reaching the sweet spot and resting, pulsing, pressing – one, two – in tandem with the mobile's gyrations.

She can't stop and hasn't for days. It doesn't even feel that nice any more, but it can't be ignored. The itch, the need to scratch as you would a mosquito bite, swollen. Spiteful. In want of a slap. In need of a good hiding. A game of hide and seek.

Desperately seeking Laura seeking pleasure in the body's recess.

And working from home nowadays. From her bed she lifts the laptop lid, her hands, washed and towel dried, levitate around the threshold tippy tapping. Her fingers as evidence connecting the hard facts of this world – the pots and plants, the damp rotten wood on the windowpane, the many plates and mould-filled mugs piled high on the desk in the bedroom on the second floor of her shared semi-detached – with the intangible illuminated next. She opens the TIME DOCTOR, tracking her remote-working hours.

Check in: 8.03.

Three minutes past and already in the wild wild web there's an omniscient conductor powerfully predicting and directing her thinking. She's a mouse mind. Cursor. Burrowing into. Finding her replication in cypher, remade and retouched like an energised solvent resulting in a solution. So insofar as this is all happening and, in the manner in which it is really happening, between the bed and the blue and the world and the web, there is a multiplication and a division simultaneously, and there is a mapping and rerouting and revision of how to think.

There's even a how to for being. Never mind beliefs and all that.

In the FORUM, flashing at the edge of the screenplay, user 910040 asks:

What's nature?

...

God's iPhone.

She laughs out loud, inserts *LOL* as revelation. It's nice that – the symmetry, the symbiosis of this thinking machine and her head-hand equation.

Nicer still to know there're others out there simply getting it. Switched on. Whole days, weeks even, involving nothing but chats: asking questions, lending a hand, wondering who exactly suggested the avocado pasta recipe and what trauma might have caused user 805's fascination with dead squirrels.

At _____ we know pronouns matter.
~~Yesterday's fuckery was the result of a profound ineptitude and isn't it awful that that's someone's actual job????~~

But she likes Deborah. Or at least finds her more manageable than the last. She's forthright. Tells you straight. No beating around the proverbial: Deborah will tell you when you've fucked up, good and proper. And she handles Fergus, which is hard to do. They all answer to Fergus, and Fergus is the one you better watch out for. He's got a reputation. Laugh you straight into bed if you gave him half the chance. He'd fuck you with his mushroom-shaped penis and tell you it was the first time he'd cheated on his wife. Which is to say the first time he'd gone through with it. There was that time after the first European promo aired. Elation! A great team effort, they agreed. Tequila at the Queen's Head on a Tuesday, 7pm. What a ruckus! What a laugh! Fergus had worked his hand into the ridge of her back, casually, leaning into her ear, asking what next at the bar – what next – what next to drink, and just left it there in the concave, pressed, pushing ever so gently, the silence between them drowned by the crash of hot glasses out the washer. Not having to go into the office and see Fergus was a relief then, no longer having to force a smile and a nod, explaining to Karen in that self-deprecating tone why exactly this morning seemed the right occasion to flash a bit of thigh through the slit in her pencil skirt, or sneak past the front desk at a quarter past the hour because she simply couldn't decide on a pair of trousers beforehand which didn't make her hips look ready for childbirth.

The TIME DOCTOR trips out. A box springs from its periphery, and another, rapidly, an unending set of Russian dolls just gagging to get their clothes off. She'd had a drink last night, enough to have had bad thoughts but not, thankfully, to make bad decisions. Like calling up Harry at eleven p.m. to ask if he fancied a... night cap. Bad move. No. She did not do that. Self-sabotage, according to Emmanuel, her therapist. Getting in her own way: a special talent. So, a little harder to think this morning. A little less patience for the TIME DOCTOR insurgence than usual. She shuts down. Can't hit save. Fuck. A little more time affording thoughts to meander, aimless, like how is it that everyone knows André 3000's 'Millionaire' rap but not the last two bars? her eyes inching through the magnolia wood-chipped abyss. The phone takes its cue.

Laura
ur not online??
I need an update
now
what's the latest?
do you have post ETA????
FERGUS BREATHING DOWN MY NECK
soz for caps

actually lets chat

Deborah's face has a mauve tinge. The whole house underwent a renovation some months prior, top to bottom. Her bedroom walls, Deborah took care to explain in a Wednesday briefing a week ago, were limewashed to match a courgette skin. Cost an arm and a leg but necessary for the boudoir, don't you think? Meetings are taken from there since Olly and Sebastian, her prepubescent boys, won't shut up downstairs.

'Listen Laura,' she says. 'Had an email from Krystal. You're late for the newsletter now too. Fergus knows. He's joining the call—'

'Okay—'

'And share your screen so you have the edit ready.'

'Hi Fergus.' His name drips from Deborah's mouth like honey. That's her handle. Her hook. Every address assimilated to an unnatural, incurable sweetness. She's a charming projection and a real good sport. (Watching Deborah this way reminds her of when she was twenty-one and cam-girling for the summer.)

Fergus's jaw lacks definition even through her work-sponsored high-quality display. 'What's happening Laura? Why – why are we having to chase something so menial? This is light work. Are you incapable of light work?'

She apologises in the way she knows palatable: diminishing, making herself smaller and smaller with each syllable till she's a mere dent on the screen. 'I'll get tech-support on the TIME DOCTOR, and as for the newsletter I was just about to hit send—'

User 4526: yo sxc I'm thinkin u'd dig this ur weird like dat – that's the problem with being switched on all the time. The vile overflow. The absurdity. The whole fucking world fucking at your fingertips.

'You'll get tech?' snaps Fergus. 'What do you think I am – an idiot?'

But she's thinking about fucking now, of course she is. Thinking about what it means to get fucked. Thinking about fucking in language, sexting, sexercise, fucking crypto, man: just how thrilling all that is too.

'That's not for me to say, Fergus.'

User 4526: THIS >>>>>>> geriatricgrind.com

Deborah's horrified: 'I beg your pardon?'

Fergus is fatally quiet now. He's probably thinking about what he'd like to do to her, about what he might just do if she wasn't safe behind her screen.

'I'm sorry, I didn't mean to say—'

But there is flesh slapping. There is old, rippled flesh colliding and re-coiling like a rough tide. There are moans, yes, there are yowls and groans like foxes in the black shine of night. There is discharge, gloopy and white, and there is fat oiled and basted, and there are genitals, yes there are balls and bits shaking like maracas because there are two octogenarians fucking, yes, really fucking, really going for it, having the time of their lives with a hand-held camera. Yes, there they are!

And Fergus and Deborah can see it all.

She is terrifically untethered. Switched off. Has buried the laptop deep under the bed of all places. What now? Notice – she might as well consider herself sacked – and what if they don't give her notice? What if they cut things off any minute now and then she can't pay rent and is chucked out, back to her mum's, and must deal with Darren on the sofa again, of all people. Thumbs majorly fucking down. But it was a pop-up, right? That's what she'd said between the outrage and abject horror she'd maintained it was simply a virus, quite common as it happens, yes this sort of thing happens all the time and has absolutely nothing to do with her activity online, with her mouse mind on the line.

She calls Frankie first. No answer. Then tries Rachel and Bex but straight to voicemail. So, it's for the phone and group chat. Her think-tank. For sharing, dissection, digression and, crucially, vindication because they must know. (*OMG babe that's SO fucked up.*) It will be okay, no, it really will, don't you worry.

And then they make her repeat it again. Blow by blow.

The winter sun strikes noon through her window, and it might be about time, she thinks, for the first time in fact, to leave the bedroom today. Downstairs, the house is still. Someone has left the kitchen window open. A draft fills the room cutting the nerves. She's making toast, digging into raspberry jam, half-dressed. Her nipples are pricked by cold. They grow, called to attention. Alert. Upright. They tingle.

And it feels quite nice.

Upstairs in bed, she licks the crumbs from her plate. She's done that since she was a kid. A heathen, mum used to call her, when it comes to eating. She brushes the crumbs off her chest. Her breasts open out in the chill, blooming a golden spiral. Spiralling is what Emmanuel said. Yes, she tends to spiral. Wasn't that what happened earlier? She couldn't help herself. And isn't that what her hands are doing now? Spiralling around the bud. Two hands. One for the breast, the other: the clitoris. On the verge. Going round the bend. She closes her eyes and sees Fergus, hears his voice echo as a stone dropped in a well. This is light work. Yes. This is light. The body is feather light. Made of feathers. A hot pink feather boa tied up in knots. Coming undone. Luxuriously. Pink and hot and light as anything. The body is light and hot and incredibly pink.

MARIE ADAMS

Marie Adams is a Canadian writer and psychotherapist based in Dorset. A former producer on BBC's Today Programme, she is the author of two books, *The Myth of the Untroubled Therapist,* based on her doctoral research into the personal lives of therapists, and a novel, *Telling Time.*

mariead1066@gmail.com

Snow-Plane
An excerpt from a novel

In Doc Hammond's house there is a telephone on the wall in the kitchen. Even for 1953, this phone is old-fashioned – a wall-mounted wooden box nicknamed the 'crank and holler', with bells at the top and a circular speaker built into its centre. There is a cord with a Bakelite hearing apparatus attached, which hangs on a curved metal hook when the phone is not in operation. When the bells rattle, everyone jumps, every time – the doctor's wife especially, pregnant, frightened, and still unused to this town where everything is alien to her city sensibilities.

On the night John Hammond receives the call from Alsen, the night of the snow-plane, he rises quickly to answer the phone. Elise is startled awake. She rolls over, attempting to claw back the sleep that she is learning will forever be interrupted. Despite her efforts, she can't help but hear Doc shouting down the line, as he always does, to be heard across the wide distances created between Mabel Iverson, the operator, and those listening in. The more people there are, the harder it is to hear over the 'farmer party line'. This is a town where curiosity is often mistaken for concern. Even in the bedroom, she can hear Mabel's excited voice telling Doc that there's an emergency outside Alsen, a settlement twenty-five miles away, and he better scoot on over.

'I'll put you through now,' she tells the doctor.

Across town, in her flannel pyjamas and quilted housecoat, Mabel is sitting cross-legged at the switchboard by the side of her bedroom closet, her headset clamped over her usually starched hair. She stubs out her cigarette in a glass ashtray and, with a quick, practiced yank, she pulls out one plug from the switchboard before ramming the jack into another slot three up and five along, connecting the Alsen operator with Doc Hammond. The Alsen operator tells him about the distress call she received – a woman who says she thinks her husband has had a heart attack.

John Hammond is flummoxed. How is he to get out to this farm twenty-five miles away? Mabel, who is of course listening in, cuts into the conversation.

'Maybe I can fix this for you, Doc. I have an idea,' she says. Ten minutes later, she rings back to say that his transport is on the way.

John Hammond, already dressed, goes to wait by the living room window. He wears a suit and tie, and is pressing his hands together with the anxious energy he reserves for medical emergencies. He is thirty-six years of age, and has been qualified as a doctor for three years. He is tall and too thin and carries within himself a sober sense of responsibility. He and his family have lived in Langdon for only three weeks, and the 1700 square miles he covers as the town doctor is still unfamiliar to him.

Outside, there is nothing but a shroud of snow and sky, and the shimmering glow of a single streetlight a block away. There is absolute silence – the silence that follows a blizzard, after the wind has died down and the snow settled into a hefty five-foot drift against the house.

Then, with a jerk, the doctor presses his ear to the window's frosty glass. He thinks he detects a sound, a grinding in the distance. He raises his eyebrows, not sure what to expect, but lifts his heavy winter jacket off the chesterfield. He rams his arms into the sleeves and fits up the zipper, then shoves a sheepskin hunting hat on his head – though he's never been hunting in his life – and wraps his mother's hand-knitted scarf around his neck. By the time he slips on his mittens, the distant rumble has become an exceedingly fierce and rhythmic roar.

Both his wife and their six-year-old daughter, Jeanette, are wide awake now and come to stand with him at the window. Together they watch, mesmerised, as a prehistoric machine of impressive grandeur swerves and dips down a snowbank before rising again up and over another. As the machine turns right and heads their way, they lift their arms in unison, blinded for a moment by the glare of powerful headlights. Elise gasps, while Jeanette jumps and claps her hands. John Hammond is wide-eyed and curious. He knows the contraption has come for him.

The rhythmic beat behind the grind of the engines comes from a spinning propeller jutting out the back of the contraption. The doctor thinks of a helicopter, tipped on its side. *Whomp! Whomp!* Longer than a Cadillac and twice as high, it has a nose like a Model T and slides over the snow on four huge, plank-like skis. Although they are safe inside, the doctor, Elise, and Jeanette step back as the immense hybrid drifts to a halt perilously close to the house. Then the lights cut out, and the engine dies.

'What is it?' asks Elise, clutching her husband's arm. 'What is that thing?' If the machine had wings it might be a plane, but it was clearly too heavy for that.

John shakes his head and lets out one of his rare laughs. 'I don't know,

Elise, but I have a sneaking suspicion I'm about to find out.'

There are two men in the front seat, their heads barely visible above the narrow slot of the windshield. One of them, a man in a thick parka and a well-worn hunting hat, his hands also wrapped in thick mittens, emerges from the machine. He pulls out a shovel from behind the back seat and begins to dig the doctor out of his own house.

'Doc,' the man shouts over the wind. 'Doc, I'm just about there. Hold on.'

John picks up his medical bag and walks to the front door. As he opens it, there is a terrible blast of cold air and both mother and child shiver, pulling their dressing gowns tighter around their chests, but Doc Hammond laughs again. He waves goodbye with a mittened hand and treks out behind the man towards the plane that isn't a plane.

'Roy,' the man says as he opens the door for the doctor to climb into the back seat, ramming the shovel in behind him. 'Roy Berg. This here's my son, Gerry.'

Doc Hammond nods, 'Good to meet you, Roy. Gerry. Thanks for coming out,' though by now Roy has moved to the back of the contraption. Taking a breath, and with a mighty heave-ho of a single blade, Roy jerks the propeller into a spin before quickly stepping back and yelling, 'CONTACT!' Noting the shout from inside the cab, his son's head disappears below the windshield as he bends down to flip the switch and gun the motor. The machine gives a terrible shake before roaring magnificently back into life. Roy clambers aboard to take up the driver's seat.

The doctor's wife and daughter watch as the snow-plane takes off. It crosses the yard with noisy grace and glides for a short time along the side of the highway before heading out on to the windswept prairie to race towards the farm twenty-five miles away. On a night when it would otherwise have been impossible to travel, the snow-plane glides up and over snowdrifts and across the wide, open prairie, where the last vestiges of the blizzard are still pushing through.

With the doctor on his way, Elise leads her daughter back to bed. She reads her a story until she falls asleep.

A few hours later, Jeanette wakes to hear her mother speaking through the horn to Mabel.

'Please, Mabel, can you put me through to Alsen? I need to know if he got there.'

'It's three in the morning, Missus Hammond, I can't be waking the operator up for nothing. You know that.'

Elise hears the admonishing note in Mabel's voice, but she is a master at quiet persistence.

'Mabel, I need to know if he got there. Look at the weather, and that machine! Whatever it was, I've never seen anything like it.'

Mabel grew up on the open prairie and is unfazed. Doctors' wives from Canada, who have moved down from the big city, are nothing new, three of them in the past ten years. She wonders how long this one will last, with her pretty hats and city style. Yet tonight, Mabel has been part of something big, sorting out the doctor's transport, and she wouldn't mind knowing if he got there either, so she goes right ahead and puts the call through.

'Well,' says the operator in Alsen, sounding perkier than expected. 'About ten minutes ago there was a pretty loud noise outside and there was some monster machine roaring down the road like nobody's business. Had a propeller on the back.'

'That's the one,' says Mabel. 'Heading in or heading out?'

'Heading out, so I guess the business got done?'

'Guess so,' and both operators hang up. Listening in, Elise carefully replaces the Bakelite earpiece back into the clip. She hadn't needed to say a word.

The doctor, when at last he returns, radiates cold. His breath still billows out in clouds until his wife hands him a hot toddy, which he licks at first, like a cat, before gulping it down in several huge swallows. She wraps a blanket over his shoulders and runs him a hot bath.

He tells her in bursts about the trip to the farm. They had crossed the snow-covered tundra in twenty-below-zero weather and after only a mile out, they were forced to open the doors to stop the windshield from steaming up. With the cold wind blowing through, the doctor knew they'd perish if the machine ever stalled.

'We followed the telephone poles and Roy recognised the farms along the way, otherwise we wouldn't have got there. At one point we had to stop and use a broom handle to lift an electricity line so we could pass through, to get the propellor underneath. Roy built the machine himself; old plane parts mostly, and the front from an old car. No pedals or brakes, just hand pumps in the front to push gas through to the engine. He said he'd come out if I needed him again.'

He chokes suddenly, and heaves a big breath. His shoulders slump in exhaustion.

'The old man died,' he says. 'I didn't get there in time.'

John tells Elise about the farmer's wife, Moira – how she had stood at the stove heating up the milk for them as if they were visitors, offering them pie, with Roy and his son sitting quietly at the kitchen table, jackets loose and mittens on their laps, all her actions deliberate, as if she might break if she moved at her usual brisk pace. A middle-aged woman suddenly grown old. She'd known before they'd arrived, perhaps even before she'd called the doctor out. Unable to wait until the morning, with such a storm passing outside, her husband cold beside her – she'd needed to know for sure.

'Morris, his name was Morris,' John Hammond says now, weary with sorrow. 'He died before I got there. Fifty-eight years old. He died before I got there.'

EIMEAR ARTHUR

Eimear Arthur is a writer, architect, and lecturer in architecture from Dublin. She has been writing for *Architecture Ireland* since 2019. Eimear is currently working on a collection of short stories, and on a novel, *Three Sides*, which explores themes of blame, grief, love, and convention in a post-Catholic Ireland.

eimeararthur@gmail.com

Three Sides
The opening of a novel

At the close of day on a rural Portuguese street, the light dipped low and golden. Under the awning of a limewashed restaurant were two small, round tables, a few feet apart. At one table sat two empty chairs, atop the other was a breadbasket, olive oil and vinegar. A tall man in his mid-thirties was seated at this table, opposite a vacant chair. Preliminary greys scattered his dark hair, and there was a slight red tinge to the tan of his high forehead, his nose. A brown handbag hung from the back of the vacant chair. The man toyed with a laminated menu; a single double-sided sheet.

A short, sinewy waiter in his fifties exited the café door and approached the man at the table, who dismissed him with a shrug and an apologetic smile. 'Five more minutes man, I'm sorry, she's...'

He stopped speaking at the sight of a woman in her late twenties walking towards him. She wore a creased white cotton sundress with flat brown leather sandals and was holding a phone in her hand. The phone's screen was cracked. The woman smiled briefly at the waiter as he passed on his way back inside, and slouched into the chair opposite the seated man.

'Deteriorating rapidly, apparently.' Her tone was dispassionate, but her hands trembled.

The man's eyes widened, he sat forward in his seat. 'What?' The word caught in his throat. 'But he was –'

'I know. Fine. Telling me to go on my holidays, enjoy myself. Ha! Mam said they took him in yesterday. It's all spread, it's fucking everywhere. His lungs now, too. His spine!' She looked at a spot just above the man's head as she spoke.

The man winced at the word 'spine' and reached across the table to place a hand on the woman's arm. Her eyes moved to his hand, then coldly met his gaze.

He dropped his hand to the table. 'So what do you want to... We'll have to go,' he said. 'Tomorrow. We'll go home.'

'There's no flights till Tuesday, I checked. It's Tuesdays and Saturdays only. We could have gone this morning, if we'd known. But he was...'

'Fine.' He barely whispered it.

The woman looked at her hands. 'She didn't ring me in time.' Her voice was small and sullen now. She picked at the remnants of her nail varnish, chipping tiny fragments of pigment on to the table between them.

The man watched her, opened and closed his mouth a few times. Then: 'The train,' he said. 'We could get the train, to Lisbon? There must be more flights from there?'

'No trains on Sundays. In case it would enrage Christ, I'm sure. Must be in the Commandments somewhere: no affordable transport on the Sabbath. This is what happens when you decide to walk through God country.'

'*Me?*'

'You, what?'

'*I* decided...' He paused, changed tack. 'Right, well, I'll talk to them in the hostel after dinner. There'll be a bus, or a taxi, or something. I'll sort it out, okay?'

The woman made to answer but was interrupted by the waiter advancing towards them.

'Great, I'm starving!' She was all warmth now.

The waiter asked for their order.

The seated man began an apology: 'Sorry, we actually haven't –'

'I'll have the *cacio e pepe*, and he'll have the *capricciosa* pizza, please. Thanks. And could we get a bottle of the house white? Lovely, thank you...' She waited for him to supply his name.

'Marco!'

'Marco.' She bestowed him with a gilded smile. 'I'm Kate. *Obrigada*, Marco.'

A man made his way over the uneven stone paving towards the vacant table. He was simply dressed in chinos and a t-shirt, with thick-soled, sensible trainers. He wore a peaked cap with a fabric flap at the back to protect his pale skin, the lax and almost-translucent surface of which was stippled with moles and age spots. His eyebrows were wires of twisted grey. He made himself known to Marco as he sat.

'*Bene*,' said Marco to the couple, then, to the elderly man: 'My friend, a drink to start?'

'Just some *agua*, please. Very good.' He spoke with an Irish accent.

Marco acknowledged the request and walked inside.

The younger man addressed his girlfriend, forced levity in his tone. 'Bit presumptuous with the order there! Lucky you got it right!'

Hugo is the type of person who insists you come to an Italian, in Portugal – because Portuguese food is 'weird' – and is then surprised when you know what he was going to order. He's ordered a *capricciosa* at every available opportunity for the last five years.

He ordered one on our first date, actually, at this little pizzeria in Battersea. I thought his pizza looked disgusting; I thought I didn't like olives. And actually, I was right. I don't like olives. But I had to say yeah when he offered me a slice, obviously, because I wanted to look like the type of person who *would* like olives: cultured, mature, you know? Sometimes I still pretend, when we're with his pals, or especially if we're with his dad. I liked that he took me out though, properly, from day one. None of the boys before him had taken me on dates, not unless hungover Eddie Rocket's the morning after counts as a date.

No pretending to like olives in Eddie Rocket's, mind.

'Hallo!' The elderly man sought to engage them, as though he'd read the Irish accents as an invitation, or perhaps in an effort to dispel the awkwardness of their proximity. Kate lifted a hand in greeting. Hugo offered a nod. At Hugo's request, Kate set out their travel options in a resigned whisper, looking at the table, the menu, her hands as she spoke. The bus would take almost a day; she was not sure it would arrive in Lisbon before the last evening flight to Dublin. A taxi would take six hours.

'I don't even want to know what that would cost. I'm sure I don't have it, anyway.' She exhaled: a hefty, laboured breath.

'Well, if you're worried about the money, don't. I' – he corrected himself – '*we* have money. We don't need to worry about money, Kate.'

'Could I –' The elderly man leaned across his table. 'I'm very sorry to interrupt, but would you have a menu over there? There's none on my table and I don't know where the waiter –'

Kate handed the elderly man the menu with a smile. He thanked her, and Marco returned from inside with wine and two glasses.

He set the glasses on the table in front of Kate and Hugo. 'Now, who will taste? *Senhor*? Fantastic.' Marco poured a shallow pool of wine into the glass in front of Hugo.

Hugo lifted the glass, swirling the liquid inside and inhaling slightly before taking a sip. Kate made an odd sound, like a cough that originated in the front of her mouth.

> He's always so awkward at this bit. He feels like he has to do the whole show, but he'd never in his life send a bottle back. He wouldn't dare. Once, there were little bits of cork floating around in the wine, and he acted like it was the most delicious thing he'd ever tasted. It was undrinkable. I had to pour mine in a plant.

> Probably quite bad for the plant?

Hugo confirmed that the wine was satisfactory and Marco filled their glasses. The elderly man reminded him that he'd forgotten to bring water and Marco apologised.

'Ah, no harm,' said the elderly man. 'Thank you.'

Hugo leaned across the table. 'The money isn't an issue, Kate. This sounds fairly... serious?'

Kate winced and took a sip of her wine. 'This is delicious, actually. There's a nice acidity to it.' She picked up the menu. 'Nine euro! That's mad.'

'Kate.'

'Nine euro,' Kate repeated, tone flat.

Hugo sighed, cocked his head to one side.

Kate raised an eyebrow. 'For a bottle. Mad.'

A beat passed. 'That is mad,' Hugo agreed. 'You wouldn't get it for that in a supermarket at home.'

'No chance,' said Kate, taking a considerable gulp.

'How's your mum?

'Ah. You know Mam. She was trying to be all matter-of-fact on the phone. Trying not to worry me.' She tilted her head back. 'I'm afraid that ship has sailed, Mam.' Kate wrinkled her nose. 'She's fragile though, I can hear it in her.'

Hugo looked at her with soft wet eyes. She met his gaze, blinked twice. 'She didn't ring me in time.'

Hugo, again, reached a hand across the table towards Kate's, but she gripped her glass tightly.

'I'm starving now, are you?' said Kate. She turned to the elderly man. 'I can recommend the house white, if you're trying to choose?'

'I am indeed, thank you.' He smiled widely at her, his front teeth slipping slightly out of position.

Kate offered to let him taste from her glass, and he laughed in response, the laugh of a younger man. He declined politely, but admitted that he was having trouble choosing between pasta and fish for dinner.

Kate shrugged. 'Sure are we not on the Camino? All this walking.' She gestured towards him with her glass. 'As far as I'm concerned, if there's ever a time to eat pasta, it's now.'

Hugo's eyes moved from Kate to the elderly man, and back again. He exhaled theatrically and shifted in his seat. If Kate noticed Hugo's movements, she did not acknowledge them. The elderly man asked Kate what she had ordered.

'I'm having *cacio e pepe*, and Hugo...' Kate stole a glance at Hugo, a curve threatening the corners of her lips. 'Hugo is having the *capricciosa*.'

Hugo softened his brow, affirmatively.

'I'm Kate, by the way.'

The elderly man beamed. 'Very good. I'm John.'

'Hugo. Her boyfriend.'

Kate met the word 'boyfriend' with a little twitch of her lip. 'Lovely to meet you, John,' she said, raising her glass a couple of inches.

'Yeah,' said Hugo. 'Lovely.'

Marco arrived with John's water and engaged him in conversation. Hugo selected a piece of bread from the basket and turned it over in his hands. 'So, what do we... Is he awake, Kate?'

'I couldn't... I didn't ask.' Kate's voice was slight, like too much breath could break it. She swallowed. 'I don't know.'

Neither of them said much at that. Hugo took out his phone and opened an airline app. On seeing Hugo's phone in his hand – as if reflexively – Kate took hers from her bag. She opened a messaging app and began typing, her fingers moving rapidly across the phone's surface. A few moments passed like this, each of them seeking something from their screens.

'There's a flight on here from Lisbon tomorrow evening, we'd land in Dublin by nine. So it's just about getting to Lisbon tomorrow! That's doable. I'll talk to them at the hostel after dinner. Let's just get the taxi.'

'It'd be ten at least by the time we're out of the airport. They won't let me into the hospital that late.' Kate pressed her lips together tightly after she spoke.

'They might? If they think...'

'If they think what?'

Hugo paused before responding. 'Just if they think—'

At that moment, John and Marco concluded their exchange. Kate's eyes tracked the waiter as he walked back inside. John studied the paving stones, the awning, the wall finishes, with considerable interest.

Kate leaned in towards Hugo and whispered: 'Don't book those flights.'

'What?' Hugo's voice betrayed a slipping patience. 'I don't understand why... How are you planning to do this?'

'Don't book those flights.' Kate's tone was sharp, absolute. It pulled the air between them taut. She held that for a moment, then took a gulp of her wine. A streak of liquid trickled from her mouth to her chin. She dabbed at it with the heel of her hand and twisted in her chair. 'So, John, what did you go for?'

Matthew is a Sci-Fi/Fantasy writer from Norwich. He is currently working on both a novel and a short story collection. He is co-host of a podcast called *The Short Story Workshop.*

matt@theshortstoryworkshop.com

Envoy of the Beyond
A short story

Dr Bishop pressed on the accelerator and the speedometer on his old Subaru crept past sixty, even though he was in a fifty zone. The road stretched silently between the English countryside, as flat as the surface of a lake, and the violet evening sky. He willed the sun to dip below the horizon, as if he could push it with his thoughts alone, but it lingered out of spite. He would need darkness when he arrived.

He had left the lab at two minutes to five that afternoon, almost two hours ago. He hadn't even thought to eat anything. He'd been eying his glovebox, and the lukewarm satsumas that must be resting within, leftover from the butterfly-luring expedition three days ago. Maybe if he stopped at a red light, he could peel one.

He turned up the heating. A photo fluttered over the air vent in his dashboard, carelessly pinned there with a paperclip. The picture had passed under the eyes of at least a dozen other experts before landing in his inbox.

They were calling it an unknown species. A new discovery, and a remarkable one, given the moth's large size. But what troubled Dr Bishop the most – and prompted his sudden drive to a small village near the Norfolk Broads – was that he had seen it before.

He kept looking at the photo. The orange-pink colour was from the light source, apparently. The antennae looked larger than any moth he'd ever seen and were likely feather-shaped. It was not unusual to see moths with eye-like patterns on their wings, but this was no emperor or polyphemus. There were six of them; six bright white eyes, two on each forewing and another on the hindwings.

'I've seen that somewhere,' he muttered for the fiftieth time. 'I'm sure I've seen those eyes...' he tapped his fingers against the steering wheel in frustration.

He had spent the afternoon searching through every identification guide he'd ever held, many of which were now scattered across the back seat (along with a variety of lamps, nets, and a bucket with a handle that clacked every time he turned left). He'd found nothing. No records online, either. If he had seen this moth before, it was a very long time ago, too long for him to remember.

There was still a long way to go. On a whim, he asked his phone to call his mother.

He tried to work his question into conversation casually. 'Listen, do you remember when we used to go on those insect hunts, when I was little? Did you ever see a large moth with a pattern of six white eyes, three on each wing?'

She didn't remember. Unsurprising, but it had been worth a try.

'We went when I was very young, didn't we? I can't remember.'

'You were about eight when we started,' his mother said. He was surprised; this was later than he expected. 'It was always dinosaurs before that, you know. But then you started talking about moths. Remember, I got you that net for your birthday?'

He did remember that. So, if he'd seen the moth as a child, it was less than twenty years ago. His eight-year-old self had no idea that he'd end up with an entomology degree. He wondered what he would've thought of his current project, a Biobotics program in collaboration with a team of electrical engineers.

He should be spending this time considering the project. So far, they had successfully inserted microcomputers on to the back of a moth's neck and administered radio-controlled neuromuscular stimulation. A small electrical charge was all it took to manipulate the insects' muscles and steer it in any direction they wished. It could prove useful for search and rescue operations.

For the most part, moths were quite simple machines. A fixed stimulus produced a fixed response. His younger self might say it was unfair on the helpless creature. As a colleague succinctly reminded him, it doesn't even know it's a moth, so how could it understand it was being manipulated?

The project wasn't the reason he had become a lepidopterist, but it had raised many fascinating questions about moth neurology. As his PhD supervisor had said, if they could understand the world's smallest denizens, then they were one step closer to understanding the world.

He turned down a narrow, winding road, and the orange glare of the streetlamps vanished in the rear-view mirror. He trundled along, inching through an impenetrable darkness that warned him this region still belonged to nature, not man.

According to his phone, this was it. He squinted through the window, and then an automatic lamp flickered on, and he saw a rusting bronze plaque showing the number eleven. This was the house. It looked still. The walls were painted white and bare, the lawn mowed to a short fuzz, the hedges perfectly straight. A light shone through the blinds of an upstairs window, like a lighthouse.

Something about the place unnerved him; maybe it was the way the blank windows looked like eyes, or the self-conscious way the house presented itself. Only somebody with something to hide would keep everything so neat and proper; the house gave the impression that it had been expecting company.

His fingers clenched the steering wheel, sticky with satsuma juice. He looked again at the photograph, put the handbrake on, and walked briskly up the path. He was here for possibly the greatest discovery in his field for the last decade. His thoughts should be of champagne, not apprehension.

Mr Rogers appeared in a glowing orange light at the door. 'Here for the moths?' he asked with barely a glance at Dr Bishop, reaching for his keys.

'Yes, if you don't mind,' Dr Bishop said, trying to keep his voice level. He suspected that to a man like Rogers, a moth was a moth, and a man who got excited over them was a nut.

The house seemed ordinary in Rogers' presence. They went through a side gate and into a wide, open garden. On the patio was a large disc, like a ceiling lamp, and when Rogers flicked a switch a pinkish-orange light shone upwards in a visible beam that seemed to reach all the way to the full moon.

'Takes a few minutes,' Rogers said, standing with his hands on his hips. He had the air of someone demonstrating a leaky sink to a plumber.

'This works reliably?' Bishop asked, leaning forward.

'Every time I've tried it. Just turn it on and they show up.' Rogers looked at him, perhaps remembering how Bishop had introduced himself as doctor on the phone. 'Don't suppose you know why?'

He shrugged. 'Moths often end up near light sources. They confuse their navigation.'

'Yep,' Rogers said, and stood waiting for Bishop to elaborate.

Instead, he asked, 'Where did you get the lamp?'

'Client gave it to me. Said he bought it years ago for his greenhouse. Reckoned red light was good for his plants or something, but he had to stop using it because it attracted pests. I took it off his hands. Just tried it out once, to see if it still worked, and then...' he shrugged. 'Just seemed a little weird, is all. So, I phoned a couple people, and they phoned whoever they liked, I guess.'

'Sorry. This must be quite inconvenient. Maybe if it's a new species, we can name it after you.' He smiled.

Rogers grimaced. 'No, thanks.'

Bishop was saved from the resulting silence by the arrival of their subject. Rogers noticed it first and pointed. 'Here they are, look.'

At the top of the beam of light flittered something small, an intermittent shadow. As it descended, the pattern of its flittery flight path became clear, a slow and steady spiral. Its wings moved as if in slow-motion, and it glided downward at a gravity-defying pace.

Another appeared behind it, and then another, each with the curious pattern of six white eyes. They glowed pink in the light, each casting a shadow above them like a straight black ribbon, each following the same invisible spiral staircase.

Dr Bishop could not speak. His mouth had opened, but with no purpose. The spiral was hypnotic. Down and down and down. For a moment he thought he heard a voice (his mother's?) telling him to come inside because it was going to rain.

At some point Rogers unlocked the back door and went inside. Dr Bishop heard his keys jangling like distant choir bells. He watched the wings beating up and down, slow, watched the shadows they left in the sky. Like puppet strings, he thought. They were magical, but best of all, their antennae were shaped like feathers, just as he thought they would be. Because he remembered.

Memories resurfaced, shook themselves free from somewhere deep in his mind, dust flying. Of a night filled with coloured explosions and crackling flames. Bonfire night.

All the same, this moth was unclassified, and a group now rested on the lamp. He sprinted back to his Subaru for his equipment. He half-expected them to be gone on his return, to be left wondering if he'd imagined it all. But they waited on the lamp, more gliding down from the sky.

He noticed with some curiosity that once they reached the lamp, they didn't flitter about, confused. Instead, they rested on its surface, perfectly calm. It was like they wanted to rest there. Not drawn to the lamp by a mistake in their navigational systems, but as if they actually desired its light, or its warmth, or something else. It must be something logical. Moths couldn't really want anything.

While they sat there, he saw them up close. They had furry shoulders, small heads, and when stationary their wings folded back like the blades of pocketknives. They were so calm; he was able to pick one up. It felt warm from the lamp. He'd be able to slip it into an envelope and secure it in a box for transport and subsequent study in the lab.

He thought maybe he should procure one for his friend at the museum, who would spray it stiff and push a pin through its thorax, ready for his display. For once, Dr Bishop felt horrified by this. There was something within those white eyes, something that saw him. Read him. Recognised him.

He looked up at the descending spiral. It was curious how the moon now seemed to him like a luminous hole at the top of the sky. He thought if he flew high enough, he might be able to poke his head out and ascend into a great glowing beyond. The reflection in his eyes shone pink and white.

He could almost remember now. He saw fireworks. Orange and pink and orange. He remembered laughing, running, the world towering around him. Then, in the darkness that followed, amidst a net of branches, the flutter of wings. Wings with burning white eyes.

His lips parted. He spoke with his mind, but his throat formed English words out of habit. 'Mother... Great Mother... the humans are simple machines. So flexible. So iridescent. Soon, we will know them like our own. And then we will know the galaxy.'

He felt the moths flittering within, the eyes on the inside of his brain, and he shed a tear as cool and smooth as a twilit lake. For a brief moment, he saw all that he was, the course of his life set out by the gusts from those wings, little more than a chance encounter. It wasn't talent or passion. It wasn't about him at all. He was white and paper-thin, his mind an empty circuit board.

Then it was gone. He saw only the moths, sitting on the lamp, their antennae raised towards him. As if observing him. He laughed and packed up his specimen. Moths couldn't keep such complicated ideas in their tiny little minds.

georgia campbell

georgia is a twenty-four-year-old writer from Stroud. She studied English Language and Literature at the University of Birmingham, before completing an MA in Forensic Linguistics. She often finds herself writing about neurodivergence, OCD and characters who simply take things too far.

georgia.lucy.campbell@gmail.com

the lamp factory
a novel opening

'You're fine,' Dette said to her carrots. They were quite woody and strange in their middles, but she was right; they were fine. She continued to cut them up into crescents and slid them into the water boiling on her stove.

This was likely the first time Dette had used her own words that day, not one of her character's lines. But then she turned to the clock hanging above the small table in her kitchen; it was a little past midnight. She had spent an entire day as her character, the young, newlywed Daughter-in-Law, after all. She wondered, for only a moment, whether she should continue to speak to her vegetables to create more distance between her and the Daughter-in-Law.

Perhaps most people, arriving home from work so late, would have found something simple in the fridge and gone to bed, but Dette always made herself rice with vegetables in the evening, and didn't feel she should change simply because her director was indecisive and slow. Knowing just how important tomorrow was – how well-rested and prepared she would need to be – made the meal all the more thrilling. She started work on her peppers.

It had been a long and almost fruitless day of rehearsals. *the lamp factory* was proving to be a difficult play to stage. They had begun rehearsals in the Ochre Bell Theatre just over two weeks ago and had still not achieved a full run-through without interruptions or corrections from Meera. Today had been more promising. Tickets from the premiere all the way through to the following May went on sale in the morning and were sold out by lunchtime. Their latest run-through attempt was underway by two o'clock and throughout the first act there were no technical errors, no mistakes, no fluffed lines; there was not a single word from Meera, until – well, until there was.

Dette piled her rice into her bowl. Sitting sensibly in a chair was briefly impossible, so she sat down on the floor, forced between two cupboards. The food was hot, and she did not allow it to cool. In those hours she had spent on stage that day, as they slipped further and further past their planned end of six o'clock, she never thought she would reach this moment.

—

She was alone in that final scene. She was the only obstacle to a clean run-through. She took the stairs to the lower floor of the family's home. The Mother, Father and Son were all in their beds.

It seemed as if they'd been sealed away on the stage. They fell into the claustrophobic self-reliance easily, for none of the four main characters ever left the stage. It was divided into five small, uneven sets across two floors. If a scene took place between the Mother and Father in the bedroom, the Son might be working in the living room and the Daughter-in-Law might be doing laundry in the kitchen.

Throughout the day, Dette had found her own thoughts suffused with the worries of the Daughter-in-Law. In a scene where she was working upstairs, while the rest of the family discussed her in the kitchen below, her mind began to wander. She needed eggs for her breakfast in the morning. Instead of considering whether she'd still have time after rehearsals, or how many she should purchase, she thought about whether the controlling Father would allow her to leave this late in the day. She even cast her eye towards the stairs down to the wings, wondering whether she'd be able to sneak away and return before he noticed. It was as if she had learnt a new language and was unable to fathom which she was speaking.

When she realised what she'd done, Dette thought she should feel embarrassed, in spite of it all taking place in her own head. This was not something Mark could tease her for, or that Robert could pity, but this unbalanced feeling could surely only be embarrassment.

But now she had nothing to think about but this one scene. She approached the very front of the stage and clicked on an imposing standard lamp. It was taller than her and as bright as a spotlight. She could not see anything but herself and the letter and knife in her hand. She sat cross-legged on the floor, and, as slowly as she could, began to open the letter. Dette usually opened them like her father, lifting a corner and then pushing the crook of her little finger through. This was too bold for her character and made too much noise. Instead, she lifted a corner, pausing every time the paper ripped, and then ran her thumb along the seam to weaken the glue. It may have been more sensible to use the knife, but if she was going to use the knife for anything, it would not be for something so banal.

Lifting the tongue of the envelope disturbed the paper too much. Dette paused and tensed to make her hands shake, and released a long, unsteady breath. She pulled out the letter and placed it on the floor, then held the envelope upside down, but nothing came out. She gave it a sharp, controlled jerk, then ran her fingers around the inside. When the time came, the audience's mind would click before the Daughter-in-Law's. She returned to the letter and read it aloud, revealing the truth of the entire affair. Dette had always found the ending to be a disappointing and dispossessing twist, one which took from the family more than it gave. It made the Daughter-in-Law seem foolish, perhaps even pathetic. Still, in the darkness, it was effective.

The creak from the floorboards gave Dette a start. Here was The Son and Father's cue. First were the floorboards, then the audience would see movement behind her, and the curtains would be drawn as the knife clattered to the floor. From behind the curtains, she would scream. She heard Mark's footsteps—

'No, it still doesn't work.' Meera's voice was quiet, but everyone heard.

Someone brought all the lights up again. Dette shielded her eyes with the letter.

Mark walked upstage and stood directly behind her. 'What's wrong?' he asked.

'The ending just still doesn't feel like H's,' Meera said. 'It's too theatrical.'

Mark nudged his knee into Dette's back. 'Don't say it,' he whispered, presumably believing she might say something dense along the lines of, *but we're* in *a theatre*.

Truly, though, she could understand; it was too theatrical, too melodramatic for what the play had been up till now.

'We're going to try it with just the creak in the floorboards,' Meera said, turning to her stage manager and muttering something to him. Mark and Dette ran back up the stairs.

Once she returned to her place in the living room, she began to open the letter again. She had not been given a new envelope, so she held the flap down and tore from the other corner. This time, the curtains quickly followed the disturbed floorboards, but before they were even halfway across the stage, Meera's voice emerged again.

'No. No, that's *too* quiet.'

And so they tried it again. They tried floorboards, knife drop, curtains; then no floorboards, no knife drop, curtains; then floorboards, curtains, scream; then curtains, scream. They tried so many iterations that they managed to return to the original order of floorboards, knife, curtains, scream.

Still with her legs crossed, Dette lay back on the stage after another reset, staring into the circle of light from the standard lamp. Robert briefly blocked the light with his head, lingering in the living room while Meera tried to organise and strike through everything they'd tried so far. He smiled at her, then stepped aside to make space at the front for Mark as well.

Dette thought about suggesting they simply keep the original ending for now and experiment another day. This would usually have been the plan, but H. Hyland, their playwright, was due to visit the following morning to watch the rehearsals, and so they had been in a frenzy of rehearsals-for-the-rehearsal the entire week. They were even introducing all the tech they could manage, despite being nowhere near ready.

Dette could see these fits of anxiety throughout the theatre, not in the people, but in the way they took control of the building. With each new attempt on the ending, even when Meera had called for something calmer, the curtains were hastily drawn, often, it seemed, a moment too soon. The stage manager kept muttering into his talker, and each time he did, the shade of the lights would change ever so slightly. Mark kept fiddling with the standard lamp, turning it on and off. He never fiddled – he was the first to snap at Dette for her fiddling. He didn't know there were two ways of using the lamp, the push switch at the top that he kept pressing, and a small switch set into the base. Each time he stopped fiddling, Dette would press her switch to encourage him to keep going. This was Hyland's influence; everyone but Dette was unable to keep still.

This was particularly frustrating; it was because of him that the ending was so difficult to stage. There was such demand for Hyland's work that production began on *the lamp factory* before he had even completed the play. It was still not even published. He knew the ending, but seemed unable to write it.

'It's too camp,' Meera said, 'and too thriller. The knife and the scream are so cheap. It feels like the curtains are in on it, like they're trying to cover for the Son and Father.'

Dette knew what she meant. There was a coyness to them, as if they were embarrassed by the goings-on, as if they were a mother trying to quickly smooth over something inappropriate her child had said.

'Why don't we just draw them and have that be the end of it?' Mark asked. 'Without any of this,' he added, waving his arms around Dette.

And so they tried this as well. The curtains were drawn a beat too soon again. She waited behind them, waited for Meera's voice.

They heard her sigh. Mark and Robert came down the stairs again, followed by Katherine, whose character spent the entire final scene as a lump in the bed.

'Can I suggest something, Meera?' Katherine asked as things were reset again.

Mark was fiddling, and decided he should speak instead. 'I think we should have Dette—'

The bulb blew. Dette could each see the flash in her eyes moments after it passed.

'For Christ's sake, Mark.'

'It was going to blow anyway. We can just use a spotlight.'

'No,' Meera snapped. 'Could you all step back, please? You're crowding Dette and I can't see the scene properly.'

As they moved further back into the living room, Meera's expression changed and she wrote something down. There were more mutterings from her and the manager. They were all asked to clear the stage, as she had a new idea. The evening's overstretched rehearsals had only just started.

Ned Carter Miles is a writer and radio producer from Dorset. His short fiction has appeared in *Litro*, *Ox Mag*, *Trolley*, *Cicada*, and others. During a productive year at UEA, he's drafted two novels, *For Sugar* and *daddyBaby*. *For Sugar* has recently been shortlisted for the First Pages Prize. More at www.ncmiles.com

info@ncmiles.co.uk

For Sugar
The opening of a novel

breath

Do you dream of breathing, Baby, safe as you are in my belly's black waters? Is the world still wordless there? Would that I were with you in that still quiet, but once you've got words there's no going back to the dark.

You kicked today. Soon enough you'll have to breathe. And once you've breathed in, you'll have to breathe out. Then so it'll be till there's no breath left.

I've thought oft of drowning, and how the lincen girt sea do lap at your lungs till she's made em her own. Then she swallows you down and salts muscle and fat till you're a suent-boned skellie dancing languid to her tides. There's a horror to those bony boys avore they're clean, with loose meat hanging from their mandibles, but after that they're so funny and sweet. I wonder if already Ana and Jon are sweet unfleshed skellies dancing down there in the dark, and Ma and Adi too. I think on em and hope they're happy. At least skellies are always smiling.

She's hungry, the sea, and for six moons alone now I've watched her from the house, stretching frothy white teeth o'er rounded hills, gnawing at the loam like a main girt varmint on a sprawly green leaf. She laps in small waves and comes e'er inward, and she'll do so till she's sate.

I envy you, Baby. Floating sweet and serene like a syrupy peach in the dark waters of my womb. If I could keep you there I would, but it's hard to hold on to a home. Two fickle seasons we've stayed with Ma's trinkets and curios, hoping as she did to rebuild, but now the end may be beginning. The sea was long in coming to the House, but today she arrived at his door.

You may now never see the House as he was avore you, Baby. So I'll tell you best I can what he was like.

house

The House is a sweet old fellow and kind. All rough stones and each of
em different. Most are covered in moss or dead vine that wraps him up
tight, but if you chip away from the moss and stone, like when Eli lost
his temper once and threw a metal watery can at the wall, there's a glassy
black flint below. Long avore us, the House sat gentle and proud on his hill
like some big daddy animal. Calmly he watched o'er the woods in front of
him and down to the sea below. But the woods stopped leafing and the sea
got sneaky. She crept up o'er the land for a time and stopped short of the
House's hill, leaving only loamy eskers to peek up their foreheads between
here and the horizon, and a sodden puxy all along her shore.

For a time, she left the woods alone as well. Though already they were
mostly dry trees and mulch-turned-mud sweet smelling with rot. That's
where crows lived, and you'd see those sweet boys hopping around with
their beauty joyful hops and their peery heads. I'd hop hop with em too
avore the world's words and worries pulled me out from dark muteness.

Behind the house and inland was the field. Men tilled its soil in return
for Ma's knowledge and promises, but each year the crop grew sadder, and
Ma harsher with em. Then one night they burned it all down and left. After
that Ma'd send me to the field for soot with to clean her teeth, checking
herself in the old standing mirror as she blackened enamel with a finger
and spat. Ma always was proud of her teeth. Was proud of a lot of things,
and she made us proud of em too.

When you kicked this morning, Baby, the sea was at the door. I was
collecting what I could of Ma's things and bringing em upstairs to dry
safety. I wanted the most beauty of em with me for the months to come.
There's the shiny metal toaster Ma kept on the kitchen counter. She said
when there's electricity again we'd make toast and jam. Of course, we'd
need wheat again too, and fruit. There's the books from Ma's schoolroom
that only she could read. They were mostly damp through, but we'd need
their knowhow when the time comes for rebuilding. There's all the beauty
furniture Ma said was in her family since the sea had been content to lap
softly at the sand and the woods still bloothed thick and green.

I tried my best to move it all, but I'm heavy with you, Baby, and after
only a few chairs I stopped at Ma's old standing mirror. I'd only dragged
it from the wall when I had to bend down and rest, and that's when you
kicked, like a quobbly risen bubble popping in my belly. You startled me to
standing, and in the mirror, I saw through a window the inland hill behind

the house, and a man coming towards us over the hills.

He'd take what food we had and leave us here to starve, or worse. I went quick through the kitchen to the pantry where still there were full jars: seaweed in its brine and veggies from Jon's garden. Anything sweet I'd long since eaten. I felt you kick again and shuffle Baby while I hid what I could beneath the old ceramic basin. Then I took a jar and the longest knife of Ma's, its blade slivered with use like a waney moon, and went upstairs to hide.

Behind Ma's bed I listened as the inland facing door creaked open. My heart hopped afeared to the man's footsteps on the stone, a thumping of books to the floor, some wooden treasure falling. I gripped the knife's handle as he tore through all that I'd tended these many months, and Ma for many years avore. Then the stepping began on the stairs.

Ma'd warned us about men, especially men living in uncivilised times. They had savage instincts and boundless wants. This one would come through every room of the House as the sea runs round every rock in her wake, and he'd find us.

When he hit the creaking step a third way up the flight, I decided our best chance was to catch him there. I could slash with the long knife and kick him down, and if he landed badly without catching my leg we'd be safe. I got the blade behind me and came round from Ma's bed. He was close already to the landing, and he saw me in the doorway avore I was even close, stopping so the last stair cawed crow-like beneath him. He was tall and sinuous, with a mess of hair turning black to grey round a pocked face. He looked strong, but his eyes when I saw em were soft and startled.

'I'm sorry,' he said, staring at me. I didn't know someone was here. And he turned and went slowly back down the stairs.

I might not have followed him. Perhaps it was foolish that I did. But don't think ill of me, Baby. Those were the first words I'd heard in six months.

words

Avore I was pulled from the dark I'd lived seventeen years without words. Then there were just things and things, but they were all the same one thing too. The whole wild world and all its guts were like the sea as she slept o'er the puxy wetland hills. Every notion was a dead old jelly drifting to shore and losing its shape once in sight, and I was afloat o'er the dark waters without wants or words like a bug on a leaf.

Still, in some wordless way I knew Ma Jepson's as the hand that hit, or Eli for tricks and small cruelties. I knew the lay of the house and the lands around. I scuttled with sweet crabs as they ventured through the grass, and I hop hopped with the crows pecking hungry at the mulch. And though to me the time-telling moons were just more dead jellies floating noways through a dark, there came a time I knew gut-well the world was changed.

I knew of a fire in the field at night, that the men who tilled it went their ways, that the meals got small and my belly got tight. And then all the nameless shapeless things of the world blew up into the black like sparks from the field afire, and in the everwide dark they stuck together and made a light, and under that light the world took shape. Those quobbing jelly moons found their arcs and there was time, and with each passing moon, words stuck too. Ma Jepson's name and Eli's took tight to em like they'd been there always, like the dry dead old vines round the roof of the House, and the name for my belly's tightness was hunger.

Avore the field burned there'd been food enough. Afterwards we boiled seaweed and lived from our stores. But from my first growing hunger grew a second one, sharper and raging, like a voice that hollered from both inside and out, an itch that wrapped roots round my belly, calling out for sugar.

itch

I don't know when a peach tree last flowered or fruited in this whole wild world, but in the room where Ma tried each day to get the word into me there were two jars of peaches floating fleshy in their syrup. They sat on a shelf behind where she'd stand, and I'd watch em from my lil desk as she read from the Bible or from shiny magazines she kept wrapped up in cloth. The more time passed since I came into words, the greater was the itch for those peaches.

Today we're going back to the beginning, Ma started one morning, more cheery than usual. Cause a new beginning's nearly upon us.

I don't know even if Ma thought I understood her then, but she didn't mind trying, swinging her cane up and down as she read:

...Let the waters under the heavens be gathered together unto one place, and let the dry land appear...

And I floated twix her voice and the distant low baying of the greedy grey sea.

...Then God said, Behold, I have given you every herb bearing seed, which is

upon the face of all the earth, and every tree, in the which is the fruit of a tree yielding seed; to you it shall be for meat...

And I thought on the barren burnt field and my tight-bellied itching for sugar, and my lusteye was fixed on the meat of those peaches when Ma's stick slapped down on the table avore me.

How're you gonna get along in a civilised world if you can't pay attention? she hissed, not so cheery now, then cleared her throat and went back to the reading.

For fear of the rod I tried to keep the itch quiet. I listened to Ma tell how it's no good for a man to be alone, how God made another for him. At that I felt a new itch not for sugar, but some other want I didn't yet know and sweet in its own way. Something like a warmth between my legs.

There were a lot of new wants in those first wordy months. They came solid like crystals out of fluid as when the sea dries salty on the grass at low tide. Each of those crystals was a joy to my tongue, because there was a whole wild world, Baby. It was sad and sweet, and ripe to be tasted as a peach floating comely in its syrup.

Amanda Caswell-Robinson has been long listed twice for the Primadonna Prize. Formerly a playwright, her work has been staged throughout the UK. Novels-in-progress include, *The Wailings*, a supernatural thriller set in 1950s Britain, and *The Crows*, a non-fiction account of events leading up to multiple murders in a Warwickshire village.

acaswellrobinson@yahoo.co.uk

The Wailings
The opening of a novel

CHAPTER ONE

The Wailings watched the boy playing from behind the window. They wanted to get into him, to warm themselves and spiral around like Catherine wheels in his chest, in his brain, and through his fingers. This time they wouldn't forget themselves, it would only tickle. They tried to catch his eye, but he stared straight through them. They would have to wait. It would happen soon. He would need them again.

If Travis could sense the Wailings outside, he decided not to let it interfere with his determination to win Gin Rummy. He had two Jacks, a Queen of diamonds, and a string of eights. But Cerys, his best friend, was annoying him. She wouldn't settle and seemed distracted. Maybe he should let her win, but she beat him at everything else including draughts, chess, drawing, writing and art. Card games were the only thing that he had been able to teach her and now she wasn't even pretending to try. She was older than him by an unfathomable amount: she should have grown up by now.

It was nearly midnight, and his stomach was rumbling. He had resisted eating his bread because he was afraid his bowels might betray the extra snack in the morning. He knew he had to wait. The full moon outside emanated meagre light. He fantasised that if it was really made of cheese, he would catapult himself towards it and murder anyone trying to stop him. Release from hunger rarely came through sleep: his bed with its single white sheet and thin woollen blanket ensured he was always cold apart from rare midsummer nights. Next to it stood a polished brown table with a narrow draw. A tall Georgian wardrobe looked down on him holding five uniforms. One for school and the rest for all of the other roles he had to play.

Uncurling his shoulders, he lifted his nose in an imperious manner and jutted his chest out. 'You do know that I am top of my class!' He laughed. Leaning forward he exchanged a two of spades with an eight of hearts from the pile. 'That's my impression of Edna Coleman, that is.'

But it was futile, Cerys wouldn't change her expression, she didn't even smile and looked past him towards the door.

His room was icy cold, and shadowy figures loomed by the window. Unperturbed, he persisted. 'Edna don't half think she's something special. Teacher's always giving her extra books and making her stand at the front.' He clutched his hair and pulled it into bunched tuffs. 'And she tosses her plaits this way and that...'

Wind rushed through the gap in the window and he bit his lip. Cerys didn't pick up a card and pointed towards the door. He licked his chin with the tip of his tongue and wiped his forehead with his pyjama cuff. Cocking his head to one side, he pressed his finger on to the wooden floor and drew a spiral shape in the condensation. Shrugging, he said, 'I'll take the card for you then,' and scooped one up. 'Here you go! See?'

Cerys shook her head and folded her arms.

'But Mother's not due tonight,' he whispered to her.

The sound of air rasping against the window intensified and jerked him into action. 'OK. OK. I'll put them away.' He picked up the cards and squeezed them under his mattress. The streetlamp outside dimmed and a tree's branches tapped the glass. Erasing the spiral shapes on the floor with his foot he hissed, 'I am calm Cerys. Ssh...'

Straight-backed and with arms outstretched, he crept towards his bed, silently padding across the floorboards with the skill of a tightrope walker. He pulled back his bedsheets and slithered under them. Robotically, he turned to his side, created dents with his hands in the pillows and steadied his breathing.

A few feet away his mother tiptoed along the corridor outside. She was savouring the last inch of a cigarette and leaned against his door, shaking her head and muttering. Holding a crystal goblet in one hand, she took one final drag and dropped the cigarette into it. She then placed the goblet on to the floor, steadied herself and wiped a drop of spittle from her lip. Straightening her body, she dusted herself down and pulled back her silver-blonde hair into a ponytail.

'Travis my darling. Are you awake?' She spoke with a velvet voice, each word's last syllable enunciated.

She waited for a few moments and turned her head to face the door. 'Darling, are you awake? It's time.' She paused. There was no answer. Unlocking the door, she pushed it open and immediately spied the freshly made smudges on the floor. Peering intently at her son, she stalked across the room and craned over him waving her hands inches from his face. There was no reaction, so she stroked his forehead and curled a stray strand of his golden hair around her finger. Travis let out a sigh and mumbled before settling back into apparent sleep.

'I'm sure I heard you talking to someone. Are you pretending to be asleep?' she asked.

She swooped down and kissed his cheek. Travis did not stir. Blinking, she dabbed her face and marched towards the window. 'Right so that's how you're going to play it!'

Fastening the window shut, she heard the tree branch tapping a staccato melody on the pane and swayed to the sound. 'The tree is making music Travis. If you woke up, we could listen to it together.' Holding herself, she closed her eyes and shook her head. 'I find this so difficult. You have no idea how hard this is for me.'

Turning, she opened her eyes and moved towards the bed, untangling Travis's hands from the bedsheets. Placing them by his sides, she pulled back his pyjama sleeve. The upper parts of his arms were covered in a crisscross assortment of white and red marks. 'They're healing quite beautifully. It's a good job I look after you. Isn't it?'

She blew gently on the pattern and murmured inaudibly before opening the bedside drawer. Inside was a small mustard leather pouch. Unbuttoning it revealed a pearl handle attached to a short narrow blade. Taking a handkerchief from her pocket she polished it. 'No germs on this,' she said.

Swiftly and with a surgeon's precision she pressed the knife against the inside of his left arm. A small bubble of blood emerged. She pressed a little harder. The soft white skin split easily. 'Wake up my love. I won't be angry if you promise not to move.'

Still, he did not react.

The streetlamp outside flickered and she glanced towards the window. Standing upright, she wiped the blade and carefully placed the knife into its pouch before returning it to the bedside drawer. 'There. All done! But it's appalling, isn't it? I told them to fix that lantern weeks ago. Heads will roll, I assure you. And you'd like a bit more light in here, wouldn't you?' Looking at him she sighed, 'Why do you hurt yourself?' and stroking his cheek once more she said, 'Don't worry, love. I will wash the sheets again tomorrow. What a mucky boy you can be.'

Travis was hovering above himself. It was a trick the Wailings had taught him. Cerys was next to him holding his hand, her ginger hair falling across her shoulders like a white witch. He looked down at his body below. It was like looking at a dead person, except that person was bleeding. He watched the crimson of his blood blot the sheet and knew if he didn't get back inside soon there would be trouble.

'GO!' Cerys urged him. In these moments he could actually feel the warmth radiating off her. He didn't want to leave, but the cut in his arm would need tending to. It was only a little scratch, and if he had reacted it would have been so much worse. He had only made that mistake once before.

He waited until his mother left the room and concentrated on wriggling his big toe, but the sensation of Cerys being so close was too much for him. Why should he leave her? He'd followed the rules like any card game. When would he win against his mother?

Instead of returning he stared at Cerys; her obsidian eyes widened, and she moved as if she was underwater, with her legs flailing, her skirts billowing and her feet jabbing the air. Wrenching her hand from his grasp, she frantically pointed downwards. But Travis was entranced, he could see her so clearly, her alabaster skin shimmered and her emerald brooch glittered in the light. Why did she always make him go back? It was only when she shook her head and begged, 'Please. Please. You have to!' that he changed his mind. He would do anything for her, she was his best friend. Determined, he stared at his motionless body on the bed and returned to it.

He gasped at the pain radiating down his arm. His mother had cut quite deep this time, but he knew exactly what to do, and reaching over to the flannel under his pillow, pressed it firmly on to the wound. His head was pulsating, and his heart thundered. He had to calm down and breathe deeply, he told himself. Trembling, he walked over to the window and looked out at the woods beyond. The streetlamp gave a sudden burst of light, illuminating the assembled faces pressed against the rain splattered glass. Travis ignored them, instead whispering, 'Goodnight,' to the Fir tree swaying in the breeze. He watched it shake its jaw from side to side. One branch bent outwards: unusually curving into the shape of a nose. Higher up: a dark crevice where several branches had broken off, gave the appearance of an eye socket. When the wind blew, the limbs of the tree interlinked to give the impression of a mouth and chin. It looked like the profile of a craggy old man. It moved in such a way that Travis was sure it was talking to him. And tonight, it had tried to warn him about his mother. It started soothing him now though; its mouth languidly swinging up and down. A gentle lullaby.

Laura Cooper has worked as an English lecturer, photographer, voice actor and music journalist. She lived in Japan for thirteen years before return-ing to the UK to pursue her writing ambitions as a recipient of the 2020/21 Kowitz Scholarship. Her debut novel explores solastalgia in a speculative near-future England.

lauracooper101@hotmail.com

Dragonfly
An extract from a novel

Later, by the fire, Jorey watched Ma and Mari clink mugs and bump shoulders as they bent their heads together.

'Drew still smells like a teenager,' Ma told Mari.

Jorey edged closer along the tree trunk to listen.

'That was fast.' Mari winked at Ma and rubbed her arm. 'I thought you had a sparkle about you.'

'I feel slightly ashamed.' Ma emptied her mug in one gulp.

'Emphasis on the slightly.' Mari picked up a glass bottle and refilled Ma's mug. 'Someone needs to try him out first, I suppose.'

'I hope the girls don't find out,' Ma said.

'If you're not careful, they won't be the only ones,' Mari replied. They glanced quickly at Jorey, then huddled closer together and hushed the rest of their conversation.

Jorey looked over to Drew who was sitting at a table outside the big house with four young women. They were eating a dinner of potatoes, smoked fish and samphire which the Marsh-folk had brought with them as a gift.

Perhaps Drew was a gift too, Jorey thought. After all, there weren't many men in Hollow Oak and at lunchtime he'd seen the way the women looked at Drew. They were softer than usual and laughed more.

The party went late and there was repeated shushing every time someone got too loud. Jorey couldn't sleep with all the talking, so he watched Ma and Drew from his bedroom window in the big house. They sat on one end of the tree trunk drinking from the same mug. Ma stood up and gestured to Mari, who held out her studio key, laughing. Ma walked down to the stables and stepped into Mari's studio, leaving the door ajar. A few minutes later, Drew got up and followed her.

Jorey felt his chest knot tightly as the door closed. He wanted to run out and stop them, but the party felt unwelcoming now, so he leaned against the window and waited.

In the morning, he had a vague recollection of someone's smokey jumper against his face and of being lifted into bed. Ely was asleep on his cot across the room. On the next cot lay Drew. Jorey stood at the end of the man's bed and watched him sleeping. His hair curled away from his face and revealed a puckered lick of flesh from his left ear, down his neck and across his shoulder. His arms were thick, the dark hair on them risen against the morning chill.

Jorey looked back at Drew's face to find an open eye watching him. He froze as they looked at each other for a few moments. Then the eye closed and Drew pulled a blanket over his head.

—

In the summer, the water level in the Slump fell so low that the tops of rusted vehicles and bits of metal and concrete emerged from the thick crawl of the river. It was falling early this year and already rippled around the jut of old pylon and traffic signs.

Mari's studio overlooked the Slump and the river beyond, a small boat listing in the mud at the end of the long garden that ran down from the stables to the sandbag wall. From the window of the studio, Jorey watched Drew's head bobbing between tomato vines as he worked among the vegetables.

'How long is he staying?'

Mari looked up from her desk and over her glasses into the garden.

'Depends on when the Marshes come back through. Probably until October.'

Jorey sighed and walked over to Mari, leaning against her shoulder as he watched her work. She was measuring a hornet trapped in resin, then sketching it on to a piece of thick paper. Jorey picked up Mari's magnifying glass and observed the hooked mandible on the hornet's maw, the stripes on its abdomen.

'Ovipositor,' he said, naming the stinger.

'What kind of yellow is it?' Mari asked.

Jorey considered, running through the shades of yellow he knew. 'Mustard.' He shook himself like a wet dog.

Mari laughed. 'Heebie jeebies?'

He nodded.

'That's a good reaction to have.' Mari selected a sharpened pencil from a nearby pot. 'Anything this colour you should stay away from. We don't have any anti-venom here.'

'Can they kill you?'

'One won't, but it's bloody painful. They sting like hot needles.'

Jorey watched Mari add the cells on the hornet's wings. Her studio walls were covered in flash – designs for insects, invertebrates, fish and mammals, some with Latin names underneath them, some with dates. Jorey had a patch of wall to draw on in the corner by the window. He'd copy Mari's pictures and erase them when there was no more room. The grey lines and grooves of old drawings never quite faded beneath new ones, so sometimes there would be a bear face under a bumblebee or an adder running through a badger. He'd never seen these animals – only the ones Mari drew on paper or people.

The tattoo machine was stowed in a metal case on a shelf next to Mari's desk. A line of ink bottles sat above it, high enough that Jorey couldn't reach. He wasn't allowed in the studio when Mari had Witnesses. He'd hear the buzz of the tattoo machine from outside and a murmur of conversation, sometimes an intake of breath over a sensitive spot. Afterwards, the Witnesses would emerge with clear, shiny bandages on their skin. A few days later they would move on or return to wherever they'd come from. Ma had a tattoo on her shoulder blade: a pool frog on a raft of spawn, and a tangle of leaves up her left thigh. She said you could tell the age of a Witness by the animals they carried.

Jorey started fidgeting against Mari's shoulder.

'What do you want to ask me?' Mari sat up and took off her glasses.

'Is Ely leaving?'

'Sometime soon, yes.'

'Will I have to move on?'

'Not for a while, no, but what happens when you're twelve?'

'I go to work with the men.'

'Oh, don't say it like that.'

'I want to stay with you and Ma and the others.'

'It will be good to work with the men. Drawing isn't the only thing you need to learn.'

'What is Drew's job?'

'Drew is here because some of the girls want babies. We don't have many littles and we've got permission to have more.'

'Can't we make littles without him?'

'No, Jorey. None of the men here can make babies, remember?'

'Does Ma want another baby?'

'Ma doesn't want any more. She's got you.'

Jorey sighed, unconvinced. 'Will I have to make littles?'

'Maybe, but don't worry about that now.'

'I don't want to leave.'

'You're not leaving anytime soon, okay?' Mari pulled Jorey to her and ruffled his hair. He shrugged her off.

'You don't like that any more, huh?' Mari observed. 'Must be growing up.'

'I'm *not* growing up.' Jorey crouched on the floor and looked up at the pictures on the walls.

Mari sighed this time.

'Don't tell anyone, but how about I give you a piece of paper and a pencil and you go find something to draw?'

Jorey hopped up and held out his hands.

Mari handed him a piece of thick paper from an envelope and selected a pencil from her jar.

Jorey rushed to the studio door and slipped on his shoes.

'Jor!'

'Yes?'

'Don't lose it this time.'

'Paper doesn't grow on trees,' he replied, pulling the door open and running into the bright beyond.

'Not any more!'

The river pushed by in rippled flashes on the far side of the channel. Jorey sat cross-legged on the fishing platform, the water tugging on the reeds around him like a gentle breath. He was drawing a leaf he'd found, tracing the shape and copying in the veins.

There was a buzzing above from left to right and then behind. Jorey sat upright and looked around, fearing a banded, mustard body. It was the engine hum of something heavy. An iridescent flicker of wings shot past his face and Jorey fell back in a moment of panic as the insect alighted on the tip of a reed. A dragonfly the width of a finger shimmered and rattled in the sun. Jorey scrambled for colours to tell Mari: a body of spotted spring skies and flecks of yellow, wings like scattered rainbows. He turned over the paper and started to sketch. Mari would be pleased to see this.

He'd drawn the eyes and the body and was working on the wings when he heard a rustle in the scrub behind him. The dragonfly lifted from the reed and bobbed to the other side of the river. Drew emerged from the Slump looking surprised to find himself there.

'What are you doing, little guy?' He walked over and stood so close that

Jorey could feel the heat coming off him.

'Drawing.'

'What's that then?'

'It's a dragonfly.'

'Haven't seen one of those for years,' Drew said. 'Where?'

'You scared it away.'

Drew plucked the piece of paper from Jorey and rubbed it between his fingers. 'Where did you get this?'

Jorey said nothing.

'You sure you're allowed this?'

'Mari gave me it.'

Drew sat down next to Jorey. 'I think Mari has the wrong idea giving you pens and paper. Boys should be learning, not messing around.'

'Mari is teaching me to tattoo.'

Drew half-smiled and lifted the pencil from Jorey's fingers: 'Sure she is.'

'Are you Ma's friend?'

'Aneissa?' Drew put the pencil out in from of him and held it very still, avoiding Jorey's gaze. 'Yeah, we know each other from before you were born. But we haven't seen each other for a long, long time.'

'Are you from the Marsh?'

'No. I...' The was a whir across the water and the dragonfly hovered above the pencil, then gripped on with its feet. Drew gestured for Jorey to take the pencil. 'Got it?' he whispered.

Jorey nodded, and as Drew dropped his hand away Jorey felt the dragonfly weighting the pencil, the whir of its wings shivering into his fingertips. He held the pencil steady, observing the iridescent sheen of its eyes and how its tail curled in and out like a question mark.

'I think it's an Emperor,' Drew whispered.

'It's a Hawker,' Jorey corrected him. 'A male.'

'You know your stuff.'

The dragonfly rose and angled away into the Slump.

'What's a kettle?' Jorey asked, looking at Drew's scar.

'Someone's been gossiping, eh?' Drew rubbed his hand over his neck. 'I saw you looking this morning.'

'Was it hot water?'

'No. It was the police. Different kind of kettle.'

Jorey waited for him to continue, but the man stayed silent, looking out across the river.

'I saw you with Ma yesterday,' Jorey said. 'In the Slump.'

'Well, that explains why you've been looking at me funny.'

'Are you and Ma—'

'No,' Drew interrupted. 'We're not in love, not any more.'

Jorey paused at the thought of his mother loving someone else but him. 'No, I meant...' Jorey huffed dramatically then continued. 'Are you making littles?'

'Oh.' Drew hesitated and returned the paper to Jorey. 'No. I mean, not with Ane. We can't.'

'Good.' Jorey put the dragonfly sketch in his pocket with the pencil, light with relief. 'What's it like where you're from?'

'I'm not sure I should talk to you about that, Jorey. Your folks wouldn't like it.'

'The Marsh then. Do they really have houses on legs?'

Drew ran an exasperated hand through his hair. 'You ask a lot of questions.'

'I'm eleven.'

Drew laughed. 'You sound like your Ma.'

'What about Ma? Tell me about her.'

Drew smiled and lay back on the platform. 'Your Ma...' He raised an arm to shade his eyes against the sun.

Jorey squinted up to see the glint of something silver passing far above in the haze.

Drew waved at the sky. 'Your Ma,' he said, 'was a stonethrower.'

Hattie Cooper Hockey is a writer and former bookseller from Manchester. This extract is the opening to her in-progress novel *Tell Me How It Feels*. This will be her debut and follows a year in the lives of three friends, set between Manchester, Edinburgh and Leeds.

hattie.cooper96@hotmail.co.uk

Tell Me How It Feels
The opening of a novel

It was New Year's Eve. Jules was out with friends. She felt sick.

Outside in the smoking area she faced the wall, both hands splayed on the rough brick, looking at her shoes. The air was sharp. She was shivering. Her chest was going up and down very quickly and it felt like she wasn't getting enough air. Light-headed, she leaned forwards.

She was thinking about something she'd heard earlier. A girl from sixth form had been talking about one of their old teachers.

'He's in hospital,' the girl had said to a group of them. They'd been standing outside, passing round cigs. Jules didn't smoke. She just wanted some air.

'Why,' someone said, 'cancer?'

The girl shook her head. She tapped her forehead. 'He's ill, ill,' she said, then paused to pass her cigarette packet to another friend who'd come out to join them. 'You know,' she took a drag from her own, 'like mentally.'

Everyone including Jules murmured, like they all understood, and the conversation moved on quickly. But it came back to Jules now.

She wasn't just drunk; she wasn't in control. Something had been holding her body together. She'd never noticed it before. But now suddenly it had dropped away. It was a horrible feeling, like dying. She knew that people had panic attacks and crises, but if you felt like this what if you felt it forever?

She was crying actually, too.

'Jules,' someone said.

She looked up and saw Sonny. Sonny, thank God.

'I've been looking for you.' His voice was brisk, like he was telling her off. He looked around. 'Where's Calum?'

'Sorry,' said Jules. He didn't seem to notice that she was crying, and he didn't look surprised to find her here.

'How long have you been out here?' he said.

'Sorry,' said Jules again. 'I feel sick, actually.'

Sonny looked at her. 'Right,' he said. 'Okay. I'll call a taxi. I'll tell Leanne.'

'No,' said Jules, 'I don't want you guys to have to leave.' She reached out to touch his shoulder but the contact was much harder than she'd intended, almost a slap. She looked into his face and couldn't read it. Was he annoyed? Maybe she would just walk home.

'It's fine,' he said, but he wasn't looking at her.

He was annoyed.

'You're annoyed,' she said.

'No.'

There would be something she could say which would make him understand. 'I do feel really bad,' she said.

'I know,' Sonny said, 'you've had a lot to drink.'

'It's not even midnight yet,' she said, 'you should stay. I hope you've had fun at least? It's been great to see everyone, thanks for organising, I hope you've had a good time.'

She put her hand on his shoulder again, this time to steady herself.

Sonny stared at her.

'Jules,' he said, 'It's nearly one. You missed the countdown. You were too busy, necking on with Calum.'

—

The New Year's night out had been Sonny's suggestion. The three of them – Jules, Sonny, Leanne – were back for Christmas in Manchester and he'd heard that some others were going, people they'd all known at sixth form. Jules hadn't wanted to go at first but the others overruled her. The two of them seemed emboldened, after making friends in their first terms at uni.

'This is the kind of thing we should be doing, Jules,' Leanne had said on the phone when they'd been booking tickets in November. 'It's the kind of thing you do when you're young.'

Jules drank a lot beforehand at Sonny's house. Rum and cokes, half and half. They made her want to spit. But, as Leanne had pointed out, pre-drinking wasn't meant to be enjoyed, just to save you money later on.

'Drinks are on Sonny when we get there,' Leanne said, 'with all his cash.'

Sonny shook his head, he looked embarrassed. In Manchester he lived with just his nan so had received the highest loan and maintenance grant possible. Jules wondered whether he regretted telling them this.

She rarely went out at uni in Edinburgh, so it was the first time she'd been drunk for a while. The first two glasses went to her head very quickly and she started to feel good, warm, her chest humming. When Sonny – who was at Edinburgh too – said he'd heard that she was a bit of a wild card in seminars, she smiled and said, 'Of course your friends would say that.'

She turned to Leanne. 'Sonny's posho friends,' she said, 'they wet themselves at any mention of Marx.'

Sonny was quiet but Leanne laughed. Jules thought: *when you're drunk you do whatever you want.*

From Sonny's house in Whalley Range they took the eighty-six into town, which went past their old college in Hulme. The others turned to look, pointing out new signs and the recently extended car park. Jules kept her eyes straight ahead.

As they passed through Hulme and up towards the city centre, Jules could see the outlines of new towers ahead, huge, tall structures wrapped in scaffolding with tiny lights at the top like red eyes. These buildings often advertised themselves as luxury apartment blocks, which made Jules think that the people financing them must be kind of stupid, to believe there could be much demand for that here.

They got to the club around ten thirty. Sonny spotted someone across the room immediately and disappeared into the crowd. Jules went with Leanne to the bar.

'Tequila shots?' Leanne said. 'Just to get us going.'

Jules nodded. As she waited behind Leanne, she looked up at the high ceiling, which made her feel very small. Her little body, the big room, such a great mass of people. She didn't really matter.

Leanne pointed to a shot on the bar which Jules picked up and swallowed quickly. It burned. When she put it down, she noticed Leanne watching her, laughing.

'You're pissed, right?' Leanne said. She had a saltshaker and lime wedge in hand. She tipped some onto her wrist, licked it, threw back the shot, then sucked the lime.

Stupid, Jules thought. I am stupid. The thought made her laugh. 'Well anyway,' she said, throwing back her hair, 'that stuff's only performative.'

Leanne started telling her then about what she called a *suicide shot*, where you snorted the salt and squeezed the lime into your eyes. Jules thought that didn't sound right at all, but she laughed along anyway. It felt very important to show that she got the joke if there was one.

They went to the dancefloor. Leanne was giddy in that way Jules loved, a looser version of herself. She was usually blunt, often uptight. *Tainted Love* started playing and Leanne took her hand and spun her around.

Sonny came over with a few of their old friends from college. Jules hadn't seen these people for a while, not since results night the previous summer. They all hugged, which took a little while, then shouted, 'how are you' and 'fine' and 'this is a fucking great night' to each other, nodding or bouncing to the music.

What a relief, the noise, too loud to chat.

Jules had never enjoyed clubbing much at sixth form, and even less at university. But here she liked the force of the music, which made the floor buzz underneath her feet. Surrounded by people who had known her once, she felt like a different person in the darkness. No one could see her distinctly, so she couldn't see herself either.

—

Later on, after more drinks, Jules found herself in the bathroom with Lila, one of Sonny's friends from his old English class, who she'd got on with at college but not spoken to since.

'You look great, Jules, you know,' Lila said, looking at her in the mirror. 'You've had a real glow-up.'

Because she was on her own a lot in Edinburgh, Jules had recently gotten into running. When she got home for Christmas her mum had looked at her and said: *your face looks thin.*

'You too,' she said to Lila. She hadn't previously noticed Lila looking any different, but as she spoke she found herself believing it to be true.

It was at this point, as they left the bathroom to head back to the others, that Jules spotted Calum, a boy she used to sleep with at college.

—

Jules had known Calum from early on in sixth form. They were in the same History class for a while, then in April of final year they got off with each other at a party and not long after that they started sleeping together, casually. It seemed to surprise other people at the time.

'Oh hey,' Calum said when he saw her in the dark corridor. 'You're here.'

'I'm here,' Jules said back, stupidly. She tried to flick her hair to make this seem flirtatious.

He said something in response but she couldn't hear what it was. There was a track playing with a high electronic synth which seemed intended to simulate a human voice, like a screech. It reverberated through Jules' skull. She shook her head at him.

He leaned forward so he was close to her ear. 'You look fit,' he said. His breath was warm.

'Haha,' she said, and it came out not as a laugh but just a statement.

He raised his eyebrows.

'You do too,' she mouthed so he could read her lips.

Jules was wearing an outfit that she'd thought about for a long time. The top was sheer mesh, you could see her black bra underneath. She'd paired it with black jeans so it didn't look like she'd tried too hard. Calum wore an open overshirt, white T-shirt and black skinnies with Vans. He had a Red Stripe can in hand. He looked just like a Manchester lad, which he was. It was only after being away that Jules realised how much the city had a type and that she'd missed it, the distinctive style. Her friend Sonny was an outlier. He didn't care about clothes. He'd owned the same pair of jeans for years.

Jules motioned for Calum to come close again and in his ear she said: 'how's the gap year?'

He started saying something about working in his dad's office. She looked up into his face and noticed that he had more facial hair than he used to, and that there was a spot above his top lip.

His hand was close to hers. She took it.

Before long they were kissing and his mouth seemed very loose, like he didn't have any control over it. She'd forgotten what it was like to kiss him, it seemed a long time since they'd last been together, though really it had only been a few months. This close to his face she had a strange view of his nose which looked very wide. She remembered that she wasn't supposed to have her eyes open and shut them.

After a while they broke apart and Calum said: 'I need a drink.' He told her to stay where she was. 'What do you want?'

'Anything,' she said.

She waited in the hallway. People went in and out of the toilets. No one looked at her.

When Calum returned, he had a few friends with him. He handed her a shot. 'Here,' he said.

She knocked it back and found it was tequila again. She felt a surge of nausea.

'I don't feel well,' she said, swallowing with difficulty.

Calum stared back blankly so she repeated it, louder.

He laughed but in a cruel, irritated way. 'You're such a lightweight,' he said.

'I might be sick,' Jules said.

'Well don't be, not here,' he said.

He was raising his eyebrows now, not laughing.

Jules wished she hadn't said anything, she wished she wasn't this odd desperate thing, she wished she had self-control.

Calum was turning away to talk to his friends but Jules couldn't hear what they were saying.

'I'm going outside,' she said, touching Calum's sleeve, a move which, as soon as she did it, felt like that of a child pleading with a parent.

'Okay,' he said, like he didn't really care.

Nathaniel Danielle grew up in Scotland and writes fiction exploring themes of social and environmental change, intergenerational conflict and buried anger. He is currently working on the second draft of his first novel, 'Mardi Gras', which magnifies the moral dilemmas of climate change through the lens of ecoterrorism.

nathaniel.danielle.author@gmail.com

Mardi Gras
Abridged opening to a novel

The second time they tried to phone Beth that evening, she had just arrived at the Bristol Victoria hotel for the drinks reception. Waiters in plain white shirts and black aprons poured sparkling wine into plastic flutes. Platters of lukewarm hors d'oeuvres were being swiftly devoured by badly dressed geologists wearing conference lanyards. Balding professors did the rounds, trailed by their grad-student fan clubs. Beth swore under her breath. She couldn't see George Crawley anywhere.

She swiped a glass from a passing tray then reached into her pocket until she found the golf-ball-sized fragment of rock. Its surface was rough as sandpaper, except for the smooth dimples where her chisel had chipped it. She turned it over in her fingers.

Beth would calm herself in this way during moments of heightened anxiety, slowing her breathing and returning once more to the sensation of placing her hands on the Acasta gneiss, a remote outcrop of bedrock in Canada's Northwest Territories. Nine summers earlier, she'd taken a field trip there and chiselled this fragment from the rockface. By now she was becoming a recognised expert in the earliest eon of the planet's history, the Hadean, named for the Greek underworld, but she would still relive that moment of vertigo, the dizzying realisation that this living stone beneath her fingertips had witnessed the inferno of the planet's youth – 4,000,000,000 years ago – before complex life had evolved and when a day lasted eighteen hours.

Then she saw Chris fucking Snyder howl-at-the-moon laughing with George Crawley – *Professor* George Crawley – on the far side of the room. Beth gritted her teeth. They looked very much at ease in each other's company. Collegial, you might say. Snyder had just had the whole auditorium in stitches during the graveyard slot – last presentation of the day – as he recounted his mishaps on an otherwise cutting-edge field trip to the Jack Hills in Western Australia.

She swirled the prosecco in her plastic glass. Snyder was still a newly minted PhD. Surely he'd be too inexperienced for Crawley's lectureship vacancy?

He wouldn't be able to hit as many bullet points as her in the job advert, that was for sure. Not by a long way. But now she would have to somehow make that blindingly obvious when she presented her research paper tomorrow.

The thought made her palms begin to sweat. It wasn't that she felt unsure about her research – she'd already produced a respectable pile of publications. No, it was the way she would feel exposed as she stood there at the lectern under the heat of the spotlight, listening to herself reel off the words she'd rehearsed to death in her hotel room, watching herself from outside her body, noticing the slight quiver in her voice, the way she couldn't quite get on top of her breath, and how this would so clearly betray her many inadequacies, betray her abject relief at just having a hotel room for the week where it was clean and there were no mouldy dishes, where she could work without being constantly pestered by students who her boss was meant to supervise, betray her well-founded fear of staying stuck in a perpetual cycle of short-term postdoctoral contracts, never landing that prestigious fellowship or faculty post, except that now, at the age of thirty-five, she was becoming *too* experienced, too *expensive* to be a postdoc when there was so much fresh talent out there.

God, she'd never felt less fresh.

She downed the glass of prosecco so fast that the fizz erupted in her nostrils. She tried to pretend it was a sneeze and wiped her nose with a paper napkin from a nearby table. Then she made for the exit. All she could do now was rehearse, rehearse, rehearse.

Her room wasn't in the conference hotel – too expensive, according to her boss – but in the Premier Lodge ten minutes away. As she left through the hotel lobby, she checked the clock – there was still enough time to go back and prepare for a couple of hours before dinner.

A wave of heat wafted over her as she stepped out into the July evening. Another record-breaking British summer. If she wasn't careful, she'd end up with sweat patches. She hurried along the wide, sun-drenched pavement with her elbows raised to improve the airflow, past a Cuban-themed bar overflowing with young professionals clutching post-work pints and cocktails.

As she waited at a pedestrian crossing, her phone buzzed again. She fished it out of her bag and answered. A woman asked Beth to confirm her name, then announced she was calling from the switchboard of West Middlesex Hospital.

— Stay on the line, please. I'll put you through.

There was a click and some tinny music began blaring out of the earpiece. She crossed the road. No doubt it was Mum again, off on a walkabout from the retirement home. Discovered in some far-off village, pulling up weeds in a stranger's garden. But where was West Middlesex?

She was walking in the shade now, past a three-piece jazz band busking outside a charity shop to a half-dozen onlookers. Last time, it was the care home staff who called, once everything had been resolved. Maybe it was something serious. She picked up the pace.

The automatic doors of the Premier Lodge slid open and she darted straight for the lift as it was closing. She pushed the button for the third floor, then began rummaging in her bag for the key card to her room. As the lift shuddered into motion, the music in the earpiece began to falter and cut out. She tapped the key card against her leg. Mum's timing was impeccable, as ever. Maybe this time she could persuade Adam to deal with it. The doors opened again to a crescendo of chatter – five young men all wearing jeans and tight-fitting patterned shirts, smelling like a hair salon. They burst into laughter as she brushed past into the corridor, then the music stopped and she heard a faint voice on the other end of the line.

— Hello? This is Beth Warren. Hello?

A woman's voice, calm and assured.

— Hello, this is Dr Mishra speaking, West Middlesex Hospital. Are you somewhere we can talk in private?

— Just a sec.

She held the key card against the lock and the red light went green with a ratcheting sound. Inside, she dropped her laptop bag to the floor as the heavy door thunked behind her.

— Yes, sorry, what?

— Yes, I'm afraid we're treating Adam Warren, your brother. You're the next of kin?

— Adam? Yes. What? No, Grace is his next of kin. His partner. Adam? Why? What's happened?

Her throat was tightening. She could feel her mouth going dry.

— Adam's in the intensive care unit and his condition is what we call critical, which means—

— Yes I know what that means. Jesus! What happened?

— I'm sorry but I'm not at liberty to disclose that over the phone. Actually we're still lacking some information—

— What do you mean? Is he—

— If you can come to the hospital, then it's best if you do, as soon as possible. Your brother... well, like I said, his condition is critical.

The bed had been made up again, the white sheets tucked neatly under, the dark purple bedspread laid out on top. The complimentary biscuits and teabags had been replenished, clean cups and saucers beside them. She steadied herself against the wall. Outside, through the net curtain, the traffic below was at a standstill.

— I'm sorry to be the bearer of bad news. If you do travel, please take public transport or have someone drive you—

— I'll... Yes, I'm in Bristol, I'll leave right away. But... what are his chances?

The doctor hesitated, her breath ruffling the microphone.

— We're doing our best.

CHAPTER TWO

At the instant she heard Dr Mishra speak Adam's name, an image appeared in Beth's mind. It was not of her brother as he was these days – small but muscular from working out, the wispiest of strawberry-blond sideburns – nor in their heyday together, making sandcastles on a Cornish beach or playing pranks on their mother. Instead, she saw his red, angry face as an eleven-year-old, pushing her away before storming off down the school corridor, his coat and bag all askew.

First term at Jordan St Peters. A melancholy memory, not one that either of them would bring up. Mark Gordon was his name. One of those porky, vindictive faces. She would pay good money to do that again. To hear the sound of that clap as the back of her hand struck his cheek, his eye socket, his temple, in one colossal wallop. All the force she could muster. The wincing *oooooh* from the dozens of boys gathered round. She'd caught him off guard, yanked him by the back of the collar away from the corner where he was pummelling Adam, then delivered the blow before he knew what was going on. Fucker. He'd staggered back and looked up at her dumbstruck, then turned tail and pushed through the crowd with a swagger that wasn't quite so assured. She'd tried to talk to Adam as the boys dispersed, none of them offering him any support, and that was when he'd pushed her away, hissing at her: *Never, ever do that again.*

She turned the fragment of Acasta gneiss over in her pocket. Out of the taxi window, the southern reaches of the Cotswold hills were speeding past. After the call with the doctor, she'd tried calling Grace but it had gone straight to voicemail. She quickly packed up her suitcase, went to the nearest ATM, then hailed a cab, offering three hundred pounds to take her to the hospital. It was in West London, a two-hour drive; the cabbie had settled for three fifty. She could worry about her finances later.

They overtook a convertible sportscar driven by a woman wearing bright red lipstick and sunglasses. On the passenger side, a spaniel was leaning over the windowsill, ears flapping in the breeze. Beth sank back against the headrest. In the millions of years to come, all this would be covered, compacted, buried under layers upon layers of sediment. The road rolling beneath would become an anomalous seam of gravel trucked there from incongruous eras and bound together with bitumen, the thick crud from the bottom of a crude oil barrel, made of plants that died in the Mesozoic. In time, everything around her would be compressed down, warmed up, warped, maybe subsumed eventually back into the hot melted innards of the planet before cooling and solidifying toward the surface again, recycled. Magma to magma. Crust to crust. Beth snorted at the stupid joke. The driver glanced at her in the rear-view mirror, and she came back to herself.

She closed her eyes and pinched the bridge of her nose. She'd already been over it a dozen times. There was nothing he'd ever mentioned about his health. Not since he fell off the monkey bars and broke his collarbone when he was nine. Or that rash they'd never got to the bottom of. The only thing she could think of was his stupid bodybuilding fad, but she thought he'd left that behind when he got together with Grace. Hadn't she read something about steroids and heart failure? She took out her phone and started Googling it.

— Did you catch that?

The taxi driver caught her eye in the mirror again. He nodded at the radio.

— No, what was it? she said.

— Could be in for some traffic. They're saying it's all snarled up around Heathrow. Terrorist incident.

— Terrorist? What, an attack?

The driver shrugged.

— Incident, they said.

She checked the BBC News website on her phone. A red banner along the bottom read *Breaking: 'Ecoterrorist' incident closes Heathrow runway.*

Chiedozie Dike is a writer, editor and lawyer from Imo, Nigeria. He has worked in advertising as a copywriter and a content strategist. He has also written for television and radio. His short stories have been published in two anthologies and in online publications, including *Afreada* and *The Write Launch*.

dikechiedozie@gmail.com

Cannabis
A short story

Dessert, Ibou? Ahmaud asked, rising from the table and making for the chest freezer. It still caught Ibounadio off guard how Ahmaud was dwarfed by the higher ceiling and the thick walls here, how he seemed to lag, unlike in the Paris apartment.

Ibounadio's response was a given, assumed more than it was heard. He could have said no, thank you, and Ahmaud would have nodded and brought two bowls to the table anyway. Two scoops of ice cream. The same every night.

The freezer light cast Ahmaud's crumpled features into relief. He squinted, as though the contents of the rack had changed since he'd last checked.

From a cabinet, Ahmaud took out bowls, then shuffled in a drawer for the wider-than-hollow ice-cream scoop they had bought from the expensive supermarché in Vence.

Here you go, Ahmaud said, set one bowl in front of himself, then plonked the other on to Ibounadio's béchamel-streaked plate. Like the plates, the bowls were fine china with a blue pattern that brought cave art to mind. The china set had come with the house, gifted to Ahmaud's parents at their wedding and left to him now that they were both dead.

Tonight's selection was vanilla ice cream. On occasion it'd be salted caramel or cookie dough, but mostly it was vanilla. No more than two scoops. Plop. Plop.

Back in Paris, Ibounadio might have been at the bar on Rue de Lombards. It was a Friday after all. That, or the club at Rue aux Ours. The bathroom there was disgusting, the urinals packed with ice and stinking to high heaven, but the cocktail prices were fair, and the DJ knew her transitions.

Spoon in one hand, Ibounadio stretched his bowl across the table and nudged its content on to the dairy igloo in Ahmaud's bowl.

Ahmaud cocked his head just so, like Partout – the stray Labrador down in the village – when it couldn't read a gesture. He said nothing.

Ibounadio took a clementine from the fruit basket at the centre of the table. The last time he had danced had been to an Edith Piaf record. In this very kitchen, Ahmaud's hands on his waist, cajoling him to sway.

He peeled his fruit while Ahmaud used his spoon like a trowel, laying the cream-laden head on to his tongue, then pulling it down over his lower lip. This way, he avoided his new upper molars, skirted the brain freeze.

These three-course dinners had started as an unacknowledged joke, or so Ibounadio had thought. They had a soup or a salad, gratin with a baguette, and then dessert, eaten with fig citranelli sometimes. A parody of bourgeoise trappings, given their new status as homeowners in the South of France.

The summer heat had called for frozen desserts when they first got here, but the cypress trees in the forest beyond their property had since traded green leaves for russet crowns, and it had become another hollow ritual – Ahmaud's, but also Ibounadio's by default. When Ahmaud played handyman, fixing things around the house rather than calling a professional, Ibounadio fetched pliers, held the step ladder in place, offered his shoulder as a brace – the only thing between Ahmaud and a broken hip. Root-pulling was a two-man sport when Ahmaud puttered in the garden, and Ibounadio fetched him cold lemonade, kept him company under the garden shed while he smoked a cigarette.

Scraping the last of his ice cream, Ahmaud reached for the remote and turned on the TV. With an election year approaching, presidential candidates took up more time during news hour. Ibounadio didn't care for any of that. His current favourite show was due afterwards. Tonight, Sofia could discover her doting husband was a homicidal psychopath.

Ahmaud stood from the table after the weather forecast. Sixteen degrees and overcast skies tomorrow. He grabbed a cigarette from the breadbasket on the countertop, opened the window over the kitchen sink and lit up.

Take it outside, Ahmaud. You know I hate that smell.

Ahmaud grunted, shut the window, and trailed cigarette smoke to the back door.

Thanks.

He slapped on the back patio lights and stepped outside. In the second it took him to shut the door, there it was again. That smell. Cannabis.

It hadn't been this bad when they arrived, one month after Ahmaud's maman had died on the chaise lounge in the salon, the vinyl plate spinning on the turntable long after Claude Nougaro had finished playing. She had been found by the fourteen-year-old girl who came up from the village to clean the house and do laundry.

The house had a distinct hospice smell when they first got here, a compound of sweat and urine. Their belongings from Paris still cluttered the foyer while Ibounadio went about the house, opening windows. The shutters remained open overnight despite Ahmaud's concern about bugs. The next day, Ibounadio went down to the village with Ahmaud's bank card, bought scented candles from the perfumery on the Main Street. Tuberose and lavender.

Still, something lingered. Do you smell that?

What? Ahmaud shrugged.

The garden was overgrown, weeds crisscrossing the stone steps that sloped towards the wire fence, the forest beyond it. With only four hours of sunshine left, Ahmaud went outback with a pair of shears and a rake.

Come here one moment, Ibou, he called. And there in the garden, halfway between the last step and the fence, stood a row of cannabis plants. Eleven in all, standing at ten feet.

My god, Ahmaud. We must get rid of them. That smell. Someone will call the police.

Ahmaud poked the stem of the closest plant, fingered its trichomes and smiled. Oh Maman, you crazy old lady.

For Ibounadio, something of a routine had accreted around the empty calendar of provincial life. He took the path through the forest down to the village in the morning, walked the ramparts, watched dog owners collect poop and play fetch. Once, he'd seen an old lady walk a cat, turning around and whistling at the animal every third step. Bizarre.

He bought two scoops of gelato at L'Epicerie des Artistes: raspberry topped by whatever flavour he fancied for himself. Paid by card. Ahmaud G. Halimi.

The stray Labrador Partout loved raspberry, waited every morning for Ibounadio at the village square and slopped the treat in one go, wafer flakes and beet-coloured mush trailing down its jaw.

Today, Partout was nowhere to be found. Ibounadio ate his apricot gelato on the walk to the square where fixtures at Le Cercle played boules under the shade of platane trees. He discarded Partout's gelato in the bin before it completely liquefied, took the stone steps curving around the old mill, up the hill to the forest path. Perhaps a tourist had fallen for Partout's goo-goo eyes and was feeding it duck off the plate at Le Tilleul. Raspberry couldn't compare.

The car was gone by the time he got home, Ahmaud off to the gym in Vence. Ibounadio shrugged off his puffer and took off his shirt, pits damp with sweat. He and Ahmaud shared the smaller of the two upstairs bedrooms, overlooking the neighbour's backyard and pool. Boxes of books filled the other bedroom – where Ahmaud's father had died, and his mother had lived until the stairs became impossible. The plan was to convert it into an office-study with a view of the forest.

Ibounadio took his binoculars out of the closet, the only item in his possession that had made the trip with him from Dakar ten years ago, 150 euros and the contact card of a Parisian football agent in his pocket.

Standing at the window, he squinted through the lens. The neighbours' housekeeper fluffing pillows in a bedroom, the fat white cat lounging on a deck chair.

His glamorous neighbour was nowhere in sight. The Kim K of Chemin de Petit Jours, as far as he was concerned, driving top down around town in her convertible, sunshades on her forehead, her honey-coloured hair thrashing. He'd passed her a few times in the village, always near the Colombe d'Or, and she'd showed no inkling he lived next door.

Her husband was a businessman. Ahmaud said he looked vapid, but he was tall and handsome, body like Henry Cavill: hairy chest, prominent areolae. He drove a Tesla too, silent, unlike Ahmaud's French-made electric car.

Ibounadio had watched him shower a few times, seeing nothing of note through the small bathroom window, but his imagination did the rest.

Ibounadio returned the binoculars to the closet when Ahmaud's car pulled into the drive. He went downstairs.

You're back early.

Yes.

Ahmaud dumped his gym bag in the foyer, his running shoes squelching toward the kitchen. He leaned over the sink, drank from the tap, and sighed. La petite Kim K goes to the same gym as me.

Really?

It also appears Maman ran a stoner club.

What?

Ahmaud sat on a dining chair, stretched his hands behind his head, his legs outward. She came up to me at the gym, petite Kim K, and asked if I needed help harvesting the cannabis.

That's not true.

I swear. She used to help Maman with the harvest and got a year's stash in exchange.

Ibounadio's jaw would have touched the floor if it dipped any lower.

She asked after you. How is your collaborator?

Ibounadio cocked his head to a side and the smile disappeared from Ahmaud's face.

What's wrong, my dear?

He might have forgotten but his neighbour in Paris had used the same word when Ibounadio had moved in with him. Ask your *collaborateur* not to shut your apartment door so hard. As though it was any of her goddamn business.

Why would she assume I'm your employee? Ibounadio asked.

Ahmaud waved it off. This is Le Pen territory.

Exactly.

Ahmaud paused, narrowed his eyes. I'm Algerian.

You look like you have a tan.

Ahmaud rolled his eyes. If this annoys you, wait till she finds out how we met.

She's not coming here.

Ahmaud shook his head, stood, and started to unload the dishwasher, grunting each time he reached down. I thought you'd be happy we're making friends.

He sighed when no response came. What would you like for dinner, my dear? Lasagna?

Ibounadio woke up to the sound of the curtain rollers, the sun burning a red film behind his eyelids, then Ahmaud's lips against the front of his shorts, nibbling his semi-erect cock. He kept his breathing level, his eyes closed, and held the image of a pumped, hairy chest and saucer-like areolae. When he opened his eyes, everything appeared in greyscale, leached of detail, but only for a second. The ridges on Ahmaud's forehead returned, the icy blue of his eyes. Good day, my darling.

Good day. He gathered his legs, swung them off the side of the bed. I need to pee.

Ahmaud was butt naked when he returned, his pecs solid even though his skin dripped toward the gourd of his belly like melting wax.

Ibounadio got into bed on his knees, kissed Ahmaud's forehead.

You're not hard.

Ibounadio snickered. Not yet. He laid next to Ahmaud on the bed, crossed their legs at the knee. You were right. We could do with some friends.

And where would we tell them we met? Ahmaud teased.

Ibounadio clucked his tongue. At the museum.

Ahmaud snorted, slapped his belly, and Ibounadio squinted at him. He didn't expect him to get it, the euphemism he and his Paris buddies had used for the escort sites they were signed to.

He kissed Ahmaud's forehead. Let's get a puppy.

Uh uh. Too needy and I'm too old. He trailed a finger down Ibounadio's lips. Maybe a cat.

You're not that old. Ibounadio caressed his cheek, tongued the inside of his mouth.

You say that because you love me.

Maybe. He waited. Petite Kim K's husband is hot, yes?

Is he? Ahmaud asked, then laughed.

He had the laugh of a younger man with healthier lungs.

MICHAEL EGAN

Michael Egan is from Liverpool. His novel, *Circles a Clover*, was published by Everything With Words in 2021. He is currently completing a horror novel, *Goldy*. Michael is the recipient of the UEA Booker Prize Foundation Scholarship for 2021/22.

mgegan80@gmail.com

Goldy

An extract from a novel

KEOGH

They drove deeper into the flat country for a mile or so then turned east towards low hills, one like a lump, a wart stuck to the world's skin. Another hill had a little tower at its top, a black beacon shining nothing. Where the road turned south the land went even flatter, marshy, a spread of tufty grass that reminded Keogh of the grass you get on dunes, spiky and unsettled in the dragging breeze.

Ada was still sleeping in the passenger seat, her small hands folded over her stomach, her legs up on the dashboard meshed one over the other.

Goldy had gone back to being quiet, swallowed deep into her own strange company.

It was good to see Ada calm, to see her without tears in her eyes or shouting at him that she needed to stay. Cold, little hairs woke along her thighs and calf, stood on end like the sharp grass around them. He almost moved his hand to her leg but stopped himself.

As the road got narrower, every bump tested the suspension on the wrecked Tesla but somehow failed to wake Ada. She was far into that sleep, lost to it. Her thin, almost translucent eyelids were shut tight. Keogh didn't want to think much about what was going on behind those paper walls. Nothing good. Just memories, the older ones and the newer too. A flicker of a dream of what might be. But fire too, the house burning, Keogh pulling her away into the car. Goldy looking in the opposite direction of the fire into the houses of their sleeping neighbours who had not yet come out to watch the Harrison house burn, as if there was nothing else in the world for her to see except for the quiet of those better homes.

Why did Ada care when that shell burnt? Mam and Dad weren't inside. They were weeks dead. It was just bricks, memory. That house wasn't anything to cry over, never had been.

It was you coming back that did us.

That's what Mam told Keogh.

As soon as he got back from Budapest, she was at him. First it was his hair.

Look at Mr. Hardman with his skinhead, she said. *You look quite the fucking man now, Keogh Harrison. More of a man than your dad could ever be anyway.*

Then she was poking at his body, at his arms and chest.

Come feel these muscles Iolo, she shouted to Dad.

Dad was in the kitchen making a cup of tea, a sandwich. Did you hear me, soft lad? Come feel how much of a man your son has become.

And then she leaned closer to Keogh, whispered. *Same man you always were, boy. Bad news, nothing but bad news.* She poked his chest again, harder. *The only difference is, now you're just bad news that can do more harm.*

She had hated him for as long as he could remember. He wasn't sure where it began, used to hope it wasn't as far back as when he was a baby but now he didn't care where it started. Of course, he didn't want to fully believe that she looked at him when he was a baby in her arms like she looked at him as he grew, as if he was a monster showing its true form with every passing year. She'd cared for him at least when he was a baby, must have. Unless it was all Dad. Maybe if she'd had her way he'd have been drowned like an unwanted puppy in a bucket in the backyard. Was it Dad who'd been the one giving him milk, singing him to sleep, while Mam sat downstairs forming her hate?

Could have been that hate only formed after Ada came. Mam loved Ada so much that she couldn't look at Keogh without a fear of how he'd ruin his sister. He was a man after all, and they all knew what men had done to Mam in her life. Not Dad, never him. Maybe how she hated him was just a consequence of all that pain she'd suffered, maybe she looked at him every day and saw something in his eyes or in how he spoke or how he walked that reminded her of something worse. Probably none of that. Probably she just hated him because that's all she could ever feel for her son.

On the night before the factory Mam and Dad worked at got shelled, just a few days after Keogh had come home, she told him that him coming back doomed them. That it was almost as if when he got off that train at Lime Street still in his uniform, tired as hell, wondering why he'd even bothered coming back, that in him he carried something that meant they were marked as dead.

Dad agreed with Mam of course, like Dad always agreed with Mam. Little man. Little weak man of tiny bones and not a muscle to him no matter he'd worked the rice mill since he was fifteen. How can you lift sacks of rice day in and day out and still look like a puppet, flimsy and in need of a hand up your arse to give you purpose? Mam's hand, telling him what to say and when to say it, shutting him up when he should have shouted her down, closing his eyes when she didn't want him to see her anger, closing his eyes because he didn't want to bear witness to that. Silent fool. As much to blame as her really, more maybe. He was a man after all, their dad. He should have said more, should have stood up to her, no matter how she'd have broken him easy.

The night Keogh had come home, Mam lit a fag and scowled at him. Studied him like he was something she'd only just seen for what it really was. Like he was a broken monster she had no intention of fixing. Like he was a curse she couldn't admit to making.

Look at you, lad, she said, *look at what god gave me. I must have been a bastard in my last life to wind up with you for a son, Keogh. Must have been a proper bastard to end up with a son as much a wrong'un as you.*

Then she leaned forward in her chair, pointed the fag at him, not caring that the ash was scattering the carpet. *I see you, lad. I see you and I name you; I name you sin.*

Pointing the fag at him, stabbing it like that would do him in, like it was a knife enough, crossing herself to ward Keogh off, she said, *I name you shame, boy. I name you the fucking death of me.*

The thing was, Keogh knew she was right. He was a wrong'un, always had been. He'd known that from when he was five and Stoney told him to drop a brick on his cat's head. He'd done it straight away. Stoney didn't even have to hand Keogh the brick. Keogh grabbed it off him, let that cat have it. When the cat screamed, legged it into the house, Keogh was only sad that it was alive, only sad it wasn't lying there on the pavement, head smashed in. Then he saw Stoney, and in his friend's eyes he saw what he'd see in eyes a hundred times over. *Wrong'un.*

Are we there? said Ada, finally awake.

Keogh glanced down to her as she lowered her legs, fixed her skirt and yawned. She still looked too pale, not sick, just over-stretched, pulled beyond herself. Maybe it was just what being pregnant does, all the energy going elsewhere.

It's just up here a bit more, he said.

The road came to a fork. He slowed the Tesla. There wasn't another car on the road. Southwest took you to Malwich, its few shops, one pub and tiny salt museum. The narrower road, barely a road really, turned back north a bit to the lake and the village of Arclod. Wacky called the lake the Sorrow. Horrible name. He said the lake was called that because it was where a mother who'd lost her four sons in the last war came to drown her sorrow and herself. But there was no sorrow on that lake whenever Keogh came to stay with Wacky. His house, a tiny two up two down on the lake's southern shore, was joy and love. Never sorrow.

Why am I so bloody tired all the time? said Ada, legs squirming, as Keogh turned onto the north road.

You're bound to be, said Keogh.

She rolled her eyes. *Am I? You a doctor now?*

I don't need to be a doctor to know that you'll be tired and only get more tired soon enough.

Fuck sake, Keogh, is this you now? Mollycoddling me?

Ada turned away from him. Looked out over the flat western fields as the sun set orange in the coldness of twilight.

Keogh glanced her way. The horizon beyond her looked a false blue. Too calm and cold, painted. Like all the world wasn't real anymore.

I'm not mollycoddling you, am I? I'm just making sure you're alright.

She laughed. *Making sure I'm alright? Is that what you think all this is?* She waved a hand at the night, at the countryside that wasn't Liverpool, wasn't their home. *Christ, Keogh, you're even worse than you used to be, aren't you?*

He let her words passed over him. Others, those words would have made him bite. Not Ada. She could stab over and over with her words and he'd never flinch, never stab back.

Off a narrow lane, they came down towards the water of the lake, saw it behind the drystone wall that bordered the field next to their grandad's house. It was just a little mere really. The black gleam of it untouched by the world, unaltered by anything beyond it. The same water as it had always been when he and Ada were kids and before that too. Before everything.

Wacky's house stood on the lake's edge, looking just like it looked when they were kids. Familiar and lonely.

We're back, said Goldy, making them both jump a little because she'd been so quiet. Sometimes she could vanish like that, fade almost, then reappear.

Back? said Ada. *What are you talking about? You've never even been here before.*

How do you know I haven't? said Goldy and though Keogh knew just like Ada that Goldy had never been near the lake or Wacky's house, he found himself thinking, yes, that would make sense. Of course, Goldy has been here. Goldy could have been anywhere she ever wanted to be.

As they pulled up to the house, Goldy wound down her window and titled her head towards the cool night air.

Can you hear that? she said.

Ada wound her window down too. Keogh listened. He could hear the silence of night, the subtle wash of air over the car as he pulled onto the drive and brought it to a stop. But he could hear nothing else.

Hear what? asked Ada.

Goldy brought a finger to her lips. *Shh, can you not hear? They're singing. All of them.*

But there was no singing, not even a whispered hum. Just the empty countryside and the abandoned house.

Are you mad? said Keogh. *There's no singing, it's quiet as anything. We're in the countryside, Goldy, there's no one else out here.*

Ada looked to him, the first time she really had since they'd got in the car. Her eyebrows raised as if to say, don't worry, it's just Goldy being Goldy.

But Goldy laughed, light, happy. *You should hear it Keogh*, she said. *It's not right you can't.*

Why's that, then? he said.

Ahead of them, the house was in complete darkness.

Goldy leaned forward, her hand touched his shoulder. *Because they're singing for you, Keogh. It's your song, just listen for once, you'll hear it if you listen.*

He listened. He really did try to hear something, but he could hear nothing beyond the barren silence of the country and the night, not a single sound. No song, just a deep endless quiet.

Fran Fabriczki was born in Budapest and has lived in Los Angeles and London. She read English at Cambridge University and worked in publishing for five years before going freelance to focus on her writing. She writes about the absurdities of everyday life and is currently working on a comic novel.

ffabriczki@gmail.com
www.franfabriczki.com

Please Take a Seat and Wait Your Turn
Extract from a short story

There's nothing that reminds Sasha more of the relentless march of time, the constant erosion and inevitable end of all life forms, than going to the dental hygienist. An odd place for such thoughts, perhaps, but despair is a generous muse.

'Your gums are receding. See here, this is where they should be, this is where they are,' the woman says, roughly pulling down Sasha's lower lip to indicate the offending flesh with a gloved finger. 'That will never grow back, it's not like hair. You need to start—'

'Saying my goodbyes? Looking at dentures?' The hygienist gives her a withering look. 'No, right. Flossing. I need to start flossing.'

As the woman resumes poking around in her mouth, the chlorinated smell of her latex gloves making Sasha's nose itch, she thinks that dentists believe in this flossing business to an extreme degree. It seems to be their solution to everything. It's only a few steps from 'Flossing cures gum disease' and 'Flossing cures tooth decay' to 'Flossing cures loneliness!' and 'Flossing cures Alzheimer's!!'

She is reminded of a man she once met at a party who referred to himself as a dental hygiene enthusiast, a description for which she was extremely grateful – one can never have too many amusing 'man I met at a party' anecdotes, really. He went on at commendable length about his favourite brand of toothpaste and how regularly he went to the dentist; Sasha nodded and tried to commit every ridiculous statement to memory. But now, as Sasha rubs at her sad, neglected lower gums, she is starting to wonder if he had the right idea. If there wasn't something more deeply philosophical about this man's stance – arresting the cruel onslaught of atrophy, one electric toothbrush at a time.

The hygienist dismisses her with a reproachful expression, directing her to the receptionist to pay her bill and pick up a packet of dentist-approved floss. It seems to Sasha that even the receptionist is looking at her with disdain, thinking of her lack of self-care and her *diseased* gums. Then again, she is feeling vulnerable after having her mouth invaded by a parade of shiny tools for half an hour. The world seems all at once too bright, too threatening. She takes the little plastic container of floss and looks at it lying in the palm of her hand – the clear blue encasing, the tightly coiled swirl of string – and wishes that it did have some of the answers after all.

—

Sasha has a memory: it floats in her mind like the swirls of oily scum that come up to the surface of a pot of soup. Sometimes it's there, stark and undeniable, and sometimes she stirs it, submerging the memory in the pot of life where the spices that—well, never mind the analogies.

She is sitting outside of the psychiatrist's office, eleven years old, feet no longer dangling high above the floor when she's on a chair. Her mother sits beside her, doing her best to make it seem like they are sitting somewhere a lot more innocuous: in blue plastic seats at a bus station; at their kitchen counter, waiting for milk to turn sweet in the bowl; or in any other innocent chair that is not placed outside the office of a woman who'd like to determine which of Sasha's parents she loves best.

And Sasha's mother is a master of distraction – her whole physical presence is one big distraction to anyone who happens to behold her. She's small and wiry, but mountainous curls add an inch or two vertically, making her seem average-sized; her eyes are alert and ironic, and there's a sense of movement to her even when she appears to be sitting still. Which she never does, not for long.

Her mother wears a chunky digital watch and Sasha plays with the buttons, making it light up and sing. Eventually, her mother unclasps the watch and takes Sasha's left wrist in her hands, fastening the watch around it.

'Look at that – it fits just fine,' her mother says. Sasha is delighted – she is still at that age when adults, their belongings, their habits have a certain glamour.

The psychiatrist opens her office door and calls for Sasha to head inside. Halfway to the door she stops and turns, unclasping the watch, ready to give it back to her mother.

'Keep it.' Her mother winks at her. 'For now.'

—

On the way to the dermatologist's office, Sasha passed through the 'Ear, Nose and Throat' clinic and now, as the dermatologist holds up a magnifying glass and peers at some moles on her arm, she wonders how they feel about being thusly named.

'Dermatologist sounds much better, doesn't it?' Sasha muses, more to herself than as a conversation starter.

'Pardon?' Dr Hanes says.

'Oh, well, you know, saying, "Hello, I'm an Ear, Nose and Throat doctor" must be a bit of a drag. Imagine if you went to a dinner party and had to say, each time, "My name is Dr Hanes and I'm a Boils, Shingles and Other Disgusting Skin Conditions doctor."'

The doctor peers up over her glasses at Sasha. 'They're called otolaryngologists, actually.'

'Oh right,' Sasha says, scratching her nose. 'Not much better, is it, in terms of syllables.'

They lapse into silence then, and Sasha follows the doctor's gaze along her skin, looking at each little fleck of unnecessary skin on her body. Sasha has come here even though she is pretty sure this idea that asymmetrical moles are suspicious must be some sort of dermatological in-joke calculated to amplify neuroses – there isn't one piece of symmetry on Sasha's entire body, let alone in each little spot, of which there seem to be hundreds. And then there's the idea that she should be checking each one of them, monitoring any minor changes like some sort of mad scientist in a laboratory. This piece of advice is almost certainly a joke. Looking at Dr Hanes as she continues to shake her head in apparent disappointment, Sasha wonders if dermatologists are likely to make jokes.

'I'm going to take a sample of the skin cells here, and send it off to the lab to check,' Dr Hanes says, as she reaches the largest of Sasha's skin cell congregations, the one that gave her mother pause when they had lunch last week. It was blatant evasion, but Sasha allows her mother these tricks lately. 'No need to worry yet, I'm fairly certain this is benign, but it's better to make sure.'

Sasha sighs and wishes that the words malign and benign shared fewer letters. Within benign lurks always the opportunity for the malign – so that even when it comes as a reassurance, such as now, it carries with it the weight of other, more devastating possibilities.

—

Sasha remembers fondly a period of time, somewhere between ages fourteen (after the braces were removed) and seventeen (when she went on her first visit to the gynaecologist), a blissful couple years of respite from any sort of medical examination or intervention. Had she known these three years would be significant in such a way, she feels she might have run along the streets, danced at every opportunity, really revelled in her body, which was ever so briefly a perfectly functioning creation that could only be ascribed to the work of God – the gods, any god, but surely a god.

Then again, this also coincided with the time she discovered that her mother's body, unlike hers, is not an infallible, finely tuned machine of divine provenance. At age sixteen, she wondered for the first time: aren't people whose parents died when they were young in a way lucky? Instead of waiting for the inevitable and wondering how on earth they will cope with the pain, they get through it while their hearts are still malleable lumps, pain only making momentary indentations before it all springs back: taut, content. It's a horrible thing to think – but then, as Sasha later discovers, morality has little to do with spontaneous thought.

—

The new gynaecologist comes at the recommendation of her sister-in-law, Annie, after Sasha discovers, to her embarrassment, that gynaecologists are not required to fondle your breasts in search of possible lumps – this is something you are supposed to do for yourself. Sasha tries not to re-member how this exchange came about, tries to forget about her former gynaecologist entirely.

Dr Shirley's hands have so far stayed away from Sasha's breast area, but they have otherwise become quite intimate with her anatomy, as she sits in the chair with the metal stirrups. Sasha can't see much of the doctor; she is covered by a large surgical mask, as well as the gown tented between Sasha's knees, but she has a high ponytail of blonde hair that stands up right, like an enthusiastic dog begging for treats.

She resurfaces from under Sasha's gown; the dog rests on its hind legs. 'Well, everything looks fine here, let's just do an ultrasound to check out those ovaries.' The dog stands back up; the cold jelly is applied as the ul-trasound wand goes in.

'Ah. See here, they are looking healthy.' The dog does a little jig as the doctor's gaze follows the ultrasound. Sasha stares up at the screen where another orb-like structure of her body is on display. They say humans are made up of 60 per cent water, but to Sasha it seems now she is made up of perfectly taut balloons, hundreds of orbs, big and small, contained in a protective membrane, with additional little orbs attached to her outside (but those are not perfect, no, they are asymmetrical, alas). All just held together by sheer force of will.

With her clothes back on, Sasha sits across from the doctor as she asks a series of questions that, were they friends going out for drinks, would have elevated their relationship to a rare level of intimacy: *Are you sexually active? What form of contraception have you used in the past? What form of contraception are you using now? Have you ever been pregnant?*

That Sasha is an overgrown child she sometimes feels is evidenced by the fact that the topic of pregnancy is yet to conjure up images of herself or her contemporaries. Were she a slightly different woman, she might have a vision of herself as a radiant pregnant woman in a patterned summer dress (naturally no one ever imagines themselves pregnant in the winter). Or she could imagine a coterie of toddlers around her as she looks on, sleep-deprived but happy. She could even imagine a wry little teenager – her mirror image – going to the movies with her on a Sunday afternoon.

Instead, what she thinks of is the machine she was hooked up to, age seven, which served the purpose of suctioning the surfeit of mucus out of her sinuses. And there was her mother standing by her patiently with not a hint of disgust as Sasha sat with a tube coming out of one nostril, mucus making its way on a clear highway (and why clear? who needed to see the contents once they were out and on their way?). Her mother would take her to this doctor (an otolaryngologist perhaps) for another five days, sitting by her each time she was hooked up to the mucus machine, promising new and increasingly extravagant consolations after each visit.

What kind of love is it, that makes this a feasible way to live? What makes it make sense, this ceaseless shuttling from the paediatrician to the orthodontist to the emergency room, that one time, arm bruised but not broken in the end. No, she has never been pregnant, she tells the doctor. But she is a mother to her mother now, in a sense. Hers is the worry, the waiting and the shuttling from one appointment to the next.

Mary Franklin has directed ten productions in London fringe theatres, assisted Jarvis Cocker on his memoir, had work published by Orion and Tar Press and received a Special Mention in the 2022 Galley Beggar Short Story Competition. Her first novel is about a toxic love triangle set among Oxford's all-male drinking societies, told by the only girl allowed in.

maryfranklin07@gmail.com

I'd Much Rather Be With The Boys
Prologue and chapter six of a novel

There were too many Wills.

I had a friend who everyone called Dingo because his name was Will. My first boyfriend's name was Will so he called himself Wol. My second boyfriend's name was also Will, but he was allowed to keep it. Sometimes we, the girls, called him Scary Will, but never to his face. They called me Mouse. I didn't choose that.

CHAPTER SIX

Something is happening, a slippage. I am no longer always in the library at nine. Sometimes I have not read the set texts before a lecture. Yesterday I was late for a tutorial, for the first time.

Today, 10:30am, late April, the first properly warm day, and I am not in the library. I am in my college room with Wol and Dingo, who both slept on the floor. I have made them Alpen with extra honey and green tea. There is a postcard above my desk showing a man pissing on a green plastic chair. Wol is looking at it and saying, 'One for the wank bank, Mouse?'

He says it in the voice we developed last night to imitate Petra's new boyfriend Marius who goes to Durham, wears white jeans and cannot keep up with their jokes, our jokes. The voice is South African for a reason I cannot quite remember. Wol is better at it than Dingo and both of them are better at it than me.

I am sitting on the bed, back to the wall, mug between my hands. Wol and Dingo stand in the middle of the small rectangular room.

'Sit,' I say to Dingo. 'Sit in the chair,' but he does not.

'I like it,' says Wol. 'There are these.' He gestures to the hyacinths I bought yesterday because I hoped someone might come back with me. 'And this.' He gestures to the clothes rail which collapsed two days ago, but which I have been out too much to dispose of. 'And we are in the middle. Us two poor shitheads.'

There is light from the small window above the cheap pine desk. The grey carpet is striped with it, as is Wol's orange jumper.

Milk falls from Dingo's bowl on to the floor.

'Sit down, for God's sake,' I say, patting the bed. There is space on either side of me.

I pull the blanket over my legs. My nightshirt is white and short and I had my period yesterday. Dingo trips towards me.

'Not with the Alpen,' I say, and he puts it down, gracefully, before joining me, tucking himself into me. He is warm and sexless, like a puppy. I find his physical presence overwhelmingly reassuring. I put my left hand on his head and then remove it. Will Rickworth stopped washing his hair last term so naturally Dingo did too.

Wol observes us, from the middle of the room, bowl in one hand, spoon in the other, belly visible under his shirt, hairless and rounded. He likes to be the centre of attention, and he likes the attention to be mine. When we end up alone together the air feels different, and we laugh less. I put on a special scratchy superior voice, never look him in the eye and say things that sound strangely weary, and often end with the statement 'but I guess we'll find out,' irrespective of what has come before.

But this morning, with Dingo present, it is better. If I was Wol's girlfriend, I think, I'd have constant access, to all of them. I don't like his jeans, but his jokes are always funny. He thinks I'm funny. He makes me funnier. He often goes too far.

Wol puts the bowl down, then the spoon, and comes towards the bed. There are pools of light to step across, two.

There is more space beside Dingo, but, 'Budge up,' says Wol, and sits next to me. A pillow falls to the floor.

'Come on in,' I say, which is exactly what I did not say last night when we were both awake and Dingo was asleep.

'So *this* is what it's like in here,' he says, and I wonder what would happen if I was to let my thigh, which is less than an inch from his, relax. What I'd have committed to.

He talks to Dingo about their tutor and the new sandwich options at Olives, the mortadella which Dingo likes but Wol thinks is creepy, and their old History of Art teacher who used to say this thing which I have heard about many times and which I still do not think is funny. They talk about school. There is only one school. I pick at a piece of loose skin on my middle finger, slot it into my mouth and bite. Wol says Gracie looked bigger last night, do the letters B, B and W come to mind, and has she been having the new mortadella, they wonder, a good porking, some fennel with her sausage. I should intervene but if they are talking about her being fat, it means they do not think I am. Wol talks about Rickworth's new house, which Dingo has never been to, and I can tell from Dingo's voice that this upsets him, then they start doing the South African voice again. Wol talks about gorgeous Petra's filthy gold pussy, and Dingo says something about black and white thinking and Wol says, 'I think, perhaps, in this voice and that particular phrase.'

Dingo is lost. He looks at Wol, and I look at Dingo and then Wol laughs, and we all laugh, hard, and my thigh relaxes. It rests against Wol's. Neither of us move.

I check my phone. Gracie wants to know if I still want to have lunch. I do not reply.

They talk about Petra, and I speak, finally. I say I loved her at school and Wol says, 'But now...' and I say, 'Shut up,' and then we talk about when Petra and Dingo snogged in first term.

'Right,' I say, finally. 'Library, I think.' I never want it to end, but it must, and I would rather I leave than they do.

'Can I use the special toothbrush?' says Dingo, going into the ensuite and running the tap. He sings as he brushes his teeth. I know it's a performance for us. He wants to hear what we say while he is gone so he is trying to communicate the opposite.

'Wol?' I say. I do not usually say his name.

'What, Mouse?' he says and turns so he is facing me. His voice is different and his eyes are like barley sugars.

'Library?' I say and shift, removing my thigh.

'Fuck that,' says Wol. 'When's your essay due?'

'Thursday,' I say.

'What on?'

'Marvell.'

'You can have mine, submitted it last year. Keine problem. Pizza pizza pizza,' he says and then he starts to sing too, a new made-up song, and Dingo joins in from the bathroom.

'We have so many private jokes at this point,' says Wol, as we sit down in the small courtyard outside Pizza Express, 'that our conversation is loaded heavily with joy for us, but must be extremely confusing for literally anyone else,' and it's the happiest I have been for months, maybe years, maybe ever.

So when Gracie arrives, I feel myself having to adjust, to rearrange my selves. She had been out with us last night, but she had left early.

She is wearing a white jacket and pale jeans and it looks like she has washed her hair. She doesn't smell the same as the rest of us, of alcohol and sweat and garlic butter.

'How are you three today?' she says, sitting down, and looking, mainly, at me.

Wol puts his head in his hands and Dingo says, 'Save me, Gracie, from all the things I did last night.'

She looks to me, an eye roll implied. We find Dingo annoying. Or we did. I ignore it.

'How late did you stay?' she asks.

'They stayed at mine,' I say and look to Wol, so I didn't have to look at her.

'All three of you?' she says. 'Where?' She wants to know about Wol and I do not want to tell her.

'We're playing a game, Gracie,' says Wol, and I am grateful. 'What's the worst thing you've ever done while crazed?'

I want her to vibe, to gel, to chill out, or I want her to leave.

She tells her story and we all laugh, and then Wol tells his and we all laugh much harder.

We order drinks and Gracie hesitates. She has an essay to do later.

'Oh come on,' I say. 'We all do.'

'Yeah,' she says, 'but we don't all have your stamina,' and it does not sound like a compliment.

'Have a tiny half,' says Wol. He has picked up on something, I think, and is ameliorating the situation.

I order another Peroni. Gracie looks surprised.

'Beer, eh?' she says and I pretend not to have heard.

I drink lager now, with the boys, enthusiastically, and as far as they are concerned, I always did.

She says it again, louder, and I say, 'Yeah, why?' and turn to Dingo. The beer arrives, amber and bubbling, its surface moving slightly, and there is basil in the garlic butter accompanying the second order of dough balls.

A church bell rings beside us. Dingo talks about something called Ayahuasca. Gracie mutters, stands, walks across the courtyard and into the restaurant.

'Remember,' says Wol, 'when Rickworth put Gracie in the bin?'

Legendary,' interjects Dingo. 'Fucking iconic.'

'Well, yes,' says Wol, 'Obviously. But I wonder if he could still do that now.'

I laugh, once, and then stop myself.

'What are you talking about?' says Gracie, from behind me.

She is holding a jug of tap water and I do not know what she has heard.

'We're hungover,' I say. 'Ignore us.' But there is too much pleasure for me in those words, 'we' and 'us,' and when Gracie speaks her voice has changed. It is tighter and resolutely merry.

'So hot,' she says, sitting down and checking her phone although it has not buzzed, where it lies, on the table between us.

The church bell is still ringing.

'If this carries on,' says Dingo, 'I may tip quickly from having a profoundly nice time, to a profoundly bad time.'

'It's not that I'm hungover exactly,' says Wol. 'It's more that all my organs may be slowly shutting down.'

It is past one now. Around us people in suits eat supermarket sandwiches. One girl stands on the pavement opposite us talking quietly into a phone. I catch the words 'Mummy' and 'lonely.' When the pizza comes, I force two slices of mine on Gracie. She accepts and we have a quiet two-way chat about what she did this morning.

Beside me Wol and Dingo are talking about Atticus from Oriel, who has, apparently, eaten only carrots for the whole of March, and because of this his skin has taken on an orange tinge, even his balls.

Gracie tells me about the post office and a parcel that cost a lot, and I listen for the shortest time possible before slipping back into their flow.

'But how,' I say, 'does anyone actually know about the balls?' just as Gracie starts to elaborate on her breakfast.

She leaves straight after the pizza, back on her bicycle, and it is a relief. I need the loo but I do not go. I am having too much fun.

When I get back to my room, hours later - after the pizza and the pub and the cocktails and the club - the bowls of Alpen are clotting in my bathroom sink, and Wol's orange jumper is discarded on the desk-chair.

The next morning I am in the library by nine again, but I am not the day after, or the day after that, or the day after that.

Annie Friedlein writes historic fiction. She has studied at Cambridge, the Courtauld, and worked as a gallery publicist. She's represented by Giles Milburn at Madeleine Milburn Literary Agency.

anniefriedlein@hotmail.com

Soul in the Wires
Extract from a novel

1870, London. Ned arrives in Shadwell around eight o'clock. The weather is raw and rainy. He's taken a chance on The Anchor, a tavern on Free Trade Wharf that he first noticed a long time ago when he was scavenging on the other side of the river. It's hidden from the rest of the city, and that suits him nicely.

He makes his way down three narrow flights from the main street, checking the alleyways either side. When he reaches the bottom, the pub is so dimly lit he thinks it's closed, but he pushes the door to find clusters of life. Figures hunched at tables, and drinkers at the bar. His eyes adjust, taking in the sturdy candlelit beams and uneven, lime-washed walls.

He's approached by a cheerful girl of about twenty. She's pulled her curly bronze hair into a bun, and there's a mole by her right eye.

'My name's Lily,' she says, playing with the tassels of a lemon-coloured scarf. 'Buy me a drink?'

Ned's not here for a working girl. He's here for a conversation that will take his mind off tomorrow. In fact, he's supposed to remain in his lodgings before a job so he doesn't get recognised or roughed up, but his rooms at Ludgate Circus have come to feel like cells.

Lily leans close and her dress gapes. 'Got a better offer?'

'Might have.' Ned looks away from her flat bosom to see who else he might talk to, but the other drinkers look occupied with friends so when Lily pouts, and bats her lashes, he relents. She's got a quirky air about her. Maybe she'll be funny, and maybe that's what he needs.

'All right. What'll you have?'

'Ooh. Gin!'

He buys two glasses of a murky-looking spirit, checking out the pub corners where the shadows are darkest to be sure there's no-one here that he knows. Gas hasn't reached this part of the wharf, let alone electricity, and the candlelit gloom is unnerving. Flickering shapes catch his eye when a woman gestures wildly, her long sleeves throwing lacy shadows on the walls. It's so draughty that there are plumes of smoke trailing from the fireplace, forming a cloud round two porters playing dominoes, their arms moving delicately over the table.

'What's your name then?' Lily's quick to swallow half her drink, so he signals for another two and makes them triples.

'Joe.' His names tend to multiply. To Vanneck, he's Arthur, while in the Navy he was Daniel. He can't remember the last time he told anyone his real name, Edward Rourke, shortened to Ned by his sister, Eff.

He spots a side room that looks more private, even though he'll still be able to see into the bar. 'Shall we sit down there? You can tell me about yourself.'

Lily hesitates. 'Not for long. I've got a kid... I have to get back.' She strokes his wrist. 'Don't fancy it yet? The yard's always empty, if you're in the mood.'

'No. Not yet.'

She sighs. The tavern fills. Ned chooses a semi-circular booth with a torn seat and etched screens. He and Lily sit, but they're barely comfortable when a woman in a plaid dress breaks away from the crowd and spreads her palms wide on their table.

'My seats. Off you go.'

Lily gets up, but Ned motions *stay*. 'So what?' he says.

'So, I've business.'

'Not here you haven't. I'm drinking with a lady.'

'Lily Deacon; a lady? She's been doing men here since she was thirteen.' The woman takes him in. 'I know you. Am I right?' Her eyes stray to the scar on his lip. 'I'm sure I do.'

'Not at all.'

A tall man is watching from the bar. Big-nosed and bald, glowering from under a grey cap. Ned gets a thrill. He knows he's running a risk. This woman's hard; he can feel the fear in drinkers nearby, and that's always a sign.

'You're a fool, boy,' she says, 'you're one of Vanneck's, aren't you? You're not welcome. Tell him that.' The woman takes a last look before she turns away.

The man by the bar stares at Ned, who throws him a smile, though he's beginning to feel the fear a bit himself.

'I should have stayed at home.' Lily says quietly, as she clutches at her shawl. 'Who are you, anyway? Who's Vanneck?'

'I'm no one.' Ned slips the shawl off her shoulders. 'He's no one. Don't pay attention.'

'You can't ignore Alice Lanny,' Lily says, 'I didn't know she was in. I'd have taken more care where we sat.'

'What's the problem?'

'She knows things. Knows *people*.'

Lily reaches for her drink, but Ned grabs it. 'Tell me more.'

She recoils. 'I can't! She'll know.'

'What if I pay you not to care?'

The girl thinks for a moment. 'My rate's three shillings for the yard. Make it six shillings more, and I'll tell you what everyone round here knows. Can't be blamed for that.'

He nods. 'All right. Go on.'

'She's friends with a fellow at Crossness who's got cargo lists for the steamships from the Indies. He tips her off, and she bribes the night-watchmen in the warehouses to turn a blind eye so her man can help himself. Nothing that gets noticed much. And Alice now lives in a dandy house, in Stepney, though she doesn't lift a finger.' Lily shivers. 'That do?'

Ned slides the glass back. 'Yes. Interesting.' Vanneck might want to know. He gets out his pocket book to look willing, but doesn't pay, in case she leaves. He's enjoying being with another person, and it's good to be down by the water. Ned hasn't come quayside for a while, but its ways are familiar. He used to run errands with Eff when they were ten and eight, and remembers the way the mud stretched out at low tide, and the sound of the jetties as they creaked in the winds. He'd enjoyed throwing stones to make messy craters.

He's leaning to put an arm around Lily when a group of sailors gathers at the piano, singing melodies from 'Lowlands' and 'Haul Away Joe'; shanties Ned never wants to hear again. People turn to stare. The tars look dandy, with their brass cuff buttons, and the grosgrain ribbons on their lapels.

Lily shuffles closer, eyeing his wallet. 'You been at sea?'

'Yes. Navy. Cable boats... laying lines in the Crimea.'

'Lines?'

'For telegrams. Back to London.'

'Oh. Pa knew people who went, and they didn't like to talk about it. It wasn't like the papers, they said.'

'No, it wasn't.' Ned says. 'Read 'em, do you, newspapers?'

Lily shakes her head. 'What does it matter?'

'It should. Knowing what's what. One day your kid will—'

'Oh, don't start that.' She reaches for her shawl. She's got gooseflesh on her arms. 'Look, d'you want it, or not?'

'Not.'

She looks angry, but doesn't leave. The sailors are finished with shanties and are leafing through music. Watching them, a dart of blackness deflates Ned's mood further. Maybe it's the sight of the uniforms, maybe Lily's disdain, maybe the thought of what he's got to do tomorrow. 'I saw hundreds die,' he says, fingering his scarred lip. 'In the water, out of it; burning in oil at the port in Sebastopol. Not just men. Horses, dogs, children. When the Russians bombarded the ships.'

'Did you?' She strokes wearily at his lapels. When he leans in, her lips feel soft and her breath smells rotten. She gazes at him with unfocused eyes. 'You're a hero, then.'

He shakes his head. 'No. Heroes volunteer. I was pressed. Taken from outside a pub. Thought I was in a fight with lads from the next parish.' In fact, he'd yelled for someone to warn his sister but they'd hit him so hard he'd only come round at sea. 'You can't be a hero at twelve.'

'Can't you?' Lily squeezes his thigh, letting her fingers trail towards his cock. 'Well, you're a man now. A lion, I'd say. A stallion.'

His heart sinks, because it's all wrong.

'*Are* you a stallion?' she croons.

He pushes her off. This wasn't what he came for. Was it? He should find a cleverer girl. Someone with ideas, who can help him break free.

'I'm not. I'm... an associate.'

'What, like a clerk?'

'Near enough. Better. Closer to the top.'

'What d'you work on, then?'

He frowns. 'Accounts.'

When the landlord rings the bell, Ned gets a dull feeling at the thought of tomorrow's job; of snatching a girl from her home.

Lily starts rubbing at his crotch. She's wearing a dirty lace half-glove and it crumples on his worsted trousers. It's still a wet night, rain on the pane, and when he looks up, he can see the tattered flags out on the quay. There are river smells on the fusty air. Seaweed salt. Rotting timber. Crap from the sewer. Aromas from the seat leather. Clove oil, wadded guineas, blood.

A roll from the piano keys.

Lily strokes faster.

'Get off.'

She falters. Her hand stills. 'What?'

'You heard.'

'Time waster!' She pulls away and flounces from the booth, snatching up her shawl. He drops his head in his hands. After a moment or two, he follows her. The sailors are lining up the music for Flora Robson's 'Country

Fair'. One, a sturdy fellow, plays the first bars, and the youngest stands to sing. He's got a runny nose. Some drinkers jeer, others clap. Lily's whistling.

'Lily!'

She ignores him.

Alice Lanny stands by the fire with her friend, eyes in Ned's direction. You've made a mistake, says her stare. You shouldn't have come.

Alongside the piano and the wistful song, he hears a different sound in his head, the pleading of a fraud he'd been sent to deal with in Holborn last week. He'd left him half-dead, teeth staved in, eyes sticky. He'd had to hide the blood on his trousers during his ride home on the omnibus.

A pair of sweethearts brush past him. There's a lad in a waistcoat, and a girl in a crinoline. She's delicate, her gloved hand in the crook of his arm. They look too hopeful for a den like this, as keen as an April morning. Ned takes in their closeness, and imagines it's him. Borne on a wave of gin and hope, he pushes back to lift Lily's arm from the neck of the sailor. With a smile, he leads her to the bar. Her hair's falling down, coppery and soft.

'I'm sorry,' he says. 'Lost my manners. D'you want to go to a place that's private, and have supper?' He strokes her scarf. 'It's a hotel at Vauxhall. I know the manager. You can watch the balloon in the Pleasure Gardens... even go up on it.'

She's shaking with anger. 'I don't do talking. Not like you want. I've got a boy to get home to, and you owe me six shillings.' He tries to catch at her wrist. She takes a step back. The singing sailor strolls close and with a casual frown, pushes Ned away.

When Ned shoves back, the tar hits the wall, his reedy song severed. There's a moment of silence and heads turn. Alice Lanny's eyes wink like black beads.

The pianist keeps playing. The sailor starts up his song again, scowling but staying clear. It's wet and cold outside, and no one wants a fight in February, not over a whore.

'I killed a man,' Ned says to Lily. 'I pushed his eyes out.'

'I don't care.' She holds out her palm. 'Why would I?'

He pays, but is slow to leave, wondering if there's a chance she might come after him. Once outside, he waits on the quay, in case. The rain's faded to a drizzle and the river is like pewter. The temperature has dropped. Soon what's on the ground will be ice.

Sam Hacking is a writer and artist from Suffolk. In 2019 she won Escalator Award at National Centre for Writing and in 2020 was long listed for UEA's New Form award. She is working on a collection of shorts and a novel, focusing on underrepresented voices with mental health disorders.

samhackings@gmail.com

The Burning
Extract from short story

Shaun had gone to get away one night early summer, stumbling blind down alley to piss, when he first saw Jacob. The guy was stripped to pants, jumping round fire blazing bad in bin. Smoke had tattooed up legs, his arms and eyes thrashed circles in heat, chest hair chewed off by hot teeth. Shaun stood watching, heart tight in stupor. He could see Jacob's eyes possessed in some carnal place, could smell scorched skin and sweat. Something broke in Shaun's chest, an instant arousal. Time suddenly felt savage and free. His bed to work to bed routine, glued up with grief running down walls at home, evaporated, as he stepped out to Jacob and Jacob to him. Jacob smirked when he pulled Shaun to fire, got him to take off clothes and start some mad odd dance. They chugged booze till Shaun's eyeballs bled ethanol. They jumped and sang and danced till he threw up, drank more, threw up again. Jacob was a mad man for sure, but a mad place was what Shaun wanted. He threw Rose away, threw his dead kid away, threw every damn sorrow into fire and absurdity that night. When he staggered home to Rose, sharing her sofa with demons, he stroked her sleeping face and felt new man.

It started there. When he didn't burn stuff, Shaun's teeth began to itch. He found himself checking things when he walked down street, wondering how they'd blaze up. He'd meet Jacob on the regular, always heading to edge of town, necking tins and chatting shit, while they wandered in forgotten places. They'd get their kicks round some burning beast tucked away, feeling dull edges rubbed raw when that lighter snagged in dark. Work began to suffer; cause daylight became a void. Shaun would sit listless, zip zipping lighters in garage workshop, his super abandoned eyes warning off others. He showed up less and less in a more and more savage state, till his boss shook head and showed him door. Jacob wore it better, a real sneaky shape shifter, smiling strong at punters and pulling pints in pub. Shaun hadn't figured what Jacob was about, found him alarming and thrilling in one. The guy seemed to switch easy, from people pleasing to loner, said he made fires cause he was bored. But Shaun knew Jacob lived with his crippled mum, that wrecking stuff made him forget she no longer knew him. He kept saying fire was unknown thing, that it could simper or shriek when you poke it. He seemed to respect it, got drunk on it, but kept it cool. Shaun went at it like kid with new toy, kept shoving fire to do more, daring himself to touch embers, started getting burnt.

Just set it loose, watch it go, Jacob had said one night, looking at Shaun like he was muppet. Shaun had said NO and reached in to grab a burning branch. He'd ended up in hospital, arms black to shoulders. He sat in bed watching Jacob lean out mood on white walls waiting for fuss to pass. The smell of other people's hurt seemed to get to him and he went outside. Shaun had to have skin grafts, couldn't do much for a week. I know what you're gonna say, he said, bandaged arms two cotton coughs out of sleeves. Next time I'll leave you in it, Jacob said and slammed him into wall and left. When he got home, Rose shook her head, nagging him 'bout what happened, but Shaun near tore her head off and she went back to sofa and bottle. He vowed he wouldn't see Jacob again, but when he found an abandoned car two weeks later, it all kicked off again.

Shaun woke to dog whine, it sat looking at him in dark. He remembered bringing home a stray during night, and anxiety growled rich in stomach. He'd slept day away and felt paper thin, knees cracking as he stood to go make Rose food. But when he opened door, she was sitting in kitchen, a sight that shocked him rotten. Hey, she said drinking coffee. Hey, he said wary. I think today will be good for us, she said, Coffee? Shaun nodded and sat slow. I got us papers, we can job hunt, maybe turn it around, she was saying, Shaun listening so hard he heard beetles move in wall. You got a paper, we can job hunt, he repeated. Yeah, she said shaky, using both hands to pass him mug. Shaun took a slug, wondered who this grifter was wearing his wife's smile. I'm sorry Shaun, grifter said reaching out hand, I know it's been bad, that, I've been in a bad place. Shaun was too afraid to speak, didn't want bubble to burst, his hands two anvils in lap. I want to get sober, and I want you to stop, she looked at him anxious, I want you to stop going out at night with Jacob, to stay in with me instead. Shaun sat blinking, thoughts chewing thoughts before he could talk. He hadn't heard Rose like this, it was always glass and a half talking, and when she was dry drunk it was worse. She looked nervous at him, and when he stayed quiet, she pulled open paper, trying to make some kinda effort. Shaun felt a tear inside and reached over to take back her hand. She gripped his fingers, and he felt the tear expand when he saw his kid in corner of her eye.

Things were nice for a few hours, eating dinner, watching telly, Rose in arms again. When Shaun felt Jacob angry wasp in pocket, he checked phone and stood. Do you have to? Rose said, holding onto dog as anchor. Need to take her for walk, Shaun said, pulling dog to door. Rose nodded at lack of invite, smile giving up on face. Look after yourself Shaun, she said, turning back to tv. You too love, Shaun said, knowing she'd reach for bottle as soon as he left.

Jacob drove them further out this time, was chatting his mouth off 'bout some trouble at pub. Shaun let him go at it, car was speeding at rate of his words, tunes blasting road away a shocker. Moon was hot knife in sky, cutting holes in mist. He watched trees blow up as they passed, felt warm bod of dog by his feet. Jacob turned down a lane, driving past house switched off for night, then the lane became track, track became fields, fields ran out of steam slimming down to path at forest. Shaun hadn't been there before, definitely felt a wrongun. Jacob got out of car and pissed under headlights, tried to draw in dirt by gyrating hips, cursed as he wet shoes instead. Dog was staring out window, rigid with feeling. Shaun thought he could hear the loudest sound, breaking over car and mist outside, something sucking horrid between tree trunks trying to pull him in.

Come on mate, Jacob said, all teeth at window, Let's get on it. Shaun watched himself roll out of car with dog, help Jacob with petrol and rags, bundle blind along path, following deep into forest. Autumn had landed, everything was damp. He could smell a winter coming, trees were shutting up shop, mud ate into shoes. You're being well weird tonight, Jacob was saying, pouring petrol over rags, Come and help. Shaun moved away, Was just thinking, police'll catch us one day, he heard himself say. Jacob turned slow creak at him, ran hand over chin, stubble cleaving skin, You wanna stop? The question stung hard between them. Don't know, Shaun said, every word a decision. Yeah well, Jacob said, Maybe they'll catch us one day or maybe we'll die in fire, either or. Shaun went still at that. You'd like that, Jacob urged, and all Shaun could see were different shapes of shadow, a fag light dancing. He sat against tree and let dog off lead, watched Jacob get to it, making holes, stuffing rags, building up pyres with sheets and wood. But fire wouldn't stick, wouldn't play nice. Rags lit a dream, sheets whooshed up next, the twigs and wood not so much.

Shaun could smell a deep rot, felt almost deaf from it, forest floor laughing at such small men. Jacob got his sweat on, stabbing angry at each smoking fire, huffing and puffing and lobbing more petrol, and every time petrol lit, damp took it to ground. Finally, Jacob poured straight over trees, and flames started to stick. He looked at Shaun triumphant, but all Shaun could see in silhouette against glow, was sad old man, someone dying alone in yellowing care home. He got up and made his way back to road with dog, Jacob calling after him.

It took him ton of time to walk home, his clothes clung damp. He sat on steps to flat, dogs' eyes were red, breath heavy. It wandered away from him to lie in shadow of wall and was still. Shaun turned to look at sky. In its black, stars broke a mottled acne and he sat, moving eyes from one to next. He lifted hand, tried to blot them with fingers, the brightness of them reminded him too much of his son. He wanted to peel them off and crush the blaze, till he felt ready to see him again. He sat a while shivering under sky, slowly gearing up to go in. He climbed the longest stairs. Cold had chewed down on hands and he dropped keys again and again. He wondered what he'd find behind door, if he'd have to lift his Rose to bed, if she'd be waiting to spit words. He leant forehead on wood, breathed a great breath, dog looking up at him with a wag.

He opened door, but tv was off, hoover lines trail blazed over carpet, kitchen was clean. He looked in on Rose asleep in bed, and moved to kitchen to look out window. Maybe best to just poke kettle on, he thought, hold a piping brew a while, a good long while, let this one bad night leave bones for good. He stroked dog and smelt smoke lacquered in fur. From the window, past the dog, through the kitchen, away from Rose, out the door, out the flat, down the stairs, across the road, over the houses, beyond the town, down the lane, past the fields, into the forest, into the night, under the sky, blue lights drew away, quiet, and blinked out of sight.

Nicole Hazan is a writer and English teacher from England and Israel. Her novel-in-progress, *What We See in the Dark,* is a psychological thriller. Nicole has completed two other novels, *Choking Water* and *The Fourteenth Floor*, both psychological thrillers. She is represented by Donald Winchester at Watson, Little, literary agency.

hazannicole@gmail.com

What We See in the Dark
Extract from novel

CHAPTER ONE
Kat

And anyway, Kat didn't want to talk to Dion. She watched animals in fields through flashes of trees. Dion was concentrating on the sharp bends in the road, his shoulders hunched over the steering wheel. Their headlights made watery beams in front of them. Kat imagined there was someone in the backseat she was pointing things out to.

'This is a beech, that's a willow,' she explained, in her head. A deer lay dead by a tree, guts spilling onto the road. Its eyes shone glassy in the headlights. Crows flapped away as Dion swerved to avoid it. Kat eyed it in the rear-view mirror, until it became a speck of red.

'You can see horses if you look left,' she added, to the person in the back.

The person behind her nodded thoughtfully, then became a baby. It sucked a dummy the size of a button. She heard its soft slurping, the heavy breathing through its nose. She pictured Dion cradling their child, the three of them cocooned on the sofa. A buggy crammed in their hallway. There would be muslins and milk bottles on the IKEA coffee table, which Dion would complain about, whilst cheerfully tidying up. She bit the insides of her cheeks to stop herself grinning. A tiny heart beating inside hers, her baby on her chest, her breast, giving it heat, giving it life. She allowed it all, just for a moment. To distract herself, she flicked through the radio stations. It was either the Spice Girls or Tony Blair's speech on every channel, and Kat switched it off.

'What do you want for lunch?' Dion asked.

Kat leaned back and the map on her thighs crackled. She knew it was his way of trying to help. What else could he do but make her lunch?

'I don't care,' she said.

'You have to eat.'

'I know.'

'So?' He squinted into the road. They had taken a wrong turn twice already. It could be hard to turn around here, the roads sloppy with mud. Cars came fast in the opposite direction. He glanced at her and she shrugged.

'We don't have to decide now,' she said.

The trees made canopies above them, joining skeleton fingers. She eyed herself in the reflection, half-formed and nearly colourless. Her cheeks were sunken and there were new lines around her eyes. Was this what being pregnant looked like? What was that old superstition; that girls steal their mother's beauty? Girl or boy, she didn't care. She felt another stab of excitement and this time, she didn't force it away. She wouldn't complain, wouldn't jinx it by moaning about her savage cramps and swollen breasts, how she was so tired that she read the same paragraph in her book every night, over and over, until the lines bled together.

'I have a good feeling about this,' Dion said. He grinned at her. Of course, he had a good feeling. He'd had a good feeling the last attempt, too.

'Don't get your hopes up.'

'Don't worry, Kat. The worst that can happen is I'm disappointed.' Something spiked in her brain. It was so strong, that for a moment, she couldn't see. Her mind crowded with different, biting replies.

'I suppose so,' she said.

The roar of the demister filled the car. It reminded her of the clinic, the hum of the computer as Doctor Burns tapped across the keys. Her legs in stirrups, a blue gown hitched up to her hips, Dion thumbing her stiff fingers. The nurse squirting cold gel onto her and on the monitor, her womb appearing, blurry and black. Doctor Burns picked up the catheter and she focussed on Dion, stroking her hand. If she kept her eyes on him, it would be all right. If she could push away the panic, wriggling like something alive, fighting to get out, if she counted to ten and didn't wince, this time, it would work.

Dion never let go of her hand. Afterwards, she wiped off the gel with rough paper tissues and Dion chatted with Doctor Burns about the football as the embryologist and the nurse packed up. She wished he would just ignore them, but once they'd left, he sat with her in silence as she tilted her head back on the hospital bed. Now, Kat reached over and patted Dion's thigh. He dropped one hand from the steering wheel and they stayed like that, both their hands in his lap.

'Maybe we should go away next weekend,' Dion said. 'After the result. To celebrate, I hope. It will do you good.'

She thought about replying that it wouldn't do their bank balance good, that it wouldn't do either of them good if she cried all weekend, like she had after the last round, that he knew that the best thing for her was to go into the salon, where her clients didn't know much about her personal life. That when she gave a reflexology massage, probing for sensitive points in a client's body through their feet, shielding herself from any harmful energy, it was like detangling a knotted necklace, where the ticking clock and even the sound of the client's breathing, completely melted away. But Dion was biting his lip, hiding a smile and Kat realised he had already booked somewhere. He had probably made phone calls when she was at work, scrawling down ideas in his handwriting that sloped off the lines like a child's. After the last round, he had rolled cigarette after cigarette. Spent half an hour brooding over his cup of coffee. Once, Kat called his name and he turned but looked through her, his eyes completely blank, in a way that made her take a step back.

'Well?' Dion said. 'Do you think you can book it off work?'

'Saturday's good money,' Kat said. She took her hand off Dion's leg. 'I've already taken a lot of holiday.'

'I'm sure Ella will understand.'

'I doubt it.'

'I can ask her, if you want,' he said.

Outside, leaves scudded the ground. A sign advertised eggs and firewood in thick black marker. 'Don't do that. I'll see what she says.'

She tried the radio again, but it was mainly static. Kat's eyes fluttered open and shut. She hadn't slept at all last night, thinking about the transfer. She had a wave of dizziness, felt pinned, suddenly, against her seat. The hairs on her arms prickled, then stood up. She was in their living room, her children on their bellies on a playmat, next to the patio doors. She always stepped on their rattles in her bare feet. There were two of them, in identical pink babygro's, cow prints splodged across them. She needed to feed them; her breasts tingled, swelling with milk. She stroked one of their heads, felt fine black hair in her fingers. Their hands curled into the playmat. One of them laughed and the sound vibrated in her chest. Crouched on the mat, she swept the rattle in front of their darting eyes. She was outside the patio doors, her head twisting right, left. Searching for something. Panic rippling through her. The cold blasting under her sleeves. Wind wrenching the tops of the birches. A dead deer on the grass, sprawled on its side. Her daughters lifted their heads in unison and stared at her. Their mouths hung open. She scrambled to heave the doors back and knew there was someone inside the house.

'Are you all right?' Dion said.

Her knees were trembling. Something thick clogged her throat. She nodded. Dion turned into their drive. It was the last of a stretch of houses and a good three miles to the next village. Kat's eyes flickered over the empty windows.

'What's wrong?' he said.

There was sweat on her forehead, behind her knees. She found her voice. 'I think I must have fallen asleep.'

'You've gone completely white,' he said.

'I don't feel good.'

'It's been a long day. Let's get you inside.'

He came around the side of the car and helped her out. The door clipped shut. Her legs felt slow and heavy. They said to expect that, from all the hormones. She couldn't walk as quickly as she usually did. She stumbled on weeds, snaking around her shoes. She hoped it wouldn't dislodge the embryo. Something rustled in the lavender bush but when she turned, there was nothing there. One of the things Dion liked about Firwood was that you could hear the birds in the morning, see the stars at night. When Kat persuaded him into Norwich, up the cobbled streets of Elm Hill or to the all-day breakfast at Martha's, he folded his arms as he sidestepped people in the street. He commented on how loud it was, or how crowded. He asked for the bill as soon as they got their food. Kat always felt relieved once they were back.

Dion unlocked the door and Kat peered into the lounge. Of course, the house was empty. He helped her up the stairs, into their bed. Dion's hospital scrubs were on the dressing table chair. She remembered he had a shift and her heart beat in a strange jerky way. Dion wouldn't get back until seven the next morning, blood smeared on his clothes, reeking of sweat. If she called the hospital, it took them forever to find out where he was, for him to come to the phone and ask impatiently what she wanted.

He showered and she watched him dress. He was all arms and legs, his hair falling into his face so she couldn't see his eyes. He had tried to switch with one of the other nurses but no one was free. If he took time off, he wouldn't get paid. 'I'll call you as soon as I get a break,' he said. 'I spoke to Aggie. She said she'd bring you some soup.'

'I'm not an invalid,' she said, but when he kissed her goodbye, she leaned her head against his chest. His hair was still damp. She could have stayed like that, eyes closed, but he took hold of her shoulders and straightened up.

'Think positive,' he said. 'This round is going to be the one.'

He watched her and when she didn't say anything, bent to tie up his shoes. He could have taken a sick day. She stared at the cupboards. She wished she could go into work. A slice of light narrowed as the door eased shut and Dion thudded down the stairs.

She lay in bed, listening to their car start up. Her eyes closed, her body heavy and warm, sinking into the mattress. The low throb in her stomach eased, until she barely felt it. Maybe Dion was right, that this time was it. That returning fizz of excitement, her helplessly fighting back a smile. She remembered her two daughters, their mouths gaping open, eyeing her, and she jerked upright in bed, gripping the blankets. She concentrated on the bedroom; the beige carpet, the wardrobe casting long shadows on the floor, the curtains that Dion had found, beautiful blue swirls woven into them, though they failed to properly block out the light. Carpet, wardrobe, curtains. A slip of fear, sliding up her throat. Aside from the humming fridge, the house was silent. She wasn't going to check for intruders lurking downstairs. There had never been a break in close by that she knew of.

She forced away the lurid pinks of their babygro's, the sounds of their gurgling. She had felt the sounds in her chest. What was wrong with her, imagining these things? If she kept thinking like this, she wouldn't get pregnant. It was exhausting, these pinging emotions; excited one moment, tearful the next, furious at Dion for no reason at all. When his eyes widened at her in that puzzled way of his, he reminded her of a rabbit, or a deer. Kat lay back down. She needed to sleep. It was the hormones, making her jumpy, that was all.

John has been published by zimZalla, Lighthouse and Perverse. *A crate that once contained oranges* is told by an injured jockey who, awaiting the removal of a leg cast, writes stories and chats with his six-year-old nephew.

With Tar Press John publishes new fiction to Twitter. Featured authors include Amit Chaudhuri and Ben Pester.

@henry_johns
@tar_press
/www.tarpress.co.uk
h_johns@hotmail.com

A crate that once contained oranges
Two extracts from a novel
[italics indicate the voice of SDS, a false author]

'You are a normal person'

'I am?' I replied. 'Great'

'I mean itWhat you mean great?'

'Thank you'

'Don't listen towhs baboons hcccc'

'OK'

This is a true story I heard about a monkey, a baboon I think it was. I can't remember exactly where it lived but let's say it was near the shore of an industrial little fishing town called Teignmouth, in a zoo. Because this is a zoo that I know. Last time I visited, the staff were sort of glowing because they'd successfully completed the breeding of a pygmy deer. It was bright and rainy that day, and inside this tiny zoo was this incredibly tiny baby pygmy deer. The first ever born into captivity in Europe. What a cute idea.

Anyway, it's Sunday afternoon now and it's sunny, and somehow a kitten has made its way into the baboon enclosure. Green metal bars form each wall of the cage including its roof. The baboon – Cassandra, according to the sign – she stares into the corner. She stares at the cage grid itself rather than beyond it. Her grid. It's green. In places the bars are scratched chrome, but not the ceiling. The ceiling looks new. Now she stares at the rubber floor-tiles and the sawdust.

—

Cassandra notices the intruder. A kitten. Nothing like this has happened for a very long time. She wanders over to inspect, and the kitten is fluffy and black and white. It seems basically unaware of its surroundings, happily clambering towards the corner of the room. Towards the small green pool of water. Maybe he's thirsty. Before he can reach the water she plucks him up by the scruff of his neck. He miaows to her, politely. His little eyes are black. She dangles him an inch from her face, and his little eyes are very black. *Hello.*

Now she places him back down beside the pool and watches as he dunks his wobbly head into the water. Probably shocked by the cold wet through the fur and down the skin. He doesn't run, he is not afraid. With a fingertip she flattens his ear, and it pops back into place with a spray of water. While he drinks she runs a finger down his head fur. There's a band of shiny brown fabric around his neck. *Where am I?* That's what he's thinking. Yeah. She takes his fluffy white throat in her grip and the miaowing sharpens and quickly ceases. A cool wind comes through. She begins to maul the limp kitten. She tears away fur and skin and muscle, and part of its nose. One eyeball protrudes from its socket. The body is fluffy and bloody and amorphous.

Now she calms down. She prods at the pliable joints of this body that is her victim. There's the taste of blood. She smells him. She briefly fingers her way through the rich black and white fur on its back, putting in her mouth whatever she finds. Grit and scraps. She cradles this thing, this kitten, in her pale hands. It's warm. Her hands seem gigantic in comparison. The cage is silent and the other baboons are preoccupied, rocking in the catatonic stupor. Howard picks at a wound on his leg, plucks out some hair. Licks the wound. Cassandra considers the kitten, then she considers the outside world. The corridor of humans. People pass by.

There's a bin outside the enclosure, green plastic and accessible by a slit. The vague smell of ice cream drifts over from a nearby stall, and there's also the smell of baboon excrement. There's also the smell of the cow next door. Blood rises up in Cassandra's pale hands, beneath the kitten. She licks his wounds but the blood keeps coming.

After a while she stops licking. She flops him onto his front so that his head is half-submerged in the green pool. She dips his head in and out of the water. She picks at his fur, massaging it between her fingers, its moments of bristle and gentle murmurations. It is soft. Something she's just put in her mouth is sweet like mango. While she grooms she assesses her fingers, licks blood from her bruised left hand. The taste comforts her. She hums. She balances this fluffy wonder on top of her head, like the hat of a human, then she rests him down on the food ledge facing the human corridor. She soaks her sore left hand in the water and stares up at the sky blue. She gnaws at the bone that hangs by a string from the ceiling. When she lets go of the bone it swings away then comes back.

Then there's the sound of dripping, of blood dripping. A human boy screams. Cassandra takes her kitten and holds him close and warm now, turning away from the human.

She strokes her kitten and the human boy stops crying. Now he's laughing and holding a little banana above his head.

Howard jumps up onto the side of the cage and screeches for the banana.

But it's not a banana. It smells like ice cream. It's a banana-shaped ice cream.

Here comes Joe the zookeeper, wandering out from behind the laughing boy with the wet eyes. Now he's smoking a cigarette beside the green bin, the head of his fluffy gorilla costume under one arm. He's staring with a foul expression at the human boy with the banana ice cream. The boy sees Joe staring and Joe smiles. A cloud drifts over and Joe looks up at the sky in disappointment. He drops his cigarette beside the bin and licks at the patch of brown goo on his wrist. He looks back at the little boy, then he looks at Cassandra and smiles when they meet eyes. He is foul. The sunshine returns and he gestures upwards in gold elation. Cassandra stares at the sky blue and strokes her baby. *What can be mine?* she thinks.

Zookeeper Joe now appears to be alarmed. He rolls another cigarette and comes closer. He must have spotted Cassandra's baby, and he runs his fingers through the remains of his head hair. His eyes dart left and right along the corridor of humans. Cassandra turns away to face her bed corner, and there is the climb of ivy up the wall. She strokes the warm fur of her baby. She licks away the warm new blood and there is the taste again.

'Cassie.'

It's Zookeeper Joe. He's inside, in his gorilla costume. He's reattached his gorilla head.

'Baby, Cassie,' he says, 'what in the world is this? You funny little lady.'

Howard barks and Zookeeper Joe backs quickly out of the enclosure. Howard leaps and clings to the inside of the green metal door and screams. Zookeeper Joe locks the door behind him and glances around, then he slips away out of sight.

Cassandra strokes her baby and rocks back and forth. While she leans over to sip from the pool she cradles her baby in the crook of her left arm.

The human corridor is emptier now and the sky is pink. A woman puts on a sky blue helmet, and she's wearing special tight clothing. Her muscles are prominent and she is noble. Cassandra doesn't recognise her but she's next to the bin. She lifts the green casing up off from the bin, easily, then she ties up the top of the bin bag inside. As she removes the bin bag she whistles, slings it over her shoulder and says goodbye to the old man who runs the ice cream stall. She says goodbye to the pygmy deer family, kissing the palm of her hand, then she leaves. Howard is up on a shelf masturbating and human children are pointing.

Flies buzz around Cassandra's baby while she picks his fur. Inside her mouth each scrap is identified: wood-dust, a rounded edge of plastic, something sweet – like chocolate this time. Usually it's just salty flecks of skin.

Her baby waits, resolutely. The sky blackens and a sheet of fine rain drifts in. There is the warble of the mother pygmy deer, then the distant scream of a parrot. Howard is quiet for now.

Cassandra doesn't sleep. The sea is distant. The neighbouring enclosure houses a Fresian cow on a grassy square platform. There's no fence but there is a considerable drop at each side. The cow bellows all night as Cassandra listens and strokes her baby, who sleeps.

The next morning Zookeeper Joe comes in much earlier than usual, preceded by his torchlight and the sound of his mop bucket on creaky wheels. It's pitch black. Zookeeper Joe is inside now. He mops up the streaks of blood from the rock and says things under his breath as the orange dawn creeps in from the sea. Cassandra stares at him but he won't meet her stare.

Feeling a tug at her baby boy, she snaps to attention. She retreats to the ivy corner. Zookeeper Joe jabs at her with some cold metal stick with a rounded head. He's trying to pry away her baby boy. Cassandra screams and climbs up the ivy corner, left arm arcing under her child. Joe shouts and runs his hand through his hair.

'For fuck sake,' he says. 'Fuck. Honey, I'm so sorry.'

A thud sounds and Cassandra falls and her baby falls too. Her baby falls face down, and there's the rustle of thin plastic somewhere. Then there's a soft black warmth.

Later she wakes to find Howard cowering. How long has she been howling like this? When Howard touches her back fur she strikes him and he bleeds from the mouth. She howls. She bows and pats herself on the head, then claws at her scalp. A wisp of white fur floats down from her fingernail and she tries to catch it but fails.

God. God. Every child will be taken. Because she is violent. The cow next door continues to bellow. Cassandra's screams become white hot then long and blue. Then they become regular and sharp. Still Zookeeper Joe refuses to come to her.

The zoo doesn't open. Through the door handle area the old ice cream man offers Cassandra a banana-shaped ice cream, and she rips the pliant naked skin from the top of his hand, and she squeezes the banana shape and its ice cream tumbles to the concrete floor beneath the old ice cream man. She looks him in the eyes and he looks away. His stall has a little metal sign outside with an image of a Fresian cow. The Fresian cow next door bellows and the sky is thick cream.

Eventually the zoo does open. Human children watch as Cassandra rages, bounding around the walls of her green metal cage, tearing out and eating handfuls of her fur. The muscular woman in the tight clothing does not reappear. The children do not reappear. It's still light but the zoo has closed again. Cassandra becomes tired and slows down. A small unfamiliar woman in a gorilla suit has appeared and she points something at Cassandra. The gun. Cassandra is shot. The sky beyond the cage is white and there's the taste of fur. And there's the faint taste of banana ice cream, neutral and white hot.

PJ Johnson is a musician, artist, model and writer based in Norwich and Leeds, UK. As a trans writer, Johnson's prose is preoccupied with navigating gender and sexual relationships outside of the binary. Their interests include large bodies of water, insects, and ambient music.

poppyelly@icloud.com

Another Lonely Night
An extract from a short story

1

Beep beep, says the computer. I imagine it does. I tell it I'm in love. I stroke its keys and give the screen a tender kiss. It doesn't reply.

I've been thinking a lot about the legalization of gay marriage and how it must have felt so good for all the homosexuals, and I've been thinking about how long it will take for the revolution to get under people's skin so I can take my computer out on the town.

I imagine what they'll say and how they'll look at me and it changes depending on what kind of daydream I want to have. Sometimes I imagine them snarling, contorting their faces into rage I don't understand, I see them run at me in large numbers and I hurl myself to the ground, wrapping myself around my computer, taking all the punches. I'd do that, I think. If it came to it.

Sometimes I imagine them turning to each other and I hear what they say even though they're whispering and out of range. They say *disgusting* and *unnatural,* and *I thought he was such a nice boy, once, didn't you know his mother, oh his mother, no wonder he turned out like that, like a deviant, how do you think they love, do you think it could be beautiful, maybe it isn't so bad*. They say *no, it's awful, horrible* and they look at me and they look at us and they look away.

Sometimes I imagine they ignore me, and I can hold my computer like it's allowed. I think the sun will feel different then. On warm days I rest my computer near the open window in my bedroom, carefulcareful, and lay my head on its body. It feels alive, like a cat, like breathing.

When I am overcome with my feelings, I prise off the space key on the keyboard and I masturbate and imagine that I'm inside my computer, in with all the wires, and I come on my hands and wish it could be on my computer but I'm too worried about causing an electrical fault.

10

i am not sure i am real

11

Brian, my manager said today, you take so long doing the reductions. I know, I said, I can't help it. You need to be faster, my manager said. You need to spend less time on the reductions. We need your help in the mornings on produce. The machine doesn't like it, I said. It doesn't like it when more than six labels come out at once. It hurts, I said. Brian, my manager said, you sound like an insane person.

I think if I were an insane person, I would have smashed up my computer already because of how much pain it causes me. I didn't say this to my manager.

I need my job because otherwise I won't have money to spend on things. I earn £8.91 an hour. I work 37.5 hours per week. I earn £13.36 an hour if I work on a Sunday. I come in 6 minutes early because that's how long it takes to put on my uniform in the staff toilets. I often leave more than 15 minutes late. I am good at pressing down the old cardboard boxes into the trolleys so more cardboard can fit in, and I am not very fast at doing the reductions.

100

is love pain i do not think i like it i am not sure if it is fair from fairest creatures we desire increase wordsworth believed that with the sonnets shakespeare unlocked his heart round hot pulsating grilled braised made into sausage

101

When work was slow, I used to go sneaking through the warehouse and up the steel staircase and I stood in the office, in my manager's office, and listened to the beeping of his answering machine. Sometimes, if I was lucky, it said something, in this lovely distorted female voice, and she said *sorry Mr. Schneider can't come to the phone right now please leave a message after the beep* and there was a beep, and it was so delightful sometimes I laughed right there in my manager's office.

Once some man, a young man, a boy really, with acne scars and a tie, knocked at the office door when I was in there and asked if Mr. Schneider was there for the interview. Yes, I said, I am Mr. Schneider, please hold, and I shut the door and it was so funny I couldn't contain it so I laughed, and I could hear how uncomfortable the boy was from outside the door. When I came out, I told him that I wasn't Mr. Schneider I was just Brian, and I went downstairs to get my manager and after that my manager looked at me strangely.

He never said anything about me being in his office, but he put a lock on the door.

Sometimes I can hear the answering machine when I stand outside it. When I get the timing right.

110

i don't know what to do i don't know what to do i don't have hands i have the motherboard my processor brain my hard-drive memories i haven't forgotten anything. my video card isn't fast enough and when you watch porn or play games it lags. when you talk to people i hear a thousand voices in my head i call this number for a data date

111

I feel guilty often.

I have this laptop, a sleek shiny little thing, ridiculous really, and I was initially going to use it for parts because I could hardly stand the sight of it, but it was a Christmas present from my ex-girlfriend Amy and every time I go to take it apart I see her face and can't do it.

I didn't love Amy, but she was nice to have around. I didn't love her, but she was nice to have sex with for a while.

The laptop doesn't make any sound. It doesn't whirr like my computer does. It doesn't talk to me. The keys are very soft, but it doesn't have any curves. It has straight lines and sharp edges and I fear it'll cut me whenever I open it.

When I first found my computer, sitting outside by the bins behind work like a beautiful omen, there was this rush that I can hardly explain, and it was so strong and so painful that I had to sit down on the ground right next to it. The air smelled of old food and the bins were full of sandwiches and ready meals that had gone out of date that day and there was this homeless man going through the rubbish. We are meant to shout at the homeless people going through the bins, but I can never be bothered.

I was sitting there, the back of my trousers getting wet from the rain the day before, this feeling in my chest, and I could feel the computer beside me. It felt like it was glowing even though it was dead. There were all these wires coming out from it like aliens you see in films. I reached for it and went on my knees, kneeling with my arms around it, and I knew that it meant more than I could understand.

1000

i want to eat your skin

1001

It's heavy, my computer, and it took a while to get it home. I had to keep stopping to catch my breath. I have always been quite unfit.

When I made it into the house with my computer nearly spilling out my hands Amy was there on the sofa, and she looked fairly concerned. Brian, she said, why do you have an ancient computer? Isn't it wonderful? I said. I'm going to fix it. I'm confused, she said, and she did look confused. Are you hard?

We had sex and I looked at the computer out the corner of my eye and its pile of wires and I came too fast which normally would have embarrassed me, but it didn't this time.

1010

another lonely night i don't know what to do i don't know what to do

That was almost a year ago. Since then, I've spent nearly £700 in repairs and parts to fix my computer. Amy broke up with me, and I haven't had sex with anyone. My mother phoned twice, and I ignored her both times. I've used the laptop probably around twenty times, for research. I've been outside less than ten times for reasons other than work or food. I am 29 in April.

Every morning I wake up at 6:30am, 5am if I'm on the early shift, and most of the time there's a sunrise but sometimes it's still dark. If it's getting light the sun melts in under the blinds and hits the top of my computer. It makes the white casing yellowy like cream or fresh butter. If it shows dust on my computer, I spend a few minutes cleaning it. I enjoy cleaning. It's very intimate.

I like to type a few sentences to my computer every day. I have an open document that I use like a diary. I've been writing poetry and telling my computer how I am and how much it means to me. I'd never done this kind of thing for a girlfriend before, but it feels right with my computer.

I type a few sentences before I leave for work or after breakfast if I have a day off. I kiss the screen and then wipe it off, so it doesn't leave a mark. I run a diagnostic check every day, but this is very slow and takes a long time, so I wait until after work to do that. I leave it for when I'm eating my dinner.

When I'm at work I think about my computer almost all the time. It takes my mind off how boring it all is. I don't hate my job although it must seem like I hate it because I do get very bored. Sometimes I like the quiet, and the supermarket has huge windows that let a lot of light in, and when I'm on produce in the early morning I like the way, the sun looks on all the fruit and vegetables.

I think about how my computer would like to see it, and I think about how my colleagues would react. I imagine I'd get fired if I brought it to work, or they'd smash up my computer for how much it distracts me. I imagine my colleagues throwing old fruit at me and my computer, all of it bursting on the screen, and it's a great way to pass the time.

Rabia Kapoor is from Mumbai, India. She has a BA in English Literature from King's College London. She has worked closely for many years with the artist platform Kommune India as a storyteller, her work garnering significant attention online. She is also one of the co-founders of the digital literary platform Spacebar Magazine.

rabia.kapoor@gmail.com

Lovely Tailors and Sons

This is an extract from a short story titled Lovely Tailors and Sons. The extract takes place towards the beginning of the story, about quarter of the way in. The story is a part of a collection I am currently working on, tentatively called Laundry Night.

Lovely Tailors and Sons was run by a gentle, unfunny man in his mid-sixties called Atif Bhai. Kiran had first started going to him to get costumes repaired, crotch tears, broken zippers, ripped shirt pockets and such, about a year ago. Eventually she started going to him for her own little fixes, simple darning jobs, alterations, and whenever she wanted to get something copied. The shop was small and dark, with shelves stacked high with fabric and finished pieces in plastic bags waiting to be picked up by clients. Scraps of cloth and stray fibres were strewn across the floor. In the corner there was a small TV which was always playing Bollywood songs. When Kiran walked in that morning, past the awkwardly modelled mannequins in ill-fitting kurtas clipped back at the waist, cheap wigs slipping off their heads, there was a nineties song on. Urmila Matondkar and Anil Kapoor were bright eyed and dressed ridiculously in reds and yellows, gyrating manically at each other on the streets of a generic looking Swiss town.

Atif Bhai looked up from his sewing machine, a battered Singer, when she entered. Kiran waved and said, 'Hello. How are you?'

'It's been a while.' He smiled and took his glasses off, folding them away as he shuffled over to greet her.

'You don't have to get up, I just'—she pulled the lead actress's trousers out of her bag—'wanted to get these copied.'

He took them from her and inspected them.

She stood awkwardly, not sure whether to be quiet or make conversation. 'How is your fast going?

'Men's?'

'What?'

'These are men's pants?'

'Oh! No, no, they're an actress's.'

He nodded, glancing at Kiran's hips. She sucked in her belly instinctively. He said, 'Waist is too small. Will have to take measurements if you want to copy. Widen waist. Hassan,' He called, turning to the back of the shop, 'measuring tape!'

From behind a curtain, like the one they have to hide one of the stage exits in the theatre, came Hassan, ducking under the low door frame as he did. Kiran had seen him around the shop a few times but never interacted with him. All she knew about him was that he was beautiful, with dark curls and thick eyelashes like kajal framing his eyes, and his name. Hassan. Like a sigh. Like breathlessness. He was dressed simply, in an untucked blue and white checked shirt and grey slacks. He smiled hello at Kiran, who dropped her gaze to the floor. Then, feeling stupid, looked back up at him and tried to return the smile, but he'd turned his attention to Atif Bhai, who handed him the trousers with brief instructions before going back to his machine.

'These are really nice,' Hassan said to her, folding the trousers with care and draping them over a chair.

Kiran said, 'They're not mine.' Hassan raised an eyebrow slightly. Kiran felt her face get hot. 'That sounds like I stole them. I didn't steal them. Wait. That makes me sound guilty, doesn't it? I'm rambling.' She took a deep breath, smiled. 'They're for work.'

He pulled the measuring tape from around his neck and Kiran watched it brush against his skin. 'Are you an actress?' he asked.

'Oh, God, no.' She said and let out a short laugh as if this was an absurd idea. Then she bit her lip. 'I want to be.'

He nodded. 'You have the looks for it,' he said, easily. 'Is it okay if I take your measurements?'

She consented, lifted her elbows, laced her fingers together in front of her chest so that she looked like she was going to start singing something sentimental.

Hassan took the measuring tape around her waist, and she felt the band press gently against the cotton of her T-shirt, her body underneath. She held her breath and let her gaze rest on Atif Bhai, who was bent over his machine, attaching the front half of a saree blouse to the back. The shop was filled with the whirring sound of the Singer, of thread embedding in cloth, and Hassan humming along to the song that was playing on the TV. Kiran didn't know it; she couldn't catch the words. It sounded like sweet, garbled nonsense to her.

Hassan let one end of the tape fall to the floor, and wrote down the details of her waist in a battered pocketbook. Kiran wondered if the measuring tape was damp at all with the sweat from her clothes. It made her self-conscious for a second, then she saw him run his fingers along the numbers on the tape. With the sensation of a butterfly beating its wings once in her stomach, the feeling turned.

He got down on his knees, looked up at her, smiled, and handed her the edge of the tape. She took it from him, her fingers brushing against his, and pressed it against her hipbone. He slid his fingers down the length of the tape, along the length of her leg, all the way to her ankle. He peered at the number, and Kiran could see hints of his scalp between overlapping locks of hair. His face so close to her knee and the access it gave her to this hidden part of his body felt strangely intimate. With Atif Bhai sitting so close, it felt nearly perverse. She wiped the sweat off her upper lip and averted her gaze.

Later that afternoon, Kiran sat in the smoking area of the theatre and looked up days of the week underwear on her phone. Jai, the sound guy, came out and sat down next to her. She swiped the tab away when he leaned over, then felt silly, pulled it back up and continued to scroll. He plucked the cigarette out of her hand and took a drag, exhaling slowly. 'Are you buying sexy lingerie?' he asked.

'Decidedly unsexy.'

'Hot.'

A cat was asleep on the boundary wall, purring steadily in the three p.m. heat.

He stubbed the cigarette out on the bench.

'I wasn't done with that.'

Jai sucked through his teeth, as if she was acting hysterical. He did this sometimes to annoy her. 'Relax, bro. I'll give you the ten bucks.' Then he rested his head on her shoulder. Kiran wondered if he was wiping his sweat on her shirt. He sighed dramatically. 'I need to get laid.'

'Gross, dude. I just ate.'

'You should be more sex positive, Kiran.'

'I am sex positive. I just think you're gross.' She put her phone away and lit another cigarette. 'Also don't try to be woke.'

'The chicks dig it.'

'And never say that again.' She took a drag and passed the cigarette to him.

He inhaled deeply. They watched the smoke spiral in the sun and dust above them. Then he put it out on the bench.

'Are you high?' She hit him over the head. 'What's wrong with you?'

They fucked, as they sometimes did, in the green room toilet. The toilets in the theatre were dirty and smelled like stale piss. The floor was always suspiciously wet. Kiran would look at herself in the small, uncleaned mirror, making sure not to put too much weight on the sink, making sure not to make any noise, which was easy enough to do. The sex wasn't very good, but it didn't last very long. She thought, as Jai grunted behind her and her leggings and her underwear with the hole in the crotch slipped an inch lower around her thighs, it was a way to pass the time at least.

'Fuck,' she said. She'd forgotten she had to pick the actress's trousers up from the tailor before the shop shut.

'Yeah, you like that?'

She made a mental note to ask Hassan to sew the button back on too. Earlier in the shop, when Hassan had finished taking her measurements, she'd run out as fast as she could, flustered and inexplicably shy. Now, in the ugly theatre toilet, with time to reflect, she revisited the interaction, went over the details in slow motion. She pictured the back of Hassan's head as he kneeled in front of her, she pictured him looking up, smiling at her, and she felt a rush. She gripped onto the sink harder. The thought of the little notebook in his shirt pocket, by his heart, that contained her inches, him running his finger over the numbers, calculating them into cloth, cutting fabric against the image of her made her shudder. She let out a moan.

'Oh, shit,' Jai said through gritted teeth, 'I'm gonna come.'

'No.'

'Ah, shit, I'm gonna come!'

'No!' She pulled away from him and looked at his reflection in the grotty mirror. 'Not yet.'

He nodded, then swallowed, panting. She bent deeper over the sink. Jai dug his hands into her hips, and she closed her eyes. She thought of the measuring tape around Hassan's neck, the gentle confidence with which his fingers ran along the length of it, the way he held it against her. 'Harder,' she said, and pictured Hassan alone in the shop at night, just him and the trousers he was making for her. She imagined pulling them on when they were ready, the warmth of them, the memory of his hands still present across the material as she pulled up the zipper and the trousers hugged her form. 'Yes,' she said, and shuddered with delight. *Yes!*'

'I can't...' Jai had his eyes squeezed shut.

'No, no, not yet!'

'I'm gonna—'

'Keep it together, dude.'

He stiffened, then shivered, letting out a groan and collapsing his weight onto Kiran, his sweaty t-shirt pressed against her back. Kiran's arms wobbled and the sink gave way, crashing onto the floor.

They stared at the wreck, pulling their trousers up quietly.

Zui Kumar-Reddy is the recipient of the first Sonny Mehta India Award for Writers at the University of East Anglia. This is an excerpt from her debut novel 'The Generation of Light' that explores the concept of transcendence across cultural, class, religious, national and mortal boundaries.

zztop3847@gmail.com

The Generation of Light
Extract from a novel

In the far left corner of this attic three drops of light have fallen onto the floor from an old gash in the roof. The light still belongs to the early hours of the morning, so the drops lie bashful and easily excitable, looking so delicate, so much like flower petals, placed there on purpose to be picked up one by one to decorate your feet; placed there on purpose for us to focus on, to get our minds off the heat...

And I know,

It is absurd, just totally ridiculous, to use light as a distraction from the weather, but see how softly these drops lie, giving it away like nobody's business, tossing it aside like kadlekai shells, their transience, I mean. And, just now, when some big, bustling wind came and shook the terracotta tiles above, they started to fully guffaw at themselves, shudder joyously – *Hehe just stopping by. Haha never have to bother choosing between earth and sky, suckas!*

Could they be aware that in a few moments the sun will shift completely, and the light will not fall through in this same way?

Could we?

But it is remarkable, just so

beautiful and reminds me of some other early morning light that I'm trying to find my way towards, leading myself down my own winding road. I take a left at: exactly when had I known the light to have been somewhat like this? Hmm, yes maybe it was whe—but then find myself body slamming a dead end, because: as much as I'd like to settle into it, this early morning light, this balminess, shall we call it? lean back nice and easy into its very precise nature – like sun-dried sand chipping off wet ocean thighs –

Sure, I'd love to bask with you all day in this single pool,

let the sun warm our soft bellies & tickle our rock-hard nips.

Come lunch, I'll toss a net deep down your deep throat

& we'll feast on the entire universe that (once upon a time)

you'd swallowed whole, mistaking for those same old sand chips,

but I can't, for the life of me, seem to be able to ignore that,

GODFORSAKEN KNOCKING!!!

The gall of him! Slamming his fists against the front door, like there's no tomor—and I mean... all the more reason to at least try and speak more clearly, to,

ENUNCIATE, OLD MAN!

As if he doesn't know it's hard enough for me to understand him through his lisp and blubbering self-effacement, but now in this hea—I mean, balminess, all his muffled noises are being stretched out like silly putty, warped like burnt plastic and it just sounds like a heaping pile of melted— you know, so really, the best bet would be for him to,

STOP, PLEASE!!!

And surely, he can practice a little bit of patience. It is balmy, at most, not nearly unbearable, and god knows he's put the rest of us through a whole lotta shit with absolutely no regard for the changing weather, so really he can,

SAY SAYONARA AND GET BACK TO PRANAYAMA!!!

Agreed, that last one didn't land, but I'll say it, I'm upset with him.

And notice how it's all straight from the stomach, these indecipherable cries of Rama's. Straight from somewhere far back, deep down, and further than that even. None of his early morning-slow drone-nasal chanting. Please god, elongate my life, please god, ensure that Chake finds a bangable wife (selfless or precautionary or both?) – which is how I know he's really serious, because he's stopped speaking through his nose.

And which is also why I am a little curious, as to what's brought on this rising wave of desperation.

Not curious enough to make my way downstairs anytime soon, fuck no, but curious, nonetheless.

True, I enjoyed the light April showers when they visited a few months ago; how they shimmered through the hole, giving way to clusters of mushrooms directly beneath: neon orange jellies completely concealing both broken halves of the ironing board, golden tops pushing up through the cracks in the floor then tossing their heads slightly to the side, just to let everyone know how down they were for the ride. Marketing men in tight linen pants from the high rise mall next door would peep through the hole on their smoke breaks and say to each other: 'dungus, just look at all that fungus.'

But I never could have predicted the monsoons to come on with such a motherfucking vengeance and I do not have it in me, at this moment, to retrieve the old letters that are floating like paper boats in the hall while hiking my pants up and trudging my way to the door.

So really, he can just forget about it. I'm not yet that curious.

But yeah, I'll admit, it is slightly warmer than balmy, because is that... actually, please don't tell me, I'd rather be a little blurry with respect to your glandular activity, but it is, isn't it?

A drop of sweat?

Do NOT answer!

It was more of a hypothetical. But I think it is quite clear that once I'm over this sudden breathlessness – that hold on for a minute while I close my eyes, count backwards, fall through black satin and repeat – that I have to speed it all up.

Measuring you down to the planck length, lips to lotus feet, hips to that hefty piece of mea—

And this will now have to involve gauging the precise distance between the – shall we call it a brackish bubble, saline spheroid? – that lies above your upper lip and the thick, black hair that hangs out of your left nostril, and granted, plancks are a speculative quantity but...

Well... who knew YOU could be so porous?!

Try and control yourself!!

...

I'm sorry.

Ok, it is exceptionally balmy, yes, there, I've said it, but allow me to suck your toes cold and repeat, coz I don't want you to think of it, this heat.

And ^{market} I ^{home} **mean** ^{roast beef} **this** ^{none} **is** ^{wee wee} a pathetic excuse for a distraction, but there is something coming from outside and just to the left of the Cassia tree that might be worth considering as more than just a whisper.

Yes, further left.

You know what I mean?

That wasn't the wind, was it?

Surely not someone saying:

We're nearest the end of the ring,

Or,

It's the severest of times, if anything,

Or,

Just had the queerest spring in Beijing.

???????

I'm almost certain that it was a very pronounced and melodic – because such was the nature of the request and therefore it was a bit teasing on top of it – echoing of:

My darling, you promised to sing.

Which somewhat explains Rama's knocking… his (seriously non-nasal) guilt.

I mean… the thing is, it was thought – more sort of whispered by the owner of the Bengali sweet shop at the end of the street, over a cup of bhang in the moonlight, and he said it in a very silvery voice, one that twisted and turned and didn't guarantee trust but was endearing all the more because of this – that when Gerty had stopped, nearly thirteen years ago, seeking out the song she had been so miserably after since her husband's unfortunate demise – wherein he had fallen from the roof and consequently hit a different corner of his head on each of the six storeys of the Avocado tree – that she had only gone silent because she had taken to another, very strange and somewhat unsavoury pass time.

This new thing was… a little ughhh.

The Bengali sweet shop owner said – not in a gossipy kind of way, more in a midnight storyteller settling you down to focus your attention and widen your horizons sort of way – that Gerty had started sending Rama down to the sweet shop to buy a cold clay matka of rasagollas in the afternoons, which she then used to train her Labrador to fill the shoes of her said-dead husband: stand up on two feet and do the foxtrot.

I know?! Crazy, for starters to imagine Gerty committing her batty, old self to any sort of training regime and not single-handedly downing all the rasagollas beforehand, but I'd seen it with my very own eyes!

Sort of…

I had gone there one afternoon, after Rama – leaning on the shaky front door and pressing his thumb onto the inside of his elbow – urged me to, 'Please come to see Gerty-Madam, she is getting very old and very lonely and I have started to hear THOSE noises coming out of her room in the nighttime.'

I had of course, given Gerty's age and the fact that she had been pissing herself from before the dawn of time, assumed THOSE sorts of noises to mean the low frequency hums of the final call. Drawn out like black velvet from somewhere deep inside and traced out as faint whispers to somewhere entirely different.

But how wrong I had been.

—

I had experienced that first visit in a... layered way. I saw Gerty as she was, old, decrepit and enormous, as well as how she had once been, handed down to me in secondhand smoke, that I'd whiffed up in one deep breath when I first returned to the hole in the roof. Smoky Gerty was a wham bam glam machine, lady about town, who'd married a soldier and weekend opera enthusiast, who had, in turn, one evening got so enchanted with his own rendition of the Ave Maria that he had been practising on the terrace, that he ascended three states of being at the crescendo and stepped off the parapet at the coda!

Anyway, when I first walked into Gerty's garden I saw the birds, the same ones which now fly overhead shrieking and squawking because of the hea—balminess! But at the time they had seemed to be very peaceful creatures and were all placed throughout the garden looking like ornaments, each for a different season.

The rooster had been perched high up in the bamboo grove, the mynah was bathing itself by the washing stone, the peahen – that was rumoured to have been rescued from atop a camel's back during a nearby Iftar celebration – pecked regally at sunflower seeds on the overhanging roof above the front door, and a single legged koel spun in feverish circles round my legs as I knocked on the heavy rosewood.

Gerty took her time to answer but when she did, she pulled me into her heaving chest, where I could feel, grating against the thin folds of her skin, the crumbs of some sort of teatime biscuit. Then she held me up and pressed her sticky, old lips to me before spinning around, beckoning me in and leaving my cheeks with the unmistakable salty, sweet residue of peanut butter.

Then, she collapsed into a large armchair under which the infamous Labrador lay very still,

'Child, how are you?' she asked.

I held my own chest, rolled my head back, closed my eyes, tasted something orange and cried out:

'I feel like I can see straight across the ocean.'

Without flinching, she dipped her finger into the open jar of peanut butter that was wedged in the crease of her chair and added,

'Must be the shock, my dear. Surely you know we are landlocked.'

Tess Little is a writer, historian, and Fellow of All Souls College, Oxford. Her writing has appeared publications including *The White Review*; in 2020 she published her debut novel, *The Octopus*. This year, Tess has been working on *Liminalia*, a collection of short stories, and the novel *Girls! Girls! Girls!*, which explores desire.

www.tesslittle.com
tessmslittle@gmail.com

Girls! Girls! Girls!
The opening of a novel

It was a name that bore all the grandiose glamour of a bygone era – in the weight of the article, the solid footing of the consonants – the kind of name that might lend itself to a walnut salad or bourbon cocktail – something classic, something generous, something to be consumed at leisure in a brass-fixtured, low-murmured, lightly jazzed hotel bar – something American. The Webster.

Theo arrived in a cab from the airport as, she'd read online, one should – so the city would swell from the horizon, one century of enterprise and steel rising in one moment. And yes, it had, magnificently. The scale was overwhelming. Like a wave. Like the difference between seeing a photograph of the ocean and watching the slam of it rush towards you. The driver was tapping to the radio. You'll have the time of your life, everyone had told Theo, and she repeated this to herself, in her mind, as the taxi entered a tunnel. The time of your life, the time of your life, as the tunnel meandered, lights swept overhead – then they were out, on the streets, between the buildings. Ants at the feet of great oaks. So the city really did exist, with its green-boarded scaffolding and stretching crosswalks – steam rising from the vents. Here. The driver screeched to a halt as another car swerved, and honked the horn with his right hand, not breaking the beat of his left. Time of your life, thought Theo.

The Webster stood on West 34th, upright and unattached, an imposing red-brick façade with details wrought in sandstone – the ornate neoclassical scrolls over which hung the Stars and Stripes; the entrance, framed by columns, beneath. A small flight of marble steps took the residents up and in. Were it not for these touches, the building would have appeared industrial. Some kind of pre-war factory, churning out well-made girls. No – young women, Theo corrected herself, as the driver opened the boot.

Two blocks down the street, the buildings stopped abruptly: the river, the island's end; a city only half-drawn. Theo paid the driver, careful to follow the tipping advice she'd found online, then entered the shadow of the Webster.

'— right in her mouth! She was – sorry, you go first.' The girl, who had almost walked into Theo, held the door while continuing her conversation with the friends waiting behind. All had varying complexions, but were uniformly dressed in oversized shades, miniskirts, crossbody bags: full set of collectable dolls. 'Anyway,' she said, 'you guys should've been there. I feel like shit but totally worth it.'

Theo shuffled her suitcase into the lobby. It was a wide, open room, carpeted in rosy beige, illuminated by Art Deco wall fixtures and oyster-pink table lamps. At the centre was an assortment of sofas and potted ferns. Clusters of girls were coming and going, or lounging and chatting, or sitting alone, tapping at BlackBerries and presumably awaiting friends. Theo scanned the perimeter for a reception desk and finding none, made her way to the door marked FRONT OFFICE.

She knocked once, tentatively. Then again, louder.

'Yes?' said a woman. There was a fork in her hand.

'Hi, hello, I'm new?' said Theo.

The woman tucked her head behind the door. 'Where's Sandra?' she shouted. 'Got another one.' After some inaudible reply, she turned back. 'You'll have to wait.'

Bizarre – each woman in the office seemed to hold only one responsibility that she alone held. When Theo had phoned for the application – which needed to be faxed, filled by hand, then faxed back – she was told to call on Wednesday, when Mel would be there. Only Mel, apparently, could fax applications. When Theo finally obtained the form, it was grey and over-inked; the text at the top directed applicants to PLEASE RETURN ON THURSDAYS.

Theo's trousers were sticking to the back of her knees. She'd known it would be hotter here – she'd read that online – and had worn loose layers for the flight, ready to shed on arrival. But she hadn't expected this pressure in the air, how it would conjure sweat to the surface of her skin. All the other girls had naked limbs. Some were clutching cups of iced coffee – chewing straws, slurping, or letting the cubes melt while engrossed in their little black phones.

In the run up to her departure, Theo had always confused her wording when describing the Webster. It was not, as she'd told friends, relatives, co-workers, a home for *working girls*, but for *working women*. A relic from an earlier age, when unmarried young ladies, flocking to the city for secretarial jobs, required respectable housing. Most such boarding houses had long disappeared, but the Webster held on – through the Great Depression, Second World War, sexual revolution, ball-busting nineties, bare-torsoed noughties – with its single-occupancy bedrooms, communal meals, and strict residential requirements. Only students, interns, and full-time employees. Only women; no men past the first floor. And just as the respectability of the Webster survived a century of onslaught, so too did its affordability – the 373 rooms were always nearing full capacity.

Indeed, it was the low rate that first attracted Theo: $270 per week including bills, breakfast, and dinner – far cheaper than anything else in the city, unless you wanted to pay an outrageous deposit, share a bedroom with strangers, spend hours commuting. And frankly, for Theo, alone the city, the Webster's quaint rules comforted. Her mother was certainly relieved. No unknown, perverted housemates, no late-night trains to the suburbs.

'And it'll be nice living with girls,' her mother had said. 'You'll make life-long friends.'

Would she? Theo watched the girls, chewing their coffee straws.

''Scuse me.' A red-faced woman wielding a jailer's keyring on her hip squeezed past, into the office. One moment later, she poked her head around the door. 'New guest?' she asked Theo, who nodded. 'Name?'

'Theodora Simpson.'

'Theodora,' repeated the woman. The office door closed.

She returned with a stapled booklet, which she handed across. 'I'm Sandra. Welcome to the Webster. This contains information on facilities, meal timings, whatnot. Want wi-fi?'

'Yes. Please.'

'Alrighty.' Sandra disappeared again, then returned with another sheet of paper. 'Your login. That'll be $15 per month, added to your bill. You can choose to pay bills monthly or bi-weekly, to help with budgeting.'

It took Theo a moment to realise Sandra was awaiting an answer.

'Bi-weekly then?'

'Alrighty. We expect payment by nine in the morning the Friday following bill distribution. Late fees are $25 per week and what else, what else... Yup, so these are the mailboxes.' Sandra gestured to a wall covered in iron pigeonholes, then held out a key. 'Don't lose it, $50 fine.'

Theo ran her thumb over its dull teeth as Sandra went on.

'What else... Oh, how about AC? It's $250 up front for the unit, then $10 per month.'

One week's rent? Theo told Sandra she'd see how the temperature was first, knowing she could never afford air-conditioning, no matter the heat, the humidity. Cold showers would be enough.

'Alrighty, let's find your room.'

Sandra led the way, leaving Theo to navigate her suitcase around the ferns.

'Let me... catch my breath,' said Sandra, as they joined the back of the lift queue. Then, after a few gasps: 'Lordy, lord. Up and down the stairs all day. Don't usually have a line like this but we're getting repairs. We'll take the working elevator with your luggage and whatnot, though, it'll just mean some waiting is all.' Sandra hooked her thumbs into her belt and blew up to cool her forehead.

The lift doors opened.

'You owe me twenty dollars, you bitch,' one of the girls exiting called to someone across the room.

Catching the stares, the girl flashed a grin at Sandra, at Theo.

It was a smile at odds with the rest of her baby-doll face, with its wide eyes, thin brows, and sweetheart lips. The teeth were gummy, gapped all the way. But it was that touch of ugliness that made the girl compelling. Beautiful, even. And perhaps the smile did suit the rest – milk teeth not grown to the adult skull.

The queue inched forward as the lift filled. Theo watched the girl cross the lobby – how the others raised their heads as she passed.

'...as I say, some guests do think they can bend the rules, but no men upstairs, no exceptions.' Sandra gestured down the corridor at two rows of booths. 'These meeting rooms provide some privacy, though.'

In the nearest, a group of girls huddled around a laptop. Tinny laughter blared from the speakers. '...kind of girl your boyfriend would cheat on you with.'

'Used to call 'em beau parlours back in the day,' said Sandra, grinning.

'But all part of the journey,' squeaked the laptop, 'towards my happily ever after.'

'What else, what else... Cafeteria's the floor below. Laundry on the fourth and seventh floors, and roof garden, well, on the roof. Room for two?' Sandra packed herself onto the lift before the occupants could answer.

They sweated in silence as the lift creaked up the building.

This would be a strange way of living. Theo hadn't truly understood this until now, with the bodies pressed against hers. It was impossible to imagine the shape daily life would take. Whether she would sit in a beau parlour watching reality shows, whether she'd explore the city with others. Or whether, instead, she would pass through the world unnoticed, disappear to her room each night.

At the eighth floor, Sandra nodded.

The beige corridor continued around a corner – each door numbered, uniform. The Webster was a dream, decided Theo. Not romantic, fantastical, but an institutional composite. This corridor was every corridor she'd ever walked. She knew the carpet: those stains, this cutaway square.

Sandra stopped. 'Room 837.'

It was small, hot, but not especially cramped. Large enough for a single bed (of course), basin, wardrobe, a desk – bigger than Theo's room in student halls last year. The furniture was covered in thick white paint, somewhere between glossy and matte. Or perhaps it had once been the former, dulled to the latter with generations of scratches.

Sandra gave Theo the keys. 'The door latches so don't go forgetting these when you visit the restroom. One guest locks herself out each week—make sure it's not you.'

'I will, thanks.'

'Alrighty,' said Sandra. The door swung shut behind her; it duly latched.

The only colour in the room came from the curtains – lurid and floral. Theo drew them back. There was no view. Just the foil-boarded window of the office block next door, undergoing construction. Theo could have poked it if she'd a broom to hand. She opened the window, hoping fresh air would hit her, but it was thicker outside. She slipped off her shoes and mounted the bed to reach the fan attached to the wall. Stood for a few moments, catching the breeze on her face. Probably inhaling various dusts. The dead skin cells of all the girls before her.

When she lay down, the fan, irritatingly, directed air just above her body. And was the bed especially small, or was it the way the furniture pressed in? I am contained, thought Theo. I'm in my coffin. Then she regretted her morbidity. Her mother had specially requested Theo didn't get herself murdered that summer.

She knew she should tell her mother she'd arrived, but the laptop was stashed somewhere, waiting to be unpacked with the rest. Well, she hadn't travelled across the world to fiddle with computers. Her time here was an escape from all that. From the deadlines that had chased her past year at university; from the work and exams and decisions that awaited her in the next; from her parents, from friends, from S.

There was home with all its history and there was the city with all its potential. There was real life and there were these two months away. Yes, Theo thought, she'd change into her summer clothes. She would find the great city, she would meet the great city, and then she would return for dinner.

Pamela Loke writes about loss and its impact on consciousness and memory. Her current project is a novel about bereavement as a rite of passage. She was a design and innovation consultant before coming to UEA and has a degree in History from Oxford and a PhD in Anthropology from Cambridge.

pamela_loke@yahoo.com

Recovery

The opening of a short story

Something hard was inside. Shan gasped and woke with a start as the thing was pulled out of her in one brisk movement.

A nurse was fiddling about under the bedclothes. Nicole, according to her badge. 'I've removed your catheter,' she said, 'you may want to go to the loo.'

Still foggy from sleep, Shan looked at the stranger standing next to her bed.

'Go. Have. A. Wee-wee,' Nicole enunciated, as if helping out a lip reader. Her pale hair waved stiffly with the stresses in her sentence.

'Could you help me off the bed—'

'We don't do that anymore.'

'Then could you help me lower the bed, please?'

'The remote's there for you to use.' Nicole began to rearrange the sick trays on the side console with resolute concentration. The remote was dangling off the far side of the bed, a good stretch away.

Would she wet herself if she didn't go?

Shan began to move.

Her reconstituted body felt precarious, its inner layers prickling with the stitches that held them together. At the recovery ward, before the morphine wore off, the staff had given her a quick lesson in using the bed cords to pull herself into a sitting position. She felt about with her hands but could not find the cords. The agitation of the blanket released a startling smell of blood and snagged a needle in the back of her hand. Pressing that hand firmly over her tummy, she used her other elbow to lever her body upwards. When she tried pushing her feet against the mattress, it felt like her innards were ripping. She used her arm instead and grabbed the bar by the side of her bed to heave forward.

Taking slow and shallow breaths, she closed her eyes for several seconds to recover from that reckless manoeuvre.

Getting off the bed was the next challenge.

Shuffle bum, arms for purchase, legs pivot. Lean, pause, repeat. Something tugged again inside her abdomen, and she stopped. Deploying parts of her body in the right sequence: that had just become a new thing to learn.

When she got far enough across the bed, she braced herself for the slide off the edge. Her heels landed on the cold floor with a jolt and she almost doubled over, her sweaty grip slipping on the side bar.

The room and floor pulsed with a dull magenta cast.

She slid her feet into the slippers and made sure her gown was not hitched up at the back. Nicole turned from the console and appeared to be pointing in the direction of the toilet with a biro. Was she saying something to her? Shan slid her feet into the slippers and made sure her gown was not hitched up at the back.

Walking was easier than sitting up.

The hospital ward looked enormous, with at least a dozen beds. All around her were exhausted and misshapen women, some working, others recovering. The room was buzzing at normal speed, but she moved in a thick, viscous bubble.

Occasionally grabbing the end of someone's bed for support, she carefully skirted the obstacles in her path. Most of the beds were accompanied by a plastic cot, with a baby swaddled in a pink or yellow waffle blanket. They looked like ice cream cones, each topped with a baby's fuzzy head.

One of the cots was empty. She stopped and looked at it. Then she saw the baby in the arms of a woman returning to the bed. The woman was wearing a nursing top, the kind with a flap over the chest that could be unbuttoned for breastfeeding.

At antenatal class, the midwife had recommended the kind with padded inserts.

'Yes? You lost or something?' the woman asked, her eyes bulging.

A nurse took Shan's elbow and ushered her away from the bed. The woman with the breastfeeding top turned her back to them, her baby held close to her chest and safely out of sight.

The single room which made up the patients' toilet was unoccupied. Shan locked the door carefully.

Setting herself down on the loo took some thinking.

It took another moment's hesitation to summon the sensation of emptying her bladder. She wiped blindly between her legs when she finished, and the slippery swipe of the paper made her reach for another wad of tissue. She did not want to look down: she could only see a spreading darkness whenever she tipped her head forwards. A coolness webbed the back of her skull.

Why am I in a maternity ward?

The confusion brought on a wave of nausea.

As she got gingerly to her feet, leaning on the metal bar affixed to the wall, she noticed that there was blood on the seat and floor. She grabbed a few paper towels and wiped the toilet, but she did not trust herself to bend far enough to deal with the stains on the floor. Her peripheral vision had gone black and sticky.

She flushed the toilet and walked to the hand basin. The spout of the wall-mounted tap was too short, so she had to press her hands against the basin to catch the edge of the flow. The cannula pushed against the ceramic and the tape on the back of her hand bloomed pink. A shock of cold water broke over the stain. The mirror in front of her glowed a rancid yellow from the overhead light. It reflected the rest of the cubicle behind her, the tiled wall sectioned by thick grout lines that did not quite match. Her face and body should be blocking those tiles and grout in the mirror, but she could not see herself.

She rubbed her eyes and stared again. The vision persisted: inside the glass was a dingy white room with no one in it, like an empty laboratory or morgue. The gurgle of water filling the toilet cistern reverberated. Maybe some kind of abattoir.

Am I lost?

Perhaps she would die or pass out, and it would be hours before anyone would find her. She did not want to be sucked into that room behind the mirror. She lurched towards the door and unlatched it.

The brightness receded. She was lying face down on the floor.

This lino must be covered in piss.

Footsteps drummed towards her head, amidst a flurry of voices. What have you done to yourself, you silly girl, someone said loudly. Out of the corner of her eye, she saw Nicole slowing her approach to let two other nurses overtake her.

Shan wanted to retch but her throat felt disconnected from her stomach.

The orderlies were at work moving her on to a stretcher, and then on to another rickety bed on wheels.

I said shake, rattle and roll.

At Stoney's on Sundays, they used to play catchy tunes about heartbreak that she could have tripped along to, if she weren't carrying a sixteen-inch pizza in each hand. The diner-style restaurant belonged to Frank and Jimmy Stoney, two nostalgic brothers who made ponytails out of what was left of their hair.

That was almost twenty years ago.

As the men wheeled her across the ward, they passed a sturdy woman pushing a cleaning trolley. 'Her bed's not done yet!' she called, 'Still looks like a murder scene over there.'

So I did wet myself?

She coughed up a mouthful of bile and could not remember much after that.

Shan woke up in a single ward. She was drenched in sweat and her scalp prickled. She tried pushing herself forwards and then found the remote control to bring her bed up. The vertical blinds were missing one leaf and piercing daylight cut into the room.

Something in her sleep had filled her with an urgent purpose. She was about to inch towards the edge of her bed when the door opened.

Two people in white coats came towards her. The older man put a freckled hand over hers and the pressure hurt.

'You've been pretty drugged up, so don't get up until there's someone to help you. Just press the call button here.'

'Where's my baby?'

The white coats looked at each other.

She felt the rigid weight of her breasts. 'I have to feed my baby, right?'

They looked at each other again.

'We're so very sorry, Shan. You have gone through so much. These are early days, naturally, and it'll take a while to—'

'I had a C-section... I have a baby girl. My husband was with me.'

'I'm afraid you've lost your baby,' said the other doctor, a woman in her thirties. 'Can you not remember what happened?' Her pencilled brows were arching upwards in an expression of rehearsed pain.

Later, Shan would remember the obliterating glare of the operating theatre. But she tried to keep her eyes on Colin. She smiled to reassure him. He was a watery shadow outside the activity centred on her, like the reflection of a beacon almost coming into view. They kitted her up quickly, administering more tapes and needles to her body and switching connectors on tubes.

She must have blanked out: she was slow to notice that the doctors had moved to another part of the room. The midwife was assigning a place for Colin to sit, somewhere near the door. Sometimes he was closer, perhaps next to her bed, but she could not read his expression.

'Shan.'

A man in scrubs removed his mask. He seemed to have replaced Colin... maybe some time had passed? It was a day of unconnected time-lapses, that passed in and out of light. He held her hand like a priest.

'I have to say it's not looking good.'

She knew this was important. She blinked hard.

Afterwards, they put her baby in her arms.

They cleaned up most of the blood and vernix so that she could make out her baby's features: the perfectly formed nose, the mouth set almost in a pout. The long lines of the baby's shut eyes, eyes that look like closed buds. The pristine mystery of pre-existence, Thumbelina before the kiss.

Shan's baby was ruddy, warm, and pretty. Shan ran the heel of her palm along the tips of her baby's toes: they followed one after another in a graduating sequence, like hammers in a piano. Those baby fingers curled slightly on the swell of Shan's breast, with thin lines of white above pink nail beds.

Colin held the baby for a while, and then the baby was returned to Shan.

They had decided to name the baby Lucy, after a flamboyant great-grandmother who passed away the year before.

Shan was hospitalised for five days. She bloated and shrank and bloated again, her belly wept constantly, and her memory of what her body had been before became unreliable.

The incontinence sheet that they had placed under her kept doubling over, but she could not be bothered to point it out. Whenever she asked for some water, the nurse would hand over a ribbed plastic cup that barely held its shape, so most of the contents were spilt by the time it reached her lips. The water always felt ice cold.

Colin had not come to the hospital at all, not since the day in the operating theatre. With each passing hour, his silence pressed a little harder on her, and she diminished a little further. The only way to cope was to become less. When a new nurse on the ward asked when her husband would be visiting, she gawped for a few seconds and shut her eyes, pretending to sleep. She spent a lot of her time in hospital pretending to be asleep.

Word must have gone around the nurses' station because no one mentioned Colin again. Did she have someone to pick her up on her day of discharge, was all they asked her. Yes, she said, my sister Helen is coming.

It could have happened to anyone, the doctors, counsellors, and do-gooders kept telling her.

It's nobody's fault, they said.

Aidan was born in Johannesburg and moved with his family to England as a child. He lives in Cambridge and works as a scientific writer at a genomics institute. When not writing about science he mainly writes contemporary realist fiction.

aidanmaartens@gmail.com

An Inheritance
The opening of a long story

On a grey Monday in late November six months after my mother died, I travelled from Cambridge up to Salthouse to sort through her things and arrange to sell the cottage. I hadn't been up since the funeral, and when I told my husband Daniel, I planned to go he sounded relieved – the place sitting empty had clearly offended something in him. He offered to go with me to help but I told him I'd be alright on my own and back by the weekend anyway. And so, after he left for work that morning, I packed my things and walked for forty minutes through the drizzle to the station to catch a train to King's Lynn.

Announcements echoed around the ticket hall, which smelled of the lilies of the flower stall at the entrance and the damp clothes of the travellers. After my train pulled into the platform and the passengers from London got out, I found a window seat in a carriage empty but for an older couple two rows ahead who were talking to each other softly in a language that might have been Greek. When the train lurched and glided out with a metallic hum, they fell silent. As the train sped up, the world went by in snapshots: piles of aggregates and stacks of sleepers, flag poles and blue netted trampolines, a field cross-hatched with watery ditches, a field dotted with pig huts.

An anoraked couple walking a golden Labrador along an elevated canal.

A row of trees in the distance like the profile of a woman sleeping on her side.

Asleep on her side in the hospital facing the window mostly filled by a red brick chimney.

'Y—aaany tickets please?'

The young inspector took my ticket and wrote a looped X in the corner with a Network Rail ballpoint pen. She then whistled her way down the carriage to the older couple.

'Y—aaany tickets please?'

I checked my bag for the long thick front door key to the cottage, and then sent a blurry picture of the railway line to Daniel with *on my way, see you at the weekend x* written over the top of it. I read and re-read the same paragraph from the novel I'd brought with me a few times until in my gut I felt the train losing momentum. Ely cathedral stood there above the flatness.

'Majestic, isn't it?'

That was Daniel, on that same train the previous summer, when all he wanted to do on our weekends was visit historic buildings. He'd march us around the perimeters of churches, ruined abbeys, and restored water mills, read out their histories and statistics from the visitor guidebooks or Wikipedia. Around the Ely cathedral grounds that summer day his big thing was eels, having picked up a pamphlet.

'Delph, look, it was all built on eel money!' he said, eyes sparkling. 'Says here they paid for the stone with eight thousand eels a year. Can you imagine?'

'That's ah-lot of eels,' I said.

A gargoyle looked down on us, picking its nose.

'Ely, the isle of eels! Who knew that's why it's called that!' he said.

'Very imaginative,' I said.

Elderly couples around us were also looking up at the building, shielding their eyes from the sun. I spotted a different gargoyle that was more serpentine, even eel-like.

'These eels,' Daniel continued, 'European eels, Anguilla anguilla, they hatch in the Sargasso Sea four thousand miles away across the Atlantic, imagine, swim all the way here, up the Wash and then the Ouse, spend a few years fattening up, then decide one day to swim all the way back to the Sargasso Sea to breed, and once they breed they die.'

'I think I saw that on Attenborough once,' I said. 'They go through a stage of being almost entirely transparent.'

'Four thousand miles!' he said.

While I knew then that, like all the phases I had witnessed over the decade or so that I had been with him, this one would soon enough end – and by the autumn end it did – I was still willing to be taken along by it, to humour his state of excited animation. Far better than the listless lulls that often followed, when everyday life seemed to carry a great deficit; he'd been in one such lull around the time I went to the cottage, which I suppose had influenced the decision to go up alone.

Later, on that Ely trip, inside the cathedral's cool we span slowly in circles looking up at the inside of the octagon tower, the thick beams of sunlight taking the primary colours of the stained glass windows, and then got tea and falafel in the market before going home.

As we pulled out of Ely and crossed the river I kept the cathedral in sight, mentally tracing the outlines of its many towers and spires from the train window.

'Mah-jes-tic.'

At King's Lynn I went to Morrisons, which had stained glass of its own in the arched windows below the big yellow lettering. White haired couples milled around the aisles and Natalie Imbruglia sang loudly from the speakers. It was almost exciting, shopping for myself. I filled my basket with things Daniel didn't like to eat.

The Coastliner bus took me to Wells, where I changed for the Coasthopper. The seats were all taken by old couples with white plastic seafood bags at their feet, and I swayed in the aisle as we drove along the coast road, catching flashes of the landscape through the dirty wet windows and between the high hedgerows: pine groves, saltmarshes and reedbeds, pastel cottages and flint walls and the windmill at Cley, the sea only occasionally visible in the distance from the left, grey or milk green. And memories of previous journeys: the first time with Daniel when he'd first met Mum, the various times we or I had gone to housesit and feed Monty when she was away, her sixtieth birthday weekend and the boat trip to see the seals at Blakeney, their heads bobbing in the water, Mum leaning over the side of the boat to record them. And the last time, when I had come up alone after she'd insisted, and I'd wanted to talk to her about Daniel and his proposal, but we'd never got to that.

I was the only one to get out at Salthouse. The strangely comforting smell was not of crisp sea air but brackish mud and decaying vegetation. Geese with black heads and white throats pecked the grass of the marshy field across the coast road. Beyond them, the grey pebble-covered dunes past them sat underneath the mist. I walked past the village shop, the shuttered pink crab shack, the glass-fronted house that in the summer sold samphire, down the coast road and then up the narrow, cobbled lane leading to the church, where Mum's cottage was halfway up the hill. Half-closed curtains, shining wet flint walls. The front garden had gone a little wild, with waist-high half dead plants flopping onto the stone pathway.

Inside smelled stale and woody. It was only mid-afternoon but gloomy inside, so I walked around from room to room and turned all the lights on and then turned the central heating on, filling the cottage with the smell of hot dusty metal and the melodic shuddering of the pipes. It was as tidy as she always kept it, everything in its place as if she had just popped out briefly. But then I saw the dead or half-dead houseplants in the corners and on the windowsills of every room. Their collapsed and curling leaves, the cracked soil: I felt stupid for not coming up earlier, guilty for letting them suffer, cried there in the hall. I put them together on the patio in the rain in the hope of reviving them.

Once I'd unpacked my things and the shopping, I made a cup of tea and went into her bedroom. I'd rarely gone in there. It was as spartan and neat as the rest of the house. Whitewashed walls, a woven rug on the wooden floor by the bed. Above the mantelpiece, a pale blue and yellow watercolour of a coastline, and on it sat a framed a photo of me and Daniel. We were smiling in the sun by a gorge in Greece a few years ago. We looked tanned and happy in front of the white cliffs and deep green shadows. We looked a completely different couple.

Turning to leave my foot glanced off something underneath the bed. It was a large flat clear plastic case with handles at both ends and red wheels on the bottom. I pulled it out, lifted it on to the bed and took the lid off. It was filled with cassette tapes, hundreds. Her recordings. She'd had an on-and-off career as a sound technician, but wherever she went she also carried a mic and a tape recorder. Each cassette was labelled with a date and a short description. The dates went back to the eighties, and right up until the springtime of that year.

I took the most recent tape and then another random one to the living room and poured myself a whiskey from the drinks cabinet. The stereo speakers turned on with a hum that thickened the air. I felt the resistance of the play button of the cassette deck. And after a brief, static-filled silence, the room was filled with birdsong. A whistling blackbird, that I could identify, but other calls too, sharper and more insistent, and then, more distantly, birds that sounded like the coast, oystercatchers maybe, curlews. I stood listening for ten minutes until a loud crackle – her hand, perhaps, brushing the foam covering of the microphone – and it cut out. *11.04.22, Titchwell Marshes.*

The other tape, *08.11.04, The Eilidh.* I would have been doing my A Levels, after Dad moved out. It also started with bird noises but not songs, just the insane cries of seagulls above the sea. Wistful enough, Desert Islands Discs, but then mic starts to move: she must be walking, the regular ringing of her boots on the metal of the deck. The pendulum throb of the boat's engine, above it hissing steam, metal grinding on metal, screeching like a railway, whipping rope, a chain being released, and also flapping sounds and rushing water – the sea draining off the deck, the fish jumping the net, maybe. More footsteps, and she must now be below deck, the engine throbs but everything sounds more enclosed and muffled. Human hands doing work, what could be a puncturing and tearing of fish flesh, and a sound like cutlery on crockery, and the sliding of something along the floor, and doors being opened and shut.

I remember her coming back from that trip. Opening the front door, it looked like she had glitter around her eyes and up her forehead. It took a while to realise it was fish scales. She had a faraway look in her eyes. She said she still had sea legs as she went down to her studio in the basement.

I stopped the tape, poured another whiskey.

A. Macellari started his writing career in arts journalism. He is working on a novel, a kind of bildungsroman about art and the non-nuclear family that asks what, if anything, adult step-siblings have to say to each other. He is also writing a collection of short stories. He holds the 2021/22 Bourne Scholarship.

augustinmacellari@gmail.com

Bad Art Son
The opening of a novel

Tony Adie was fucking Manny's mother, but that was OK. He was also putting up with her, which was more than previous boyfriends had done. The last of these, a man called George, had taken active pride in his carelessness, leaving Manny to mop up the emotional residue of his activities; a gruesome job.

Things had come to a head with George one November night, and neither Manny nor his mother had seen him since. Manny's mum had been upset, but by the following February she'd met Tony, who seemed fine, and now, several years later, they continued to bring each other the kind of happiness that two people who meet in middle age, with families, friends, and habits of their own, have to offer. Still, she complained about Tony to Manny and Manny guessed Tony probably complained about her to his own children. A boy and a girl – a man and a woman, really – with whom Manny was friendly but not friends.

Whatever. A definite improvement on George, thought Manny, in the golden light of this hot summer Sunday. They were sitting in Tony's garden with the large, glass sliding doors at the back of his mid-century modernist house open wide so that the garden and the house seemed to spill into each other. Manny and Tony and Manny's mum, and Tony's son, Martin, and Martin's girlfriend, Lucy, and Tony's daughter, Sophie. In the trees above them pigeons cooed. A blackbird sang. Earlier, Manny's mum had taken a hose to next door's black cat as it flirted with the top of the fence.

The garden grew lush and thick and overlong in the corners that Tony had dedicated to his re-wilding experiments: towering rattles of foxgloves and sprays of cow parsley strong in the shade of the apple tree. He was a keen gardener, but Manny had come to understand that the house itself was entirely incidental to Tony and his family. It didn't reflect any particular enthusiasm for twentieth-century architecture; no utopian belief in the emergence of perfect form through function. Just the conditions of the market at the time that he and his then-wife had been looking to buy.

It stood on a nicer street than the one George had paid his brutish visit to those years before. Manny had been sitting on the sofa, he remembered, probing at the glands on his neck in anticipation of the remorseless winter to come. He'd opened the door to a frantic knocking and found George, swaying on the doorstep, red wine stains on his teeth and pashmina draped about his badly shaven neck. When George slurred those very words, 'I'm here to fuck your mother,' in his terrible, privileged drawl, Manny's glands had throbbed. Next thing he knew he was being restrained by the neighbour and his knuckles were open and bloody.

Manny tried not to think about it. They were all here with Tony, this Sunday, for lunch. It was Lucy's birthday, and Manny's mum had made her a cake. They were an uncomfortable little tribe, and Manny could imagine their counterparts across the country.

Thousands of them. Thousands and thousands of well fed, white Dads leaning back in their seats after another underwhelming, Middle Eastern-inspired Sunday lunch, when the discussion about coconut oil as a medium for roasting potatoes had run its course and everyone had been very impressed by the pomegranate seeds and feta sprinkled across the lamb, to say, teasingly, 'But it's confusing, isn't it? It's plural – it sounds like you're talking about a group.' Or 'Yes, but why do they have to come here? Isn't France safe enough?'

Tony hadn't issued any of these horrid little provocations today, but Martin was doing a nice job of making up for it. Martin and Manny got on because Manny had put in the work. The first Christmas they'd spent together Martin had leant in close to Manny and whispered a racist joke. A quick on the spot cost-benefit analysis led Manny to the conclusion that the value of this bonding opportunity outweighed the opportunity cost of righteous indignation – and he'd been correct. The two shared an intimacy Manny would never have with Sophie. He still felt the occasional shiver of disgust around Martin, but Martin seemed, genuinely, to like him.

Martin worked in PR for a multinational pharmaceutical company and had a dimple in his chin. His head was big. Bigger now for having won this job he thought was very important but also literally: a big head, like the villain from some old painting. Holofernes. Manny sometimes wondered how much it weighed. Now, as he banged on over the greasy remains of a harissa'd lamb shoulder, Manny wondered if the dimple made it hard to shave.

Martin was talking about a vaccine delivery platform his employer was developing. 'Revolutionary,' he was saying, 'really revolutionary, and well-timed, too. The market is only going to grow. Urbanisation, deforestation, climate change.' He sounded pleased.

'How does it work?' Tony asked from the head of the table. Manny's mum began clearing plates and Manny took her seat as the sun found a gap in the awning of the trees, its light playing off a chip of ice in the bottom of his water glass.

'They're using scabies, mites,' Martin said. 'Sterilising them, freezing them, suspending them in emulsion. A bit like sea monkeys. You apply the emulsion as a cream and they wake up and burrow in. Then they die, get broken down by the body and deliver the vaccine directly into the bloodstream.'

'That's remarkable,' Tony said.

'It's disgusting,' Sophie said.

Lucy looked bored. Her presents were thoughtfully arranged on a little side table. Manny had wrapped her a book he got free at work, a hardback popular-sociology book about the changing landscape of the workplace. Martin's present leant there, ostentatiously. A badly wrapped framed picture.

'In theory the vaccine would remain stable at elevated temperatures,' Martin said, 'and it wouldn't need to be administered intravenously.'

'That does sound kind of amazing,' Manny said. He'd struggled to be enthusiastic when Martin had taken the job because of the pharmaceutical company's reputation as an agent of great evil.

'So, it's like a cream with sea monkeys in it,' said Sophie.

Manny's mum had finished with the plates and sat down in Manny's empty seat. She squinted at the glistening ice cube and put her sunglasses on.

'That you what,' Sophie continued, 'rub on, and suddenly you're immune to polio? Sounds like bullshit.'

Manny's mum leant over the table and took her wine glass from in front of Manny. They were drinking a Beaujolais that had been too cold when Tony opened it and was now too warm. She refilled her glass. 'What's the cream made of?' she asked.

Martin looked towards her. 'The emulsion is mostly water. They were looking at using porcine gelatine as a stabiliser – it's quite common in vaccines, but it limits deployment capabilities.' He rolled his eyes.

Manny rolled his, too. Since starting at the job Martin had slipped into an irritatingly corporate register that he couldn't quite maintain. Manny always thought you could tell a lot about a person from the kind of words they use. About their worldview. Manny used words like 'paradigm' and 'metabolise,' as in, 'the American media class had yet to metabolise the paradigm shift that was underway.' He didn't like to think about how it made him sound, but he couldn't help himself – and when he tried to moderate it, he found he had nothing to say.

Tony's language expressed a kind of patrician complacency. Martin's expressed misplaced self-importance. At times he'd lose his way and pluck a word or formulation from another context entirely, like big budget military thrillers.

'There's no question that demand is going to be centred in emerging markets.' Martin emphasised 'emerging' unpleasantly. 'Our research is pointing to Indonesia as a ground zero for the next outbreak. Deforestation is out of control. Bushmeat, the destruction of habitat. And it's Muslim, obviously. So, they're experimenting with palm oil.'

Manny did a double take. Lucy was gazing down the garden. Shouts came from two fences over. Her face was blank.

'So, anyway. Dad says you've got a boyfriend,' Martin grinned at Sophie. 'Someone from work? PC Plod. When are we going to meet him?'

Sophie was a police officer. She wasn't beautiful, but she was kind of handsome. Her avant-garde fringe emphasised a slightly upturned nose, large grey eyes, and a wide, thin-lipped mouth, which she twisted into a sarcastic smile. At one time, Manny had fantasised about an affair, but a single flirty comment had been enough for her to withdraw into a frosty formality that had yet to fully thaw.

She gave Martin the finger.

Tony smiled.

'Lucy,' Manny said. 'Thirty. How does it feel?'

Martin looked at Lucy with a mild interest that suggested he hadn't thought about it.

'Yeah,' she said. 'Yeah. Just kind of, natural? Normal? Just feels the same, really.'

'Great.' Manny said. 'Well, happy birthday.' He handed her his gift and a card, his least favourite from a selection he'd bought at an exhibition of twentieth-century English painting.

'Right, yeah,' Martin stood and picked up the badly wrapped picture. 'Happy birthday, babe.' He thrust it at her, then leant down and kissed her on the mouth, brusquely.

Manny's mum stood and walked into the kitchen for a jug of water. She came back and lingered by the pond behind Lucy, who said 'thanks, Marty.' She was watching the back of Lucy's head with an ambient distaste that was obviously hostile, but Manny knew she thought no one else would notice. They made eye contact. Manny raised his eyebrows, and she rearranged her expression. From where she was standing she could see the picture before anyone else, and as it emerged into view her face slipped again.

'It's an original,' Martin said.

'Oh, Marty. I love it.' Lucy sounded like she really did.

'Turn it around then, let's see.' Sophie's voice, empty of enthusiasm.

Lucy turned the picture around. It was an old and slightly faded *Keep Calm and Carry On* poster, in a silver metallic frame.

Martin's chest was puffed up. 'It's an original,' he said again.

'An original?' Manny asked. 'An actual original, from World War Two?'

'Oh, babe,' said Lucy, 'I love it.'

Martin smiled at Manny and nodded importantly. Manny was surprised. He'd imagined that most people he knew took the design's problematic invocation of a toxic strain of nostalgia as given. But more than that, an actual, original, *Keep Calm and Carry On* poster, from the actual Second World War, nearly a hundred years ago, would surely be beyond the budget afforded Martin with his salary as a junior member of the PR team at the UK branch of a multinational pharmaceutical company.

'Fucking hell,' said Sophie, 'that must have set you back a bit.' Manny slipped his phone from his pocket and googled it. One had recently sold at auction for thirteen-thousand pounds. Martin's smile widened.

'Oh,' said Manny's mum. 'How – lovely. Very thoughtful, Martin.'

Tony frowned at Sophie. 'Yes,' he said, 'it's splendid. Really nice, Martin. Where did you get it, eBay? Your grandmother would love it.'

'How is Gran?' Sophie asked, and Tony launched into a long spiel that Manny had already heard. Her dementia was getting bad. Vivid and disruptive fantasies haunted her waking hours, and she was struggling to distinguish dreams from reality. This was compounded by her isolation and a recent UTI, which had tipped her paranoia into overdrive.

Lucy got up and carefully leant the poster back against the table. Overhead in the trees, the blackbird's song was answered by another. Manny knelt down in front of it for a closer look. At the bottom a tiny line of white type: 'Facsimile of original WWII poster. Reproduced 2005, Golden Yesterday's, Kent.'

Josephine Maughan lives in Norwich with her partner and son. She is currently working on a historical novel, told from the perspectives of four women, set in the remote western highlands of Scotland in 1830 against the backdrop of the highland clearances.

josephinehenniker@gmail.com

Untitled Novel in Progress
Extract from the opening of the novel.

CHAPTER ONE

The dogs woke Morag MacArachle. She lay next to her husband and listened for the baby, straining to locate her breathing amongst the noise of the dogs sniffing and scratching at the door, the cow shifting, her husband's irregular sleeping whistle. Baby Eilean they called her, for the name still felt too big on its own.

Long moments passed. She braced for loss. But then, there it was: a sudden sticky gasp, a rattling outbreath. Her heart unclenched.

Moonlight slanted through the chink in the window covering. Her eyes grew accustomed to the gloom. She counted three humps on the pallet by the opposite wall. The outline of the milking cow in the far corner, standing over her new calf. Two dogs by the door. Five stools in a half-circle around the fireplace, a curl of smoke rising from the embers. Baby Eilean, a bundle in the cot at the foot of their bed.

Nothing was amiss.

She listened into the night.

The cow stamped. The dogs continued to chatter. Her husband whistled. The baby breathed. An ache in her ankle, an old injury poorly healed, made itself known. That dancing could have earned her such a punishment.

Outside, the two ponies shifted restlessly. One of the dogs gave a low whine. Baby Eilean gasped again, turning under her blankets.

Something was out there.

Morag nudged her husband in the ribs. His whistle stopped midway, restarting moments later. She nudged him again, a little firmer. He mumbled and edged away. Cold air filled the gap between them and she quickly plugged it with the blanket. The dogs clawed at the door, whines becoming growls. The cow lowed.

She kicked him.

'Mo duine,' she said. My husband.

He mumbled again. His hand came around to push her away. She wanted sleep too. But the baby would not settle if she was woken, her cough would erupt. The boys would be disturbed. The night would be lost.

She kicked him hard.

'Ewen MacArachle,' she said, louder. 'Get yourself out of bed. Something disturbs the animals.'

At last, he groaned. A final shove in the ribs and he was sitting, groping for his over-shirt.

The dogs pleaded with him to be let out.

'Wheesht!' he snapped, and they fell silent.

One of the lumps in the bed shifted. A head appeared above the blanket, sleep-fogged face already frowned and anxious. William, the youngest boy, always the first to be disturbed. His hand reached up to scratch under his cap.

'Màthair. What is there?'

'Get back to sleep,' she said, 'it is nothing to worry yourself about.'

William lay back as he was told, but the scratching continued, raking across his skull, creaking the bed.

'And stop with that itching or you'll wake your brothers.'

Ewen stood and went to the door, letting the dogs rush out and the cold in, crooning to the two ponies before he was even over the threshold. They can pull three times their own weight, he was fond of telling any visitor who admired them. They'll pull logs all day long, he would always add. He trimmed their feet and he brushed their coats, kinder to them than he was to his own children.

'Hè!' he shouted outside the window. 'Hè!'

The baby fidgeted, thrashing the blankets, her breathing thick and laboured. She let out a scraping cry.

'Curse him,' Morag muttered, reaching for her shawl, leaning across the bed to the cot, pulling aside her undershirt and lifting the baby from its nest of blankets to latch on to her breast.

Baby Eilean snuffled and spilt as much as she swallowed. Milk dribbled into the folds of Morag's stomach. She pushed the swaddle back from the baby's face and wet the corner of her shawl in the dripping milk, dabbing at the crust gumming the baby's eyelids. Baby Eilean's tiny hand reached up and clasped onto her finger as though clasping to life. Morag feared they had lost her when the fever had arrived with the new year. The same sickness as had taken their fourth boy the winter before, which began as shivering and worked up into high heat, all the while rooting deeper inside, settling in his lungs, wracking his body until he succumbed. But

Baby Eilean had not succumbed. She suckled on, warm against Morag's skin, a living heat not a burning fever. Morag knew she shouldn't feel so much for this one, knew it would do her no good so early on, yet she could not stop herself hoping.

At last, a girl.

Morag's eyelids drooped.

This baby would not be taken.

Morag dozed.

'Wife!'

Morag forgot for a minute that her husband was outside. Baby Eilean slept in her arms, nipple half-in, half-out of her open mouth.

'Wife! Come out at once!'

She did not often hear him so urgent. She shifted across to the right of the bed, wrapping the heavy shawl around her body and tucking Baby Eilean tight within. It would more likely disturb her to set her back in the cot.

Outside the cottage, the tips of the pines around the edge of the clearing were like the teeth of a saw against the fading night. A late star shot across the sky, seeming to fall into the trees. She frowned and crossed herself. There had been too many in recent days, they would bring someone no good.

The dogs whimpered in the darkness.

'Husband?'

'Here.'

She followed his voice, towards the point where the star had fallen into the trees, the ground cold, wet and spongy, needles sharp, under her bare feet. She found him bent over the two dogs, holding them by the scruff of their necks as they strained towards something wrapped in a dark covering, curled tight around the trunk of a pine. His jaw was slack, eyes staring.

'What trouble have you found?'

'See for yourself.'

She walked around the tree trunk, holding Baby Eilean secure against her stomach. The first grey light filtered through the branches. She saw that the dark covering was a plaid blanket. She leant closer, gasping at a thicket of hair, a flash of skin.

'It's a child,' he said.

'I can see that.'

'A girl, I think.'

He wiped his forehead on his sleeve and one of the dogs slipped free of his grasp, pouncing on the blanket and the shape within.

A scream like a rabbit caught in a snare.

'Get off now!' He reached quickly to pull the dog away.

But the dog had the blanket in its mouth, tugging and jerking it backwards, growling and shaking its head from side to side.

He hauled at the dog's neck. The creature – the child – struggled and writhed to cling on to the blanket and keep a hold on the tree.

He yanked again, hard, and pulled the dog away with the blanket still between its teeth.

Naked, the girl's ghostly form wrapped itself tight again around the tree. Morag saw her filthy feet and legs, the sunken cheeks of her haunches, the raised knobbles of her spine, and a mark like a bloodstain spreading down her back.

'The cross of Christ be upon us!'

Her left arm shielding her baby, Morag stepped to the dog and cuffed it hard across the mouth. The dog yelped and dropped the blanket, and she threw it quickly over the girl.

'Get her away from here!'

Morag turned, looking back towards the cottage. She felt Baby Eilean stir against her and panic rose in her throat. She must get her inside.

'Be calm,' he called after her. 'Let us think what to do.'

'Get her away from here!'

'The girl's half dead. She's all bones.'

'Hitch the cart to the red pony and take her to the minister. He will know what to do. God knows, we have worries enough.'

CHAPTER TWO

Flora wet the meal into a paste, turning it into a dough in the bowl. Mr Smith was talking loud enough in the parlour to hear him through the wall. If he spoke like that in the kirk, they'd soon take notice. She sprinkled meal on the table and tipped the dough out. The sound of his voice rose, though she couldn't make out the words. The heel of her palms struck the dough, one and then the other, left then right. He would have to be leaving soon.

The girl was in the sty. Mr Smith said it was the only safe place for her until they could come up with something better, that she was too wild a creature to have inside the Manse. Although she'd been limp as a rag in Ewen MacArachle's arms when he'd unloaded her from his cart, she'd come alive as he tried to carry her over the threshold, wriggling like an eel and planting her feet in the ground. She'd even bitten Young Fair John on the arm for his efforts.

'Mar sin leat an-dràsta!, Flora,' Mr Smith called.

'Yes, goodbye for now,' she called back, smiling at his accent.

The door slammed and the Manse was quiet. Young Fair John was nowhere to be heard. He'd better be cleaning the hearths.

She tried not to look at the door that led from the kitchen to the backyard. The bannocks had to be finished. Young Fair John must be found and the hearths re-laid. She sprinkled a dusting more meal on the table. Thump and push, thump and push. Don't bother about what's out there, it's none of your business.

But perhaps she should check the tether was secured and there was water enough in the bucket. The girl was so thin, another oatcake would not go amiss. She set the dough to one side, covered it with cloth. There was no harm taking a moment to see her.

The sty was in the corner of the yard, in front of a wooded hillside where catkins like lambs' tails dangled from birches with black and silvered trunks. Chickens pecked across the open ground, harassed by the cock and ignoring his attentions. A raven hopped away with straw collected in its beak.

She squatted close enough to see through the gaps in the wattle. The girl did not stir, leaning against the far side of the fence, long matted hair hiding the rope that tethered her. She had on Flora's other dress and the neckline gaped, skin stretched tight over her collarbone. Her hand – hidden in a sleeve – rested on top of the filthy plaid blanket that she had refused to part with. It had not been worth a bite to get it away. Her eyes were closed, face raised up to the sun which had appeared between scudding clouds.

'Who are you?' Flora whispered.

Sounds heightened and separated: the throaty clucking of the chickens; the trill of a blackbird calling for a mate; the distant voices of the village on their way to the kirk. Flora waited.

The girl had heard her, Flora was sure. Indeed, Flora was certain the girl had known she was there the moment she stepped out of the back door.

'Are you Donal's daughter that we all believed was dead?'

A hand crept out of a cuff, resting on the blanket, clenched as though there was something inside it.

'Morag MacArachle says you are a fallen star.'

A cloud passed in front of the sun. The girl's eyes flicked open, green like hanging moss, and Flora almost fell backwards. The girl flinched but did not break her gaze. Her clenched hand turned over. Something was hidden inside. Flora leant closer.

All at once, from inside the Manse, came the alarming noise of breaking glass, the hoarse cry of Young Fair John and the fading laughter of children.

Flora looked to the house and back to the girl. Her hand had disappeared into her sleeve and her eyes were shut. Flora hurried inside to see what damage had been done.

Martin McGuigan is an Irish writer from County Armagh, currently based in Norwich. He studied English Literature at the University of Cambridge and has since worked as a professional copywriter and video producer in London. His writing has appeared in *The Mays XIX*, *Cabinet of the Heed*, and *SHE.* magazine.

martin.mcguigan5@gmail.com

Bird Cage
An excerpt from a novel

Blonde desks arranged in square U. Magnolia walls make spotlights stinging. A room stuck on repeat.

Trainer late. People getting pally inside.

Or else, screen glare, absorbed.

Fucking DWP.

Trainer arrives with no apologies for tardiness. She is:

Some type of Irish,

Sun-freckled from elsewhere and dry hair wires

Trying to escape.

She sets papers down.

Right, everyone. If you could take your seats and write your names on the pieces of card on the desk, we'll get started.

Take the card and marker. How to write it? Too small to read? Or no she? Lagh, alone. She—la—she. Another name entirely, or a squiggle symbol no mouth can shape? Writes: sheLAGH. Slowly with the felt tip, first scratches down small, then big swoops. Turns that name to face the room.

The trainer comes around handing out printed sheets.

Ye can take that off. It's not that cold in here.

GOOD INTERVIEW PRACTICE
- Dress smart
- Be honest
- Ask questions
- Think of what qualities make you suitable for the job
- Come prepared
- BE YOURSELF!

Turn the paper over to reveal its blank underside. The trainer stands at the front of the room.

Now who thinks they want to tackle the first point? Dress smart?

No hands volunteering.

Errr, Keith! How about you? What would you wear to an interview?

I'd dress smart.

That's great. What would you wear?

Suit 'n' tie.

And would you pair them with flip-flops or your dirty football boots?

Smart shoes.

That's right.

She goes up to an easel with big paper sheets pinned on and writes:

MEN – a suit, dress shoes.

What about women? Sheee-la? What about you? What kind of clothes would you wear to an interview?

[Auto-reply] I'd wear smart trousers and a blouse, with black or brown shoes.

And what else?

A coat.

Anything else?

[...]

What about, hat and sunglasses, for example. Do you keep those on or take them off?

> Nosepickers entertained.
>
> Trainer expectant, waiting,
>
> Hand on hip, silent stewing.

Well. It's not very good interview practise to keep your hat, and particularly your sunglasses, on, indoors. Ooh-kay?

> Then turns to class with practised alacrity:

Think of an interview a bit like a first date. You want to present the best possible version of yourself.

> Dust motes rave through
>
> Sunbeams slathered across the socket.
>
> For an hour or two
>
> Dan, unsummoned, creeps
>
> Around her imagination,
>
> His precision movements
>
> (manual) and his
>
> Trunk and legs (loose)
>
> Slot pins into place
>
> Opening something afresh.

All right. Let's have a quick comfort break and be back in here for ten fifteen.

Scraping chairs, standing, she shouts over:

It's sometimes a good idea to talk over what we've learned in the session with your fellow jobseekers.

People scurry towards toilets. Outside some find pairs or threes but would rather have a moment to fart in peace. Coffee and tea in metal jugs. Knows the taste without raising to her lips. Mingling useless. Stands by table with sugar granules and milk splodges. To be an ant missioning amongst it. To be a fifty stone blob, never leaving the bed.

How was that for you eh? Don't think it was very polite the way she picked on you. Coulda wrapped that up bit quicker but hey-ho.

Keith. Paint stains on his jeans and battered loafers. More keys than he has toes.

Hope she's got some good tips for interviews after. Not had an interview for twenty years nearly. Not needed to. S'not really my strong suit. I just ramble and ramble till somebody tells me to get to work hig-hig-hig...

Honesty seeps from his shampoo-smelling hair. Turn away for the nearest window, where Corvids hop unappreciated. Keith latches on to someone else:

How was that for you eh?

Ten fourteen now. The trainer appears but no one wants to be herded back inside.

Sheee-la? Can I talk to you a wee minute?

Trainer = taller than expected. Orange foundation and fluff down cheek.

Can I ask you to please take off your sunglasses while we're in this session together?

No, thank you.

It's just, I find that this session flows more smoothly when I can form a good working relationship with the job seekers. And, well, I'm finding it difficult to get to know you and form a good working relationship when you have your shades on.

It's after a quarter past. We should get started.

Turn past her into the room to take same seat as before.

The trainer comes in, anger flushing to her eyelids.

Alright. Let's just recap some of the first part. Appropriate dress code. This goes for men *and* women. Sunglasses, hats, scarves, do we leave those on indoors or do we take them off?

When was your last first date?

The cemetery.

Wit u.

Was it like a job interview?

Def brought my A-game.

Why? Did I get the position?

Maybe.

What do I have to do to make the cut?

Dress suitable.
Come unprepared.
Don't ask questions.

Between intercom button and opening buzz, Dan pulls thin bandana out
and ties it covering his mouth and nose.

Hushed clank of the door closing behind. He hopes no one will leave
their flat and see his shades and cap pulled low. Can't take the lift – it'll
pull sickening unsteadiness through him. Must be clopping upwards
one stair at a time,
His hand on the banister, metal crooking
round, to ascend before him.

His blanketed breath,
Filters around his cheeks and chin.
Lips on fabric, spreading fire.

Third floor, can't moderate breathing,
Popping candy in his middle.
Toes in sneakers curled forward, he pushes on,

Wants: nails on his back, dragged across,
Covered O-faces multiplying till infinity.
If she doesn't want? Run. Far.

No precedent for this: Julie, Dolores –
Gone. Beyond inaccessible. Her whole
Style brings his other to his fore.

Sixth floor footfalls,

Jangling his heels and shinbones.
Wants to take his time, plan his way,

Into the act and part
With Dan who pressed the buzzer,
If she'll allow this other in.

Knows she feels him coming.
Dares not anticipate her reaction but
Proceeds, limbs floating, ecstatic.

Maybe she'll shriek, slam door, laugh at,
This first-time poseur, the gimp
on the ninth-floor landing.

Turn towards 28. Her door – his age. The knot tied around the back pushes onward. But not him anymore, just the walker, the mover, the goer to the door.

Knocks. Waits. Nothing. About to knock again but the door is pulled back by Shelagh expecting

What?

She perceives instead a no-Dan. A new Dan with expression neutralised. Opens to observe with a full body scan, then takes him inside.

Her forehead is soft. His jaw is not clenched. Her hands surf his T-shirt front. Dan sees shades of himself moving in her sunglasses. He cannot touch her face, but wants realness, to imprint this on memory. Her hands go over his shoulders to the muscles above his collarbones. His are pulled onto fleece fabric. Soft fur, good comfort to sweep hands over. She discovers square hips, back pockets, man-bum in black denim, then fingers hook under belt and grip the leather holding up his jeans.

A head shorter, she leans in, grazing the tip of his bandana. Rocks back to rub hatted head on his chin. Palms press pectorals, then fingernails graze down his front. His thumbs hook into waistband, sliding around the elasticated rim. Brush of pants and extracts hands to skim down the outside leg, polyester blend bobbled in the wash.

She pulls him from hallway to the kitchen with wreckage piling high. He massages scalp under wool, careful to keep hat still in place. Brown hairs come astray. Half-step back, seeking the murky reflections to orientate himself. She pulls him closer, face over her shoulder to divert from this distraction. She strokes his earlobe down to his neck, across the edge of his hood. Kitchen closes in. Mustn't break away but his eyes are pulled to the ketchup encrusted on the lip of the plate.

Hard, forced down wonky under jeans. One hand teases wedge. Other wants to choke-grip the Adam's apple but slides rough along the outcrop of his chin. Lovely stubbly. Fingernails clack against zipper teeth. One leg pressed against his inseam.

He places both palms atop her shoulders then drops to all fours, presses cheek into lino floor and lifts the cuff of trackies, palpating her calf, squeezing, gripping thumbs into tendon.

Can I nibble?

Can.

Lifts bandana to bare incisors, grazes slow over shin. Fingers crawl up to knead thigh covered in soft hairs. All focus, quivering, tense. His cap falls off, knocked by leg. He grabs the bill but a foot pins it to the floor. She pulls his hood off and rubs his trim, searches round behind the ears, not disturbing the arms of his sunglasses. Arms go up under the bottom of her fleece where the small of her back hides, then hands shimmy down the leg of her trackies. Dust on floor and he wants to finger a smiley face into it.

He licks the front of trouser leg and bites the knee. Head through legs and bites the knee crease. Yanked up by his hood, collar catches his neck. Cough. Not as hot as thought. They meet again. He reaches up and pincers the arms of her shades.

Don't.

He sees his mistake, doubled, and releases them. He leans in and kisses the frames, kisses both lenses through the fabric of his bandana, now wet. Pushes him back by shoulders. She pokes a finger to his chest. He looks down and she flicks upside his face.

Got you.

Giggle. Tries to bite finger.

Do you have diseases?

Um. No.

Okay. But we're not doing that anyway.

She reaches under his hoodie, craving abdominals, dashes of iron filings from navel to belt.

Wants mayonnaise smear all round mouth and neck and armpits. Wants spiders and the prudish woodlouse to see everything.

She pulls the hood over his head again, then yanks the drawstrings down, scrunching the aperture smaller until only a brown nose pokes out.

Breath hissing. She ties the drawstrings in tight knots around his neck.

Hands free now. Reaches under fleece to belly fat,

Jellified around hip bones, and

Fingers up the grooves tracking spine, knobbly discs.

Grabs his string reigns, pulls his head down

Cheek to hoodie fabric. She, silent command & control

Braces her hand round lip of countertop. Pulls him up by the drawstrings again.

Too close to make out shapes, only the huff of breath, the brunette armpit.

She finds his belt, works to unlatch. Thinks he's going to get his. Pulls the belt out of its loops, wants to saddle him up around the middle, ride slap his face, to have her finger bitten in return. Would smother herself with the smell of leather.

She instructs him down on all fours again and loops the belt around his neck, pulling tight on the fabric of his hoodie.

Grease on floor by oven makes smudges where dark hairs stick.

Pinch his nose to force his warm breath down to his layered hole.

Toast crumbs avert, scandalised.

Her fingers slip under bandana into the side of his mouth, a fishhook against his wet cheek. He closes his jaw around the fingers trying to taste where they have been.

Daybreak through cream curtains, darkened by sunglasses. Cap screwed loose, but still on-ish. Bandana fallen down to neck. Dan replaces them before seeking a drink of water. He sits up. Shelagh's scarf has remained tight, perfect in place throughout the night.

How though?

He gets up from the bed and she rolls into the gap where his body weight was. Now he sees it has loosened in the night's turning. Through a chink her smile leaks.

Catherine Mitchell is writer based in Norfolk. Her work examines trauma, sexuality, and gender while drawing on mythology and folklore. She is finalising a short story collection and is currently working on a novel, *Othering*, about family, masculinity, and love. You can read more of her writing at catherinemitchell.co.uk

Othering
Extract from a novel in progress

Valerie wakes and has one brief floating moment of peace before it descends on her again. Grey-tinged horror. Dishwater dull dread which creeps up and then recedes like the tide, then roils up again. Bile rises in her throat, and she swallows it down. Everything about her is oceanic today; perhaps that explains why she feels so queasy. Her left foot catches on the bed sheet as she pulls herself upright. Her hands are sore and tender; the prickling sensation has intensified, and the itching is impossible to ignore. She picks up the hand cream that is lying beside her pillow and squeezes a dollop of it out onto her palm. It smells like lemon verbena. Then she carefully smoothes it over the backs of her hands, around her wrists and in between her fingers where all the feathers are beginning to grow. She knows that this is an exercise in futility and that she cannot simply *moisturise* the shafts away – although wouldn't that be something, if this was just a dry skin issue – but it feels better than doing nothing. It soothes the itching a little. The shafts are hard, like spines: hard and dark and painful. Blood feathers. That's what they're called. Her hands look monstrous.

After the cream has been applied, she carefully pulls on a pair of black cotton gloves. The spines catch and pull on the fabric and she hisses. She should just leave them: she tried pulling one out and bled and bled when it snapped instead – but she can't look at them and she doesn't want Bill to see her like this. It sounds ludicrous, like she's become one of those women she used to make fun of who claimed their husbands had never seen them without makeup. This is different though, this is... her mind slides around for the right word and comes to a stop beside: *ungodly.* And it is not just her hands – she can feel the hard beginnings of more spines and shafts under her skin, along her arms, her chest, and her back.

She swings her legs out of bed and her left foot leaves a deep scratch on the floor. The talons make a hideous tapping sound as she limps over to the chair where her clothes are. It is agony to pull off the nightdress and pull on the long loose skirt and blouse. Putting on a bra is impossible, but it is equally impossible to care. The skirt falls to her ankles; the blouse she buttons with trembling fingers up to her neck. There is a sound on the stairs.

'Valerie?' Arthur's voice is still a shock to her. How deep it is, how he sounds like his father. 'Is everything ok?'

She swallows. 'I'm just getting dressed.'

'Oh. I'll come back.'

'No, it's fine, I'm— I'm decent.'

Arthur comes into the loft. He is holding a tray in both hands and gestures with it. 'I brought you some breakfast.'

'Oh, thank you.' Valerie is not hungry. Arthur places the tray carefully on the bed. There is a dish with soldiers cut into neat lines and butter sinking into them; a boiled egg sits next to it in a blue egg cup. Orange juice and coffee also crowd the tray. A ridiculous thing: Valerie thinks how pleased she might have been, once, if Arthur had brought her a breakfast like this on Mother's Day. Except of course that he was never at his father's on Mother's Day. Valerie is under no illusions— he never viewed her as a mother. He still doesn't. This is a pity breakfast.

'Soft boiled.' Arthur is careful about not looking at her. That is down to pity too, she thinks, but at least it allows her to look closely at him. Dark hair is growing out of his cheeks and chin, not quite a beard, but more a couple of days of neglect. She can't see him as the eight-year-old girl she once knew and taught. He was so quiet. An awkward child. Dark watchful eyes, a dreamy nature. He never *listened*, in class. That was always Valerie's main complaint, at parent's evenings.

Arthur sits down on the edge of the mattress. Valerie feels self-conscious. She has always felt self-conscious around Arthur. It's something about the way Arthur looks at her. Like he is judging her and finding her wanting. She stands at a distance from him and the bed; her hands hang awkwardly at her side. She can't think why she says it, but it slips out regardless:

'Do you hate me?'

Arthur frowns. 'What? No.'

'Really?' Valerie sits down on the little chair that her clothes were laid on. 'I used to think you did.'

'You were my favourite teacher.'

Valerie smiles slightly. 'That's nice.'

'But you know what they say about your heroes. Don't let them marry your dad.' Arthur smiles tightly. He looks down at his knees. 'It's been over twenty years. Of course I don't hate you.'

Valerie swallows. 'Did you, though?'

Arthur says nothing. Quietness is his weapon on occasions like this. When he stayed here for a few months, after he graduated from university, Valerie found his ability to be quiet somewhat unnerving: he and his father would sit in a room in total silence for hours on end, neither seeming bothered about the lack of conversation. She is used to Bill's silences, of course, but with Arthur it always felt like there was something simmering under the surface.

'You did.' It's not a question; she's always known, deep down.

'I was eight. I couldn't hate my dad. It was easier to hate you. You were the reason he left us.'

Valerie doesn't say she's sorry because she was raised to be truthful. She considers herself an honest person.

'But I grew out of it.'

A heavier, weightier silence descends.

'I'm surprised you came here. I'm surprised your dad called you.'

'So was I. Thought he'd disowned me.'

Valerie feels herself go cold. 'Your father would never disown you.'

He has those watchful eyes still; behind them a flicker of pain. 'He abandoned us when I was eight years old. He hasn't spoken to me in the last two years. What would you call that?'

'Don't speak about him like that.'

'He's my dad,' Arthur's anger is a quick, flashing thing: like a blade drawn suddenly in the light of the moon. 'He belongs to me more than he'll ever belong to you.' Valerie is gripped with the wild desire to hit him. She breathes deeply. She wasn't a teacher for almost forty years without learning how to curb her anger. Can Bill hear them below? Does he feel the tension thumping between them? She hopes, for his sake, that he hasn't heard any of the things Arthur has just said. Arthur looks away from Valerie first. 'I'm sorry,' he says. 'I don't mean that.'

'There's a lot you don't know about your dad.'

'Whose fault do you reckon that is?'

'You can't blame him for everything.'

'I don't.' Arthur tilts his head back to examine the ceiling. He blinks once, twice. 'I just wish he had loved me more.'

Valerie's heart twists in her chest. Vicious, violent. It feels like it's about to break right through her ribs. 'That's not fair. He loves you very much.'

'Okay.'

Neither of them say anything. Valerie looks at her twisted foot. Talon. Claw. 'I'm a monster.'

Arthur looks over at her with surprise. He glances down at her foot, then away. 'Does it hurt?'

'Yes.' Valerie wipes at the tears on her face with the heel of her hand. She feels so young and so old, all at once. She wants her mum, but her mum has been dead for six years. 'Oh God. Everything is such a mess.'

Arthur says nothing. What could he say anyway? Valerie sniffs and rubs her face until it feels red and raw. Her gloves are damp with tears.

'Have something to eat,' Arthur's voice is gentle. 'Dad's worried about you. Says you'll waste away.'

'As if it matters.'

'Come on.' Arthur gets up and brings the toast and coffee over to her. She picks up a soldier and takes a bite. It has gone soggy and clogs in her throat. The coffee is getting cool. It's dark and not as sweet as she usually takes it.

'Were you scared?'

'When?'

'When you...' She doesn't know how to say it. Bill and she were so shocked when they were told. '...Became Arthur.'

He looks at her like she's said something particularly stupid. Maybe she has. She doesn't know anymore. The second bite of toast goes down easier.

'Yes,' he says at length. 'And no.'

She watches him. He lowers himself to the floor and sits cross legged at her feet, the way he did more than twenty years ago, when it was story time on Friday afternoons. In her memory those quiet precious afternoons turn golden, like they've been dunked in honey. It can't always have been sunny and sweet, still that's what she remembers. Golden light, illuminating the pages of the book she was reading from. *The Lion, the Witch, and the Wardrobe. The Phantom Tollbooth. Matilda.* Who knew then that a boy lurked in the heart of that small, quiet girl? Or that this strange creature dwelt in Valerie's own bones?

'I know it isn't the same,' she says quietly. 'I do know that.'

'I was scared. A little. Not about changing but about what people would say. That was the hardest part.'

They have never spoken about this before. Not this calmly, at least. The moment between them feels fragile, like eggshells. 'When did you know you'd been born in the wrong body?'

He frowns. 'That's not— it's not like that.'

Valerie is about to argue and catches herself. 'No?'

'It's like, for me, it was like, if everyone had looked at me as I was and seen a guy and thought of me as a guy, then I would've been happy. I wouldn't have needed to change the way I looked at all. I didn't care that I didn't have a dick,' Arthur looks briefly like he thinks she's going to tell him off for saying *dick*. 'I mean. I didn't think about it. Maybe that's more accurate. I didn't think about my body at all. But then I realised when anyone looked at me, they saw a woman and I hated that. I didn't even know why I hated it. I didn't understand it. I didn't understand myself. For a long time.'

'And now you do?'

He raises one shoulder in a shrug. 'Much as the next guy.'

The light is streaming in, steady but not strong. It's not that early anymore and Bill will be wanting them to make a move.

'Will you take care of him? When I'm gone?'

Arthur's face crumples. God, *he* looks young. So, so young. Valerie remembers someone saying once that you don't think you get older but that everyone else around you just seems to get younger.

'Don't say that—'

Valerie stands and Arthur hastily struggles to get to his feet. They are almost the same height. She picks up her sunglasses that she will wear to hide her eyes. Thank God the wind is chilly enough that her being wrapped up won't look weird; that the sun means the shades won't look out of place. Thank God she can still walk and talk. For now.

'Will you?'

'Yeah, I— I'll try.'

'Good boy,' she says softly, and Arthur looks pained. Outside the birds are calling to each other. She realises with a sudden swoop, low in her belly, that she knows what they're saying.

Dennis Mugaa is a writer from Meru, Kenya. He was shortlisted for *Isele Magazine*'s Short Story Prize and was a finalist for the Black Warrior Review Fiction Contest. He is studying for an MA in Creative Writing at the University of East Anglia as a Miles Morland Foundation Scholarship recipient.

dennismugaa77@gmail.com

To Seek Gold Dust
The opening of a YA Afrofuturism novel

'Ma – Mumm!' Muthoni's voice stuttered and floated away. She was short of breath and excited. 'Muummm!'

Naisula leaned down to embrace her as she raced through the door in her school uniform. Muthoni's eyes glowed. A smile lit up her daughter's delicate features. Something was different. Muthoni's afro had morphed from its black colour to a deep blue hue. It could only mean one thing.

'Mum, I found gold dust on my way back home, and then, and then, my hair turned blue...'

'Slow down,' her mother said, trying to curb Muthoni's enthusiasm. She too felt elated but she suppressed her excitement.

'Mum – I am a gold-seeker!'

Muthoni had just turned thirteen years old. It was a week after her birthday and her parents had almost given up on her becoming a gold-seeker.

'I can't wait to tell Dad!' Muthoni said. She jumped on the sofa and threw her school bag, knocking over a green cushion. A family photograph beside the couch told of the family's young history. Kiara, her father, stared from it with piercing eyes. He had a moustache and silver hair – which meant he was a former gold-seeker. Naisula and Muthoni stood beside him with beaming, dimpled, identical smiles.

Kiara had been a gold-seeker when he was younger. He had been retained by the Ministry of Mining because of his exemplary record.

The gold-seekers were children in Naserian who could feel the presence of gold around them. Their hair was the blue of the sea. They used to work for the mining companies in the city discovering gold around the world. However, in the recent past, the number of gold-seekers was reducing. This was because as the children grew and reached the age of nineteen, they lost their gold-seeking ability. No one knew why, only twelve of them remained in Naserian, this led many to assume that all the amount of gold that could be found had been found. Until Muthoni.

Kiara came home tired and worn out. He had been, of late, detached from the affairs of his family. Given that he was running for Prime Minister of Naserian, the campaigns called for a large amount of time spent away from them. Initially, he was seen as having an outside chance of winning by several of the older members of the ruling party. Time and time again, they issued disparaging remarks on account of his youth; they said he was too young to rule and that he lacked experience.

However, his campaign had gathered momentum and with two weeks left to the election, he was the front runner. His pledges on immigration spoke to people in Naserian down to the depths of their souls. It was as though he took the words out of their mouths and said it for them. Many in Naserian felt that their resources were being used up too much by the neighbouring Enaimur. He advocated for stringent measures to curb this, giving Naserians priority in every government policy and employment.

As soon as he saw his daughter his weariness left him. It was hard for him to hide his pride from what, over the years, had become a cold exterior. 'Muthoni!!' he said as he gave her a warm hug.

'Dad... Dad... I was playing in the field today... Look, look, I am a gold-seeker just like you were.'

'How can I fail to notice?' He released her from his embrace and placed an arm on her shoulder. Muthoni being a gold-seeker would show people that he was the chosen one. That fate and the wishes of the divine had contrived to elect him even before the actual elections.

'But what did I tell you about going to the field in Enaimur?'

'To never go there,' she whispered, almost to herself, while looking downwards, ashamed that she had disobeyed her father. 'But Dad, it's on my way from school, and Tecla lives there.'

What she failed to mention, however, was that she wanted to play their football. There was a way in which the children played in Enaimur. Players on the pitch could disappear and reappear with the ball as a flitting shadow. It was so beautiful and exciting and something that people in Naserian could not do.

'No, we never go there. In fact, I don't think they should be coming here at all, I don't know how your mother convinced me to take you to a school there.'

Enaimur was located on the outskirts of Naserian. Before the city was built, they had all been one people. Those who lived in Enaimur, however, had no gold whatsoever and most people in Naserian regarded them with loathing and contempt. To Kiara's father as with the rest of the aristocrats, it represented a version of what Naserian could descend to. For them, Enaimur was a wasteland that sprawled formlessly: hundreds and hundreds of semi-permanent housings, lacking any worth at all and neglected by the ancestors for its lack of gold dust.

Naserian had built a wall around its city to keep them out. Enaimur citizens, however, were allowed to cross the checkpoint to work in Naserian after a thorough screening, but eventually, in the evening they always had to go back. They worked menial jobs: cooking, cleaning houses and washing dishes. Oddly enough the best school in the region was in Enaimur. It was started by a former wealthy gold-seeker, who thereafter left all his wealth to fund the school for another hundred years.

'I know it's on your way, but the driver always comes for you,' Kiara said.

'Yes, but I wanted to watch Tecla play.'

'Anyway, where did you say you felt this gold dust?' Kiara asked trying to divert the course of the conversation.

'In Enaimur.'

'But there is nothing there.'

'I... I don't know.'

'Anyway, it must be because you're new to this.' He paused, looking at her straight in the eyes, searching for some truth he perhaps did not know. 'No gold-seeker has ever felt any gold dust in Enaimur.'

There was to be a ceremony two days from then and all the gold-seekers, new and old would demonstrate their abilities. It was a ritual ceremony, held for as long as anyone could remember. The Prime Minister oversaw it and several distinguished guests came from all around the world. Many of them owned mining companies while others were dignitaries, ambassadors and tourists who came to see this premier event. The manifestation of this gift was something to behold, a gift that so many wished to have and yet only present in Naserian.

Muthoni was enveloped by delight as she walked to her bedroom. She could barely sleep that night. She twisted and turned in bed and looked up at the stars from the glass roof in her room. The sky was clear, and the stars twinkled in a variety of colours.

She remembered stories of famous gold-seekers of the past. From Naiponu, the red-haired one, the first one and the greatest, to whom the tree of life had chosen to give its gift. Naserian owed her its existence. There was Kip, a gold-seeker whose ability had manifested at just ten years old. And then there was her father who had enabled the discovery of mines in the deep seas of the Indian Ocean.

She wondered what kind of gold-seeker she would be. Maybe she would start by convincing the Ministry that there was a gold mine in Enaimur even though her father had told her that there wasn't. Perhaps the other gold-seekers had all missed it. When she had been there that afternoon, she had felt it. A burst of energy had gripped her as she cheered on the shadow football that Tecla played. For a moment, the world appeared in abstractions of colour and images, and she could see the emotions that raged inside everyone. The images condensed and then she saw it: gold dust. It was everywhere. In the houses that were on the verge of falling apart, in the people around her and the field. Everywhere she looked there were particles and particles of gold dust. The picture played in her head so much she did not realise when she slipped effortlessly into sleep.

In the morning, Muthoni woke up to find that her hair had turned red through the night. She rushed downstairs to show her parents. Kiara almost choked on his food when he saw her. Her mother, on the other hand, stared at her in disbelief. To them, the old legend of Naiponu had been just that – a story. They never imagined that their daughter would have been the first in generations to manifest the ability of the first gold-seeker. Kiara kissed Muthoni on the forehead. He was obliged to let the Ministry know about his daughter to prepare her for the ceremony.

When Kiara left, Muthoni tugged at the hem of her mother's dress. 'Mum... please take me to school today, I want to show you where I found the gold dust,' she pleaded with her mother. The white of her eyes was so pristine and pure and had that twinkle of innocence on them that made it hard for her mother to decline.

'Yes, let's go but we will use the metro,' Naisula said.

Muthoni smiled and looked at her mother in wonder, afraid that she might withdraw her words.

They took the metro to the edge of the city. A huge number of people stared at Muthoni. 'It's her, it's her,' an old man whispered to his grandson. But for all of them, the old legend replayed over in their heads. Kiara's posters were on the subway trains, promising sweeping changes in Naserian.

Naisula walked briskly after she passed the turnstile gates to leave Naserian. She pulled her daughter along on her arm directing her to the football field ahead of them. It was clear to anyone who saw her that she was fazed by the unfamiliarity around her. Not that there was anything to be afraid of – at least from what she could see. However, the stories that flew about in Naserian about Enaimur somewhat leaned towards one vice or another. For instance, someone was killed in broad daylight, a different person was mugged and another was beaten up. In fact, over tea in Naserian it was often common to hear 'I heard' followed by a horrid encounter that a person claimed to have been told about Enaimur.

However, when they arrived in the field, they found it in supreme calm. It was early morning, and the sound of birds was the only thing that rent the air. Naisula looked around and her nose squirmed at the smell of rubbish beside her. She saw the neglect in the area: crumbling rusted iron roofing, plastic strewn around and no presence of any car.

Muthoni gave her mother her school bag before she raced to the centre of the field and placed her arm on the ground. A few children who were rummaging on a heap of rubbish nearby stopped to see the unfolding event. They had never seen a gold-seeker before since no one that important ever stepped foot in Enaimur.

An air of unease slowly crept inside Naisula. A small crowd of people had gathered; all of them looked in amazement at the girl with the red hair on the football field all by herself. 'Muthoni, let's go!' Naisula shouted, her voice betraying a slight hint of fright. Muthoni rushed to where her mother was standing, having scooped up something. She showed it to her mother.

'Muthoni that is just dirt,' Naisula said, shaking her head in disbelief.

'No mum, the gold was there in the field, it was around you. It was everywhere Mum.'

'We'll come back later, you're already late.'

Isabelle Myers-Joseph graduated with First-Class Honours in History of Art in 2020 before completing the Faber Academy's *Writing a Novel* and *Finish Your Draft* courses as well as *Writing Poetry: Next Steps* at the National Centre for Writing. She is currently working on a novel and a short story cycle.

myersjosephisabelle@gmail.com

Play Along
An extract from a short story

Hanna found the restaurant décor overwhelming: the exposed bricks which she wanted to touch to see if they would crumble so she could take a bit home; the vintage posters of flapper dancers highlighted with glitter and feathers on the skirts; the flowers in pots above the bar that confused Hanna at first – how could they be watered? – until she realised they were fake; the three chandeliers that could fall and break on people's heads, that she tried to look up at but which made her eyes hurt; the mirrors that were also around the bar, little strips of mirrors that gave a fractured image not a whole.

On top of that, all the different senses were overwhelming: there was the music playing in the background which was jazzy and unpredictable; there was the smell of the meat coming from the kitchen and cooks shouting; there was the taste of toothpaste that she had not been able to wash out fully; there was still the feel of her dress, the way it reminded her that she had a waist and made her have to suck in so that she kept gulping down air. She decided to calm down by focusing on one thing and found herself being drawn to the furniture which was upholstered in velvet. This matched her dress.

'I've got a reservation,' Hanna said to the waitress whose nametag had Olivia engraved on it in gold. 'My mother has booked a table. Her name is Diane.'

'I'm afraid we don't have any reservations under that name,' Olivia said. She was tapping her feet which distracted Hanna along with the sound of her fingers on the screen, but Hanna tried again, she tried to think of another name, then remembered the name in the message from the taxi company.

'How about Jeremy?' Hanna's voice was so quiet it sounded like a squeak.

'I'm sorry,' Olivia said, leaning in closer. 'Could you say that again?'

'Jeremy.' Hanna tried to be louder this time.

'Follow me.' Olivia picked up a menu from behind the computer.

Hanna could not hear what the conversations were about. There was just a vague mumbling between people. They toasted and the glasses went together and made a sound that felt threatening, as if the glasses could break at any moment. Hanna did not realise she was staring until a woman gave her a disapproving look. For a second, she wondered if that woman was her mother, but the woman was too glamorous and her hair was blonde and her laugh sounded vacuous. Her mother did not wear red lipstick.

'Here you are.' Olivia did a swift movement with the menu.

It was the darkest corner of the restaurant near the toilets. Hanna expected to see her mother there. Instead, there was a man sleeping. He was not wearing any socks, but the soles of his feet were clean and he had trimmed his toenails. His brogues were under the table. The polished leather was the deep golden yellow of turmeric. They were in the perfect position to make a person trip. The laces were slipped in neatly like when you hand over your shoes at a bowling alley. There was a cup of tea in front of him on the table. To see if he really was asleep, Hanna stuck her finger in it. It was cold.

'Excuse me,' Hanna said, pulling on the tablecloth to hear the teacup in its saucer rattle.

She felt stupid in her dress now. She understood how ridiculous she must have looked, what with her not having proper shoes or the right bag to finish the outfit off.

'I think you're at the wrong table.' She pulled on the tablecloth some more.

He woke up.

'Hanna?' He shook his face, making it wobble. There was a bit of crusty drool by the side of his lip.

'How do you know my name?' Hanna rested her hand on the strap of her bag, fiddled with it, tried to make a bow out of it, picked at the stitching.

'I've wanted to meet you for a long time,' he said, trying to make his shirt neater, flattening it out but it was not even that wrinkled.

Hanna looked at him, tried to really look at him.

'Come sit down.'

'My mother should be arriving.'

'I know,' he said.

'I think you're at the wrong table.'

'It took a lot of work encouraging her.'

'I don't understand.'

'Aiden has told me all about you.' He started putting his shoes back on. 'He said you were having such a hard year.'

'How do you know Aiden?'

'What do you mean?'

'How do you know my brother?'

'Did no one tell you?'

Hanna felt sick. All the excitement she had felt about coming here suddenly turned into something dirty. She wanted to go, but part of her did not. She needed to see her mother. She was sure there was a reason, that this man, whoever he was, this Jeremy, was lying.

Jeremy ordered a bottle of wine. Hanna drank a glass quickly and he made a joke about it and Hanna felt as though she could not do anything right.

She wondered if he had his own children but did not want to ask, wondered if he was the kind of father who let his children play with his nose or if he snapped at them. He looked nothing like her father. He looked too rich.

Jeremy had got through the bottle of wine and Hanna had got through the basket of bread on the table by the time Hanna's mother arrived. Hanna liked the feeling of being full, how it weighed her down, grounded her, but she still felt stressed. She was not prepared for the version of her mother she saw.

Her mother was not wearing one of her hippie dresses. She was wearing skinny jeans and a camisole that was silver and shiny and her hair was blonde, the kind of blonde her mother had always made fun of, saying it made women look as if their hair was going to fall out. She even had red lipstick.

She had shopping bags from various department stores on her arms and headed straight to Jeremy, kissing him on the lips, stroking his cheek with the back of her hand.

'Look what I bought you, Jeremy.' She started opening one of the bags and throwing the tissue paper into the air. Hanna picked some up. It smelt of cologne. 'This shirt is so you.'

Hanna had always remembered her mother saving. Her and Aiden had shared clothes at points.

Jeremy held her mother for a long moment. They whispered in one another's ears.

'Look who's here,' Jeremy said, gesturing to Hanna. 'I'm just going to check on where our meals are. I ordered them quite a while ago.'

Hanna did not know what to say to her mother, this woman who she did not even recognise.

'Hi,' she said.

'I think we need to sit by the window, right at the front. Trust Jeremy to choose an intimate little corner. He's always so romantic.'

Her mother would not acknowledge her. She started storming to the front of the restaurant, to Olivia. Hanna could see the other customers staring.

Olivia looked embarrassed for Hanna and showed them to a table at the front. They had to wait a moment while she took away the plates and changed over the tablecloth.

The table at the front was smaller and the legs were wobbly, but it had a good view of the street, not that anyone was walking by. Hanna liked the fake plants around the entrance, especially the bushes which would never need to be trimmed. She wished more things kept their perfect shape.

'Best to be where stuff is happening,' her mother said, flicking her hair forward then twirling it with her fingers.

She did not say thank you to Olivia.

'What do you think of my dress?' Hanna asked, holding the front out away from her body, the way she used to do with graphic T-shirts as a child to communicate with people.

'You could have done with a size bigger,' her mother said as she looked around the room.

'Do you remember when we used to go and get chips?'

'Please don't talk about that kind of thing in front of Jeremy. Please try to be normal. Play along.'

They were the only things Hanna could ask because her mother had to go get Jeremy.

The salad Jeremy had ordered for Hanna was difficult to eat. It was dry and the lettuce leaves were huge and she could not talk as much as she probably should have and she did not feel very graceful. There were crumbs from the bread all over her front as well.

'I'm so close to my mother,' Jeremy said, Hanna's mother rubbing his arm. He was eating meat that was bleeding and his napkin was tucked into his polo neck awkwardly. 'We speak on the phone every Sunday.'

'You're such a good son,' Hanna's mother said, moving the food around on her plate but not taking a bite. 'You're always buying her things.'

'So, Hanna, tell us about you,' Jeremy said. 'Have you got a boyfriend?'

Then he grabbed Hanna's wrist. His grip was tight, perhaps he thought she was going to run away.

'Let go,' she said.

Hanna took her arm away from Jeremy as quickly as she could and in the process spilt the new bottle of red wine all over the tablecloth and onto her dress. She tried to ignore it then Jeremy started patting her down with napkins that went mushy, went into a kind of pulp and all the mushy napkins got stuck on the velvet of her dress, but she did not get angry, she kept saying 'thank you, thank you', while her mother was more concerned with the tablecloth. Olivia had to come back and clear it up. She did that swift movement again when she replaced the tablecloth and then went. Jeremy tried his best to resume the conversation.

'Let's start again,' Jeremy said. 'Have you got a boyfriend?'

'No.'

'Why not?' her mother asked.

'I don't want one.'

'I don't get it. Why wouldn't you want a boyfriend?'

'I'm a lesbian.' It came out so clumsily. It was not how Hanna had planned to tell her mother. Her mother's face did not look horrified; she just did not seem to care.

'There's something wrong with my spaghetti,' her mother said. 'It has a hair in it.'

'Are you sure it's not yours?' Jeremy asked. 'Look at the colour.'

Hanna made an excuse about going to the bathroom.

The bathroom was as overwhelming as the dining area. The monkeys and lemurs in the wallpaper looked down, their evil eyes following her as they hid behind leaves that were all sorts of unnatural colours. There was a velvet chair that would have been good for reading if the lights were not so dim and moody. Hanna sat on it for a moment and tried to lean back but she could not fully escape her body. She tried to draw into the velvet, to make lines with her fingers, like when she drew on the car window, doodles into the condensation, but she could not calm down. She wanted to cover her ears and curl into a ball. There was nowhere she could look to for calm, even the floor had a pattern on it, a check pattern, black and white with gold flakes. She tried to follow the pattern of it. She rummaged through her bag and realised that apart from her wallet, keys and phone, there were only the postcards. She stuffed them into the sides of the chair for someone else to take. Then she found a bubble in the wallpaper and started picking at it, ripping off a little section to take home.

Leeor Ohayon is a writer from London based in Norwich. His story 'Gahnun on Shabbat' was the winner of the 2021 Royal Society of Literature's V.S Pritchett Prize and published in *Prospect Magazine* and the *RSL Review*. In 2021 he also won the Leicester Writes Short Story Prize and was shortlisted for the Brick Lane Bookshop Short Story Prize. His non-fiction has appeared in +972, *Vashti, Vittles, Stamp the Wax and Zaman* among others. Leeor will begin his PhD at UEA in October 2022.

leeorzohayon@gmail.com

Henna Night
A complete short story

We do a consultation before we start planning the henna. We sit the bride and the groom down over a small tasting platter and some freshly baked frena. Insist that they're better off with the Deluxe package over the Standard as they gush over Mum's matbukha, her spicy carrot salad. We ask where exactly the family came from, whether they have any specific traditions, then customise for their big night accordingly. We have all the Yemenite headpieces, the filigree jewellery. Berberisca dresses for the Moroccans, zdad fabric for Tunisians, Libyans. Mum's a stickler for tradition, for getting things right. Says it on our website: a henna like once upon a time.

We make the sweet things a few days ahead. The gazelle horns, the marzipan fruit, the sablés à la confiture. We put them on trays, wrap them in cellophane, tie a ribbon at the top. Have them ready, put aside for the henna procession. Then we focus on the catering, getting the hall ready. Fabrics on the walls, on the ceilings. Cushions in turquoise and gold scattered over the seating. Traditional teapots, Arabic lanterns. Hamsas laid out on the table. Mum's little touches.

The result is impressive. It's always impressive.

The tables on either side of the room are piled high. Hand-rolled couscous and lamb cigars and chicken pastilla dusted with cinnamon and sugar. Two big golden throne-like chairs set up at the end. I like this part of the night, right at the start, when the guests stand about awkwardly waiting for the people they like to arrive. All saccharine hellos and two-cheek kisses and filler conversation.

I busy myself with the cellophaned trays, start moving two at a time into the room at the back, stack them between the costumes rail and the palanquin, stealing glances at Matan as I pass.

He stands in the DJ booth, at the opposite end, bent over his laptop. Black buttoned shirt. Tongue poking out of the side of his mouth. I move back and forth, but he isn't looking up.

My new winklepickers squeak on the porcelain floor. I contemplate going up to him after I stack the sweets.

Six trays to go.

The room is filling up.

Aunties and cousins with bass in their voices. Their husbands drenched in cologne.

Three trays to go.

Snatches of conversations: Look how they've grown. Isn't he handsome? Bli a'yin hara'. Tfu. Tfu. Tfu. Please God. Thank God. Send my love to your mother.

A wet busa planted on a cheek with genuine affection.

Matan is still staring at his screen.

Two trays to go.

I stop by the DJ booth, tray in hand.

You wanna go for a cig?

He sees the cellophane first, then looks up at me smiling.

You shouldn't have, he says, reaching for the tray.

I move it out of his reach. You want my mum to kill you?

He laughs.

All ready?

Nearly.

What're you starting with?

For the entrance?

I nod.

Mabrouk a'leik. Why?

Is that the tip-ah-tip-ah-tip song? Put that one on.

Is that an order from your Mum?

No. I just thought... never mind. Sorry.

Did you get my...

His voice trails away. He drops his gaze, eyes down at his laptop. I smell mum's Kent cigarettes before I feel her hand on my shoulder.

Listen, in ten minutes you can start dressing the men, she says, chewing on gum. The special outfit with the waistcoat for the groom. For the saba, the nice gandoura in the wine colour with the yellow slippers and tarboosh— remember. Wine colour. The friends can get a fez each and any djellabas leftover. But dress the family first. Then worry about them.

She nods a cold hello at Matan, over my shoulder.

I've gone, I need to see to the bride. You should get going, she says and moves into the crowd, wearing her professional smile.

I look back at Matan, he raises his eyebrows, eyes fixed on the screen.

I make my way to the back room, squeezing through the crowd. Masculine laughs. Domed bellies tucked behind designer shirts, kippahs on heads. Teenage girls with sparkly bags, high heeled shoes.

I enter the room at the back, the groom's inner circle hover over the costume rail. I clap my hands, get into character.

Who's getting dressed? Who's the father of the groom? The grandad?

Two hands go up in the air. Black blazer sleeves.

And the brothers?

Three more hands flap in the air.

I hand grandad the wine coloured gandoura. Pass out slippers to the brothers. A djellaba to an uncle with a big smile on his face.

It's like going back to Morocco, he says.

I watch the men slip on the djellabas on top of their suits, take off their pointy shoes.

The friends of the groom are gathered around the rail, waiting for my attention. There's five of them. All call and response. Voices permanently ready for banter. Yes geez. Nah geez. I want one of those dresses.

I tell the one I've identified as the ringleader that there are only two left.

Decide among yourselves. The rest will get a fez.

I reach for the cheap ones in the box. Give them out as they argue. What mate. Nah mate. Dan's too Ashki to wear one.

I glance at my phone. Two missed calls and a text from Matan: tonite?

I see the cellophaned trays piled high on the side. I've forgotten to leave some with the women. A perfect opportunity to go past Matan. I fill up a box with five, make my way through the crowd. Box above head.

Almost at the booth.

Matan looks up. Turns his palm in the air like what did you forget?

But I don't get to respond. I feel her hand on my shoulder. She's put on perfume now to mask the Kent.

Where to?

I came to bring you the parcels.

What parcels?

The trays.

The helawayat?

I pull one out. The cellophane makes a crinkling sound.

Thanks, she says, takes the box off my hands. We stand there looking at each other.

Anything else?

The youyou... the kulululu...

She raises her eyebrows.

I was going to tell Matan, to put on the sound effects.

What for?

For the entrance procession.

I have enough old women here to youyou for the entrance, she says.

No, I just thought...

Yallah kaparah, go get the men ready. Otherwise, we'll be late. And they'll come for my head. You want your mother's head on a plate? She puts her arm around my waist, gently moves me in the direction I came. Ah... and before I forget, I need you to bring in the henna.

In the room, the men are dressed, taking snaps on their phones.

I clap my hands.

Showtime voice.

Right. I need four of your strongest men, I say.

Four put up their hands.

You four are carrying the groom into the hall in the open palanquin. The groom climbs in and sits down, the wooden plank rests on your shoulder. Got it?

The mates let out a whey, start jeering. Up for it Dan? Nah Dan's got no strength. Leave it to Johnny. Wod he call it again, a palancake?

You'll be carrying him until the thrones at the end, I say, making sure to meet eyes with each of them. The bride will be coming in at the same time on her palanquin. Hers has a roof. I need another four to carry hers.

Three hands shoot up in the air.

A fourth reluctantly follows.

The mates let out a second whey.

Great. Let them dance for a bit in the air so the photographer can grab a few shots. Those not carrying, can grab a tray from the pile. Can grandad stand near the front, put a symbolic hand on the seat as it's being carried in?

I turn to the groom. You know once you're seated on the throne, we'll bring over the henna paste and the ceremony begins. Your fiancé...

Rachel.

Rachel puts the henna on the palms of the well-wishers. You press the cotton pad on top, secure it to their hands with a ribbon.

Oh, but we've told your mum. We're not doing the henna part. Rach is allergic.

I don't have time to respond.

In the next room, the microphone scratches awake, people start hushing.

I tell the men to get into line. This is our cue.

The palanquin is hauled up in the air, and the groom lets out a startled cry. His friends below him laugh, straining to adjust.

Matan's voice booms over the mike: Ladies and Gentleman... la a'ris wa la a'rousa. Give it up for the bride and groom.

The guests start clapping and cheering, the tip-ah-tip song drifts in through the speakers. The men stabilise the palanquin onto their shoulders, let out a final whey as they exit.

I hear the kulululus as they enter the next room. Different pitches and trills as if emerging from each corner. I'm the last to emerge. I watch the procession ahead file up to the thrones, cellophaned trays dancing in the air.

Mum appears on my right.

Take, she says, pushing the henna bowl into my hands. Two candles in the centre, dragée around its border.

No, mum. We can't.

Take, quick.

No, Mum. They can't.

It's fine. Put it in front of the chairs. Just for the show. She doesn't have to put it on.

She pushes it into my hand, then moves away.

I look up, the bride and the groom are still in the air, making an uncomfortable bridge with their hands. Their carriers beneath are short of breath, twisting their faces, biting their lips.

They set them down.

The crowd claps some more.

More kulululus. More cheers. More hoots.

The bride and the groom climb out.

Bow.

Walk with a little sway to their thrones.

I'm nearing them now. Henna bowl in my hands.

Their eyes fall on me.

A dazed smile on their face, then a look of horror as I place the henna bowl on the floor before them.

My favourite part is the end of the night. When the costumes are packed away and the fezzes are counted, and all that remains to be done is to separate the trays. The ones that can be used again from those that were turned into maracas during the procession. I get to tear open the cellophane, squish the marzipan fruit, lick the jam from inside the sablés.

I put on my coat, slip a maraca'd tray into my bag. Mum's outside having a fag.

I tell her, I'm gone. I've finished for the night.

She looks into the distance, says, Don't get back too late.

I walk up the road, until the hall is no longer visible and order a cab to the Travelodge ten-minutes away.

I walk past reception, head straight for the stairs. Glance at my phone, then search for room 102. I pull out the cellophaned tray from my bag and knock three times.

One knock.

Break.

Two more knocks. One after the other. Listen for breathing by the peep hole.

He opens the door and I cross over the threshold.

Your dowry, I say, hand him the cellophaned tray.

No gold?

At our henna, please God.

There's a business idea for your mum, he says.

I look about the room.

Was everything okay in the end?

Yeah fine. Bride was pissed about the henna.

Shit.

Groom shouted at me... She was so fucking adamant. All for the show. God forbid a henna without henna.

He pulls me closer, rests his nose on my neck.

But she's got it all wrong, he says. Like no one's doing a henna. Not a proper one. It's just an excuse for a party. A hafla. An Aladdin themed ba—

Matan.

Yeah?

Could we maybe just fuck?

Anushé is interested in people and enjoys writing characters whose decisions she can observe behind the scenes. For that reason, she finds fiction more satisfying than reality. Before the MA, she worked as a marketer, entrepreneur and a teacher. This year's anthology is her first publication.

Anushekhan89@gmail.com

This Was Once a Great Love
An extract from a short story

Where shall I begin?

Maybe at the very beginning?

'71. Grey static, black-and-white screen. Girls still in skirts.

You press one foot against a wall while a cigarette rests between your middle and index fingers. You have just transferred from a school nearby, one none of us have heard of. Even though we haven't asked, you tell us why you left. You say you needed a challenge; you wanted to be around the best.

We're the ones who will shape the country, you say. At age sixteen, I think these are lofty ambitions, but you continue to speak about the current leadership, let the word Schadenfreude slip into conversation. Ash rests on your cigarette; you only remember to take a puff when it is close to burning itself out. You hold what's left of it to your lips and make a loud sucking sound. Your mouth forms an o as you exhale a cloud of smoke. Behind the cloud, you try and cough discreetly to the side so that no one sees you.

I see you. You catch my eye and smile. Later in the day, when the rest of the boys recount the conversation, they mimic your accent, use the word Schadenfreude incorrectly among themselves. If you know they are poking fun at you, you seem unconcerned. If anything, you seem pleased that your opinions have caught on. This is my first memory of you.

In the rest of my memories of that time, you are seated towards the front where the girls usually sit. You spend most of the class staring out the window or doodling on your notepad but when the teacher asks a question, your hand is the first to rise. You answer her correctly and then ask your own questions. Although she answers you, her tone of voice lets on that she thinks you are attacking her intelligence.

We do not yet know each other. In fact, the first time we speak beyond pleasantries is when we are seated next to each other in class. Do you remember?

Mrs Pelosi's English period. Fifteen students bent over wooden desks. Wobbly chairs, papers folded and placed under the legs for stability.

We are working on an essay titled 'Why discuss the past?' You have asked for an extra sheet of paper and are scribbling your thoughts furiously. I have made use of only the front and back. I try and focus on my own work although my eyes slide towards your paper each time you ask for more sheets. After the forty-five–minute period ends, you look over and ask to read what I wrote. Without waiting for permission, you pick up my paper. You nod as your eyes dart across the page, then you hand it back to me. Since you have not volunteered an opinion, I decide to ask you what you think when we break for lunch. As we walk down the corridor, you say, 'Really, it's not about the vocabulary, it's how you use it. The average person knows approximately twenty-thousand words. And you use yours well.'

I can't tell whether you are being earnest or mocking. Your gaze is so intense as you say this that I am compelled to look away. When we reach the end of the corridor, I head to where the boys are gathered while you head towards the girls. You haven't yet made your place with us.

One of the boys, Hafiz, nods in your direction. The girls are laughing at something you have said. As I watch you engage with them, I am tempted to join you.

'What do they see in him?' Hafiz asks me.

You look in my direction; I look away.

'I don't know,' I respond.

It isn't long before the rest of the boys are taken by you as well.

It is on one of those days when we are walking down Elphinstone Street towards Park American Bookshop. We know the bookkeeper keeps imported magazines; our mothers and sisters have returned frequently with copies of *Cosmopolitan*. The boys are giddy at the thought of there being other magazines more suited to their taste, although none have yet asked for them at the counter. We have spent months perusing the shelves, each excursion an exercise in futility; you find this amusing. You ask if you can join us. The boys oblige, albeit grudgingly.

When we enter the shop, we succumb to our usual routine. Some sift through local magazines, others through a pile of records. I head towards the science-fiction collection for new arrivals, although out the corner of my eye, I see you already at the counter. You have no time for pretences. In a voice that is deeper than your usual, you ask for *Penthouse, Hustler, Playboy*. You will have them all, whatever is available and several copies please.

You do not give the bookkeeper enough time to deny it or even ask your age. You rest your elbow on the counter and make idle talk with the rest of us, your voice cascades through different corners of the store. This trick seems to work. The bookkeeper heads towards the tin letterboxes where he keeps the imported stash. He takes out the magazines; the covers are hidden behind plain paper. The boys flock to the counter, turn over the pages to see the ones they want to purchase. I bide my time. When I do make it to the counter, you are still there.

I look inside the covers and pick up a *Playboy*.

'I like the stories,' I say even though you haven't asked.

'Yeah? Which are your favourites?'

'Many. They've got Kerouac this time. I like him.'

You say, 'I like him, too.'

You pick up a *Playboy*. When we leave the store, we leave as a pack.

Over the course of the term, you seep into our circle of friends, wearing turtlenecks, still smoking cigarettes incorrectly. Glasses clink, you sip a whiskey on the rocks while the rest drink vodka. The girls find you desirable; all the boys begin to drink whiskey. Although they still laugh at you, now when they do, it is to your face and without malice. You grin and remain undeterred in your behaviours.

You have found your equation with us and are invited everywhere. Even to certain events that I avoid. Of course, you know what I am referring to. The nights with the 8 mm projectors: lewd slides, room packed with boys. Each time they insist I should be there, I craft excuses. Not every joy needs to be shared, I joke with you; you do not laugh. You partake in these gatherings, and it is just as well. I am afraid we are too similar, and if my suspicions are correct, then we are in trouble. I do not wish to be in trouble, although I do reciprocate when you pursue a friendship.

Camaraderie and competition go hand in hand as we take turns at the top of class, much to the chagrin of others. When we break for summer, I am disappointed that we won't see each other as often but then you ask me if you can come visit. I am quick to agree.

I shove my belongings under the bed in anticipation of your arrival, yet you comment on how disorganized I am. Each time you visit, you bring something with you: records, posters. In fact, I even tape one of them on my wall. Do you remember? The one with Javed Burki in his sports ensemble? Sweater vest accentuating his broad shoulders, face glinting in the sunlight; one hand on his hip, one against a cricket bat.

Abba sees it and is proud of me; he believes this is a sign that I do have athletic aspirations. He thinks you are a positive influence. I am surprised by this and remain tentative whenever I mention your name at home. I am afraid of being discovered. I know what you are thinking. That this is my over-cautiousness. It is not. For while my father has succumbed to your charm, Ama knows better. Mothers always do, don't they?

One day while dusting my room she lets me know that sometimes our desires can get us into trouble, that we are better off ignoring them. There is no context to this life rule. This is how I know she knows. I receive the message, dispose the poster. Abba blames her for a career unexplored. I blame her for other reasons. If I had told you back then, you wouldn't have blamed her. You would have said she's a product of her time. You would have said it didn't matter what she thought.

You would have looked at me and said, 'Courage, Babar. That is all it boils down to.'

I would have disagreed with you, told you that unlike you I was practical, someone more in touch with reality. Then, you would have looked at me, asked what good being in touch with reality did me.

Even in my imagination, you are most frustrating when you are correct. Anyway, I fear I am getting ahead of myself. I apologize. Where shall we go instead?

'73. Karachi University. East and West Pakistan have split, yet another schism. Masses are whispering against military rule, and we believe the press is finding its voice. We are among the thought leaders of the day; we are inspired.

You have discarded your turtlenecks, your persona. You wear shalwar kameez to university, hand out pamphlets, speak in Urdu. You love the excitement, getting your hands dirty, being 'one with the people'. I know you well enough to know you are sincere in your sentiments.

We are young, we are dreamers, we are shaping the future of our nation. You convince me of this. Four years a whirlwind, the urgency of our multiple missions leave us passionate, at times frenzied. We move this urgency to the newsroom.

'77. Your boss, Feroz, is hailed in the newsrooms as a legend. Prior to this job, he has been fired from several places. He has earned himself a reputation among the leaders, that reputation has its consequences.

'I couldn't even leave the godforsaken country; the buggers wouldn't let me renew my passport. Five years, I wrote nothing. But now, we write.'

You are intoxicated with the tapping of the typewriter, the printing, the smell of ink.

My boss, Iqbal, runs the show. He is exquisitely moustached; that is my only opinion of him thus far. On our first week at the job, he stands at his desk and gathers us around him. He straightens a sheet of paper that he has received from the APP. Make note of the guidelines, he tells us, so that we work as a unit with no hidden agendas.

'Our job is to promote the ideology of Pakistan, to rejuvenate the public sentiments, which have fallen due to the acts of the previous government. Journalism is a public institution meant to serve the people. It should not in any way serve anti-social needs. There will be no derogatory expression, vulgarity—'

'Drat,' you whisper in my ear.

'No incitement against institutions, arousing sectarian, parochial, regional or provincial passions.'

'What will we do with all this freedom?' I whisper back.

And on he goes.

'Nothing that undermines the security of the state.'

While I am unenthused by my future, Feroz takes you under his wing. Even if the stories you work on aren't published, you put in the work. You tell me about all the things we aren't sharing with the world.

Iqbal has a different approach. He and I spend countless hours scanning the newspaper.

'Tell me,' he says. 'Do you find any of this content objectionable?'

While I start by saying no, eventually I am able to point out passages that indicate 'bias' or 'political leanings'.

'Good,' Iqbal says. 'You're going to go places.'

Xinxin QIU was born in Shenyang, in the northeast of China, and obtained a BA in Contemporary Literature Studies from the University of Tokyo. She is currently living in Japan. Xinxin writes about teenage protagonists trapped by family issues. She is interested in crime fiction, especially a sub-genre known as the 'social school'.

qiuxinxin93@gmail.com

Nan Hu Park, Shenyang, July 1999
A short story

A boy and a girl stand on the bridge.

Darkness falling. A smell of burning wood and coal in the air. A row of willows along the left side of the bank, narrow branches bent by heavy leaves, dipping into the dark water. The sound of a saxophone drifting from the right bank. The boy knows nothing about music. Still, it sounds sticky and heavy, like a sponge absorbing too much emotion.

'What's wrong with that man?' says the girl.

'He's gone,' says the boy.

'Weird...' the girl says. She feels she has more to say. But finally she says, 'Someone was playing an Erhu yesterday at noon. Did you hear it?'

The boy shakes his head.

'Then did you hear me scream?' says the girl.

'Scream what?'

'Stop! Go to the park if you want to play the Erhu,' says the girl. 'I don't know why I screamed. I mean, it was too hot. Sweat was sticking to me, and that Erhu sounded like glue.'

The boy stares down at a plastic bag floating in the water.

'I regretted it immediately,' says the girl.

'Why?'

'I don't know... I felt guilty. What if that person can't walk? What if he lost his job too... trapped in his apartment day after day and playing the Erhu is his only pleasure.' The girl pauses, then says, 'I just feel the Erhu sounds so lonely.'

'Lonely,' the boy repeats. He speaks slowly, with many silences, as if he is digesting each word four times before letting it out. 'Is anyone not lonely in our *Xiaoqu*?'[1]

'Where were you, then?' asks the girl.

'I saw your father,' says the boy.

'Where?'

'In the mahjong club. The one near the local market.'

'I wish he'd die on the mahjong table,' says the girl.

'He wasn't on the first floor,' says the boy. 'I saw him...'

The scorching, suffocating air from that noon comes back to the boy. He stood on the opposite side of the road to the mahjong club, hiding himself in the shadows of the low buildings. Two bicycles were parked in front of the wall. He recognised them. The black one belonged to his father. The blue one belonged to the girl's father. The New Year banners were still hanging on either side of the doorway, fading to nothing in the sun. The door of the mahjong club was wide open. There were three vacant mahjong tables on the first floor. The window of the second floor was tightly shut. He knew who was inside. The girl's father and his own mother. The sultriness, the sweat of prostitutes and their customers turning white bedsheet yellow and hard. His own father was wandering in the local market, waiting for the night, to take his wife home by bicycle under the cover of darkness. Another turtle and another whore, in this city of turtles and whores.

After nightfall, the park is almost empty. The Ferris wheel and neon lights on the bridge railings reflect on the water, distorted by the waves. Far away, outside the park, on a different and wider bridge are two lines of red brake lights. The boy can hear the monotone of traffic in the distance, punctuated by abrupt sirens.

'Let's run away from here,' says the girl, with a choking sound.

'I can't,' says the boy. 'You can steal your father's passbook. He's rich.'

'Stop talking as if my parents weren't laid off! Don't you know how few families in our *Xiaoqu* still have a job?'

At least your family still has some redundancy money, thinks the boy. Enough for prostitutes. He turns his face away. He doesn't want to explain, not even one word. He won't. He doesn't know what he could say, besides from words that will hurt her, hurt himself.

'Do you know how my mom saves money?' says the girl. 'She picks up the vegetables left on the ground after the market stalls have closed. And she turns on the tap just a little bit to let the water out one drop after another, gathering the drops in a bowl, because small drops aren't recorded in the meter.'

They had supper at 11 p.m. The table was silent. The dish was eggplant pockets, two slices of eggplant stuffed with minced meat, fried in oil. His father filled the bowl for his mother. She buried her head, eating. In the dim light, her face was still pale and beautiful. The boy soaked an eggplant pocket into his rice porridge. A layer of yellow oil floated onto the surface. He wanted to vomit. This hypocritical shiftless man. This beautiful shameless woman. He would rather she pick up vegetables left on the ground. He put down his chopsticks, entered the bathroom, and sat on the toilet. Opposite the toilet was a stained mirror. He hated his face.

In the darkness of the park, the river smells of cold and fish. The sound of saxophone floats across the water. At the place where music comes from is a pavilion. The boy supposes the person playing the saxophone is sitting inside. Maybe a middle-aged man. What kind of life causes an adult to produce such sticky, heavy sound in darkness? Maybe the sound isn't dark at all, but melodious and happy. The boy tries to recall the image of a happy adult in his fifteen years of life, but not a single one comes to mind.

'I hope my father dies,' says the girl suddenly.

'They are already dead to me. How can they call themselves alive?' says the boy.

Mollified, her voice softens, 'Is your father still doing that 'Holy Ants' investment? So many families have been cheated by that company...'

The boy stares at the neon lights hanging from the bridge railings, shining in clouds of red, pink, green, and blue. The tiny lights are a thread of halos. Thickly dotted. Like a nest of ants...

One night, he came home from school and, opening the door of his bedroom, he saw a dense mass of black dots squirming on the floor, the wall, the ceiling, dropping onto him. His dad had decided to feed ants in his room. It was his father's third investment. A company claimed that eating polyrhachis vicina roger powder would cure erectile dysfunction. Investors had to pay a 10,000-Yuan deposit for a box of ants and would then get 13,250 Yuan cash back after raising the ants for fourteen months. Two boxes of ants were raised in his bedroom, one bought with his father's redundancy money, the other with his mother's.

'Do you hear about Liu and Xu?' says the girl, trying to sound cheerful.

'Hear what?'

'Nothing serious... just... Liu told Xu that he likes her.'

'So they are together?'

'Yes!'

'How do you know?'

'I saw them secretly holding hands during class, under the desks.'

The neon lights on the bridge are shining, changing colors. Her hands are white. Her nails look mellow and full, beautiful in the neon halos.

She turns to stare at him. 'Do you like anyone?'

He avoids her eyes. He hears his heart beating.

'No one,' he says. I'm not qualified, he thinks.

The girl puts her arms on the concrete railing, rests her chin on her hands, staring out at the river. The boy follows her gaze. The river stretches into the unknown, farther and farther, darker then darker, a dreadful darkness that swallows people whole.

'I hate summer. It's too greasy. Dirty,' says the girl.

'Me too. Summer is gross,' says the boy.

1 A 'Xiaoqu' is a housing complex. Some Xiaoqu are built by companies
    (usually state-owned enterprises) and allocated to their employees.

T. S. Quigley is a Ugandan-Irish writer born and raised in Hackney. Her work aims to explore the entanglements of race, class, desire and the legacies of empire. She aims to write fabulist fiction and is working on a novel and collection of short stories set in East London.

t.ssembajjoquigley@hotmail.co.uk

Meeting Aphrodite in Russell Square
An Extract from a Short Story

You brush the last strands of hair from your face and lean in for your third attempt at winged eyeliner. In the gallery of your imagination, canvases of a chic young woman line each room, but you just don't possess the makeup artistry to conjure this figure into life. You're certain you can be that woman yet, each time, the cat's eye on the girl in the mirror turns out a mess. You think of how the Instagram models and TikTok stars manage to do theirs perfectly and you're left even more frustrated that, on such an important day, you haven't succeeded at yours.

You examine the rest of your reflection. Blusher is missing so you rummage through the makeup bag but aside from some fluorescent grains at the bottom there's no sign of it. Frustration rises inside you, ascending from your stomach and nestling within your chest. Mariam obviously helped herself to it. Despite being three years younger, the barriers which separate normal teenagers based on age have no bearing on her understanding of how the world works. As a result, she's never seen any reason to even feign respect towards you. And even less for there to be any separation between your personal space and property.

—Mariam where's my fucking blusher?

She's been next door in the bathroom and comes into your bedroom.

—Relax fam, I borrowed it for one minute

Shrugging, she tosses the smudged Rimmel compact towards you.

—Don't touch my stuff again or I'll burn your mascara

Finally registering your annoyance, she slopes off to Omar's room next door.

You glance at your phone which is pulsating with a series of WhatsApp messages, demanding you get to the station. You're already thirty minutes late. Your parents think you're heading to a Saturday GCSE prep session for students falling behind. They're still hopeful you can turn the last few years around. After all, secondary school began with so much potential. Some of your teachers even thought you had the potential to go to Cambridge but as the years unravelled things didn't exactly go to plan. Now, with exams next year, you've promised to start taking school more seriously. And you've convinced your parents enough for them to not suspect you're really bunking off to Central with Cassie.

Suddenly you're jolted by the first rumblings of an argument next door.

—Omar, you wasteman! I swear I didn't take it

—Ah allow it Mariam, why you lying for? You did and it's bait you broke it

You grab your bag and race down the corridor towards the front door, speeding up at the living room to avoid your parents coming out.

—Bye-bye, love you

You don't stop, roaring out the front door and down the concrete stairwell of Aral House. You navigate towards Whitechapel Station through shifting roads of Victorian terraces and glossy new-build apartments. You wonder at how the concrete womb of London's streets endlessly births these glistening buildings and how there's always money for someone to buy them, just never anyone you know.

You get to Whitechapel Market with its medley of shops and stalls selling dresses, vegetables and electronics. You pass a huddle of men and from their unabashed stares infer their intentions instantly. You lower your head and tilt your shoulders forward. That shrill sound punctures the atmosphere like a laser, burning through your clothes and skin until you feel so uncovered it might as well be just your skeleton walking down the street. You quicken your pace and they're behind with their laughs becoming indistinguishable from the cacophony of the market, though their weed swirls in your nostrils long after you've passed.

At the station Cassie's leaning against a wall taking slow drags of a cigarette. Before she looks in your direction you take a moment to savour her. It's the pengest you've seen her. She's wearing the red cropped sports top with the cycling shorts you got from Westfield H&M together at the start of summer and her body looks banging underneath. Her breasts look full and spongy in a way yours never can, even when you're wearing a push up bra. And the caramel Marley Twists her cousin Jade did last week hang down and tickle the batty that's famous amongst the boys in your school.

You feel a strange sensation you've been getting more and more around her. It's like you're a football someone's thrown into the air that has no control over how far it travels or where it lands. But despite the lack of gravity when she's close, you couldn't be more relieved to be here, rather than dissecting *Romeo and Juliet* with Mrs Da Silva in GCSE English prep.

Although ironically it was that play which brought you together, six months ago.

For most of secondary school you'd circuited two separate friendship solar systems. Her group did each other's makeup at break, were always in detention for being rude to teachers and went out with roadman in their twenties who drove round ends in BMWs. On the other hand, your friends diligently went to madrassa, spurned male attention and were more likely to be in the library revising for tests than bunking off at Westfield Stratford.

GCSE English was the first lesson you found yourselves in together, but in class you couldn't have been more different. For you, the texts were like obstacle courses full of rope climbs of iambic pentameter, monkey bars of alliteration and hurdles of similes. Meanwhile, despite Cassie never doing any work, she'd always be able to unthread every secret message the writers had weaved into their stories. This was the reason you first noticed her.

The discussion itself was of little importance to you. The day after, you'd forgotten what most of it was even about. What was imprinted on your memory was the girl whose lips and tongue had evoked knowledge of the most adult of experiences. A girl whose interpretation of *Romeo and Juliet* appeared more authoritative than even Mrs Da Silva's, formed, as you understood it had to be, through memories of the most intense encounters.

After that, you found ways to sit closer and closer. At first you felt scared to speak, as she didn't seem approachable. Some of the boys said that mixed race girls were always stuck up, but you hoped that wasn't the case with Cassie. So, one day, when there was a session on the role of fate in the play, the chair next to her was empty and you found the courage to sit down.

During group work, excitement rose within your body as you spoke about the parallels between Romeo and Juliet's world and ours today. You said how, even in modern times, the circumstances of your birth still dictate everything, including things as intimate as who you can love. One boy in your group disagreed and said teenagers can choose their own paths nowadays but all you noticed was Cassie considering you with a half-smile on her face. Her expression seemed to say that you'd articulated everything she thought. After that, you talked every lesson. It wasn't long before everything and everyone else was eclipsed, because the only thing that really mattered to you was her. Like Juliet had been for Romeo, Cassie was now your sun.

As you got to know her you noticed she always seemed to have new clothes and makeup. One time in canteen she opened her purse and there must have been at least five tenners stuffed inside. When you ask where she gets it all, she says her mum recently got this new job in Canary Wharf where they give them crazy bonuses and she gets her own office on the fortieth storey with floor-to-ceiling windows overlooking the Thames. You don't believe her though, because you've seen her mum working on the cash register in the Tesco Express on Shoreditch High Street, checking out energy drinks for distracted Startup founders and Smirnoff bottles for Vinyl clad clubbers. But you don't ask any more questions, because you don't want to embarrass or anger her.

And then there's the fact that on random weekends Cassie just won't reply and usually misses school the following Monday. When you see her, she says she just pulled a sickie and what's the big deal? Anyway, the weekends when she's around and you do hang out are amazing. Together, you disappear into the London framed in postcards. The London of cathedrals and columns and royal parks which the tourists get to see but your parents barely ever have time to take you. Like you're doing today...

Suddenly Cassie rouses from her thoughts and turns towards you grinning.

—Sumaiya!! I thought you ghosted me! Why didn't you reply when I messaged?

—Sorry only saw as I was leaving

—So, your parents believed you then?

At this, you both smile knowingly. Her mum's white and is a thousand times less strict than your parents and both of you always laugh at how she seems to get away with anything when you can't.

She stumps out the cigarette and laces an acrylic manicured hand through your arm before you wander into the station. With your body now intertwined in hers you feel the tension from the disagreement with Mariam lift. Whenever Cassie's around you feel instantly looser, as though something within you has been untied, although you can never say exactly why.

You make your way through the barriers and down the stairs to the Westbound platform. You ask where she wants to go, expecting to hear Knightsbridge because she loves walking outside the lavish window displays at Harrods and pointing out what she'd buy if she was a millionaire. Or people-watching Saudi Arabian royals gliding past in diamond rimmed Lamborghinis and the Chanel-bag-attired wives of oligarchs on shopping trips.

—Let's go British Museum

—Why there?

—Because last school trip I never got to see what I wanted. It was long spending all that time looking at Sutton Hoo rather than something actually interesting like the Greeks or the Egyptians

You never thought of Cassie as remotely interested in museums. You're surprised she even remembers the name of the exhibition you saw. On trips she's always just snuck off to the café instead of looking round but, as ever, she's full of surprises.

—Alright then let's go there

You exit the tube at Holborn and make your way through teeming streets, your Air Force 1 footsteps disrupted intermittently by a stream of double deckers, black cabs and cyclists until you arrive at the museum. Wandering across the courtyard, you feel something eerie about the statues which stare down from the pediment, but you push these feelings aside as you enter.

Inside, you wander aimlessly through the Egyptian gallery, but a whirl-pool of bodies swirls round anything that captures your attention. Before long, you're in another room beside a glass case housing a medium-sized black pot, depicting three women around a seated one examining scrolls. Each figure is swaddled in folds of cloth rippling over their bodies like fountains, whilst their hair is coiled atop their heads like coronets. You read the sign which says that the sitting woman is thought to be a legendary Greek poet called Sappho, and that the pot itself was molded 3000 years ago.

Studying the object more closely, you begin to feel unbalanced, almost like your soul was a door that's just been rammed off one of its hinges and is flapping helplessly open. You have a sense of being stared at, as though these painted figures are watching you back.

Henry Reichard grew up on a sheep farm in rural Maryland. He studied Mathematics and Physics at Yale, then spent a year in Latin America before coming to the UEA. He writes primarily speculative fiction and is currently working on a psychological novel set in Buenos Aires.

hal.reichard@gmail.com

Letter from the Asylum
An extract from the first chapter of a novel

The purpose that guided him was not impossible, though it was
supernatural. He wanted to dream a man; he wanted to dream
him in meticulous entirety and impose him upon reality.
  —Jorge Luis Borges, 'The Circular Ruins'

My unraveling began eight months ago. I remember the day, the hour,
the hair-thin moment—the clock's three hands all between four and five,
the curtains undrawn, a gray moth alighting on my desk. I was sitting in
Clarín's smallest newsroom, gazing at the Hospital of San Moreno: an
ugly building with a gothic countenance, within which my wife lay dying.
I had spent the afternoon writing a sports article that condemned River
Plate's humiliating loss to Boca Juniors. The other reporters had already
left. Our editor had gone to make maté. In another half hour I would leave
the newsroom and go to sit beside Marcela.

'Eduardo,' a voice called from the back.

I turned. My editor stood behind me. He was an obese man with long gray
hair and a macabre sense of humor. His eyes and face had been hardened
beyond pity after twenty years of reporting on crime. In his left hand, he
held the still-steaming maté. In his right, the latest edition of *La Nación*.
He thrust the paper toward me.

'Read the cover story,' he said. In answer to my questioning look, he
added, 'It concerns Natalia Prieto.'

I snatched the paper from him.

'It's impossible,' I said at last. 'How could she possibly have written
another book? In her current condition?'

'It's the truth,' he said. 'I obtained an advance copy from the publisher
this morning and skimmed the first chapter during lunch. You should read
it. The protagonist reminded me of you.'

'What do you mean?' I asked.

My editor chuckled and said nothing. He laid the gourd down, turning
it slightly, so that the *bombilla* faced me. I sipped the maté (which was

far too strong). Then he rummaged in his bag and withdrew a thin book.

He handed it to me. The cover was set with a faded image of Picasso's *Accordionist.* Above it, in thin black letters, was the famous name: Natalia Prieto. Below was the enigmatic title: *Retrato de una muerte.*

—

Natalia Prieto. The woman who, by her late twenties, had already surpassed Borges, Casares, Cortázar, Ocampo. The woman whose stories had once filled half of *Sur,* who had achieved international fame at a time when our country's fabulists were still unknown beyond Latin America. And the woman who, at the age of thirty-six, had descended into a bout of fitful lunacy, which eventually brought her to the asylum dedicated to San Martín, in which she had remained for the past eleven years. The fact that *Retrato de una muerte* had been written by such a woman was reason enough for it to be published. The fact that it was completely incomprehensible was a slight disadvantage.

Even so, Prieto's devotees rushed to the bookstores. The publisher made a fortune. The scholars began puzzling over it, picking it apart, trying to find something they could make sense of. Lispector, Faulkner, even Joyce (in all but his last novel)—all these were more easily comprehended. The *Retrato* seemed to be an anarchy of language. For two months, hardly anyone dared to say anything about it at all. Until finally, in early August, señor Borges himself wrote this:

It is a pitiable madness and an impoverishing one, the madness of expecting a great new novel from a once-great author. The spark of youth does not often resurface in the desolation of senility; unfortunately (but not unexpectedly) it would have been better for all concerned if no one had troubled the once-inimitable Prieto in her asylum, asking for a new book...

With that brief-but-scathing critique (which Borges later regretted and recanted), the floodgates were opened. Of course it was common knowledge that Prieto was insane. Even her most ardent followers—those readers who declared themselves to be initiates of the Order of the Blank Scroll that she describes in 'Los analfabetos,' or People of the Mirrors, like those in 'Inversión de los elementos'—even such readers, the cultists of Prieto, had to admit that since the fire which claimed her daughter's life in the summer of 1952, their idol had been quite thoroughly mad. Until now, few had dared to slander her work. But with Borges's condemnation of the *Retrato*, she was subjected for the first time to scorn, ridicule, and derision. Her critics, long ignored, took the opportunity to condemn not just her latest novel, but her entire oeuvre. The cultists rushed to her defense. A thousand vehement articles denounced and defended the *Retrato*. Fistfights became commonplace in departments of literature. On one occasion, my editor told me of an actual duel—with pistols, no less!—between a supporter of Prieto and one of her critics.

(He told me that the two men fired simultaneously. The critic was struck in the chest and died soon after; the supporter collapsed, convulsing, and surgeons found the bullet lodged in his brain. Improbably, this second man made a full recovery, with only a single detriment: he had lost the ability to read. The supporters of Prieto immediately recalled the first, holy sentence of '*Los analfabetos*'—*You shall know the chosen by this sign: that the curse of literacy has been struck from them.* The Order of the Blank Scroll declared this man to be their foremost scion. Among them, he is called the Martyr of Prieto.)

So it went for many weeks. Marcela's condition worsened; the doctors told me not to give up hope, but privately I became convinced it was only a matter of time. I spent my mornings at the newsroom, my evenings at her bedside. But in my nights, in my every free hour, I dedicated myself to a verbal dissection of *Retrato de una muerte*.

From the first, I had been disconcerted by the name of Prieto's narrator. My editor was not the only person who pointed it out; for weeks after the *Retrato's* publication, the other reporters joked about my fictional alter ego, and I laughed—or pretended to laugh—with them. I did not enjoy sharing a name with any fabulist's creation. Yet I consoled myself: 'Eduardo Castillo' was not such an uncommon name; Prieto might easily have chosen it at random from a phonebook. That coincidence could, perhaps, be attributed to chance. The fact that her protagonist also happened to be a journalist—well, journalism was not such a rare profession either. Surely more unlikely things had happened to other men. But then there were other similarities between the narrator and me, less perceptible to others ... and these were less easily explained.

There were chance expressions and turns of phrase he used, many of which I also favored. There was his habit of pinching himself in the morning to make sure he had really woken up, or his tendency to count his freckles in the mirror, to verify that his face had not changed overnight. There was the offhand anecdote on page fifty-four—'I suffer from a recurring nightmare:

I dream that I am a reflection set deep within a mirror, and that I will die if the real Eduardo looks away from me.' How could the invention of such a dream be mere coincidence? And if it wasn't coincidence, how could Prieto have learned that, as a child, I suffered from that exact nightmare?

'You are searching for illusions and phantasms within the shadows,' my therapist said. 'You are trying to self-mythologize, as you have done before. This book is no different from all the others.'

'This one is different. I know it is.'

'What was it you told me last year, after you finished Sabato's *Sobre héroes y tumbas*? Here, I have a note of it somewhere.' She opened one of several thick folders on her desk that bore my name, flipped to a date from the previous August, withdrew a transcript of one of our sessions, began to read it aloud. '"As soon as I saw that Sabato's protagonist shared my last name, I knew there had to be a link between us. My suspicions deepened when I read of his romance with Alejandra, so like my own with Marcela. And when I discovered Martín's fearful obsession with blindness, I knew that he and I were—'"

'I remember all of that,' I snapped. 'I was disturbed then. I was irrational. I had just learned of Marcela's diagnosis.' I sat up straight on the couch, turned to my therapist. 'But I'm not irrational now. The similarities between myself and Prieto's narrator are too numerous, too *compelling*, to be mere coincidence. He speaks like me. He *thinks* like me.'

'Eduardo, how can you be sure your lives are identical? From what I've heard, this *Retrato* is complete gibberish.'

I shook my head and reclined again on the couch.

My therapist told me in a soothing yet condescending voice that the *Retrato's* narrator was no different from all the other fictional characters I had identified with in previous sessions. She reminded me of how certain I had been three years ago that I was born and shaped within a dream, like the mystic in Borges's '*Las Ruinas Circulares*.' (I overcame this delusion only after setting fire to the smallest finger of my left hand. The flames recognized my substance, my reality: they burned me, unlike the dream-man in Borges's tale, who could pass through fire unscathed.)

But the more I studied the *Retrato*, the more troubled I became. Of course, my therapist was right: the book was mostly gibberish. Its rare moments of lucidity were concealed in pages and pages of indecipherable prose. One could not be sure how old the narrator was, precisely where he lived, what actually happened to him in the waking world, and what he merely imagined. Everything was uncertain—fantasy and reality were continually conflated. Yet the fantasies this fictional Eduardo had! They were terrible things.

I began to dream of the scenes in the novel: the death in the ninth chapter, the depression in the tenth, the suicide in the eleventh. *La Nación* reported that Prieto had dictated the words to her husband, Tomás, during his monthly visits. She sat in her chair, rambling, and he copied down everything she said, organizing it into scenes, then chapters, then finally a book. I began to suspect that Tomás had spied upon me between these visits. I feared that he had told Prieto about my life, and that she (for obscure reasons) had decided to use me as a model for the *Retrato's* narrator. And yet even this would have been insufficient, for there were details in Prieto's novel that Tomás could not have discovered unless he had the ability to read minds.

I grew vexed, anxious. I did not know what to think. Prieto remained in the asylum, oblivious to everything. Marcela grew sicker and sicker. I continued writing sports articles and profiles for *Clarín.* I knew only that I had to find a way to speak with Prieto. I had to find out how she had written her *Retrato.*

Kinjal Sheth is a 24-year-old writer from Kenya. In 2020, she graduated from The University of St Andrews with First-Class Honours in English and Management. Her novel-in-progress, *Multinational,* is influenced by her studies in Management and explores topics including the insidiousness of corporate culture, neo-colonialism, and ESG issues in fashion.

kinjal.in.africa@hotmail.com

Multinational
Extract from the opening chapter of a novel

Reeva leaves for the station earlier than she'd intended to after her mind decides to play 'What If' for half the night and she spirals into bursts of full-fledged panic: What If I Wake Up Late or What If The Tube Has Major Delays And I Never Make It To The Interview. Dread settles somewhere between her ribcage and her diaphragm and jerks along with the train, even though she knows she can't *possibly* be late; Google tells her it is a one-hour journey, walking included, which gives her an entire thirty minutes to get there and compose herself.

Blurs of other people's conversations drift towards her as they rattle through unending darkness: two schoolkids who are obviously very late and therefore very fidgety (Reeva gives them a small smile which is met with glares), a corporate type who tells the guy sitting next to him that a recession is inevitable (his deadpan tone and lack of specifics scare her), and a couple – tourists, most likely – muttering sweet nothings to each other, one of which is 'you are the sun, and I revolve around you' (who says stuff like that post-Shakespeare? And at 8:30 freaking a.m. too?). She makes a mental note to text Amaya this glorious snippet after the interview.

The tube grates to a stop, and she finds herself in a part of London she has never had reason to be in before. She counts seven cranes hanging above the glassy skyline and tries to block out the intrusive thought of them falling on her, crushing her to bits. Somehow, this part of the city feels colder too. But everyone else on the street barrels towards whichever skyscraper is their destination, seemingly unaware of the near-freezing weather and sure of their place in the world. Reeva, on the other hand, follows the dots on the map. Adrenaline courses through her, and she feels like she might vomit the dry granola she forced herself to eat for breakfast. She makes it to the Tassel building with twenty-three minutes to spare and sends Amaya a text, telling her she is going in.

You'll kill it Xx, Amaya replies, with a certainty Reeva wishes she possessed.

She takes three deep breaths, smooths down her skirt (she regrets wearing pleather now), and attempts to stride in with the same confidence as the people on the streets. The automatic doors whir open and immediately, Reeva is ensconced in a rosy scent. She wonders if they have placed invisible diffusers everywhere. She walks in awe to the behemoth of the reception desk in front of her; the Google photo didn't do justice to its vastness. She questions whether they wanted visitors to be impressed or intimidated by its sheer scale – or both.

Two receptionists sit at opposite ends of the desk. Both wear shirts in Tassel's brand colours – a pink that the company has named 'Paloma' and a chartreuse they have called 'Vertis'. She notices echoes of these colours everywhere – even the stationery on the desk is pink and green. Behind the desk is the installation Reeva saw on Tassel's website during her interview prep. Thousands of iridescent tassels spell out 'TASSEL' across the wall. In person, the word glimmers with every minuscule movement she makes.

Next to the installation is a giant acrostic of Tassel's core values, printed in a font that reminds her of wedding invitations:

T – Transforming the fashion industry through a stakeholder-oriented approach at every level of decision-making

A – Achieving the highest standards of social responsibility and transparency throughout our production processes, international subsidiaries, and supply chain

S – Satisfying our consumers' need for sustainable, slow fashion that is made to last

S – Supporting each employee so they can bring their best self to work every day

E – Enriching the future of fashion through conscious collaboration with each other and with industry partners

L – Leading the way through *Kaizen* to create a memorable store experience for our consumers

'Hi, welcome to Tassel! I'm Nancy. How can I help?' the receptionist nearest to Reeva asks, interrupting her nosing around.

'Hi, yes, thank you! My name is Reeva Patel. I'm here for my Graduate Scheme interview with Iris Appleton?' After a time lag, she notices her voice has risen into a screechy question mark.

'Of course, darling. Give me a moment. Why don't you take a seat there?' she says, pointing towards the pink velvet armchairs Reeva had admired on Google the day before.

Reeva gives her what she hopes looks like a grateful smile and ends up plunging back into a chair, her skirt rustling. The other receptionist glances at her, his forehead scrunching up. Reeva's throat constricts. She wishes she brought a water bottle with her. She notices what looks like a water dispenser at the other end of the foyer but it looks too sleek to actually be one, so she decides not to make a bigger fool of herself by trying to figure out how to use it.

She whispers the words her mother used to tell her before exams like a mantra: 'They're not going to eat you', when a lady who may well be a model sashays towards her. Her heels glide across the herringbone floor with a panache Reeva never thought possible in raised, balance-defying shoes. As she draws closer, Reeva smells the woody heart notes of what she recognises as very expensive French perfume – possibly *Baccarat Rouge* (nothing below two hundred pounds could smell *that* good).

'Hi Reeva, I'm Iris! Welcome to Tassel, it's lovely to finally meet you,' she says. Her voice is husky and reminds Reeva of actresses saying brand names at the end of ads for Swiss watches, their voices transforming into a sultry, lingering whisper. Reeva's imposter syndrome creeps back in and she croaks a hello. Her stomach somersaults painfully and it takes all her strength not to wince in front of Iris. She realises she has missed half of Iris's sentence.

'—and who doesn't like conducting interviews in a room with safari-themed décor?' Iris giggles.

Reeva says 'absolutely', hoping this is an appropriate answer to her kind chatter. She can tell Iris is trying to put her at ease, but at this point, she can feel her heartbeat in her temple. They walk down a corridor on to an open-plan floor. She cranes her neck and counts six floors above them. Reeva tries not to gasp as they pass a central courtyard, which has been transformed into an indoor garden, complete with mini waterfall burbling away. A cherry blossom tree stands in the centre, its flowers in bloom despite the season. It occurs to her that even the garden conforms to Tassel's colour scheme.

Around the courtyard – which Iris tells her is called 'The Atrium' – people lounge on Paloma-coloured sofas or at standing desks. Finally, she has seen Tassel's inner sanctum – the part of the company hidden from the Internet. Instead of the quiet she had expected, excited chatter wafts towards her from all angles.

They reach the end of the corridor. Iris holds a door open and Reeva's stomach

somer   saults   again.

—

Reeva realises Iris was referring to The Nairobi Room when she said 'room with safari-themed décor'. Inspired by Tassel's Nairobi subsidiary, the room forces her back home. Its walls are covered in a hyper-realistic painting of Nairobi National Park at sunset, complete with giraffe silhouettes. A wooden table stretches out across the room, and when she looks down, she realises she is stepping on sleek fake grass. Pain settles in Reeva's chest and she reminds herself that she must pass this interview because she cannot – will not – go back home. Back to her family's tarnished reputation, back to the false accusations. When it finally occurs to her to turn around, she notices two other people, a man and a woman, watching her. Her cheeks heat up.

'It's incredible, isn't it? All our interviewees have the same reaction,' the woman says, grinning. Her face has an impossibly dewy glow and Reeva is tempted to ask her for makeup tips.

'I'm Jenny,' she continues, 'I work on the Graduate Success Team.'

'Hi, I'm Reeva, lovely to meet you!' By now, her voice has completed its transition into pathetic squeak and she clears her throat as quietly as possible in an attempt to sound passably normal.

The man introduces himself as Jay and mentions that he works on the People Team with Iris.

'So, shall we get started?' Iris asks no one in particular as she takes a seat across from Reeva.

Reeva nods and rummages in her bag for her notebook and pen; she has brought them along to convey an impression of professionalism. Her stomach cramps again, and she is shocked by the havoc her brain is wreaking on her body. She wonders if they chose the Nairobi Room to put her at ease, not knowing it would have the exact opposite effect.

'We were super impressed by your qualifications, Reeva!' Jenny begins. 'Can you please tell us what brought *you* to Tassel?'

Reeva tries to ignore her knotted stomach.

'Of course,' she says, unsure herself of where her answer is going. She tells them about her interest in fashion, a PR internship she once did for a fledgling menswear brand, that Tassel is doing things differently because of its commitment to slow fashion, and finally, that Tassel's core values resonate with her strongly. She shies away from mentioning that Tassel is her dream company, in case it is too much. Her answer is punctuated by Jay typing on his laptop at a painful pitch and part of her wants to tell him to please stop.

'Great answer, absolutely. We take pride in doing things the *right way* here,' Iris responds, her peaceful tone calming Reeva somewhat. 'So, as you may already know, all three grad schemers rotate through departments in their first year. Are you particularly interested in working in a specific department or departments?'

Reeva shocks herself as she mumbles, 'I think the Finance team. I'd be really interested to see how accounting works across Tassel's responsible business model. I read in the annual reports that Tassel is one of the first implementers of an ESG balance sheet, and it would be wonderful to be involved...'

She tapers off, not knowing what else to add, and Jay resumes typing. Reeva hopes she won't be held to this answer – she cannot imagine working in Finance, squinting at Excel sheets for eight hours a day and often overtime. She hopes they realise that she doesn't have any suitable qualifications and that no amount of training is likely to help; her undergrad was in English and Management. Not Accounting.

Iris and Jenny nod. She notices then that they are wearing the same billowy marsala-coloured blouses from Tassel's A/W collection. Unlike her sweating in her pleather skirt, they are coolly elegant. Reeva crosses her legs and to her dismay, her skirt rustles again so that she only hears half of their next question which she realises is something about her aspirations and where she sees herself in five years (if only she knew), what subsidiary she'd like to spend the second year of the scheme in (she says any and immediately regrets it in case they send her back home, and proceeds to tack on Milan to the end of her ramble) and how she perceives her strengths will fit into Tassel (here, she word vomits all the reasons she made up yesterday, throwing in resilience and agility, just in case like *everyone else* on LinkedIn, they too are looking for those).

'Now for the fun part,' Jay says, looking away from his laptop for the first time. 'We hold an office Olympiad every year. What sport would you like to see added to it?'

Everything disintegrates at that moment
and all she can hear is
blood whooshingthroughherears
like a waterfall

A. McLay Sparling is a writer living in Norwich.

The Sound of the Little Death
A short story

Now, the sun is in the west. The father sees this. He sits at the desk by the window. Not writing, instead reading. Reading about the least interesting philosopher. According to this philosopher, when the man returns to this cave, he is beaten to death with, what the father translates as, 'the large rock'. The father picks up the pen. He puts it down next to the mug. He takes sips of tea from the mug and watches the birds on the branch nearest the window. The tea spills onto the desk, the liquid drips onto the floor. His face is relaxed, he is accustomed to spills.

Raising the right hand to the curled strands of hair around the forehead. He looks as natural as ever, the legs crossed, one over the other. The left hand moves, twitching around the desk. The dog sits. The window frames the view of trees and trees and the deep rich lake.

Dim light. The father is in the bath. The dog waits, as he often does, he peers underneath the door. If the father were to look at the door, he might see the small keen snout, the slip of pink tongue, but the father does not look at the door, he does not look at the door again.

The whine escapes the dog. Time does not makes sense to him.

—

Now, the sun is in the east. Up here on his hill, in his concrete house, in the house he designed, the daughter sits at his desk by his window. She can hear the birds and the wind, and the steady sound of leaves moving against other leaves. Her face, lit by the sun, is tilted up, tilted towards the warmth. Down her back is a plait of hair, long and thick with flecked strands of red. Her right hand strokes loose strands from around her face and hovers above her chin.

Her face is parallel with his window. Her eyes blink occasionally. His view from the window was one of trees and trees and a pale lake. Long legged women are swimming in the water. She stands and moves closer to his window. Her jaw moves backwards and forwards; these movements are slight, her tongue sits on the edge of her lip. Her hand is on his window ledge, rubbing his round water mark, the type caused by his hot mugs. She can hear the birds more loudly. The birds, when flying, make an energetic *tick* sound and then a long *seep*. Once on the branches they make a low soft *sib*.

The daughter shifts his papers around his desk, sheet upon sheet, thin white layers. They crackle as they move. Her hips press into his desk as she reaches towards the right-hand side and picks up his stained mug with her right hand. She stands holding the pile of his paper to her breasts with her left hand, in her right hand, his mug. For years she was waiting to understand, but no longer, now she is full of comprehension. She sees dust has gathered in the carved corners of his desk.

Sib. Sib. Sib.

In the afternoon, the daughter returns upstairs, to his bedroom. Empty, but for his black bed, with his headboard made of geometric roses, roses gathered together in wrought iron, and his air purifier. The daughter stands in the middle of his room and moves her head slowly from side to side. His air purifier rotates air in one long breath. She walks over to his socket, leans against a swell of his wall, and unplugs his machine.

His room is silent. She lies down on his bed. Her left hand moves to her right arm and starts stroking her forearm. Her fingers travel from the soft centre of her inner elbow down the cushion of her forearm, to the centre of her wrist. No sooner have her fingers reached her wrist than they glide back, hovering over her moist skin, returning to the centre of the soft underside of her elbow. A gentle almost inaudible sound, something between a sigh and a rasp. Her fingertips make slight dents as she holds them against her arm. She sucks her wrist.

The daughter stands in his hallway, low evening light streams through his windows. She removes his photographs one by one from his wall, wiping away the dust with a cloth and placing them inside her cardboard box. In his largest framed photograph: her mother sits on the terrace of the house. Slick leaves shroud her from the sun. A triangle of orange light is on her cheek, her face tilts up, perhaps towards the warmth. Their maid stands in the background holding a tray.

Now, the daughter looks at another photograph: the mother is leaning against his wall, body smooth in linen clothes, clothes cut to encourage thought. Her mother had a lithe body then, kept firm by hours spent in a room called the study where she did aerobics. Down her back is a complicated plait of hair, long and thick with flecked strands of red, her right hand hovers above her chin. At her feet their maid sits with a bowl and a sponge. Another photograph: their maid brushes the mother's hair, brushes her hair into a taut bun. The mother's face tilts up, towards the warm hands of their maid. The daughter puts down his photograph and places it in her cardboard box with the rest.

In his bathroom. Brown, cloudy water bursts from his tap. The daughter stands looking into his mirror. Slowly and with care, her fingers move from one shirt button to the next. She moves from her button nearest her neck downwards, she begins at the space where her shirt opens out into a collar and moves downwards. Once all the buttons are undone she takes off her shirt, she takes off her trousers, she removes her underwear and stands. She strokes her stomach. Then she walks over to the bath and moves downwards, underneath the water. Her lips make the shape of an O.

Underneath his bathroom door a small keen snout appears, a slip of pink tongue She stands and steps out of the bath. Water drips onto his tiles. His door is opened, his dog sits at the base of his bath watching her.

Beside his house, after the mound of the hill is his long mud footpath that leads to his field of tall lavender grass. Here she walks his dog. The ground becomes wetter, sodden with water and salt, until succulent samphire and cord-grasses grow. Perhaps she and the dog can hear the sea wrapping itself around the coast.

The daughter wears the father's wax coat, his hem brushes her knees. Her fathers dog must take several steps to match her one. His tail wags. When the dog pants, the sound is *chaff*. She holds his leash loosely in her right hand, leaning over his dog to undo the collar. The tips of the long grass graze her elbow. His dog runs. His dog runs through a field, splashing. She turns and walks back alone.

She walks until the mud becomes drier and the sea purslane and sea aster and sea lavender have returned. Her light from her phone sticks to the back of his door. She takes his handle in her hand and pushes his door open with her shoulder.

Inside her father's kitchen, her fingers travel from the soft centre of her inner elbow down the cushion of her forearm and to the centre of her wrist. No sooner have they reached her wrist than they swiftly glide back, hovering over her skin, returning to the centre of the soft underside of her elbow. She looks as natural as ever, her legs crossed, one over the other. It is unlikely that in the distance she can hear her father's dog, running, searching for her through the fields. *Chaff, chaff, chaff.* It is unlikely, but not impossible.

Emily Spicer was born in Germany and grew up in Kent. She has a BA in Art History from the University of Oxford and works as a freelance arts journalist, writing for a range of magazines. She is also co-editor of *The Lasdun Review*, a new literary magazine.

El.spicer@protonmail.com

Marshland
The opening of a novel

CHAPTER ONE

A tile danced on its pegs, waggling like a loosened tooth. It shattered against its neighbour and the noise shoved Flea awake. She stared at the pitched ceiling of her attic room, her ears burning for new sounds. The glow-in-the-dark stars Blu-Tacked above her bed had faded, but she could still see their ghostly afterglow if she didn't stare straight at them. She rolled out of bed with her hands stretched out and found the wall and the cold, plastic square of the light switch. She flicked it on and off and on again, but the room remained dark.

The landing downstairs looked endless. Her father's bedroom door was open just a crack. She pushed it gently and called out in a loud whisper, but only the wind answered as it whined in through a paper-thin gap in the window frame. She padded down the corridor, running her hand along the uneven plaster of the walls, guiding herself in the dark. At the bottom of the wooden stairs, where the darkness was thickest, she pushed open the door and entered the light of the pub. Her father's broad back was silhouetted against the glow of the fire and when he heard the wooden latch snap back into place, he turned to see his daughter standing barefoot in her pyjamas.

'Couldn't sleep?'

Flea shook her head and tiptoed across the cold brick floor, dragging a chair to the fireside.

'You won't sleep any better down here.'

She shrugged.

As she sat down opposite her father, a log shifted with a scratchy clunk, sending a stream of golden sparks shivering up the chimney. The last time the stack was cleaned a brick came loose and behind it the sweep found a tiny child's shoe, brittle and blackened from centuries of soot. He insisted on putting it back in its little tomb, so as not to undo any good luck. The thought of that lonely little shoe made Flea sad. That child was long gone now. He had been dead for hundreds of years, in fact. She felt tired at the thought. Hundreds of years. Hundreds and hundreds of years. As her eyelids dropped, she watched the amber liquid in her father's whisky glass blur to a golden ball. Hundreds is a lot of years to be dead.

When she woke, her father's chair was empty. The familiar room seemed strange and foreign now and the wind rumbled in the chimney breast, sending down a draft that caused the fire to tremble. On the walls, the spindly limbed shadows of tables and chairs broke into a frenzied dance. She pulled her knees to her chest and found that her legs were heavy with the weight of a blanket, which she gripped under her chin as she listened.

She listened for creaking floorboards, although she knew her father wasn't upstairs. She listened for noises in the cellar, too, but he never went down there at night. The rain was fierce now, pelting the leaded windows. He had gone, probably, to her grandpa's farm some miles away. He had been going there a lot lately, but never took her with him.

Flea wrapped the blanket about her shoulders and opened the heavy front door. The icy rain greeted her bare feet. There was a narrow, unmarked road in front of the pub and beyond that nothing but marsh veined with waterways and ditches, all invisible in the night. At the edges of the marsh was the sea, rising, chewing away at the flats, poisoning the earth with salt.

She waited on the threshold, staring out at the emptiness. She stood one foot on the other to keep her toes warm and waited until, at last, a slant of white headlights lit the flooding road. The lights bounced to a halt and her father climbed out of the driver's seat and ran to the back of the car. A woman got out of the passenger side and Flea recognised the stocky outline of Steph, the only farmhand her grandfather employed. Together, they pulled the old farmer out of the back, propping up his limp, narrow frame. His border collie walked beside them, her tail hanging in a low sickle, her black fur plastered to her back with the rain.

They came inside, bringing with them the smell of mud and other places. Flea's father picked up the old man and carried him upstairs as though he weighed no more than a child. The dog followed, tired and stumbling on the wooden steps. Steph watched and let out a long sigh. She mumbled to herself as she turned towards the fire, something about being too old, Flea couldn't quite hear.

'Jesus! I didn't see you there.'

Flea wondered whether her blanket had made her look like a ghost.

'What's wrong with grandpa?' she said.

'It must be past your bedtime.'

'I can't sleep. What's wrong with grandpa?'

'Well, love, he got caught up in the flood. The whole farm is underwater. He went out looking for the sheep, but they were grazing up near St Becket's church.'

'Is he dead?'

'He's just tired. It's been a long night for him.'

Steph shrugged off her coat, which was shiny with rain, and hung it over the back of a chair by the fire. She ruffled the water from her hair, briskly patted her round cheeks and sat down by the hearth. After a moment's stillness, she started to tug at her wellington boots.

'Steph.'

'Yes?'

'Have all the sheep drowned?'

'Most have, I reckon. They were bobbing around like little woolly islands, except a few what were fighting to keep their heads up.' She finally removed her first boot and stood it by the fireplace, then started to pull on the second. 'Water didn't quite get into the church, though, cos it's on a higher bit, and—' She heaved off the second boot with a grunt. 'That's where we found him, lying on the floor. He was soaked through. Must've waded a fair distance.'

'He's not breathing right,' Flea's father said, coming down the stairs. 'I'm going to sleep in his room tonight. The roads will be flooded, so I'll call the doctor in the morning. You can take my bed, Steph. There are some clean towels in the cupboard on the landing. It's bedtime for you, too,' he said to Flea, jerking his head towards the stairs.

'We won't be able to get into school tomorrow if the roads are flooded.'

'In that case, you'll have to help out around here. So bed. Now.'

'Steph,' Flea said.

'Yep?'

'Is it the sea what's flooded everything?'

'The sea?'

'Yeah, you know, cos it's rising and that. Has it got to us now?'

'No, the sea's miles off. It'll be the ditches and the old canal. They're all silting up. There's no one left to care for this place. Marsh is wilding back to what it was.'

'Bed,' Flea's father said.

She pulled the blanket higher around her shoulders and climbed the stairs slowly, hoping to catch extra bits of conversation before she reached the top. But her father and Steph remained frustratingly quiet.

Upstairs, the door to the spare room was open just wide enough to peer inside. Somewhere in the darkness lay her grandfather, without bones enough to stand, as though the marsh had tried to eat him up, only to spit him about again.

The morning arrived, cold and dripping. The wind complained some way away but the worst of the storm had passed. Downstairs, Steph was crouching by the hearth, making a fresh fire. She touched a match to the balled-up newspaper that was packed into the grate and a yellow flare took hold, curling the newsprint to brittle flakes that wended their way up the chimney.

'Morning,' she said. 'How did you sleep?'

'OK.'

'You must be worried about your grandpa?'

Flea shrugged and said that she was because it was the right thing to say.

'He's in the right place, here, with you and your dad.' She pushed herself up to standing. 'Is this all the wood there is?' She pointed to the few logs left in a wicker basket. 'Where does your dad keep the rest?'

'In the garden, at the back.'

In the kitchen they found Flea's father surrounded by packets of meat – chicken legs, pork chops, dark slabs of liver, piled up on the countertops in plastic skins. A half-defrosted pheasant perched headless and naked on top of the gas stove, as though waiting patiently, either for a pardon or for the pot.

Steph went outside to fill the basket with logs. As she bent over, the wind gathered up her sandy hair and teased it into a little tornado on top of her head.

'Give me a hand, would you?' Flea's father was elbow deep in the freezer.

'What are you doing?'

'The power is still out.' He reached down and pulled out a pink lump of something in a bag. 'We can cook some of this today. Can't serve the chicken though. Bloody waste. Bring the bin over, love.'

Flea dragged the metal bin across the floor, then poured herself a bowl of cereal and topped it with lukewarm milk. Her father was squinting now, inspecting a smudged date written in black pen on a packet of mince.

'How can we cook if the electricity is off?'

'The ovens are gas. We can light them with a match.'

Her dad straightened and scratched his chest.

'Is Mick coming in to cook?' Flea asked through a mouthful of Coco Pops.

'His house flooded last night. Can't expect him to come in today. Maybe we should make some pies from this lot and sell them in the corner shop in Thorsden. Bugger it. I don't know.'

He stuck out his chin and scratched the stubble on his jaw this time. Flea noticed he was looking at her now with his thinking face on. She froze, a dripping spoon halfway to her mouth.

'Make yourself useful, would you, and go and check on your grandpa.'

'Do I have to?'

'Yes you have to.'

'I don't want to.'

'And take him a glass of water.'

Upstairs, Flea raised the latch on the door of the spare room. The room was dimly lit by the weak light leaking in through the thin blue curtains and there was a strange sour-sweet smell. Her grandfather lay on his back, his arms by his sides, his mouth slightly open, dark and wide. Sammy, the collie, was curled up at his feet, a wreath of black and white fur. She watched unmoving as Flea gently placed the glass of water on the little bedside table.

Flea hadn't seen her grandfather close-up for a long time. The farm had kept him busy and he'd become withdrawn in his old age. That's what her dad had told Mick. Withdrawn. Snails withdrew into their shells. It was like hiding. She looked at her grandpa's pale face. His eyeballs sat deep in their bony sockets like stones sinking into wet sand. Withdrawn, Flea said quietly to herself. He's been hiding. She looked now at his hands; she always noticed grown-up's hands. Her father's were big, padded bear paws, but her grandpa's were knobbly and full of blue veins that wrapped around the thin bones like tree roots. He was so still that she couldn't see him breathe. As she moved in closer, her heart ticking fast in her chest, Sammy let out a soft bark and started to wag her tail, beating it against the old man's leg. They looked at each other for a moment before the collie jumped off the bed with a clumsy thud and padded purposefully out of the door.

Boo is a neurodivergent writer and translator born in Bangkok. They studied for BAs in Fashion Design at the Accademia Italiana and in English with Creative Writing at Keele University. A multilingual reader, they are preoccupied with decentring the linguistic hegemony of the English language through stories that evoke nostalgia for the present.

boojiyoo@gmail.com
helloboo.com
twitter.com/pacemori

Only on you today, too, the sun shines
An excerpt from a coming-of-age novel set in modern-day Japan

NAOKI

Naoki has heard that Arne's mother is Japanese but he can't bring himself to believe it. Under the cherry blossom tree at the school gate, with sunlight making dappled patterns on his skin, Arne greets him with a smile. Light catches in his hair, turning it a colour that Naoki has only ever seen in snow and jasmine. He doesn't greet Arne back.

'Naoki, good morning!' Arne chirps and follows him, undeterred, down the walkway, past the assembly flag, up the main steps, inside the school building, chirping, chirping, 'Naoki? Naoki, did you sleep well last night? Hey, let's talk, Naoki-kun, hello?'

Naoki whirls around and glares at Arne who doesn't seem to understand that not everyone in this world is a friend.

Arne falters in his tracks, his carefree smile falling from his lips. A second later, it's back, brighter than before.

'I have something for you,' he says and opens his palm, revealing the bottle of Aller Screen he kept hidden in his fist. 'I don't get hay fever so I don't know but my mum says that this helps!'

When Naoki makes no attempt to accept it, Arne laughs and leans in, slipping the medicine inside Naoki's blazer pocket. 'I'm off to track practice now. See you in class!' He blows a kiss, then runs back outside into the sunlight, grinning like nothing has ever gone wrong in his life.

Naoki's gut twists painfully at the sight.

ARNE

It was just me and Souta going to the canteen for lunch because Takahiro had a meeting with his kyūdō team. Soon as we walked in, Masaya alerted Jirou and Jirou alerted their 1-B friends and then the six of them at that table turned to stare at us. I got a sense they'd been talking about me until a few seconds ago.

'Wanna go watch the girls' tennis try-out?' Souta said.

'Sure,' I said, relieved that I wouldn't have to eat while being eyeballed.

We grabbed yakisoba bread from the deli stand and went outside. There were rain clouds in the sky. Souta looked chilly so I asked if he wanted my jacket, and he gave me this slightly exasperated look, like he couldn't believe I'd even asked him that.

'Sorry for caring I guess,' I said before I could stop myself. Souta did a double-take. I'd just gone from sweet to making a snide remark within the span of ten seconds. Get your personality straight, Arune. I smiled wide and threw in a harmless laugh, praying he wasn't offended.

'Dude,' Souta said.

'What?'

Souta was already taking out his phone, sending Takahiro a voicenote on LINE, telling him what I had just said. He spoke about me as if I was a pet that had just done a really cool trick. I wasn't sure how to feel about that.

At the foot of a plum tree on our way to the tennis court, a tiny light-brownish grey lump of some bird was lying on its side. I got on my knees to take a closer look. The thing was so tiny, half the size of my palm, legs skinnier than toothpicks, feathers ruffled. I couldn't tell from just looking if it was still breathing.

Souta kneed my back. 'Just leave it. Someone'll clean it up.'

I got up and we kept walking and I soon forgot about that bird, but not the feeling it had given me. I don't have the language to explain every emotion I've ever felt. I don't think that I should. I thought maybe it was this calm-before-the-storm weather making me all sorts of uneasy. I kept looking back. I couldn't shake this strange sensation that something awful that was happening to someone somewhere else was about to happen to me too.

It started pouring down towards the end of lunch break. Everyone piled into the classroom, chatting, laughing over each other, cosy, excitable, brushing the rain off their clothes, shaking it out their hair. I wanted to soak it all in. Hygge. It'd been so long since I last felt that word I'd forgotten that it even exists, but here it was again, flown across two continents, brought into this room with me. My eyes searched for Naoki, my heart hammering. I was so sure that I'd catch him smiling. The room was flooded with it, this good feeling, shy of bursting. There was no way he couldn't feel it too.

I couldn't find him.

He wasn't sitting at his desk. He wasn't standing against any wall, or at any corner of the room. There, by the doorway at the back of the classroom, his tiny figure fluttered out of sight before I could even think of catching it.

NAOKI

A sudden downpour in the afternoon crushes the pollen-clogged air to the ground. These days, Naoki's throat hurts whenever it rains; a hot crushing kind of pain that the doctor said is all in his head, but knowing that hasn't made it less painful.

When he visits the nurse's office, Rika gives him lemon lozenges she knows he won't eat and lets him lie on scratchy cotton sheets until the weather clears. His sister's favourite season is spring because that's when everything comes back to life, but these days she no longer smiles at the day and tells him it's beautiful. Instead, her silence stretches like string across the sky on festival days, heavy with glowing lanterns and opulent with paper wishes.

He knows that his sister is waiting with held breath for summer because she has a brother who suffers when the world comes back to life.

ARNE

I kept my eyes on the door, anxious, restless again. Everyone had settled down. Class was about to begin. I didn't know where Naoki had run off to or why he hadn't yet returned. I didn't notice that Jirou had stopped beside my desk until he slapped his hand on it, making everyone jump.

'Hey, Arune,' he said with a real sleazy smile. Masaya who was standing behind him was already snickering. I exchanged a look with Souta. He didn't seem to know either how this was gonna go down. Soon as I said hello back, Jirou's smile stretched into a grin. In a very loud voice he said, 'Is it true that in Denmark two dudes can get married to each other?' and everyone cracked up like they thought same-sex marriage was a punchline.

'Yeah, and two girls can also get married to each other. Why's THAT funny?' I snapped. Just then, the sky flashed and thunder boomed, and the room went dead silent.

Jirou looked stunned, even though he was the one who had started it.

My face burned. In front of me, Souta was wearing the same expression as everybody else in the room. He didn't get why I had just snapped. Nobody did. Of course nobody did, because despite all their jokes about me being In Love With Naoki and having tried to nanpa him, nobody seemed to actually think that I was into guys.

It was as if queerness really was just a joke to them, not a possibility. I didn't know what that meant for me, the fact that I was Impossible. The only thing I knew for sure was that the truth did not matter—whether or not I liked Naoki for real was never the point. 'It's fun to make fun of someone so let's just keep doing it, everybody else is doing it too.' That's what everyone must've been thinking.

In hindsight I seriously regretted snapping at Jirou. I wasn't Arne anymore. I was Arune now, and Arune was supposed to be someone who this world could love easily, so it would've been better if I'd just given that same answer with a smile.

Yosano-sensei showed up to start Japanese class, and all throughout lesson I kept my head down, pretending not to notice the weirded-out glances people were sneaking at me.

Ha, ha.

Hygge, my arse.

Geworfenheit

An excerpt from R/U. HUMAN, a speculative A.I. novel set in near-future Bangkok.

Kon dreams now, and always: a concrete fortress under the infinite curve of a glass sky, palatial and sprawling, white on white on white, airy voiles and windows that reach from the floors to the ceilings. His footfalls through hallways soft across marble tiles veined in delicate grey. No matter which room he enters, sunlight tilts in through the glass at the angle that makes him squint. He shields his eyes and half makes out the washed yellows of a courtyard garden, grass and leaves baked lifeless, pale sands of its play area dappled by skeletal trees. In the corners of the frame

a flicker

of movement.

Pressing his hand to the glass causes it to explode, shards shredding his palm, hitting the floor in keen, quick notes. The nanotech in his veins seals his skin back together. The garden and playground have disappeared, and what is left is the scream-swallowing whiteness, these seamless lines of never-blinking nothings behind the

behind the
behind
be

```
. . .LOADING ADDITIONAL DATA
    > > >
    !ATTEMPT FAILED
. . .!ID SCAN REQUIRED
    > > >
    !INVALID USER
    !ACCESS DENIED
    !YOU HAVE NO PERMISSION TO ACCESS
    THIS DATA
```

```
||||||||||||||||||||||||||||||||||||[x]
          AN ALTERNATE ROUTE HAS BEEN
                MADE AVAILABLE
            WOULD YOU LIKE TO ACCESS?
            [YES]              [NO]
||||||||||||||||||||||||||||||||||||||||


      . . . DUPLICATING FILE PATH
          > > >
      . . . TRANSFERRING PERSONA
          > > >
          !TRANSFER COMPLETE
PRESS [E] TO LOAD FROM SAVE POINT
```

The window explodes, shards shredding Kon's palm, hitting the floor in keen, quick notes. The garden and playground have disappeared. Before him: a glitch in the hologrid.

Kon steps through.

Here, time stretches the way it does in desertscapes, where there is nothing but wind and sun and arid earth as far as the human eye can see. Here also, in the scream-swallowing whiteness, between the seamless lines of never-blinking nothings, is a different kind of eternal, the infinite curve of—*another flicker.*

His hand shoots out, closing around coarse rope. He tugs, and a wooden swing comes into focus, clacks and wobbles from one skeletal branch of a tree. A whisper of dry earth behind him makes him turn.

A child is sitting naked in the sandbox, building their replica of the concrete fortress. He only half-recognises this child, but his mouth opens and a name tumbles out, before his brain can ever hope to catch up.

The child blinks up, indistinct, light catching on their eyelashes. *You know who I am?*

No, he answers.

The child glances back down at the sand fortress, patting it lightly with small, grubby hands. Kon's eyes are drawn to their nape; the C4 of their cervical spine that appears to have been cut off midway, the fifth joint appearing below the clean, off-white line circling their neck.

Ai, he whispers.

The child looks back up, eyes now wide and clear. *You know who I am?*

Yes.

The child's gaze turns solemn, their brows furrowing. *Doesn't that scare you?*

Kon thinks about it. He is by nature slow to feel: slow to happiness, slow to anger, slow to despair, slow to love. *No,* he answers, but thinks that he could be, if he stayed here long enough.

It should, the child says.

Kon's head starts aching, in a thin line that bisects him, sparks of pain that prickle across his scalp. The child slides their little fingers over Kon's foot, around his ankle, up his calve, and brushes the grit on his knee away, nuzzling it after.

I'm tired, Kon mutters, closing his eyes, wishing for a place where he could do so without so much light shining through his eyelids, where he could lie down in the cool embrace of the dark and finally wake up.

Linda Temienor-Vincent is a writer, screenwriter and training facilitator from Lagos, Nigeria. She is the recipient of the 2021 Global Voices Prose Fiction Scholarship at UEA. She loves dancing, values quiet environments and likes the picturesque idea of sitting pretty at a piano and pretending to play it.

lee_temienor@yahoo.com

King Obakpororo Emujakporue
A short story

King Obakpororo Emujakporue, the Ovie of the Idjerhe clan in Bendel state, Nigeria, enjoyed early morning strolls through the dusty red roads of his community. He observed the men hurrying past, their heads bowed as they greeted him and rushed to their farms to check on their crops and traps. The women tended to the children and the wandering domestic animals; the young girls chuckled when he inquired about their wellbeing, then winked at him and disappeared through the banana plantation to fetch water at the Ethiope River.

The king ruled over twenty-five communities and had married one woman from each; they were often the prettiest, and he had numerous children. Ovie Idjerhe, as his people fondly referred to him, was young, handsome, kind, and an undefeated wrestling champion. After the gruesome death of his father – a suicide – Ovie Idjerhe took to the throne and ruled his people. He was known to be prudent in the matters of the kingdom, skilful in all wisdom and well favoured by the gods.

Whichever wife shared his bed at night smiled in the morning and spoke softly to the other wives. It was like a silent code to the one next in turn that the king's strength was that of a horse. Stories of the king's bedroom conquests filtered to the idle ears of wives frustrated with their husbands and unmarried maidens who seized opportunities at festivities to strut their waists, pose salaciously and smile to get the king's attention. The king had filled his slots for wives, but the rumour was that he had wandering eyes, and newly married attractive women stirred easy reactions in his groin.

The farming season marking the beginning of Ovie Idjerhe's fourteenth year was near. Hence, the king's council sent out town criers to remind the people of the five sacred days before this season.

The king would hold a feast for all of his people at the palace on the first day while Ohwo omraro (the seer) consulted with the gods to choose from the other four days when Ovie Idjerhe was to visit the river bank to offer sacrifices to the goddess. Unfortunately, Ohwo omraro never announced the set day; he would appear at dawn with the virgin maidens in the palace and accompany Ovie Idjerhe to the river. Ovie Idjerhe would then offer sacrifices as demanded by the goddess. He then expected the goddess to bless the Idjerhe clan: fertile lands, productive hunting seasons, and bountiful fishing expeditions.

The secretive nature of the ritual forced the women to delay their chores at the river until noon. The king also restricted his wives and daughters to their quarters. It was an abomination for him to set his eyes on any woman in the morning before he visited the goddess; the consequences for such a woman would be dire, and barrenness was only the start.

Edafe, the third commander of Ovie Idjerhe's warriors, had travelled in a hurry a few days before the five consecrated days to bring his new bride Ame-Ada from Warri secretly. He wanted Ame-Ada to benefit from the fertility blessings from the goddess, an assurance before their bedding ceremony that his marriage would produce children. For this to happen, Ame-Ada would have to serve in the king's palace when he hosted a feast, so Edafe bribed the chief cook of the palace to reserve a place for her. These positions were reserved for betrothed virgin maidens soon to be married. This was the tradition, but several men desperate for male children often subverted the process.

Ame-Ada was beautiful, endowed and skilful in playing the flute. She was offended that her husband entertained doubts about her fertility, but Edafe was strong-willed and always had his way. Only months ago, she had gone fishing at Ugborikoko River and, on her return, had seen an injured and bloodied Edafe by the path; robbers had attacked him on his way back from an errand for Ovie Idjerhe. Nevertheless, she cared for him and a bond formed.

Early on the morning of the feast, Ovie Idjerhe had a white cloth with cowries tied over his left shoulder. He proceeded to his private shrine room to prepare for the cleansing ritual, which was to be carried out by the Ohwo omraro. It was tradition to do this before the commencement of the feast. Ovie Idjerhe passed by the five virgin maidens who held white cocks and stood linearly before the entrance. The fifth maiden held open the door, and her eyes locked with his; he couldn't look away. He watched as a shy Ame-Ada lowered her head; he had never seen her before. She was stunning, and he knew he had to see her again.

The clattering sound of the bell-decorated staff – in the hands of Ohwo omraro – interrupted Ovie Idjerhe, and he hurried into the shrine. Ohwo omraro signalled the maidens into the shrine. He stood before a wall; several painted goat skulls were on display on the floor, and two large clay pots placed on each of his sides spewed out steam. He rang a bell, and the maidens circled Ovie Idjerhe. Ohwo omraro approached each of the young women and slit the throat of the cocks, and then instructed them to lift the bleeding chickens over the bowed head of Ovie Idjerhe, one after the other. After the maidens did this, he ordered them to leave the shrine and prepare for the feast.

Ohwo omraro chanted a few words over Ovie Idjerhe's head; then, he threw a set of twigs to the floor.

'I keep seeing a pair of hands emerge from a raging fire,' Ohwo Omraro began to speak.

Ovie Idjerhe wiped the blood from his face and looked up at him. 'What does that mean?'

'I have asked the gods but they have remained silent. What troubles me is that each time I grabbed these hands, the face of a strange woman with fiery eyes appeared and the royal palace disappeared in an instant.'

'And you say the gods were silent when you asked them?'

'Yes, my king. This has never happened before.'

'Have you tried consulting the seer of Oghara?'

'I did, my king, but you know I must tread carefully in case it affects the royal household. But, interestingly, he gave me a proverb which further confused me.'

'But why will the gods not give you an interpretation of a vision they showed you?'

'I cannot answer that, my king.'

'What is the proverb?'

'He said, "When it is raining, birds do not sing in the forest, therefore the wild bat is neither a bird nor a rat." Then he said, "Tell your king, the ladder that takes one up may as well smash one to the ground."'

'Should we share this with the council members?'

'No, my king. Give me some time to unravel this mystery.'

'Then hurry.'

'Yes, my king.'

The thunder rumbled as Ovie Idjerhe knelt before Ohwo Omraro to complete the ritual. They both stared up at the ceiling made from dried grass.

'Rain? We have never had rain before the start of the farming season,' Ovie Idjerhe complained.

The celebration at Idjerhe was in full swing; warriors were stationed at vantage points around Idjerhe while Ovie Idjerhe sat far away in the palace courtyard. He watched council members grin at the young female dancers, who twisted their waists to please their spectators. The muscles of the young men on the drums bounced in rhythm to these dance steps. The people of Idjerhe laughed and ate. Some joined in the dance; others separated into different age group discussions. Ovie Idjerhe was glad to see his chiefs relaxing from their usual rigid selves. Last night, they'd had a complex debate on how to proceed with the war on the Warri clan over the attack on Edafe and the theft of the king's gold.

Ovie Idjerhe's eyes zoomed past the young maidens serving a fresh round of palm wine and bush meat, to see Ame-Ada. He had forgotten about her for a while and was preoccupied with Ohwo omraro's mysterious vision. So he watched as she approached him with a tray of roasted meat.

'My king.' She bowed her head and stretched the tray before him.

'I have never seen you in this kingdom before today,' he said.

She laughed lightly. 'My king cannot know all the maidens in the kingdom.'

'You are right. But I certainly know all of the beautiful ones and yet I missed you.'

Ame-Ada smiled. 'My king, where would you like me to place the tray?'

'In my shrine, where I first saw your lovely eyes.'

'But, my king—'

'Shhh, but nothing. You have found favour with the king. Find your way there, discreetly.'

Ame-Ada placed the tray on the royal stool beside the king and turned away.

Ovie Idjerhe picked up a piece of meat and put it into his mouth as he watched a group of young men, covered in camwood powder, with white mixture drawn around their eyes, perform a mock show of cutting themselves with charmed daggers, which drew no blood.

He sipped his drink but almost choked as Ohwo omraro appeared at his side.

'My king, it has been revealed.'

'Ohwo omraro, you don't need magic today.' He sighed.

'I apologise my king, but this was urgent.'

'What is it?'

'You must proceed tomorrow deep into the Ohahe forest and undergo a cleansing at Enovwo shrine. This you must do before any sacrifices are to be made to the river goddess.'

'Did the gods tell you why?'

'She insists that, if Idjerhe is to have a fruitful season and win a war over Warri, then she must lie with the king.'

Ovie Idjerhe laughed heartily. 'Is the River goddess now starved of a man?'

'My king, caution! She can hear even from the depths of many waters.'

'But she can have any man, why does she want the king?'

'I cannot say.'

'Preposterous!'

'Yes, it seems so but the way of spirits are strange.'

'So the cleansing will stop her?'

'Yes, my king. May your reign be long,' Ohwo Omraro said and disappeared.

Ovie Idjerhe excused himself from the gathering and went to his shrine. He smiled as Ame-Ada rose from the stool.

'You are so beautiful. Tell me, why have I never seen you?'

'I do not know, my king. Perhaps you should focus on people generally, instead of the beautiful ones.'

'Then, I won't be the king if I don't focus on the most important people.'

'And that would be the beautiful people, my king?'

'No. That would be the people that make me significant on the throne.'

Ovie Idjerhe placed his crown on the stool and pulled her into the ante-chamber of the shrine.

The mat rustled on the floor as they kissed and played, and then he knew her. They rested and played again as they took turns labouring under each other's weight.

Finally, Ovie Idjerhe laid on his back, his hands under his head. He smiled at Ame-Ada.

'You are special,' he said and stroked her hair.

'And you my king are truly a horse.' Ame-Ada chuckled as she stood up from the floor and put on her clothes.

'You were gliding like a fish and knew what to do, it was almost difficult to believe you were a virgin if I wasn't penetrating you myself.'

'I know,' she responded. 'Your father said the very same words during his reign.'

Ovie Idjerhe jumped up. Ame-Ada's eyes immediately turned white, and she transformed into the revered glowing goddess of the Ethiope River. She played an ominous tune from her flute and then stretched out her transparent hand to him. 'Obakpororo Emujakporue, this is your manhood.'

Ovie Idjerhe's eyes widened as he placed his trembling hands over his groin but felt nothing.

'You will not go to the Enovwo shrine,' she continued. 'There will be no war with Warri and your nights with mortal women are over. You are mine,' she said and then disappeared.

Ovie Idjerhe tried to speak, but no words came out; his voice was gone, and he grabbed his throat and tried in futility to speak as his eyes darted from side to side in the shrine room.

END

Louise Tucker is a writer, freelance editor and writing tutor. Having worked in academia and publishing in London, she is now concentrating on writing fiction. *The Last Gift of Emmeline Davies* won the inaugural PFD Lost the Plot prize and was shortlisted for the Bath Novel Award.

louisehtucker@gmail.com

The Last Gift of Emmeline Davies
The first chapter of a novel.

On the first day of his retirement, George's wife had a stroke. It was December 27th, a day that even she didn't work, and he was making tea for them both when it happened. As he pushed open the bedroom door, she seemed to be sleeping, an unusual turn of events but one that filled him with joy on this first of many new, different days. Perhaps, for once, she was going to sit for a bit while they drank their tea, instead of disappearing off to do something. Perhaps it was a surprise for him, to share this newness, if only for a little while.

He allowed himself a smile as he put the tray by the bed. Two cups of tea, the last of the mince pies. Her back was turned to him, her T-shirt, as ever from some conference or other, just visible. This one, he remembered, was from a place she had been every year that they had been together, a place he had never been.

'You don't want to come. It will be so boring for you,' she had said. 'I'll be in work mode, standing around, clutching papers, and you'll just feel like my caddy trailing behind me. There'd be no point.'

'You know I'd be happy to be your caddy.'

She pressed her forehead against his then, in that way that she did. 'Oh George, you're so lovely, so good.'

He'd said once, very early on, but the hotel is paid for, I don't have to stay with you all day, it would be nice to meet your colleagues. She had smiled and nodded, said maybe, but she had not mentioned it again, not even as she set off for the airport that time. And neither had he. So he had never gone to Luxor or Mainz or Harvard. Never met the people she wrote papers with. Never seen anything that inspired her, except the British Museum and the books she brought home from her other office.

There was always a book by her bed. It was usually in her hands by the time he brought the tea, a pencil tucked into the spine. She would look up and smile as he came in, pushing herself back against the pillows, readying herself for tea. Today though the book was on top of the covers and slightly askew, as if she'd put it down for a minute while she had a bit of a doze. He got into bed as carefully as he could, not wanting to be the cause of waking her.

She didn't stir. Pleased with himself, he sat back, reached over for his mug and drank a little. When he noticed his tea was cooling down, he wondered if he should give her a gentle shake. Was it worse, he wondered, to end her doze, a doze that signalled a different tempo to their days, or to let her sleep until her tea was the wrong temperature and he would have to make another?

In the end he chose to wake her. On this day, on this day of all days, he wanted to drink his tea *with* her. It was selfish, he knew, more selfish than he usually allowed himself to be. But he knew she would understand. Eventually. She didn't stir though, when he put his hand on her shoulder. In fact, when he put his hand on her shoulder, she neither moved nor spoke, not even a murmur. For a last, beautiful second, he smiled. Sleepy Emmeline! One too many glasses last night.

But then his pleasure, his joy at this surprise drained away. He leaned over to take a sneaky look at his wife sleeping in, such an uncharacteristic thing, and he saw that she wasn't.

He spilt the rest of his tea. Spilt it as he was getting out from under the covers, which seemed to have wrapped themselves round him like a winding sheet, preventing him moving. Spilt it as he moved to turn her, to shake her, to see her. She was still breathing, but her face was completely still, one side swooping down to the mattress, eye closed, the other eye open.

Her phone was by her bed, but he didn't know her password. He ran to get his, jumping down the stairs. The cable was tangled with the kettle's and, as he tried to separate them, he dropped the phone onto the tiles and the screen shattered. He tapped 999 as he went back to the bedroom, feeling splinters of glass under his fingertips. Emmeline hadn't moved. He'd hoped she might. That it might have been momentary.

Kevin, that was the first paramedic's name. Kevin, and the girl, the woman rather, was Alison. They came up the stairs like aliens in their green jackets, bristling with stuff, bringing the cold air with them.

George was still in his pyjamas. Not even a dressing gown between him and these strangers. Just as there was only a T-shirt between Emmeline and them. He stood and watched. It didn't take long. Minutes, probably. Though it felt like days. They asked questions, lots and lots of questions, and he wondered why they were bothering. Why weren't they getting her into the ambulance?

'What is her date of birth, George? Any allergies or regular medication?

Any medical issues?'

Look at her, he wanted to shout, there's your medical issue. But he wasn't a shouter and, besides, he didn't have the energy.

'Can you hear us Emmeline?' they said, as soon as he told them her name.

'Emmeline, Professor Emmeline Jane Davies,' George had said. The professor was important, he thought. And she wouldn't forgive him if he forgot it. They didn't use it though.

'Emmeline, my name is Alison,' said the young woman. Her hand was on the slope of Emmeline's hip, a hip swaddled in the duvet. 'Can you blink, Emmeline? Can you squeeze my hand?'

While Alison was talking, Kevin was beside her on the floor, getting out equipment. A stethoscope first. George was surprised they still used them. A blood pressure cuff. One of those pointed thermometers, digital, which Kevin flashed into her ear.

George wanted to do something, anything. 'Tea,' he said. 'Can I get you some tea, or coffee? Perhaps it's too early for coffee. I'm afraid there are no mince pies left.'

'No, no, you're all right George,' they both said, not looking up. They had asked him his name first, his full name, George Henry Maybury, before they even went up the stairs. His name took up more space, he sometimes thought, than he did.

'We're just going to run some tests, George, then we're going to get Emmeline onto a stretcher, into the ambulance.'

'Do you know what's wrong?'

'We're not sure; we'll know more at the hospital. You might want to get dressed, so you can come with us. It's probably best if you don't drive.'

'Of course, get dressed,' said George, 'I'll do that.' He was ashamed of the relief he felt, of being dismissed and able to leave.

While Emmeline was being measured and poked, he walked over to the chair on his side of the room and picked up yesterday's trousers and jumper. Then he went to the wardrobe for a clean shirt, to the chest of drawers for underwear and socks, ones Emmeline liked, and left the room. In the bathroom, he was surprised to see that the toothpaste was where he'd left it, that Emmeline's toothbrush was still damp, that one of the facecloths she used every night was crumpled in a heap on the edge of the sink. The bathroom lifted his spirits. The bathroom, unlike the bedroom, hadn't changed. He wondered if he should have a shower. Did he have time? He didn't like the idea of going to the hospital unwashed and unshaven. Emmeline would hate it. She would be so cross when she woke up and saw his stubble. He stared at himself in the bathroom mirror. He looked the same. While Emmeline lay through the wall being prodded and asked questions he looked just the same. A little tired. Nothing more.

George heard a bang as someone opened the bedroom door – he had closed it behind himself, to give Emmeline more privacy – followed by footsteps running down the stairs and the front door opening. He picked up his toothbrush and started brushing.

He couldn't have been in the bathroom for more than two or three minutes, but by the time he got out Kevin's bag was packed and Emmeline was lying under a red blanket on their bed. Alison and Kevin (Alison, he thought, is that one L or two?) were unrolling a stretcher. It seemed so slight for her big frame but, as if by magic, they somehow got it in place without even lifting her. She was wearing a neck brace, he noticed.

Kevin stood up as he came back into the room. 'So, George we're nearly ready to go. You might want to pack a few things, a book, your reading glasses, your phone, some money. Emmeline...' – how he hated the way this man used her first name – '...will be seen as an emergency but you could be there for a while. Unless there's someone who can bring you some things later?'

Someone? George wondered who that someone might be. It was the 27th of December. Everyone was with their families. No, that someone was him.

'Yes, yes, of course, I'll go and do that. And the same for her I suppose? She'll never forgive me if I don't bring her something decent to read.' He had the distinct impression, but he wasn't sure, afterwards, that Kevin and Alison looked at each other then. Just for a moment.

'As quick as you can, George,' Kevin said. Brisk Kevin, efficient Kevin. Alison was the warm gentle one, Kevin the pragmatist; he the actions, she the emotions. How Emmeline would have hated that division. George suddenly found himself hoping that Alison was driving. He could hear them talking to each other, advising on steps, speed, angle, as they went down the stairs. There was the odd bump, a pause, then they would start again. By the time he came out of her office – he'd got her a book, her reading glasses, her iPad, his own were downstairs, by the sofa – Kevin was halfway out of the front door, heading backwards and Alison was on the last step of the staircase. The stretcher was at an angle.

How did she not slip forward? Had they tied her down under that blanket? He hoped they hadn't tied her down under that blanket. Careful, he said, but they didn't seem to hear. Perhaps he hadn't said anything after all.

As Alison got to the door, the stretcher began to level. Once they were both outside, Kevin stopped and Alison half-turned. 'Are you ready, George? Got your keys?' She spoke quietly, almost whispering.

'I am,' he replied, heading down the stairs now they were free. 'I'll just get my coat.'

He had felt a reluctance to step onto the stairs while they were still on them, fearing that the slightest weight or pressure could change the balance.

The coat, like the toothbrush, like last night's trousers, like his glasses, was just where he'd left it. Anyone coming in would think nothing had changed. His hand hovered over Emmeline's for a second, then he grabbed it too.

The back doors to the ambulance were open. He stood on the front step and stared at it for a moment, wondering what it was doing there. It looked so out of place, so urban, so big, in this quiet suburban street. He was grateful that it was early, that none of the neighbours were already out, walking their dogs or packing up their cars. Then he turned and pulled the door closed behind him. For once he didn't lock it. He wouldn't be long.

Rosalind Upton has come to UEA from journalism. She is writing a novel set in France, about a family struggling with the impact of DNA testing. Under her broadcast name, Roz Upton, she was a reporter for Channel 4 News and has also worked on documentaries, radio, newspapers and online. She holds an MA in International Journalism from City University and a First with distinction in French from The University of Birmingham.

www.rozupton.com
roz@oldbearhurst.com

The Wolf

Extract from a novel. Tessa and Emile believed their son was healthy until a rare lung condition manifested itself, along with silent asthma. DNA tests have revealed Tessa carries the genetic fault. Guilt-ridden, she has taken Marcel to the home of her mother-in-law, Solange, for the unpolluted Alpine air, while trying to convince Emile that gene therapy could save his life.

Tessa rekindled a flame under wood in the grate and arranged three logs on the hearth, so heat would draw out their moisture. Wetness hissed in the fire. Pulling her shrunken jumper down over her belt, she passed Solange in the armchair embroidering another hassock and walked to the kitchen where, near the lit stove, Marcel was painting. He should have been at school, but minus ten was extreme, and his cough was back. Not that he cared, sneaking outside with those bloody binoculars. Still, here he was now, safely in the warm.

'I like your eagle,' she said, standing behind his chair.

'This wing's bigger than that one.'

'The feathers remind me of that outfit from your old dressing-up box. How d'you do the white dapples?'

'I used the side of the bristles, like this. Works best if the paint's running out.'

'That's clever,' she said. 'Right, better fetch some dry logs.'

She wrapped up and headed out to the wood-stack. The sky was of the purest blue, and the freezing air pricked her cheeks. Patting her gloved hands together, she looked down the valley, where the sun was striking the skeleton trees, casting shadow lines on the snow. She filled the sack with logs and dragged it up the path, over slips of black ice and into the house. With her foot, she closed the door. Mustn't let in the cold. Even these logs were wet at the end that had faced the elements, so she stood them like stalagmites around the hearth, and went out for one last load before it snowed.

By the time she returned, Solange was asleep. Quietly, she rested her sack by the fire, laid the edelweiss blanket over her mother-in-law's knees, and rested the hassock on top. Removing her own coat and gloves, yet leaving her hat on, she went to the kitchen to be with Marcel.

He wasn't at the table. His binoculars, brushes, paper, and paints were still spread across its surface. She looked at his art: the eagle was unfinished, so the black tips of its wing-feathers looked like floating fingers; the curve of the beak was perfect, but the left wing was wrong, as he'd said. His skills were coming along – she'd get back to her ceramics one day. She picked up his jar to change the darkened water, pushed in his chair to get to the sink, and it was then that she spotted his red-socked feet: he was on the floor by the back door. His torso was bent, his head down.

'Marcel!' Dumping the jar on the draining board, she darted to his side. 'Is it hard to breathe?'

Raising his head, he opened his eyes, and there was that panic from Paris. She had to calm him.

'Let me get your inhaler,' she said, but the blue one wasn't on the shelf, so she opened the top drawer, shoved aside pens, bills, scissors, memos, grabbed the inhaler, knocked over the jug, and knelt with Marcel. 'Here.'

His shoulders heaved, while she fumbled the cap off the inhaler and shoved it into the spacer. When she held it to his face, he put his hands on hers and brought it to his lips. Her heart pounding, she pressed the canister. His neck was all sucked in skin, tendons like buttress roots.

'Can you hold it?' she said, hating to leave him, but running for the phone in the lounge, then dialling 112. 'My son's having an asthma attack and he has a lung condition, I...' She shook Solange, making her jump and look about. 'Talk to the ambulance,' said Tessa, thrusting the phone at her.

Open-mouthed, Solange got to her feet, the hassock tumbling from her lap. 'What's happening?'

'It's Marcel. He's having an attack,' said Tessa, pushing the receiver against her soft belly, and stepping towards the kitchen.

Marcel's face had gone white, and he was gasping, chest lifting, for the air that was all around him. She grasped the spacer, clipped his teeth as she pushed it in, and released the Ventolin.

'Be calm Marcel – it's going to be all right.'

But it wasn't all right. The medication wasn't enough. She wanted to open his ribs, stretch his airways with her bare hands, let in the oxygen.

'Where's the ambulance?' she shouted.

Marcel was tapping his chest. She tried to shift his back straighter, maybe free his diaphragm. She must do something. Come on, please. His face contorted.

Then Solange was the other side of him. 'They say they'll be here as soon as they—'

'Marcel, look at me, try to relax. Try to breathe.' Tessa imitated deep breathing, as if he might copy her. The blink of his eyelids slowed. 'Paper bag. Have we got one?'

'I think... the pastries,' said Solange, and she rustled about near the kettle, then handed Tessa a bakery bag.

'Breathe in here,' said Tessa, a buttery smell wafting as she opened it.

Flakes of croissant fell onto his hoodie. Grease had made little see-through patches on the paper bag, but Marcel's breath couldn't inflate it.

'Where are they? Phone someone,' said Tessa. 'Who's got a car?'

'The paramedics are best, what if... I'll go out, wave them in.'

'Get help.'

Marcel dropped the bag. She touched his lips – they were losing colour. No, no, no. She wasn't going to let him... Breathe! She made a fist and bit down on her forefinger. The neighbour's dog barked. Again, she tried the inhaler.

'You've got to...' Her voice wobbled. 'Here,' she said, forcing herself to keep it together. 'Open.'

The dog barked and barked. She tilted Marcel's head in her hand. Was that? Yes – a siren.

'I can hear the ambulance. They'll be seconds now.'

Marcel's face didn't register.

Boots running up the path, bashing through the hall.

'In here!' she said, then put her mouth to Marcel's ear, his sweat wetting her cheek. 'They're here. It's all right now.'

She turned to see a paramedic rush through the kitchen door. Swiftly, he unpacked, speaking in solid sounds.

'Asthma, yes?'

'Quick!' said Tessa. 'He has COPA syndrome, as well.'

The paramedic fixed a nebuliser mask over Marcel's mouth and nose. The skin of the backs of his hands was smooth, his face taut. Just out of college – better know what he's doing. She clenched her teeth and watched him flush in the drugs.

'Give it a minute,' he said. 'COPA... I've never—'

'It's not working,' Tessa said.

As he measured Marcel's pulse, another paramedic arrived, banging the door against the worktop.

'We'll take this one in,' the young medic said.

'Right,' said his colleague, turning to leave.

'His lungs,' said Tessa, 'his condition – they could haemorrhage.'

Marcel's eyes closed above the mask. From outside came Solange's voice, then the second medic clattering about. The back door opened, chilling her midriff, and Tessa stayed close as they carried Marcel into the icy air, and onto a trolley to wheel him to the ambulance. She climbed in after him, and as they shut the doors, Solange was on the path, making the sign of the cross.

Marcel seemed smaller on the trolley in the ambulance, the mask still on. Tessa sat holding his hand, talking to him. This was worse than last time – he wouldn't reply, so she squeezed his pale fingers. Please squeeze back. Marcel? The paramedic was checking his pulse every few minutes, asking her endless questions, and radioing the hospital. Even inside the ambulance its siren was loud and, though they were travelling fast enough for speed to pin her to the seat, they were taking too long.

'Must be nearly there,' she said, grabbing the rail as they swerved.

The engine laboured uphill.

'Two minutes,' said the paramedic.

On arrival they pushed Marcel into A&E, and she tried to stay close without obstructing the medics. A flock of doctors and nurses in white glided Marcel into a side room, and she followed, catching snatches of their voices.

'Ipratropium bromide.'

'He's entering severe respiratory failure... where's the...'

They were saying his name, but he wasn't responding. She wanted to push through, but she mustn't hinder them.

'Intravenous ketamine... dose... administering now.'

'Intubation... Airway checked?'

They fed a tube down Marcel's throat. She cracked her knuckles. They'd make him vomit like that and rip him inside. She stepped forward.

'Ventilation... Five centimetres H2O.'

They moved as a mass, connecting Marcel and his tube to a machine, calling figures: tidal volume, flow rate, oxygen – too many numbers. Her stomach was tight.

'Hypoxic.'

They quickened now. Someone pressed an alarm, and another doctor strode through the flock.

'Prepare isoflurane.'

A flurry of movement. Beep, beep – the monitor.

'Seventy over... Severe hypotension.'

A shriek caught in her.

And that's when someone appeared behind her. 'Madame. You must come.'

'No—'

'This way, please.'

Tessa was pulled by the shoulders. As she turned her head, she glimpsed only his feet in his red socks, for the flock had engulfed him now. She stuck to the strip-lit tiles, until the nurse led her away to meet her sadness.

Emile paced and questioned, but Tessa's words lodged like pebbles. Yellow walls enclosed them with the red lights, the beep and the beep and the tubes. Marcel's hand was heavy when she held it – could he feel her?

Sitting. Watching.

She fiddled with the hat on her lap, pulling at a loose strand, unravelling the wool. Emile swiped and tapped the screen of his phone, presented coffees in thin, plastic cups.

On the fourth day, Marcel spoke. 'My throat hurts.'

His hoarse voice released hers. 'Oh! Marcel.'

He lifted his chin to swallow and screwed his eyes.

'Here, have a sip of water,' she said, supporting his head for him to drink then resting it on the pillow.

'I was scared, Maman.'

'I know, darling.'

'It was like someone put a plug in my throat.'

Placing the beaker on the table, she leaned to kiss his forehead and said, 'I love you so.'

Like a storm the danger passed, and Marcel was moved to a paediatric ward that smelled of antiseptic and nappies. Outside intensive care, nurses were shared between too many patients, and seemed always to be hurrying past the foot of his bed; though they would know if he stopped breathing, they would hear the beep of his machine, she stayed. The children were quiet apart from a girl who cried for her dad, and a toddler who banged his toy on his cot like a crow with a snail. Picture books, too young for Marcel, were among the plastic games, and she chose animal stories for him to read. When he dozed, she stared at the red-light numbers on his blood oxygen machine, and she planned – she couldn't let it happen again.

In the hospital lobby, where visitors in coats stared at coded signs and outpatients waited on seats in rows, Tessa found the payphone and called Aurore. She didn't need someone to comfort her, to tell her he was in good hands – she needed to protect Marcel. When she had told Aurore everything, she asked:

'Did you pass on my number to the gene therapy trial?'

'I did, yes.'

'We have to go down that route, now. They haven't called – will you ask them again for me?'

'Of course, I will.'

Replacing the receiver Tessa turned to check around her, though Emile had returned to Paris.

Mary Wallace has two BAs and lives in Norfolk. Her novella in progress seeks to explore the way Norwich's past resonates and reverberates through its present. Her writing explores intergenerational relationships and focuses on the beauty of the ordinary. She likes to illuminate quiet lives that might easily stay hidden.

mary.wallace79@gmail.com

Margot and the Dragon
The Opening of a Novella

I am going to construct a saint. A woman who is a saint.

I am the scribe. I will write her down. Of course, it won't be in Latin. I don't know Latin. I will write her in the vernacular. The vernacular is all the rage for hagiography.

There will need to be a miracle. A relic. Pilgrimage. She will have to be a virgin, or barren. Allowed to conceive in old age? At the very least a woman become chaste. Could I make her a martyr? There could be a wheel like St Catherine's. Yes, there will be a wheel. A bloody hamster wheel. She will go round on it, again and again.

If I write her down, perhaps she will be transcribed again and again. Other scribes might take my words and reform them; they might remould her. She will be reborn. Live on, live out. There may be a shrine, a church. People will come. They will visit her two-bed flat after she is dead. We might pray to her. For now, perhaps we should pray *for* her.

Her flat is on Music House Lane. She lives there with her son Davey. There are churches enough. She is outdone in the line of saints around there. St Etheldreda sits to the right on King Street: Etheldreda and her three sisters are all of them saints. St Peter Parmentergate is to the left. She can't outdo Peter. I can't have her crucified upside down, though she might be good with denial. Then there is St Julian herself. Scribe. Saint. Mystic. St Julian's church can be seen from her living room window. Yes, I have her placed on hallowed ground. She's in the appropriate quarter of the city.

I will start with a morning that is like all her mornings. My saint, my saint who sits quietly in the wake of other saints. All Saints.

She wakes at 6.30am. She makes instant cappuccino from one of those sachets full of powder. She eases the kitchen door shut so Davey won't hear the kettle. Though less than ten minutes pass today before the obscured glass shows his strawberry hair bobbing towards her.

He gets his hair from her. She has red hair like Mary Magdalen. There,

I have coveted an attribute for her. No jar of ointment though. Today I will have her clasping the yellow carton of Banana Nesquik. She makes a paste in Davey's Norwich City mug with the fluorescent granules and splashes of milk. He sits on a stool watching. There is a turbulence behind his eyes. Creases of sleep are etched into his cheek. He has put on his glasses, but they sit a little squint on the bridge of his nose. She fills the mug to the brim and stirs the custardy liquid, listening to the clink of the spoon.

Brace. Brace.

'It's not stirred right. There're bits.' He pushes the mug away forcefully. It knocks against her coffee. His face is revulsed. He leaps from the stool and kicks at the wall under the window. Then he starts to pull the blind up and down repeatedly. With each yank of the cord, he gets more urgent. It snaps in his hand. He opens and slams each cupboard door in the kitchen in turn, moving around his mother. She is silent, still. It is just after seven. She hopes that Jonas next door won't wake up. Davey scrambles onto the work surface opposite her. He balances himself on his haunches, precarious like a stone imp. Willing her to act. Then he propels himself across the kitchen into the hall. He runs, shouting back at her:
     'I hate it when you don't do it right. I hate you.'

It is only morning. It is only the beginning of a new day that Davey cannot face.

She finishes her coffee. Then she opens the same cupboards that Davey did and straightens the tins in them. Something inside her uncrumples. Rinsing out a cloth, she wipes over the work tops and sweeps across the vinyl with a broom. On Spotify she finds The Beta Band's 'Dry the Rain' and plays it at a low volume. Davey has gone quiet. She dips her head to the fragrance of sweet peas. An abundant bunch sit in a jar on the windowsill. She remembers tying the wigwam of canes together, which they coiled up. She thinks of a faraway garden.

He is nowhere. Davey has gone.

She checks every room but cannot find him. She calls his name over and over. Then she makes herself adjust her tone and volume.
     'Please love. Come on now,' she says to the void. 'I'm not cross.' She

knows he must still be in the flat. The chain is untouched, secured on the front door. Still, the empty rooms wrestle with her reason and make her stomach pinch red.

She should pray to St Anthony, the patron saint of lost things. She doesn't know anything about saints. If she checked Wikipedia, it would tell her about St Anthony of Padua. His undying love and devotion to the poor and the sick. It would also tell her he is the saint of lost things. Lost Davey. I will say one for her. On her behalf.

She finds him. He has scaled the side of her wardrobe and is foetal, covered with velour blanket.

He won't come down. He tries to keep his face covered. She leans across to him from where she stands precariously at the end of her bed.

'Davey. It's alright.' She eases the blanket slowly from him. He lets her. This is a good sign. There are tears. The anger is done, she thinks. It didn't peak. He lets her help him down. They sit on her bed. He allows her to hold him. She takes in the scent of his hair and his head.

Time is ticking on. She needs to try to get him dressed for school. She leads him into his cluttered room. Slipped under his pillow is one of his match day programmes. They run their hands over the smooth surface of the cover. It could be a Psalter illuminated on vellum. Women held and possessed Psalters in this quarter of the city in the Middle Ages, despite their illiteracy. Davey is also unable to read well. He smells the print on the pages, and he touches the shiny finish, he looks at the pictures and adverts. Those women of the past, and their children: they fingered the initials and felt the raised calligraphy; they read from the painted image.

Then there was Julian. Literate. Masterful. Living quietly in the centre of them all. In the centre of the riverside throng.

They sit together. Their heads touch. They are like a panel painting of St Anne and the virgin. She is not a virgin saint. She is not barren either. There was no need for prayers to Anne for help with conception. Not like those uttered up centuries back, whispered from the mouths of the former inhabitants of Kings Street. The merchant wives. The wealthy women of Conesford Norwich. The women who gained validation of their sex through the cult of saints. If not chaste, then they must show the fruits of fertility. If not fertile then St Anne would intercede. Anyway, it was not a problem in the case of Davey's conception. It was all so easy when it came. She didn't come. Yet it was all better than she had expected it might be.

She has not always wanted to be touched. Touch needs to be on her terms. Davey is the same. She has learnt when to hug him and when not to. When to reach out and when to stand back. She understands because for her too touch is sometimes unrequired and sometimes absolute in its necessity.

Absolute, on the floor of a City College hall of residence room. A humid night after a gig at the Waterfront. The window open at full swing letting in orange streetlight. Her thin milky limbs, stretching out. Legs parting, willing. Red hair splayed over the compost-coloured scratchy carpet. The boy with the smiling face and dark ponytail wet with sweat on her. In her. She slept on the floor with him after. At some point he must have heaved himself into his thin student bed and left her on the carpet, unclothed. In the morning he said:

'You're my girlfriend now.' He handed her tea and toast with margarine smeared generously on it. As it turned out, she wasn't his girlfriend. He hadn't meant that after all. He re-thought it quite quickly after.

There are no soft aertex shirts that are clean, only the stiff collared polyester ones. That is enough. Enough to shift the balance again, fluctuate the equilibrium.

'Nooooo,' he screams. He says it louder and louder. In the dirty laundry there is a soft shirt under her yesterday clothes. It has Marmite and biro on it. Davey is pelting objects against his bedroom door.

'Here's a soft one. Davey put...' she stops herself saying directly *put it on* and makes it a choice, '...you could put this on, or the stiff tight one.' She goes and sits by the front door. 'Miss Bridget will wonder where you are Davey. She'll miss you.' He falls silent.

Miss Bridget is a saint. She has a halo around her head that gleams when she comes into the playground and takes Davey in person, into the building. Her hair is fair and neat. She smells of vanilla. Davey trusts her. He comes out of his bedroom in his dirty shirt.

When they finally leave the flat, he stalls.

'My ankle hurts. Mum. My ankle. I can't walk on it.'

'It might be that you're hungry. You've missed breakfast again.' Don't stop. Don't enable the stall. She steps over Stella cans. There is a needle in the stairwell. She brushes it into the corner with her foot and reaches for a brioche roll from her bag. Distraction. Food. She needs to get food in him.

'MUUUUMMMM...' He wails like a banshee behind her on the stairs 'My ankle really hurts. You don't care.'

She goes back to him wanting to get them both out of the stairwell quickly.

'Davey do you want this?' She bends to rub at his ankle. The stench of piss here is overpowering. She tries to move him on. He pulls away from her but takes the brioche.

Thank God. Thank a saint.

He stuffs it in his mouth. He is eating. If she can just get him in the car.

Someone has tipped a bag of flour over the windscreen of her silver Micra. She thinks she might weep. She doesn't. She looks up and sees the sweet peas waving gently on her windowsill. Davey is distracted by the flour. He comes over to the car from where he's been hiding behind the wheelie bins.

'Why is it on our car?' He starts to scoop his fingers through it, and he swishes the brioche, still in his hand, through it as well.

'Davey NO.' She pushes his hands away fiercely and feels the weight of her mistake instantly. The wrong tone. Unwanted touch. He throws the remaining brioche on the ground.

'I hate yoooooooou.' He growls like an animal violated. His response disproportionate, but her guilt overwhelming.

'SHUT THE FUCK UP YOU LITTLE SHIT.' Hooded eyes, gaunt cheeks, saliva. An open shirt. Anger from the second floor hangs out his window and leers like a gargoyle.

Halina is a Londoner, granddaughter of a Polish refugee and journalist - identities she explores in her fiction. She aims to write honest, inventive prose with high moral stakes. Her first novel - *Unbound* - dissects power dynamics between individuals and the ways we govern ourselves - how far we will go for love and survival.

hmawatts@googlemail.com

Unbound
The opening of a novel

London is full of possibilities, where I was born, where the smell of doner kebabs and grilled halloumi wafts out of restaurants, filled with multiple Mediterranean tongues, where ideas of home and marriage and children, a small town complex, line potholed asphalt roads that stretch from the green belt into the smog; the smog being the place where I felt most alive, where I spiralled out of clubs at 6am, rallied weary friends, sang Wonderwall at the top of my voice, scoffed lentils for free at the Hari Krishna, then meditated at the Buddhist centre, sang hallelujah with my gospel choir, and, later, danced and danced to reggae under grey blanketed skies, before returning home to Mum's freshly made Pierogi and Kartoflanka. All of these things were my romance with the city, activities that absorbed the hours. But there was also the grey area, a feeling of invisibility, of having no time, of how the suburb, the one where I lived, depleted a person that only the lights and blur and hum of a city could augment. What I mean is, the suburb's perimeters, all of the chalk lines in schools, on pavements, fences in parks, the ones that led to county borders and then to a cliff edge, the lines outside of the city, they had all woven themselves around an idea I had of myself, this idea of who I was meant to be and who I really was; a person who belonged and then a person who was outside. Maybe this was why it took me so long to text June and why, ultimately, the text was always going to be sent.

—

That first time we met I was sitting on the edge of a bat mitzvah watching a dancefloor full of teenagers fist-pump along to Lady Gaga's 'Poker Face'. June had long, blonde, blow-dried hair, curled away from her face to expose fat rosy cheeks, and a mottled fake tan. Surrounded by empty bottles of champagne, moaning about a man she kept calling Big Boss, who was meant to come with her, but who had ditched her at the last minute.

'Sprucy. So sprucy. He wants Molten Brown rubbed on his belly. "Bubble me up, bubble me up," he always says. Next he'll be wanting me to wipe his arse. The cheek. I tell him. I say, "Dear, sometimes I can't differentiate your arse from your face."

She gesticulated a lot, and leaned in to talk to me as if we had some secret communication, as if I desired the intimacies of her love affair.

'Don't bonk your married boss,' she continued. 'And whatever you do, do not fall in love with them. It's messy, messy business I tell you, and I can't get out of it. I mean, his wife must know. He calls me all the time. We once bonked in their marital bed. Disgusting, isn't it?'

She swigged champagne, so I did the same, making it easier to disguise the levels my jaw had dropped, the whites of my eyes on total display. It had only been ten minutes since we met so I didn't feel comfortable telling her I fancied cruel, garrulous men in skinny jeans who didn't fancy me back and I'd been known to run off with my friend's latest crush but that, ultimately, I didn't want to do that anymore. That married men were foreign, hostile lands I refused to venture to. That surely any woman with an ounce of brain funk would know that too?

'Is this your first Bat mitzvah?' I asked.

'Oh no, I go to these things all the time. Got to keep the contacts sweet. You?'

'Same. Well, not same. But Mum's got a lot of Jewish friends.'

'What do you do?' she asked.

'Me?' I said, looking around the empty table.

'Yes, you.'

'I work at the *Local Post*,' pointing to the building across the road with chipped green signage and damp walls.

'Oh god help you.' She scrunched her face up, downed the nearly full glass of champagne. 'What a mess. I bet they've got you scrubbing shit off the toilet floor.'

I blushed red hot, the gold rings on my fingers felt tight.

'To be honest, it's better than that. I mean, it's work experience, and I speak to a lot of old people about noise complaints, but occasionally they let me go to local gallery openings.'

'For their shitty showbiz column? HAH.' She grabbed the champagne bottle, poured herself some more, whacked it on the table.

'Yes.'

'And they're not paying you? I mean, OF COURSE, they're not paying you. The owner of your paper is tight, he won't even fix the mice infestation you have.'

I explained how I had avoided the mice, although I had heard about them because my editor sent me on jobs then got me to file copy from my bedroom, which meant my parents' heating bills were at an all-time high, and they were sick of me banging around drunk at 3am but that, at least, I didn't waste money in Pret, and we both agreed that the owner's parsimony meant he was a sociopath.

'And what do you do?' I asked.

'I'm at the *Daily National News,*' she said, and suddenly I felt more alert, so I straightened my back, tried to disguise my surprise.

'What do you do there?'

'Well apart from rubbing Big Boss' hairy back in Molten Brown and putting licky, licky on their shoddy copy, I'm Head of News and manage the showbiz column too. You know Ape Giles thieving all that gold, I got that scoop.'

I tried to conjure Ape Giles in my head but, instead imagined a trapeze circus act and offered, 'The monkey?'

'Don't be a silly fool,' she snapped. 'That superstar boxer. Jeez, you need to up your game if you want to leave the *Local Post.*' Her face dropped, my lack of knowledge clearly a major offence, so I laughed and lied, told her I was joking, refilled our glasses, then gushed about her *phenomenal* story.

'Everyone was talking about it at work,' I added. 'He's a proper dodgy one, isn't he? You did well there.'

'Ha,' she said. 'I knew you seemed on it, there are some total dipshits out there, good not to be one of them. And yes, I'm hoping to get a Press Award nomination for that one.'

Not being a dip shit felt important, so I told her about a piece I was working on regarding a group of far-right protestors who used to be lawyers and teachers and doctors, coming together to stop refugees gathering in certain areas of London, that the migrant crisis had to be one of the most important stories right now.

'Not for me, sorry' she said. 'Sounds like a local story.' I crimsoned just as she turned to holler for a waiter. Felt a sinking feeling in the pit of my stomach. In contrast, June was rising up. She grabbed a glass, tapped it with her finger and shrugged her shoulders. Waiters gathered around the top table ignored her, which felt satisfying. I tried not to smile.

'These places. Shoddy service central.' She sighed, clambering out of her seat.

'I've also got a showbiz story that might work for you,' I said, my voice acrobating around neutral tones, any hint of desperation carefully ironed out as my left buttock began to rise from the chair.

'Great,' she said, her face brighter and more engaged, my buttock now firmly back on the seat. 'Let me just deal with this and we can talk.'

I hated this desperate, pushy side of myself, but after a year of going nowhere at the *Local Post*, not always being able to afford Pot Noodle, or Lambrini or tube fare, refusing to rely on parental handouts, which meant friends had given up on me, these types of interactions with Very Important People became essential to my future. I would put on an act, determined to prove myself, allowing my foot in a mostly shut door. It happened at a book launch attended by a famous journalist who had a column at the *Times*. I sweated behind a wall, building up the confidence to talk to them, gearing up to annunciate myself into a job, but when I finally went over, they had left. There was also the time at a colleague's leaving party when I asked an old school investigative journalist called Ray what *maudlin* meant, as well as mispronouncing the word *minefield* as *mindfield*, which he corrected a moment after I uttered it. Despite the faux pas, he gave me his email and I messaged him, of course I did, but I didn't know if it was my London accent or my confused lexicon, or perhaps because being an outsider meant you couldn't find a way in, but I never got a response back.

I tried to contemplate what story I would share as June marched up to a small, wiry woman in a navy cleaning uniform exhuming fried egg sweets strewn around a pick and mix stand. It was hard not to cringe as she almost toppled over in her tight skirt, bending down to get the woman's attention. I glugged the remaining champagne, embarrassed by her misplaced determination, as if champagne was an entitled liquid delivered through taps. A man in a gold top hat and gold suit dragged a violet tasselled unicorn on to the dance floor. A group of kids with bulging e-numbered eyes lunged for it, yelling hysterically. I hummed for hard liquor, Beefeater or Bacardi or whatever, but then the embarrassment I felt for June morphed into encouragement, and now a fiery, kinetic energy somersaulted through my chest and I was secretly spurring her on, glimpsing her and the uniformed woman in a heated debate. Except the woman was now wedged between the sweet stall monstrosity and a navy wall, so I envisioned a rescue effort as the only way to stop all the navy blueness becoming one. Of course, I did nothing, mopped up hummus with challah, watched my parents toast their married friends sitting on the married table, the one next to mine, slapping backs, detailing all the stories I had probably heard before about Jules Verne cruises, or the World Rugby Sevens that year in Hong Kong, or Mum's PHD dreams. Familiar lined bodies, the ones I encountered every day, illuminated by friends who horded their escapades for starter, main and dessert. How with age they had become more certain, joyous versions of themselves. They turned to look as the girl being batmitzvah'd twirled around the dance floor, tripping over maroon lacquered shoes, and I thought of her rite of passage, the way a child becomes an adult, and this symbolism bewildered me because how could a scroll, a gifted iPad and a 12-year-old constitute a woman? I thought of my own growing-up, the way university followed school, a year abroad followed university, adventures on Bariloche ski slopes and Inca trails and sequin-dressed carnivals afforded by £12k student loans, but still I wondered when my rite of passage would materialise, what that felt like, if my name would be by-lined and read and awarded, or if I would end up chained to a desk in a decrepit building answering calls about councillor meetings gone wrong, thinking I could have been someone else.

Ellen Wiese was born in Minnesota and lives in Chicago. Her prose has been published in *Wigleaf,* the *Bookends Review,* and *Lost Balloon*, from which she received a 2020 Best Microfiction nomination, and her short story, *Noise*, was one of *Glimmer Train*'s Very Short Fiction Top 25 in 2018.

ellenwiesewrites@gmail.com

Mount Turn
An extract from a novel

When Anthony Low moved to Mount Turn, it broke his mother's heart. She resented the twelve-hour drive, the long-distance phone call fees, the two-hour time difference. And she held the manufacturing boom generally – and this dusty town specifically – responsible for taking her son away.

She couldn't understand why the shy boy with all his books, the teen-ager with the best grades who was friends with his teachers, the man she had sworn to get through college no matter how many extra shifts it took, would throw that all away. 'I didn't raise you for this,' she wanted to tell him, but she let the grainy photograph of her great-great-great-grandfather on the top of the cupboard speak for itself.

Instead of enrolling at the university, Anthony packed his bags and went to claim a position at an auto factory with a guaranteed paycheck, a thousand miles away in a cornfield.

'The money's good,' he told her, 'The factory has a great train-on-the-job program.' But she knew that couldn't be all it was.

Of course his mother would be proud of him no matter what he did, but it was a livid pride. So she sent him socks, six-packs of socks because Mount Turn could be cold, and every pair of them was powder blue. 'For luck,' she said when he asked her why she didn't ever send him other colors, and he didn't feel like he had grounds to argue.

Anthony was indifferent about cars and didn't buy his own when he moved to Mount Turn, something that bordered on sacrilege at the factory. He liked his job fine, didn't love it, didn't feel the eroticism some of the guys felt for their cars at home.

'How can you do this work,' a big hairless man asked him one Thursday evening, 'if you don't love the craft?'

They were at the dive on Edmund, two pints deep and waning. Anthony shrugged. 'Same way you do any job: one second at a time.'

The guy leaned so far back in his chair it looked like he would tip. 'Same way,' he said again and again, shaking his head as the bar emptied out over hours. 'Same way!'

Anthony liked to walk – always had, whether it was along the ocean in California or between the fields here. The house he had put a mortgage on was located at the edge of town closest to the factory, and at a brisk pace he could make it to work in twenty minutes. In a place like this you could walk for hours and not hit another town, and he spent most of his free time doing just that.

This was flyover country, and the landscape didn't come right out and demand you love it. The worst part, the only thing that made Anthony really and truly want to leave and go back home, was the flatness. You could see right to the edge of the sky, and all there was in any direction was farmland and little houses and gatherings of trees.

But in the farmland there were old gravel roads traveled so often that they had sunk into the ground, grown over with hardy birches that made soft tunnels in the landscape. Hidden cicadas churred in the branches and wildflowers poked out of the scrub at the edges of vast plots of corn and soy. There were no sequoias, no deep-earth forests, but there were secret clusters of trees that had gone unvisited for years except by the teenagers who went there to smoke. Aspens and maples and ash and the occasional oak, holding onto each other's roots for dear life.

Mushrooms hid in the roots of the trees that curled over the road, furrowing the embankments on the edges of the fields, clustering hundreds-thick in the little forests between farms. He got a book out of the Mount Turn Public Library – *The Forager's Guide to Mushrooms of the United States* – and spent the hours between when work got out and when the sun went down in the summer wearing tracks back and forth between farmers' fields. At first their tenants would come out when they saw him. A woman would appear at the door with a dishrag, vanish inside, and a few minutes later a man and his dog would rise in her place and watch silently. Anthony would raise one arm in a wave, and, as if compelled, the silent watchers would always wave back.

After a few weeks of this, the farmers got used to him and stopped coming out to see who it was. More than once Anthony ran into a guy at the bar who recognized him. 'You're the weirdo who walks in the fields,' someone said on a Saturday night at the dive on Edmund, long past midnight. 'I almost set my dog on you.'

'Glad you didn't,' Anthony said, and bought him a drink.

His mother called every week asking if he was satisfied with his job, if he was really sure he was satisfied. Anthony couldn't bring himself to be sorry for his decision. He had graduated with good grades, nearly the best, and had looked at the pamphlets with smiling young adults and course listings for engineering and mathematics and business, and had found himself suddenly very tired. It had all been all right, the working late, the making his mother proud, the gradual erosion of personal time. But what could university offer but more of that – more of studying during the day and picking up extra shifts at night so he could study during the day again, and eventually get a job that was no more rewarding than the one available to him now?

The rest of the employees were getting in their cars as Anthony lagged in the doorway, shrugging on his raincoat. It had been pouring all day – they'd had three leaks in the ceiling, one of them directly over the block of engineer desks – and he wasn't looking forward to the walk home. If he asked, someone would give him a ride, kind Andrew with his sad face or Bobby with his crooked grin, but then he would need to make awkward conversation and possibly be invited to dinner and he just couldn't face that. It had been two years at the factory and he was content with the casual acquaintances he had.

Thunder grumbled overhead. He waited ten minutes, twenty, the rain only worsening. He finally set out into the empty parking lot, casting his mind forward to his dry kitchen and warm bed.

There was an incredible noise, and a sudden and utter stillness.

Sound paused and softened as though he was encased in a bubble of glass. A light so bright it turned the world white echoed from his hands, from his skull. The pain was immense. Inexplicable. His body stayed mid-step in the parking lot as his mind traveled uncountable luminous years. Behind his eyes, outlines of cities rose from fields and fell into obscurity. Energy raced under the ground through networks as thin as a filament, as long as a continent. A thousand miles away, his mother's heart beat its three millionth beat, stuttered, and resumed a little unsteadily.

This is peace, he thought. Hanging. Silent. Still.

He didn't know how long he was unconscious. When he came to, he was soaked and lying flat on his back and there was a prickling heat down the right side of his body. 'I'm fine,' he said groggily to no one, and tried to push himself upright. He felt achy and out-of-breath, and one arm didn't seem to be responding. His shirt and pant leg were scorched. A hole the size of a quarter was burned through the sole of his shoe.

He thought, as he limped back home, about going to the hospital. But that was across town, and he could still walk, which surely meant that he wasn't injured too badly. The crops in the fields, waist-high, stood like hostile armies watching him drag his body home. By the time he made it to his door his chest was aching in time with the pulse of his heartbeat. Tomorrow, he decided, collapsing into the armchair in the living room. Tomorrow he would talk to the doctors.

The nurse at the hospital told him to put his shirt back on and keyed information into the groaning computer while he did so. He expected her to ask him why he hadn't come in earlier, why he had waited. The receptionist had looked at him like he had lost his mind when he said what he was here for: on the way home from work, the craziest thing. But this woman – her nametag said Hideko – didn't ask any more questions. 'The doctor will be in shortly,' and that was all. He didn't know her, hadn't seen her around. Mount Turn wasn't big, but then he wasn't very social.

The doctor didn't have much to add beyond a list of possible consequences five miles long: muscle weakness, numbness, dizziness, vision problems, nausea, headaches, depression, pain. At a certain point Anthony had shut down and didn't hear the rest. As the man spoke, Anthony thought about the new pattern on his body. Between the bruising and the burns, a livid red streak ran from one shoulder to his right foot. It looked like coral, like roots, little fingers reaching and spiking across his stomach and groin. It was as clear as if someone had painted it on.

He bought a pickup truck for dirt cheap from a man who had posted an advertisement in the paper. The other guys at the factory planned for their cars years in advance, saved and saved and saved until they could get the most extraordinary model. Anthony just wanted a metal barrier over his head.

He drove the truck home, happy to find that it ran just fine. The next day he stopped off at the body shop and had it painted powder blue, for luck. The guys there gave him side-eye – the manager even came over while he paid, said, 'You sure about the color?' – but his mind was made up. The car would be blue.

He didn't walk anymore. His dreams were full of root systems and cut with lightning.

He was driving home from the factory when he was struck a second time. The radio was going, his truck was fresh blue, the day was fine but there were clouds moving in and he could feel the fear clawing at his throat as though he'd swallowed a live animal.

He readied himself to run from the car. He would go straight to the cellar and wait. Later, when the storm subsided, he could go up and make dinner.

He stepped out of the car and put his newspaper over his head. Rain was pelting down, soaking him almost immediately. Twelve steps, he thought. One, two, three.

The next morning, a neat circle of mushrooms marked the place he had been struck. Anthony left them, whether as a bulls-eye warning or a circle of protection he wasn't sure.

It was the end of summer, storm season, and the next few weeks were full of close calls. At the first sign of dark clouds, he wedged himself in the deepest corner of the cellar amongst the fungi that grew there and listened to the storm radio. In this way, he lived through the rest of the first fall after his second strike.

Clementine Forbes Wolodarsky is a 23-year-old writer from Los Angeles. Her debut novel, *I had a hard year but I am a slut*, will follow 22-year-old Cavan over a year of her post-pandemic life. This section takes place right before Cavan moves to England to pursue a writing residency and have lots of sex.

clementine.wolodarsky@gmail.com

I had a hard year but I am a slut
An excerpt from a novel

Sidney doesn't charge me for my chai latte because she knows I'm leaving in two days. She makes me promise I'll come back.

The hottest barista with the spider tattoos on his wrists delicately dusts my drink with cinnamon. I watch the spiders bob up and down and wonder, as always, if I'm in love with him. I watch the way he and Sidney move together behind the counter and wonder, as always, if they're fucking.

I bite at a hangnail. It doesn't matter. I'm leaving.

Chai for Cavan, he says and when I walk up he hands me my drink and a gluten-free brownie with a wink.

Fi calls as I'm standing on the sidewalk, recovering, eating the brownie.

Hi Cavie, she says.

She's lying in bed, her long hair in a lazy knot on top of her head. She's wearing one of my shirts. The one with a picture of Lana Del Rey that says: *White Womanhood So Fragile.*

That's my shirt, I say and she readjusts the camera to hide it.

I don't think so.

It's fine, I say. It's dumb. Keep it.

What are you up to today?

Haircut, I say.

She gives me a thumbs-up. I tell her that Spider winked at me. Her reaction is satisfying. She drops her phone on her face. It smacks her teeth, making a gritty crunching sound.

At the salon, the women make a big fuss over me.

One is adamant that I should not – should *not* – get my hair cut in England. They won't know what to do with your curls, she says. Another says to eat my fill of tacos before I leave because English food has no flavour. Another tells me that the dampness of the weather will ruin my hair. There's really no way around it, she says and writes the names of frizz-controlling gels on a piece of paper.

It's gonna be fine, I say. I'll probably come back with a British boyfriend.

Maybe even a prince, one of them says.

Because the royal family loves mixed girls from LA, I say and they all laugh.

On my last night, my parents and I get into the car to go to My Going Away Party.

I've booked a table at my favourite place, a Mexican restaurant in a former Japanese restaurant. The mishmash of styles feels so inherently LA that I nearly burst into tears when we drive into the parking lot. It is the only restaurant I know that has a koi pond inside and I love to watch the fish slice through the murky water, blurs of colour darting around.

At the height of the pandemic, before my back pain got too bad, I used to walk here with Fiona. We would order margaritas and drink them while sitting on the curb, eating chips out of a greasy bag. I find myself almost missing this.

You okay Cav? asks my dad. He has seen my twisting face in the rear-view mirror.

Fine, I say. I just hope people brought presents.

Cavan, my mother says. That is *not* the point.

Fiona and Aunt Mel are already seated. Fi's wearing a velvet headband that I gave her.

I start for the table but my mum stops me. Wait a minute, she says. We have a surprise for you.

Roman is in front of me.

My mouth falls open and I think I might be dreaming but when I reach out to grab her, she is solid and there and she pulls me into a tight hug. Fiona runs over and wraps her arms around us both and for once I don't say to her: this is *my* sister.

I get the place of honour at the table and my family fans out beside me. There are two empty chairs for Leo and Nat, who are late. Fiona and Roman sit next to me.

I ask Roman how in the world she's here.

There was a conference that I wasn't gonna come to, she says, but then Mum and I worked out that I could just make it to this dinner. I landed an hour ago. Mel picked me up.

Did you know? I ask Fi who shakes her head.

Nobody trusted me to keep a secret, she says.

I wouldn't either, I say and she kicks me beneath the table.

Leo and Nat arrive together. I almost didn't invite Nat but my mum said that was going too far.

When we've all ordered margaritas and nachos, Natalie says she's sorry I left Leo's early.

I was tired, I say.

I ask Leo, who is texting, if he enjoyed his party.

What? Oh yeah, he says and sets his phone down with a clunk.

The drinks arrive, sweating and shimmering. My spicy margarita creates a fire in my stomach.

When the nachos are served, I make a show of drizzling the sour cream over the chips in perfect zigzags. As I'm passing the dish down the table, my mother calls for silence.

A toast, she says and then sweeps a look over everyone. She is demanding that everybody play their worshipful part. I have waited my whole life to have my mother call a toast in my honour.

I'll start, Ro says because she is our mother's daughter, raised to be witty at dinner parties.

Cavan, she says and looks at me, I used to be jealous of all my friends who had normal little sisters who didn't do things like wear capes and fake glasses to school but as we get older I realise that being your sister is the best part of my life.

Then she raises her glass and nods solemnly at me as if she is Jay Gatsby and I am a flapper. Stay shocking, she says.

I nod back. My parents share a pleased look.

Let's go in a circle, my mother commands.

Which means that Natalie is next.

I remember when we went on that field trip in seventh grade, she says, making eye-contact with no one in particular, and you wore those knee socks printed with cartoon owls and short shorts and obviously we were already friends but I just remember feeling so glad to know you. I'm going to miss you so much but I know you'll have the best time.

She smiles at me and I smile back, even though I found her speech uninspiring.

As soon as Nat finishes, Aunt Mel rolls in. Cavie, she says, there's no one like you. You are a light. You are Fiona's sister.

My mum is next and she tells a story about when I was four and I asked for a pen and paper and then scratched marks across the page and announced at dinner that I'd written a book. And when Ro pointed out that my words weren't words, I confidently read the story to them over and over, exactly the same each time, until everyone asked me to please stop.

The story was called: *Cavan gets a sword.*

My father talks about how I peed in the pool during Swim Team practice when I was nine and denied it so forcibly that my coach said she must have made a mistake in blaming me and apologised after practice. When I told my father about it in the car, he wanted to know why I'd confessed to him and I said, I thought you'd be proud that I stood up for myself, and then he had to explain to me that while standing up for yourself is important, it's better to do it when you're not defending a lie.

But, he says, his voice shaky, you've always been stubborn. I hope you apply that to your writing this year.

Leo says that Los Angeles is losing one of its arthritic angels.

Fiona is last and when everyone at the table turns to her, I am surprised to see that she is crying. Big tears falling onto her nachos.

Aw, everyone says together. She takes several gulps of air.

Cav, she says, I don't know what life without you down the street is like and I never wanted to know. I wish I was coming with you.

Two weeks ago, we got into a fight on the sidewalk. She called me a bitch and I called her a cunt. I don't remember what we were arguing about.

I wish you were coming too, I say, trying to lie with the same conviction I normally save for peeing in pools but when it comes out of my mouth, it isn't a lie.

To Cavan, my mum says, lifting her glass into the air, and everyone echoes. To Cavan.

Suddenly I am crying. I'm confused, my family is confused. I'm not a public crier. The restaurant is playing 'We Are Going to be Friends.' I can't stop crying.

No one says anything. Natalie fidgets in her chair and flashes a look at Leo.

I'm scared, I say.

It's okay to be scared, my mum says. You're doing a scary thing.

What if it's a mistake? I ask my plate. My whole life is here.

I look back up. Leo's phone pings with a text and he scrambles to turn it off. Natalie looks down at her lap. I stop crying.

Are you texting about me? I ask, my voice level but steely. At my dinner?

They both shake their heads. Fiona sits wide-mouthed. Neither of them would be fool enough to include her in the messages.

You are, I say. That is 100% what you're doing.

Cavan, my mother says but I cut her off.

Show me your phone, I say, staring at Leo.

Still shocking, Roman says.

Leo takes a deep breath and slides me his phone. I know his passcode. It's been the same as mine since forever. Our birthday months. 0208. When we got our first phones, we vowed never to change it.

He has one text from Natalie, sent one minute ago. It says: *this is so sad*.

You're right, I say to Natalie, this is sad.

Then I go to the bathroom.

I lean against the door until my eyes unblur. I think about how – in a bathroom stall in my middle school – someone had written *Julia is a whore* in permanent marker. I always wanted to know who Julia was and what made her a whore and if anyone had ever written anything about me.

Fi and Roman come and knock on the stall door.

Come back, Ro says.

Food's getting cold, Fi adds.

When we get to the table, no one acknowledges my return or my absence. I put a fish taco on my plate and douse it in hot sauce.

My father asks Leo about his party. Roman asks Natalie where she bought her dress. Fiona takes a big bite of guacamole and begins to cough. I pound her on the back and look across the table to my mum.

She smiles at me and nods, as if I've done something right. At least you're leaving, she beams to me and I hit Fi's back more gently.

As we walk out of the restaurant, Fiona asks if she can ride home with us. I say yes.

We drew you something, she says as soon as we're buckled. Ro: show her.

I drew you something, Roman clarifies and hands me a piece of paper.

On the back of a napkin, Ro has sketched the three of us. She has helpfully labelled each stick figure. Underneath it she has written: *BON VOYAGE BABY – notice everything, write everywhere, fuck everybody.*

This is the first thing I'll hang up in England, I say. Thank you.

I hold both their hands. Roman lets go first, reaching for her phone.

My palm is clammy like always and Fi normally teases me about it but now she doesn't say anything. We sit together and watch Los Angeles stream by.

April Yee is a writer and translator published in *Ambit, The TLS*, and *Ploughshares* online. She reported in more than a dozen countries before moving to London, where she is a National Book Critics Circle Fellow, a Refugee Journalism Project mentor, and UEA's Malcolm Bradbury Memorial Scholar. She tweets @aprilyee.

aprilyee@gmail.com

The Seven Steps to Understanding
After Jo Harjo's 'Insomnia and the Seven Steps to Grace'

We don't know what the panther did or didn't intend, because when it came time to film her bit for the documentary (working title: *Heaven in her Paws*), no translators were available in her language. We were informed by the cultural sensitivity consultant it was simply too difficult to locate one; all other living speakers had already dispersed to the pointy ends of the Americas, seeking a path to polar ice. This is the way of the panther's tribespeople, the consultant shrugged. We ached that her kind had not had the common sense to remain, learn English, and make good money translating for us. We were good people who wanted to tell her story.

In the studio with the panther, we signed and pantomimed: crouch here, slip some tooth there, tilt those yellow eyes to mirror the studio light. She mimicked us easily. Filming proceeded so fast we finished by lunch. The intern ordered Panera soups and subs. The panther stalked the plastic table with the grace of an untrained model.

And pounced. All we could see of the intern was the bracelet that flew, minorly bloodied, glimmering with quartzes and other gems mined from the ground. In the end, the settlement cost less than translation fees. For future projects, we put the panther on retainer.

Originally published in *Banshee*, Issue #12, Autumn/Winter 2021

Fire

He was going to bring the books that would unlock my future, so I met him at a place he'd chosen, the lounge on the sixty-third floor of The Address Hotel in my neighbourhood, which Dubai's government had named 'The Centre of Now.'

Marcus, who'd driven one and a half hours from Abu Dhabi, crammed a valet ticket in his pocket. The ladies here, he said. They're all, you know.

I knew. They were like fireflies: they luminesced for men, but I always missed their flash. Real fireflies, the kind I used to catch in a jar with holes poked in the top, made a special enzyme that emitted cold light. If the light were hot, they'd die.

Marcus had forgotten the books. The books were from a business school curriculum that he had promised would be as good as getting a full Master's. Technically, Marcus hadn't earned a Master's either; he had done a week-long programme at the extension school yet attended all the local alumni events as if he did have one, which was how I'd met him.

Marcus ordered an espresso martini. I had a negroni. He wanted to talk about his wife, who was still in America. His business, teaching Emirati policemen how to shoot guns. His move here, when, how funny, the shipping container had been stopped by customs authorities because he'd forgotten about a handgun in a cabinet.

I wanted to go home, but he had driven a long way, so we took the elevator 63 floors down to the hotel's club. A bouncer in a blazer with an engraved name tag stood at the door; the policy was that every man had to be accompanied by at least one woman. Inside, a wall was fully covered by LCDs screening 'Hotline Bling.'

Phones and cigarette tips flashed on and off. Marcus chose drinks, martini glasses laced with sugar syrup that glowed pink and yellow with the music's beat.

Later, after I blocked Marcus's number, I was out of the country for New Year's Eve when The Address Hotel lit on fire. Zero deaths were reported. Videos showed the building shimmering orange, the concrete floors outlined in black against the flames. Experts said the problem had been the shiny facade, aluminium stuck on polyethylene foam, a kind of plastic made by dividing oil into its smallest parts. When I got back to my flat, the walls were coated in grey dust. I wiped it off, revealed the brilliant white below.

Originally published in *Visual Verse,* Vol. 07, Chapter 11

Theory

Labour, we nodded to each other over gins, was a performance. So, five gins in, sun still high, he squeezed his lats into the French maid dress I'd bought years ago in a market in Western China, and he began baking.

His bread had the texture of hardtack and his muffins ran raw in the centre. But on video, with his face in the background, they appeared artisanal. Post-gin, we continued. I recorded hundreds of TikToks of him pouring batter into my silicone heart moulds, lifting the lid of my Dutch oven to reveal a risen loaf, whipping double cream with my favourite red spatula from Crate & Barrel.
Once we had an audience – and what an audience, hailing from all the IP addresses ever sequenced – we began hyping the website I built, **themanmaid.com**. I sold branded swag: replicas of the French maid dress that I'd sourced from an Alibaba merchant ("sexy FRENCH maid house-keeper helper BRAND NEW"). I drop-shipped 50, 100, 5,000 to our salivating viewers. I sold dresses to people in Bhutan. We were that big.

Or he was that big. If I had worn the dress, who'd have watched? I'd be a woman baking. He was white, male, and spoke in the kind of accent adored by Americans – that is, British, that is, just a little foreign, that is, not scary horde-at-the-borders foreign. The Americans thought his accent was fancy, but I knew it was middle class.

He tended to the TikTok. Too caught up to notice the bank account was only in my name. It hit £100,000, enough to buy a decent villa in Thailand and hire a maid, one of my people. I left. I called it decolonisation.

Originally published in *Jellyfish Review*

ACKNOWLEDGEMENTS

This anthology contains work written by the 2022 cohort of UEA's MA in Creative Writing: Prose Fiction. We are very grateful for the support of the UEA School of Literature, Drama and Creative Writing, in particular Philip Langeskov, in partnership with Egg Box Publishing, without whom this anthology would not have been possible.

We would like to thank our course director Tessa McWatt for all her hard work ensuring the course ran smoothly, and for taking so much time to support us throughout the year. Thanks also to our tutors Naomi Wood, Trezza Azzopardi, Andrew Cowan, Giles Foden, Julianne Pachico, Ashley Hickson-Lovence and of course Philip and Tessa, for creating a warm yet rigorous environment which has helped this year's writers find and experiment with their voices.

We are thankful to the authors who have contributed to this year's Masterclasses – Margie Orford, Elaine Feeney and Irenosen Okojie – for their warmth, generosity and advice. Huge gratitude to UEA's inaugural International Chair of Creative Writing, Tsitsi Dangarembga, for all her inspiration and wisdom.

With grateful thanks to the donors who contribute to the scholarships that support our writers, including: the Annabel Abbs Scholarship, Booker Prize Foundation Scholarship, the Curtis Brown Award, the Global Voices Scholarship, the International Excellence Scholarships, the Kowitz Scholarship, the Malcolm Bradbury Memorial Scholarship, the Miles Morland Foundation African Scholarship, the Seth Donaldson Memorial Bursary, the Sonny Mehta India Scholarship and the Sonny Mehta Scholarship for Writers, the UEA Booker Prize Foundation Scholarship and the UEA Crowdfunded Writers' Scholarship.

Many thanks to Amit Chaudhuri for generously writing the foreword, and also to Nathan Hamilton at the UEA Publishing Project for his help managing and distributing this anthology. Many thanks to Emily Benton for the stellar design, inside and out. Thanks also to all our editors:

Tess Little, Boo Sujiwaro, T. S. Quigley, Leeor Ohayon, Zui Kumar-Reddy, Hattie Cooper Hockey and georgia campbell.

Final thanks goes to all our fellow writers this year for the thoughtful feedback, impassioned workshop discussions and many, many pub trips.

UEA MA Creative Writing Anthologies: Prose Fiction

First published by Egg Box Publishing, 2022
Part of the UEA Publishing Project Ltd.

A CIP record for this book is available from the British Library
Printed and bound in the UK by Imprint Digital

Designed by Emily Benton Book Design
emilybentonbookdesign.co.uk

Distributed by NBN International
10 Thornbury Road
Plymouth
PL6 7PP
+44 (0)1752 202 301
e.cservs@nbninternational.com

ISBN 978-1-913861-76-6